ASCANIO.

BY

ALEXANDRE DUMAS.

IN TWO VOLUMES.

VOL. II.

British Library Cataloguing-in-Publication Data
A catalogue record for this book is available from
the British Library

ALEXANDRE DUMAS

Alexandre Dumas was born in Villers-Cotterêts, France in 1802. His parents were poor, but their heritage and good reputation – Alexandre's father had been a general in Napoleon's army – provided Alexandre with opportunities for good employment. In 1822, Dumas moved to Paris to work for future king Louis Philippe I in the Palais Royal. It was here that he began to write for magazines and the theatre.

In 1829 and 1830 respectively, Dumas produced the plays *Henry III and His Court* and *Christine,* both of which met with critical acclaim and financial success. As a result, he was able to commit himself full-time to writing. Despite the turbulent economic times which followed the Revolution of 1830, Dumas turned out to have something of an entrepreneurial streak, and did well for himself in this decade. He founded a production studio that turned out hundreds of stories under his creative direction, and began to produce serialised novels for newspapers which were widely read by the French public. It was over the next two decades, as a now famous and much loved author of romantic and adventuring sagas, that Dumas produced his best-known works – the D'Artagnan romances, including *The Three Musketeers,* in 1844, and *The Count of Monte Cristo,* in 1846.

Dumas made a lot of money from his writing, but he was almost constantly penniless as a result of his extravagant lifestyle and love of women. In 1851 he fled his creditors to Belgium, and then Russia, and then Italy, not returning to Paris until 1864. Dumas died in Puys, France, in 1870, at the age of 68. He is now enshrined in the Panthéon of Paris alongside fellow authors Victor Hugo and Emile Zola. Since his death, his fiction has been translated into almost a hundred languages, and has formed the basis for more than 200 motion pictures.

CONTENTS.

ASCANIO.

I.

THE TRAFFICKER IN HIS OWN HONOR.

It was the day on which Colombe was to be presented
to the queen.

The whole court was assembled in one of the state
apartments at the Louvre. After hearing mass the
court was to depart for Saint-Germain, and they were
awaiting the coming of the king and queen to go to the
chapel. Except a few ladies who were seated, everybody was moving about from place to place, laughing
and talking. There was the rustle of silks and bro-
cades, and the clash of swords; loving and defiant
glances were exchanged, together with arrangements
for future meetings, of amorous or deadly purport. It
was a dazzling, bewildering scene of confusion and
splendor; the costumes were superb, and cut in the
latest style; among them, adding to the rich and interesting variety, were pages, dressed in the Italian or
Spanish fashion, standing like statues, with arms
akimbo, and swords at their sides. It was a picture
overflowing with animation and magnificence, of which
all that we could say would be but a very feeble and

colorless description. Bring to life all the dandified,
laughing cavaliers, all the sportive easy-mannered
ladies who figure in the pages of Brantôme and the
" Heptameron," put in their mouths the crisp, clever,
outspoken, idiomatic, eminently French speech of the
sixteenth century, and you will have an idea of this
seductive court, especially if you recall the saying of
François I. : " A court without women is a year without
spring, or a spring without flowers." The court of
François I. was a perpetual spring, where the loveliest
and noblest of earthly flowers bloomed.

After the first bewilderment caused by the confusion
and uproar, it was easy to see that there were two hostile camps in the throng: one, distinguished by lilac
favors, was that of Madame d'Etampes; the other,
whose colors were blue, hoisted the flag of Diane de
Poitiers. Those who secretly adhered to the Reformed
religion belonged to the first faction, the unadulterated
Catholics to the other. Among the latter could be seen
the dull, uninteresting countenance of the Dauphin;
the intelligent, winning, blonde features of Charles
d'Orléans, the king's second son, flitted here and
there through the ranks of the faction of Madame
d'Etampes. Conceive these political and religious
antipathies to be complicated by the jealousy of women
and the rivalry of artists, and the result will be a grand
total of hatred, which will sufficiently explain, if you
are surprised at them, a myriad of scornful glances and
threatening gestures, which all the courtier-like dis-
sembling in the world cannot conceal from the observation of the spectator.

The two deadly enemies, Anne and Diane, were
seated at the opposite ends of the room, but, notwithstanding the distance between them, not five seconds

elapsed before every stinging quip uttered by one of them found its way to the ears of the other, and the retort, forwarded by the same couriers, returned as quickly by the same road.

Amid all these silk and velvet-clad noblemen, in an atmosphere of clever sayings, in his long doctor's robe, stern-featured but indifferent, walked Henri Estienne, devotedly attached to the cause of the Reformation, while not two steps away, and equally oblivious of his surroundings, stood the Florentine refugee, Pietro Strozzi, pale and melancholy, leaning against a pillar, and gazing doubtless in his heart at far-off Italy, whither he was destined to return in chains, there to have no repose save in the tomb. We need not say that the nobly born Italian, a kinsman, through his mother, of Catherine de Medicis, was heart and soul devoted to the Catholic party.

There, too, talking together of momentous affairs of state, and stopping frequently to look each other in the face as if to give more weight to what they were saying, were old Montmorency, to whom the king had given less than two years before the office of Constable, vacant since the fall of Bourbon, and the chancellor, Poyet, bursting with pride over the new tax he had imposed, and the ordinance of Villers-Cotterets, just countersigned by him.[1]

---

[1] It was at Villers-Cotterets, a small town in the department of Aisne, where François I. had a château, that the famous ordinance was signed, providing that the acts of sovereign courts should no longer be written in Latin, but should be drawn up in the vernacular. This château is still in existence, although sadly shorn of its pristine magnificence, and diverted from the uses for which it was originally intended. Begun by François I., who carved the salamanders upon it, it was finished by Henri II., who added his cipher and that of Catherine de Medicis. The visitor may still see those

Mingling with none of the various groups, taking part in no conversation, the Benedictine and Cordelier François Rabelais, with a smile which showed his white teeth, watched and listened and sneered, while Triboulet, his Majesty's favorite jester, rolled his humpback and his biting jests around between the legs of the guests, taking advantage of his pygmy-like stature to bite here and there without danger, if not without pain.

Clement Marot, resplendent in a brand-new coat as *valet-de-chambre* to the king, seemed fully as uncomfortable as on the day of his reception at the Hôtel d'Etampes. It was evident that he had in his pocket some poor fatherless sonnet, which he was seeking to dress in the guise of an impromptu conception. But alas! we all know that inspiration comes from on high, and we cannot control it. A ravishing idea had come to his mind unbidden upon the name of Madame Diane. He struggled against it, but the Muse is a mistress, not a lover; the lines formed themselves without his assistance, the rhymes matched themselves to one another as if by some magic power which he could not control. In fine, the wretched verses tormented him more than we can say. He was devoted to Madame d'Etampes beyond question, and to Marguerite de Navarre, — that too, was incontestable, — as was the fact that the Protestant party was the one toward which his sympathies leaned. It may even be that he was in search of an epigram against Madame Diane, when this madrigal in

two letters, master-pieces of the Renaissance, connected, — and note this well, for the spirit of the time is epitomized in this lapidary fact, — connected by a lover's knot, which includes also the crescent of Diane de Poitiers. A charming, but, we must agree, a strange trilogy, which consists of the cipher and arms of the husband, the wife, and the mistress.

her honor came to his mind; but come it did. And how, we pray to know, when such superb lines were evolved in his brain in laudation of a Catholic, could he forbear, despite his zeal for the Protestant cause, to confide them in a whisper to some appreciative friend of literary tastes?

That is what poor Marot did. But the injudicious Cardinal de Tournon, to whose bosom he intrusted his verses, deemed them so beautiful, so magnificent, that, in spite of himself, he passed them on to M. le Duc de Lorraine, who lost no time in telling Madame Diane of them. Instantly there was a great whispering among the partisans of the blue, in the midst of which Marot was imperatively summoned, and called upon to repeat them. The lilacs, when they saw Marot making his way through the crowd toward Madame Diane, hastened in the same direction, and crowded around the poet, enchanted and terrified at the same time. At last the Duchesse d'Etampes herself left her place, being curious, as she said, to see how " that knave Marot,[1] who had so much wit, would set about praising Madame Diane."

Poor Clement Marot, as he was about to begin, after bowing low to Diane de Poitiers, who smiled upon him, turned his head slightly to glance about and caught the eye of Madame d'Etampes; she also smiled upon him, but the smile of the one was gracious, and of the other awe-inspiring. And so it was with a trembling and uncertain voice that poor Marot, burning up on one side, and frozen on the other, repeated the following verses: —

"Etre Phœbus bien souvent je désire,
Non pour connaître herbes divinement,

[1] *Ce maraud de Marot.*

Car la douleur que mon cœur veut occire
Ne se guérit par herbe aucunement.
Non pour avoir ma place au firmament,
Non pour son arc encontre Amour laisir,
Car à mon roi ne veux être rebelle.
Etre Phœbus seulement je désir,
Pour être aimé de Diane la belle." [1]

Marot had barely uttered the last syllable of this charming madrigal, when the blues applauded vociferously, while the lilacs preserved a deathly silence. Thereupon, emboldened by the applause on the one hand, and chagrined by the frigid reception accorded his effusion on the other, he boldly presented the *chef-d'œuvre* to Madame de Poitiers.

"To 'Diane the fair,'" he said in an undertone, bowing to the ground before her; "you understand, madame, fair in your own right and by contrast."

Diane thanked him with her sweetest smile, and Marot turned away.

"One may venture to write verses in praise of a fair one, after having done the same in honor of the fairest," said the ill-fated poet apologetically as he passed Madame d'Etampes; "you remember, madame, 'De France la plus belle.'"

Anne replied with a withering glance.

Two groups, composed of acquaintances of the reader,

[1] I often wish that I were Phœbus,
Not for his heaven-born knowledge of herbs,
For the pain which I seek to deaden
Can be cured by no herb that grows.
Nor is it to have my abode in the firmament,
Nor for his bow to contend against Love,
For I do not choose to betray my king.
I long to be Phœbus simply for this,
To be beloved by Diane the fair.

stood aloof from the throng during this incident. In one were Ascanio and Cellini: Benvenuto was weak enough to prefer the " Divina Commedia " to airy conceits. The other group consisted of Comte d'Orbec, the Vicomte de Marmagne, Messire d'Estourville, and Colombe, who had implored her father not to mingle with the crowd, with which she then came in contact for the first time, and which caused her no other sensation than terror. Comte d'Orbec gallantly refused to leave his *fiancée*, who was to be presented by the provost to the queen after mass.

Ascanio and Colombe, although they were equally bewildered by their strange surroundings, had spied each other at once, and from time to time stealthily exchanged glances. The two pure-hearted, timid children, both of whom had been reared in the solitude which makes noble hearts, would have been isolated and lost indeed in that gorgeous and corrupt throng, had they not been so situated that they could see and thereby mutually strengthen and encourage each other.

They had not met since the day they confessed their love. Half a score of times Ascanio had tried to gain admission to the Petit-Nesle, but always in vain. The new servant, presented to Colombe by Comte d'Orbec, invariably answered his knock instead of Dame Perrine, and dismissed him unceremoniously. Ascanio was neither rich enough nor bold enough to try to buy the woman. Furthermore he had naught but sad news, which she would learn only too soon, to impart to his beloved; the news of the master's avowal of his own passion for Colombe, and the consequent necessity, not only of doing without his support, but perhaps of having to contend against him.

As to the course to be pursued, Ascanio felt, as he

had said to Cellini, that God alone could now save
him.   And being left to his own resources he had, in
his innocence, resolved to attempt to soften Madame
d'Etampes.   When a hope upon which one has confidently relied is blasted, one is always tempted to have
recourse to the most desperate expedients.   The all-
powerful energy of Benvenuto not only had failed
Ascanio, but would undoubtedly be turned against him.
Ascanio determined, therefore, with the trustfulness of
youth, to appeal to what he believed he had discovered
of grandeur and nobleness and generosity in the character of Madame d'Etampes, in an attempt to arouse the
sympathy of her by whom he was beloved with his suffering.   Afterward, if that last fragile branch slipped
from his hand, what could he do, a poor, weak friend-
less child, but wait?   That was why he had accompanied Benvenuto to court.

The Duchesse d'Etampes had returned to her place.
He joined the throng of her courtiers, reached a
position behind her, and finally succeeded in making
his way to her chair.   Chancing to turn her head, she
saw him.

"Ah, is it you, Ascanio?" she said, coldly.

"Yes, Madame la Duchesse.   I came hither with my
master, Benvenuto, and my excuse for venturing to
address you is my desire to know if you were hopelessly
dissatisfied with the drawing of the lily which you
kindly ordered me to prepare, and which I left at the
Hôtel d'Etampes the other day."

"No, in very truth, I think it most beautiful," said
Madame d'Etampes, somewhat mollified, "and connoisseurs to whom I have shown it, notably Monsieur
de Guise here, are entirely of my opinion.   But will
the completed work be as perfect as the drawing? and if

you think that you can promise that it will, will my gems be sufficient?"

"Yes, madame, I hope so. I should have liked, however, to place on the heart of the flower a large diamond, which would glisten there like a drop of dew; but it would be too great an expense perhaps to incur for a work intrusted to an humble artist like myself."

"Oh, we can indulge in that extravagance, Ascanio."

"But a diamond of that size would be worth some two hundred thousand crowns, madame."

"Very well, we will reflect thereon. But," added the duchess, lowering her voice, "confer a favor upon me, Ascanio."

"I am at your service, madame."

"A moment since, while listening to Marot's insipid trash, I spied Comte d'Orbec at the other end of the room. Find him out, if you please, and say to him that I would speak with him."

"What, madame!" exclaimed Ascanio, turning pale at the count's name.

"Did you not say that you were at my service?" continued Madame d'Etampes haughtily. "Moreover, my reason for asking you to undertake this commission is that you are interested in the subject of the conversation I wish to have with Comte d'Orbec, and it may well give you food for reflection, if they who are in love do ever reflect."

"I will obey you, madame," said Ascanio, apprehensive lest he should displease her at whose hands he hoped to obtain salvation.

"Very good. Pray address the count in Italian, — I have my reasons for requesting you to do so, — and return to me with him."

Ascanio, to avoid the danger of any further collision

with his redoubtable foe, walked away, and asked a
young nobleman wearing a lilac favor if he had seen
Comte d'Orbec, and where he was.

"There he is," was the reply, "that old ape whispering with the Provost of Paris, and standing so near that
lovely girl."

The lovely girl was Colombe, at whom all the dan-
dies were gazing with admiring curiosity. The old ape
seemed to Ascanio as repulsive a creature as a rival
could desire. After scrutinizing him for a moment he
walked up to him, and to Colombe's unbounded amazement accosted him in Italian, requesting him to go with
himself to Madame d'Etampes. The count excused
himself to his *fiancée* and friends, and made haste to
obey the duchess's command, followed by Ascanio, who
did not take his leave until he had bestowed a signifi-
cant reassuring glance upon poor Colombe, who was
confounded by the extraordinary message, and more
than all else by the sight of the messenger.

"Ah, count, good morning," said Madame d'Etampes,
as her eye fell upon D'Orbec; "I am charmed to see
you, for I have matters of importance to discuss with
you. Messieurs," she added, addressing those who were
standing near, "we have still a quarter of an hour to
await the coming of their Majesties, and if you will
allow me I will seize the opportunity to talk with my
old friend Comte d'Orbec."

All the noblemen who had crowded about the duchess hastened to stand discreetly aside, in obedience to
this unceremonious dismissal, and left her with the
king's treasurer in one of the window embrasures, as
large as one of our salons of to-day. Ascanio was about
to do as the rest did, but, at a sign from the duchess,
he remained.

"Who is this young man?" queried the count.

"An Italian page who does not understand a word of French; you may speak before him exactly as if we were alone."

"Very well, madame," rejoined D'Orbec; "I have obeyed your orders blindly, without even seeking to know your motives. You expressed a wish that my future wife should be presented to the queen to-day. Colombe is here with her father; but, now that I have complied with your command, I confess that I should be glad to understand it. Do I presume too much, madame, in asking you for some little explanation?"

"You are the most devoted of my faithful friends, D'Orbec; happily there is still much that I can do for you, but I do not know if I shall ever be able to pay my debt to you: however, I will try. This treasurership which I have given you is simply the corner stone upon which I propose to build your fortune, count."

"Madame!" said D'Orbec, bowing to the ground.

"I am about to speak frankly to you, therefore; but before all let me offer my congratulations. I saw your Colombe just now: she is truly ravishingly beautiful; a little awkward, but that adds to her charm. And yet, between ourselves, I have racked my brain in vain, — I know you, and I cannot understand with what object you, a serious, prudent man, but slightly enamored, I fancy, of youth and beauty, are entering into this marriage. I say, with what object, for there must necessarily be something underneath it: you are not the man to take such a step at random."

"Dame! one must settle down, madame; and the father is an old villain who has ducats to leave to his daughter."

"But how old is he, pray?"

"Oh, some fifty-five or six years."

"And you, count?"

"About the same age; but he is so used up."

"I begin to understand, and to recognize your fine hand. I knew that you were above mere vulgar sentiment, and that yonder child's fascinations did not constitute the attraction for you."

"Fie, madame! I have never even thought of them; if she had been ugly it would have been all the same; she happens to be pretty, so much the better."

"Oh, that's all right, count, otherwise I should despair of you."

"And now that you have found me, madame, will you deign to inform me — "

"Oh, it is simply that I am indulging in some beautiful dreams for you," the duchess interposed. "Where I would like to see you, D'Orbec, do you know, is in Poyet's place, for I detest him," she added, with a malevolent glance at the chancellor, who was still walking with the constable.

"What, madame, one of the most exalted posts in the realm?"

"Well, are you not yourself an eminent man, count? But alas! my power is so precarious; my throne is upon the brink of an abyss. Even at this moment I am in mortal terror. The king has for a mistress the wife of a nobody, a petty judge named Féron. If the woman were ambitious we should be ruined. I ought to have taken the initiative myself in this whim of his Majesty's. Ah! I shall never find another like the little Duchesse de Brissac, whom I presented to him; a sweet woman of no force of character, a mere child. I shall always weep for her; she was not dangerous, and talked to the king of nothing but my perfections. Poor

Marie ! she assumed all the burdens of my position, and left me all the benefits. But this Féronnière, as they call her, why, it requires all my power to draw François I. away from her. I have exhausted my whole arsenal of seductions, and am driven, alas! to my last intrenchment, habit."

" How so, madame ? "

" Mon Dieu, yes, I devote myself almost exclusively to his mind now, for his heart is elsewhere; you can understand how much I need an auxiliary. Where can I find her, — a devoted, sincere friend, of whom I can be sure? Ah! I would repay her with such quantities of gold and such a host of honors ! Seek out such a one for me, D'Orbec. You know how closely the king and the man are allied in the person of our sovereign, and to what lengths the man can lead the king on. If we could be, not rivals but allies, not mistresses but friends; if, while one held sway over François, the other might hold sway over François I., France would be ours, count, and at what a moment ! just as Charles V. is about to plunge into our net of his own free will, when we can hold him to ransom on such terms as we choose, and take advantage of his imprudence to assure ourselves a magnificent future in case of accident. I will explain my plans to you, D'Orbec. This Diane who pleases you so much would no longer threaten our fortunes; and the Chevalier de France might become — But here is the king."

Such was the way of Madame d'Etampes; she rarely expained her meaning, but left it to be guessed. She would sow ideas in a man's mind, and set avarice, ambition, and natural perversity at work; and then she would conveniently interrupt herself. A great and useful art, which cannot be too highly commended to many poets and innumerable lovers.

So it was that Comte d'Orbec, eager in the pursuit
of gain and honors, corrupt to the last degree and worn
out by years and dissipation, perfectly understood the
duchess, whose eyes more than once during the interview had wandered toward Colombe.

Ascanio's noble and straightforward nature was quite
incapable of sounding the depths of this mystery of
iniquity and infamy, but he had a vague foreboding
that this strange and ominous conversation concealed
some terrible peril for his beloved, and he gazed at
Madame d'Etampes in terror.

An usher announced the king and queen. In an
instant everybody was standing, hat in hand.

"God have you in his keeping, messieurs," said
François as he entered the room. "I have some
weighty news which I must make known to you at
once. Our dear brother, the Emperor Charles V.,
is at this moment *en route* for France, if he has not
already passed the frontier. Let us prepare, messieurs,
to welcome him worthily. I need not remind my loyal
nobility of the obligations imposed upon us by the laws
of hospitality at such a time. We proved at the Field
of the Cloth of Gold, that we knew how kings should
be received. Within the month Charles V., will be
at the Louvre."

"And I, my lords," said Queen Eleanora in her
sweet voice, "thank you in advance in my royal
brother's name for the welcome you will accord him."

The nobles replied with shouts of "Vive le Roi !
Vive la Reine ! Vive l'Empereur ! "

At that moment something wriggled its way along
between the legs of the courtiers toward the king; it
was Triboulet.

"Sire," said the fool, "will you permit me to dedi-
cate to your Majesty a work I am about to print ? "

" With all the pleasure in the world, fool," the king replied; " but I must first know the title of the work, and how far advanced it is."

" Sire, the work will be entitled the 'Almanac of Fools,' and will contain a list of the greatest idiots that the world has ever seen. As to the progress I have made with it, I have already inscribed upon the first page the name of the king of all fools past and to come."

" Who might this illustrious worthy be, whom you give me for cousin, and select for king of fools?"

" Charles V., Sire."

" Charles V.," cried the king; " and why Charles V.?"

" Because there is no other than Charles V. in the world, who, after detaining you a prisoner at Madrid as he did, would be insane enough to pass through your Majesty's dominions."

" But suppose that he does pass through the very heart of my dominions without accident?"

" In that case," said Triboulet, " I promise to erase his name and put another in its place."

" Whose name will that be?" queried the king.

" Yours, Sire; for in allowing him to pass you will show yourself a greater fool than he."

The king roared with laughter. The courtiers echoed his merriment. Poor Eleanora alone turned pale.

" Very good!" said François, " put my name in place of the Emperor's at once, for I have given my word of honor, and I'll stand to it. As to the dedication, I accept it, and here is the price of the first copy that appears."

With that the king tossed a well filled purse to Triboulet, who caught it in his teeth, and hopped away on all fours, growling like a dog with a bone.

"Madame," said the Provost of Paris to the queen, as he stepped forward with Colombe, "will your Majesty permit me to avail myself of this joyful moment to present to you under happy auspices my daughter Colombe, whom you have condescended to receive as one of your maids of honor?"

The kindly queen addressed a few words of congratulation and encouragement to poor abashed Colombe, at whom the king meanwhile was gazing in admiration.

"By my halidome, Messire le Prévôt," said François, smiling, "do you know that it's nothing less than high treason to have kept such a pearl so long buried and out of sight, — a pearl so well adapted to shine in the garland of beauties who surround the majesty of our queen. If you are not punished for the felony, Messire Robert, you may thank the mute intercession of those lovely downcast eyes."

Thereupon the king, with a graceful salutation to the charming girl, passed on to the chapel followed by the whole court.

"Madame," said the Duke of Medina-Sidonia, offering his hand to the Duchesse d'Etampes, "shall we not allow the throng to pass, and remain a little behind? We shall be more conveniently situated here than elsewhere for a word or two of importance which I have to say to you in private."

"I am at your service, Monsieur l'Ambassadeur," replied the duchess. "Do not go, Comte d'Orbec; you may say anything, Monsieur de Medina, before this old friend, who is my second self, and this young man, who speaks nothing but Italian."

"Their discretion is of no less consequence to you than to me, madame, and if you feel sure of them — But we are alone, and I will go straight to the point without digression or concealment. You understand that his Sacred Majesty has determined to pass through France, — that he is in all probability already within her boundaries. He is well aware, however, that his path lies between two long lines of enemies, but he relies upon the chivalrous loyalty of the king. You have yourself advised him so to rely, madame, and I frankly admit that, having vastly more power than any titular minister, you have enough influence over François to set a trap for the Emperor, or guarantee his safety, according as your advice is friendly or unfriendly. But why should you turn against us? It is neither for the state's interest nor your own to do so."

"Go on, monseigneur; you have not said all that you have to say, I fancy?"

"No, madame. Charles V. is a worthy successor of Charlemagne, and what a disloyal ally might demand from him as ransom he proposes to bestow as a gift, and to leave neither hospitality nor friendly counsel unrewarded?"

"Superb! he will act with no less discretion than grandeur."

"King François I. has always ardently desired the Duchy of Milan, madame, and Charles will consent to cede that province, a never-ending subject of contention between France and Spain, in consideration of an annual rent charge."

"I understand," said the duchess, "the Emperor's finances are in a straitened condition, as everybody knows; on the other hand, the Milanese is ruined by a score of wars, and his Sacred Majesty would not be sorry to transfer his claim from a poor to an opulent debtor. I refuse, Monsieur de Medina; you must yourself understand that such a proposition could not be acceptable."

" But, madame, overtures have already been made to his Majesty on the subject of this investiture, and he seemed delighted with the idea."

" I know it; but I refuse. If you can dispense with my consent, so much the better for you."

" Madame, the Emperor is especially desirous to know that you are in his interest, and whatever you may desire — "

" My influence is not merchandise to be bought and sold, Monsieur l'Ambassadeur."

" O madame, who implied such a thing ? "

" Hark ye ! you assure me that your master desires my support, and between ourselves he is wise. Very well ! to promise it to him I demand less than he offers. Follow me closely. This is what he must do. He must promise François I. the investiture of the Duchy of Milan, but as soon as he has left France behind, he must remember the violated treaty of Madrid, and forget his promise."

" Why, that would mean war, madame!"

" Stay a moment, Monsieur de Medina. His Majesty will cry out and threaten, no doubt. Thereupon Charles will consent to make the Milanese an independent state, and will give it, free of all tribute, to Charles d'Orléans, the king's second son; in that way the Emperor will not aggrandize a rival. That will be worth a few crowns to him, monseigneur, and I think that you can have nothing to say against it. As to any personal desires I may have, as you suggested a moment since, if his Sacred Majesty enters into my plans, he may let fall in my presence, at our first interview, a bauble of more or less brilliancy, which I will pick up, *if* it is worth the trouble, and retain as a souvenir of the glorious alliance concluded between the successor of the Cæsars, King of Spain and the Indies, and myself."

The duchess turned to Ascanio, who was as terrified by her dark and mysterious schemes as the Duke of Medina was disturbed by them, and as Comte d'Orbec seemed delighted.

"All this for you, Ascanio," she whispered. "To win your heart I would sacrifice France. Well, Monsieur l'Ambassadeur," she continued aloud, "what have you to say to that?"

"The Emperor alone can decide upon a matter of such gravity, madame; nevertheless, everything leads me to believe that he will acquiesce in an arrangement which almost terrifies me, it seems so favorable to us."

"If it will set your mind at rest, I will say to you that it is in reality equally favorable to me, and that is why I undertake to make the king accept it. We women have our own political schemes, more profound sometimes than yours. But I can promise you that mine are in no wise inimical to your interests: indeed, how could they be? Meanwhile, however, pending the decision of Charles V., you may be sure that I shall not lose an opportunity to act against him, and that I shall do my utmost to induce his Majesty to detain him as a prisoner."

"What! Madame, is this your way of beginning an alliance?"

"Go to, Monsieur l'Ambassadeur. Can a statesman like yourself fail to see that the most essential thing for me is to put aside all suspicion of undue influence, and that to espouse your cause openly would be the surest method of ruining it? Moreover, I do not propose that

any one shall ever be able to betray me or denounce me.
Let me be your enemy, Monsieur le Duc, and let me
talk against you.   What does it matter to you?   Do
you not know what mere words amount to?   If Charles
V. refuses to accept my terms I will say to the king,
'Sire, trust to my generous womanly instinct.   You
must not recoil before just and necessary reprisals.'
And if the Emperor accepts, I will say, 'Sire, trust to
my feminine, that is to say, feline sharpness; you must
resign yourself to commit an infamous but advantageous
act."

"Ah, madame!" said the Duke of Medina, bowing
low, "what a pity it is that you should be a queen, you
would have made such a perfect ambassador!"

With that the duke took leave of Madame d'Etampes,
and walked away, enchanted with the unexpected turn
the negotiations had taken.

"Now it is my purpose to speak plainly and without
circumlocution," said the duchess to Comte d'Orbec,
when she was alone with Ascanio and him.   "You
know three things, count: first, that it is most important for my friends and myself that my power should at
this moment be put beyond question and beyond the
reach of attack; secondly, that when this arrangement is
once carried through, we shall have no occasion to dread
the future, that Charles d'Orléans will fill the place of
François I., and that the Duke of Milan, whom I shall
have made what he is, will owe me much more gratitude than the King of France, who has made me what I
am; thirdly, that your Colombe's beauty has made a
vivid impression upon his Majesty.   Very well! I
address myself now, count, to the superior individual,
who is not influenced by vulgar prejudices.   You hold
your fate in your own hands at this moment: do you

choose that Trésorier d'Orbec should succeed Chancelier Poyet, or, in more positive terms, that Colombe
d'Orbec should succeed Marie de Brissac?"

Ascanio in his horror made a movement which
D'Orbec did not notice, as he met the searching gaze of
Madame d'Etampes with a villanous leer.

"I desire to be chancellor," he replied briefly.

"Good! then we are both saved. But what of the
provost?"

"Oh," said the count, "you can find some fat office
for him; only let it be lucrative rather than honorable,
I beg; it will all fall to me when the gouty old rascal
dies."

Ascanio could contain himself no longer.

"Madame!" he exclaimed in a voice of thunder,
stepping forward.

He had no time to say more, the count had no time to
be astonished, for the folding doors were thrown open
and the whole court flocked in.

Madame d'Etampes roughly seized Ascanio's hand,
and drew him aside with her, as she said in his ear, in
a suppressed voice, trembling with passion, —

"Now do you see, young man, how one becomes a
king's plaything, and whither life sometimes leads us,
in our own despite?"

She said no more. Her words were interrupted by
the uproarious good humor and witty sallies of the king
and courtiers.

François I. was radiant, for Charles V. was coming.
There would be receptions, fêtes, surprises, — a glorious
part for him to play. The whole world would have its
eyes fixed upon Paris and its king. He looked forward
with childish joy to the performance of the drama of
which he held all the threads. It was his nature to

look at everything on the brilliant rather than on the
serious side, to aim more at effect than anything else,
and to look upon battles as tournaments, and upon royalty as an art. With a mind well stored with strange,
poetic, adventurous ideas, François I. made of his reign
a theatrical performance, with the world for play-house.

On this day, as he was on the eve of dazzling a rival
and Europe, his clemency and benignity were more
charming than ever.

As if reassured by his smiling face, Triboulet rolled
up to him just as he passed through the door.

"O Sire, Sire!" cried the fool dolefully, "I come
to take my leave of you; your Majesty must make up
your mind to lose me, and I weep for you more than for
myself. What will become of your Majesty without
poor Triboulet, whom you love so dearly?"

"What! you are going to leave me, fool, at this
moment when there is but one fool for two kings?"

"Yes, Sire, at this moment, when there are two kings
for one fool."

"But I do not propose to have it so, Triboulet. I
order you to remain."

"In that case pray see that Monsieur de Vieilleville
is informed of your royal pleasure, for I but told him
what people say of his wife, and for so simple a matter
he swore that he would cut off my ears in the first place,
and then tear out my soul — if I had one, added the
impious villain, whose tongue your Majesty should
order to be cut out for such blasphemy."

"La, la!" rejoined the king; "have no fear, my poor
fool; the man who should take your life would be very
sure to be hanged a quarter of an hour after."

"O Sire, if it makes no difference to you —"

"Well! what?"

"Have him hanged a quarter of an hour before. I much prefer that."

The whole assemblage roared with laughter, the king above all the others. As he walked on he passed Pietro Strozzi, the noble Florentine exile.

"Signor Pietro Strozzi," he said, "it is a long time, altogether too long, I confess, since you requested letters of naturalization at our hands: it is a disgrace to us that, after having fought so valiantly in Piedmont for the French and like a true Frenchman, you do not yet belong to us, since your country by birth denies you. This evening, Signor Pietro, Messire Le Maçon, my secretary, will take steps to hasten the issuance of your letters of naturalization. Do not thank me: for my honor and your own Charles V. must find you a Frenchman. — Ah! there you are, Cellini, and you never come empty-handed. What have you under your arm, my friend? But stay a moment; it shall not be said, i' faith, that I did not surpass you in munificence. Messire Antoine Le Maçon, you will see that letters of naturalization are issued to my good friend Benvenuto at the same time with the great Pietro Strozzi's, and you will issue them without expense to him; a goldsmith cannot put his hand upon five hundred ducats so readily as a Strozzi."

"Sire," said Benvenuto, "I thank your Majesty, but I pray you to forgive my ignorance; what are these letters of naturalization?"

"What!" exclaimed Antoine Le Maçon, with great gravity, while the king laughed like a madman at the question; "do you not know, Master Benvenuto, that letters of naturalization are the greatest honor his Majesty can bestow upon a foreigner, — that you thereby become a Frenchman?"

"I begin to understand, Sire, and I thank you again," said Cellini. "But pardon me; as I am already at heart your Majesty's subject, of what use are these letters?"

"Of what use are the letters?" rejoined François, still in the best of humor; "why they are of this use, Benvenuto, that now that you are a Frenchman, I can make you Seigneur du Grand-Nesle, which was not possible before. Messire Le Maçon, you will add to the letters of naturalization the definitive deed of the château. Do you understand now, Benvenuto, of what use the letters of naturalization are?"

"Yes, Sire, and I thank you a thousand times. One would say that our hearts understood each other without words, for this favor which you bestow upon me to-day is a step toward a very, very great favor which I shall perhaps dare to ask at your hands some day, and is, so to say, a part of it."

"You know what I promised you, Benvenuto. Bring me my Jupiter, and ask what you will."

"Yes, your Majesty has a good memory, and I hope your word will prove to be as good. Yes, your Majesty, you have it in your power to gratify a wish, upon which my life in a measure depends, and you have already, by a sublime instinct worthy of a king, made its gratification more easy."

"It shall be done, my eminent artist, according to your wish; but, meanwhile, allow us to see what you have in your hands."

"It is a silver salt-dish, Sire, to go with the ewer and the basin."

"Show it me quickly, Benvenuto."

The king scrutinized, carefully and silently as always, the marvellous piece of work which Cellini handed him.

"What a blunder!" he said at last; "what a paradox!"

"What! Sire," cried Benvenuto, disappointed beyond measure, "your Majesty is not pleased with it?"

"Certainly not, monsieur. Why, you spoil a lovely idea by executing it in silver! it must be done in gold, Cellini. I am very sorry for you, but you must begin again."

"Alas! Sire," said Benvenuto sadly, "be not so ambitious for my poor works. The richness of the material will destroy these treasures of my thought, I greatly fear. More lasting glory is to be attained by working in clay than in gold, Sire, and the names of us goldsmiths survive us but a little while. Necessity is sometimes a cruel master, Sire, and men are always greedy and stupid. Who can say that a silver cup for which your Majesty would give ten thousand ducats, might not be melted down for ten crowns?"

"How now! do you think that the King of France will ever pawn the dishes from his table?"

"Sire, the Emperor of Constantinople pawned Our Saviour's crown of thorns with the Venetians."

"But a King of France took it out of pawn, monsieur."

"Very true; but think of the possible risks, revolution and exile. I come from a country whence the Medicis have been thrice expelled and thrice recalled, and it is only kings like your Majesty, who are glorious in themselves, from whom their treasures cannot be taken away."

"No matter, Benvenuto, no matter, I desire my salt dish in gold, and my treasurer will hand you to-day a thousand gold crowns of the old weight for that purpose. You hear, Comte d'Orbec, to-day, for I do

not wish Cellini to lose a minute. Adieu, Benvenuto,
go on with your work, the king does not forget his
Jupiter; adieu, messieurs, think of Charles V."

While François was descending the staircase to join
the queen, who was already in her carriage, and whom
he was to accompany on horseback, divers incidents
occurred which we must not omit to mention.

Benvenuto walked up to Comte d'Orbec and said to
him: "Be good enough to have the gold ready for me,
Messire le Trésorier. In obedience to his Majesty's
commands I go at once to my house for a bag, and shall
be at your office in a half-hour." The count bowed in
token of acquiescence, and Cellini took his departure
alone, after looking around in vain for Ascanio.

At the same time Marmagne was speaking in an
undertone with the provost, who still held Colombe's
hand.

"This is a magnificent opportunity," he said, "and I
shall go at once and summon my men. Do you tell
D'Orbec to detain Cellini as long as possible."

With that he disappeared, and Messire d'Estourville
went to D'Orbec and whispered a few words in his ear,
after which he said aloud, —

"Meanwhile, count, I will take Colombe back to the
Hôtel de Nesle."

"Very good," said D'Orbec, "and come and let me
know the result this evening."

They separated, and the provost slowly walked away
with his daughter toward the Hôtel de Nesle, followed
without their knowledge by Ascanio, who did not lose
sight of them, but kept his eyes fixed fondly upon his
Colombe.

Meanwhile the king was mounting a superb sorrel,
his favorite steed, presented to him by Henry VIII.

" We are to make a long journey together to-day,"
he said,

> "' Gentil, joli petit cheval,
>   Bon à monter, doux à descendre.' [1]

Faith, there are the first two lines of a quatrain," he
added; " cap them for me, Marot, or you, Master Melin
de Saint-Gelais. "

Marot scratched his head, but Saint-Gelais anticipated him, and with extraordinary promptness and success continued : —

> " Sans que tu sois un Bucéphal,
>   Tu portes plus grand qu'Alexandre." [2]

He was applauded on all sides, and the king, already
in the saddle, waved his hand gracefully in acknowl-
edgment of the poet's swift and happy inspiration.

Marot returned to the apartments of the Queen of
Navarre, more out of sorts than ever.

" I don't know what the matter was with them at
court to-day," he grumbled, " but they were all
extremely stupid. "

[1] Dainty, pretty little creature,
Kind to mount, to dismount gentle.

[2] Though thou 'rt not a Bucephalus,
Thou bearest a greater than Alexander.

II.

FOUR VARIETIES OF BRIGANDS.

BENVENUTO crossed the Seine in all haste, and procured, not a bag as he had told Comte d'Orbec that he should, but a small wicker basket given him by one of his cousins, a nun at Florence. As he was determined to make an end of the affair that day, and it was already two o'clock, he did not wait for Ascanio, whom he had completely lost sight of, nor his workmen, who had gone to dinner; but started at once for Rue Froid-Manteau, where Comte d'Orbec had his official residence; and although he kept his eyes open he saw nothing on the way to cause him the least uneasiness.

When he reached the treasurer's abode that dignitary informed him that he could not deliver his gold to him at once, as there were certain indispensable formalities to be gone through with, a notary to be summoned, and a contract to be drawn up. The count apologized with a thousand expressions of regret, knowing Cellini's impatient nature, and was so courteous withal that it was impossible to be angry; and Benvenuto resigned himself to wait, believing in the reality of these obstacles to a speedy delivery of the gold.

Cellini desired to take advantage of the delay to send for some of his workmen, that they might accompany him home, and help him to carry the gold. D'Orbec quickly volunteered to send one of his servants to the

Hôtel de Nesle with the message; then he led the conversation around to Cellini's work, and the king's evident partiality for him, — to anything in short likely to incline Benvenuto to be patient, — which was the less difficult of accomplishment as he had no reason for wishing ill to the count, and no suspicion that the count had any reason for being hostile to him. There was his desire to supplant him with Colombe, but no one knew of that desire save Ascanio and himself. He therefore met the treasurer's friendly overtures graciously enough.

Further time was necessary to select gold of the degree of fineness which the king desired him to have. The notary was very slow in coming. A contract is not drawn up in a moment. In short, when, after the final exchange of courtesies, Benvenuto made ready to return to his studio, night was beginning to fall. He questioned the servant who was sent for his companions, and was told that they were unable to come, but that he would gladly carry the gold for him. Benvenuto's suspicions were aroused, and he declined the offer, courteous as it was.

He placed the gold in his little basket, then passed his arm through the two handles, and as there was barely room for his arm, the cover was securely pressed down, and he carried it much more easily than if it had been in a bag. He had a stout coat of mail with sleeves beneath his coat, a short sword at his side, and a dagger in his belt. He set out on his homeward journey at a quick pace, but cautiously nevertheless. Just before he started he noticed several servants speaking together in low tones, and that they left the house in a great hurry, but they made a show of going in a different direction from that taken by him.

To-day, when one can go from the Louvre to the Institute by the Pont des Arts, Benvenuto's homeward journey would be but a stride, but at that time it was a long walk. He was obliged, starting from Rue Froid-Manteau, to follow the quay as far as the Châtelet, cross the Pont des Meuniers, go across the city by Rue Saint-Barthélemy, cross to the left bank by the Pont Saint-Michel, and from there go down the river to the Grand-Nesle by the deserted quay. The reader need not wonder that, in those days of thieves and cut-throats, Benvenuto, notwithstanding his courage, felt some anxiety touching so considerable a sum as that he carried upon his arm; and if he will go forward with us two or three hundred yards in advance of Benvenuto he will see that his anxiety was not unjustifiable.

When it began to grow dark, about an hour before, four men of forbidding appearance, wrapped in great cloaks, stationed themselves upon the Quai des Augustins, at a point abreast of the church. The river bank was bordered with walls only at that spot, and was absolutely deserted at that moment. While they stood there they saw no one pass but the provost, on his way back to the Châtelet after escorting Colombe to the Petit-Nesle, and him they saluted with the respect due the constituted authorities.

They were talking in low tones in a recess formed by the church, and their hats were pulled well down over their eyes. Two of them are already known to us: the bravos employed by Vicomte de Marmagne in his ill-fated expedition against the Grand-Nesle. Their names were Ferrante and Fracasso. Their companions, who earned their livelihood at the same honorable calling, were named Procope and Maledent. In order that posterity may not quarrel over the nationality of these four valiant captains, as it has done for three thousand years over that of old Homer, we will add that Maledent was a Picard, Procope a Bohemian, and that Ferrante and Fracasso first saw the light beneath the soft skies of Italy. As to their distinctive callings in time of peace, Procope was a jurist, Ferrante a pedant, Fracasso a dreamer of dreams, and Maledent a fool. It will be seen that the fact that we are ourselves a Frenchman does not blind us to the character of the only one of these four toilers who happened to be our compatriot.

In battle all four were demons.

Let us listen for a moment to their friendly and edifying conversation. We may be able to judge therefrom what manner of men they were, and what danger was impending over our good friend, Benvenuto.

" At all events, Fracasso," said Ferrante, " we sha'n't be hampered to-day with that great red-faced viscount, and our poor swords can leave their scabbards without his crying, 'Retreat!' — the coward, — and forcing us to turn tail."

" Very true," rejoined Fracasso, " but as he leaves us all the risk of the combat, for which I thank him, he ought to leave us all the profit too. By what right does the red-haired devil reserve five hundred crowns for his own part? I admit that the five hundred that remain make a very pretty prize. A hundred and twenty-five for each of us does us honor, — indeed, when times are hard, I sometimes find it necessary to kill a man for two crowns."

" For two crowns! Holy Virgin!" cried Maledent; " shame! that brings discredit on the profession. Don't say such things when I am with you, for any one who overheard you might confound us with each other, my dear fellow."

"What would you have, Maledent?" said Fracasso, in a melancholy tone; "life has its crosses, and there are times when one would kill a man for a bit of bread. It seems to me, my good friends, that two hundred and fifty crowns are worth just twice as much as a hundred and twenty-five. Suppose that after we have killed our man we refuse to settle with that great thief of a Marmagne?"

"You forget, brother," rejoined Procope seriously, "that that would be to disregard our agreement, to defraud our patron, and we must be loyal in everything. Let us hand the viscount the five hundred crowns to the last sou, as agreed, that is my advice. But *distinguamus*, let us make a distinction; when he has pocketed them, and when he realizes that we are honorable men, I fail to see why we shouldn't fall upon him and take them from him."

"Well thought of!" exclaimed Ferrante in a judicial tone. "Procope was always distinguished for uprightness of character conjoined with a vivid imagination."

"Mon Dieu! that is because I have studied law a little," said Procope modestly.

"But," continued Ferrante, with the air of pedantry which was habitual to him, "let us not involve ourselves in too many plans at once. *Recte ad terminum eamus.* Let the viscount sleep in peace; his turn will come. This Florentine goldsmith is the one we have to deal with at the moment; for greater security, it was desired that four of us should set upon him. Strictly speaking one only should have done the deed and pocketed the price, but the concentration of capital is a social plague, and 'tis much better that the money be divided among several friends. Let us despatch him swiftly and cleanly. He is no ordinary man, as

Fracasso and I have learned. Let us resign ourselves, therefore, for greater security, to attack him all four at once. It cannot be long now before he comes. Attention ! be cool, quick of foot and eye, and beware of the Italian thrusts he 'll be sure to try on you."

"I know what it is, Ferrante," said Maledent disdainfully, "to receive a sword-cut, whether with the edge or the point. Once on a time I made my way at night into a certain château in the Bourbonnais on business of a personal nature. Being surprised by the dawn before I had fully completed it, I had no choice but to conceal myself until the following night. No place seemed to me so appropriate for that purpose as the arsenal of the château: there were quantities of stands of arms and trophies there, and helmets, cuirasses, armlets and cuisses, shields and targets. I removed the upright upon which one of the suits of armor hung, put myself in its place, and stood there, motionless upon my pedestal, with lowered visor."

"This is very interesting," interposed Ferrante; "go on, Maledent; how can we better employ this period of waiting to perform one exploit, than in listening to tales of other feats of arms. Go on."

"I did not know," continued Maledent, "that that accursed suit of armor was used by the young men of the family to practise fencing upon. But soon two strapping fellows of twenty came in, took down a lance and a sword each, and began to cut and thrust at my casing with all their heart. Well, my friends, you may believe me or not, but under all their blows with lance and sword, I never flinched: I stood there as straight and immovable as if I had really been of wood, and riveted to my base. Fortunately the young rascals were not of the first force. The father arrived

in due time and urged them to aim at the joints in
my armor; but Saint Maledent, my patron, whom I
invoked in a whisper, turned their blows aside. At
last that devil of a father, in order to show the young-
sters how to carry away a visor, took a lance himself,
and at the first blow uncovered my pale and terrified
face. I thought I was lost."

"Poor fellow!" said Fracasso sadly, "how could it
be otherwise."

"Fancy, if you please, that when they saw my
colorless face they took me for the ghost of their great-
grandfather; and father and sons scuttled away as if
the devil was at their heels. Need I say more? I
turned my back, and did as much for my own part; and
you see I came out of it with a whole skin."

"Very good, but the important thing in our trade,
friend Maledent," said Procope, "is not only to receive
blows manfully, but to deal them handsomely. It's a
fine thing when the victim falls without a sound. In
one of my expeditions in Flanders I had to rid one of
my customers of four of his intimate friends, who were
travelling in company. He proposed at first that I
should take three comrades, but I told him that I would
undertake it alone, or not at all. It was agreed that I
should do as I chose, and that I should have the stipend
four times over provided that I delivered four dead
bodies. I knew the road they were to take, and I
awaited their coming at an inn which they must of
necessity pass.

"The inn-keeper had formerly belonged to the frater-
nity, and had left it for his present occupation, which
allowed him to plunder travellers without risk; but he
retained some kindly sentiments for his former brethren,
so that I had no great difficulty in winning him over to

my interest in consideration of a tenth of the reward. With that understanding we awaited our four horsemen, who soon appeared around a bend in the road, and alighted in front of the inn, preparatory to filling their stomachs and resting their horses. The landlord said to them that his stable was so small that, unless they went in one at a time, they could hardly move there, and would be in each other's way. The first who entered was so slow about coming out, that the second lost patience and went to see what he was doing. He also was in no hurry to reappear, whereupon the third, weary of waiting, followed the other two. After some little time, as the fourth was expressing his astonishment at their delay, mine host remarked: 'Ah! I see what it is: the stable is so extremely small, that they have gone out through the door at the rear.'

"This explanation encouraged my last man to join his companions and myself, for you will have guessed that I was in the stable. I allowed him, however, the satisfaction of uttering one little cry, to say farewell to the world, as there was no longer any danger.

"In Roman law, Ferrante, would not that be called *trucidatio per divisionem necis?* But, deuce take it!" added Procope, changing his tone, "our man doesn't come. God grant that nothing has happened to him! It will be pitch dark very soon."

"*Suadentque cadentia sidera somnos*," added Fracasso. "And by the way, my friends, take care that Benvenuto doesn't in the dark resort to a trick which I once put in practice myself: it was during my sojourn on the banks of the Rhine. I always loved the banks of the Rhine, the country there is so picturesque and at the same time so melancholy. The Rhine is the river of dreamers. I was dreaming then upon the

banks of the Rhine, and this was the subject of my
dreams.

"A nobleman named Schreckenstein, if my memory
serves me, was to be put to death. It was no easy
matter, for he never went out without a strong escort.
This is the plan upon which I finally resolved.

"I donned a costume like that worn by him, and one
dark evening I lay in wait for him and his escort.
When I saw them coming through the solitude and
darkness, *obscuri sub nocte*, I made a desperate attack
upon Schreckenstein, who was walking a little ahead;
but I was clever enough to strike off his hat with its
waving plumes, and then to change my position so that
I was standing where he should have been. Thereupon
I stunned him with a violent blow with my sword hilt,
and began to shout amid the clashing of swords and the
shouts of the others, 'Help! help! death to the brigands!' so that Schreckenstein's men fell furiously upon
their master and left him dead upon the spot, while I
glided away into the bushes. The worthy nobleman
could at least say that he was killed by his friends."

"It was a bold stroke," said Ferrante, "but if I were
to cast a backward glance upon my vanished past I
could find a still more audacious exploit there. Like
you, Fracasso, I had to deal with a chief of partisans,
always well mounted and escorted. It was in a forest
in the Abruzzi. I stationed myself in an enormous oak
tree upon a great branch which stretched out over the
road at a point which the personage in question must
pass; and there I waited, musing. The sun was rising
and its first rays fell in long shafts of pale light down
through the moss-grown branches; the morning air was
fresh and keen, enlivened by the songs of birds. Suddenly — "

"Sh !" Procope interrupted him. "I hear footsteps: attention ! it's our man."

"Good !" muttered Maledent, glancing furtively about; "all is silent and deserted hereabout; fortune is on our side."

They stood without speaking or moving; their dark, threatening faces could not be distinguished in the gathering gloom, but one might have seen their gleaming eyes, their hands playing nervously with their rapiers, and their attitude of breathless suspense; in the half-darkness they formed a striking dramatic group, which no pencil but Salvator Rosa's could adequately reproduce.

It was in fact Benvenuto coming on at a rapid pace; as we have said, his suspicions were aroused, and with his piercing glance he maintained a constant watch in the darkness. As his eyes were accustomed to the uncertain light he saw the four bandits issue from their ambush when he was still twenty yards away, and had time to throw his cloak over his basket, and draw his sword, before they were upon him. Furthermore, with the self-possession which never abandoned him, he backed against the church wall, and thus faced all of his assailants.

They attacked him savagely. He could not retreat, and it was useless to cry out as the château was five hundred yards away. But Benvenuto was no novice in deeds of arms, and he received the cut-throats with vigor.

His mind remained perfectly clear, and a sudden thought flashed through it as he plied his sword. It was evident that this ambuscade was directed against him, and no other. If therefore he could succeed in throwing them off the track, he was saved. He began therefore, as the blows rained down upon him, to joke them upon their pretended mistake.

"What fit has seized you, my fine fellows? Are you mad? What do you expect to make out of an old soldier like me? Is it my cloak that you want? Does my sword tempt you? Stay, stay, you! If you want my good sword, you must earn it! Sang-Dieu! By my soul, for thieves who seem to have served their apprenticeship, your scent is bad, my children."

With that he charged upon them, instead of falling back before them, but only took one or two steps away from the wall, and immediately placed his back against it once more, incessantly slashing and thrusting, taking pains to throw aside his cloak several times, so that, if they had been warned by Comte d'Orbec's servants, whom he had seen leave the house, and who had seen him count the money, they would at least conclude that he had not the gold upon him. Indeed, his assured manner of speaking, and the ease with which he handled his sword with a thousand crowns under his arm, caused the bravos to entertain some doubts.

"Damnation! do you suppose we have made a mistake, Ferrante?" said Fracasso.

"I fear so. The man seemed not so tall to me; or even if it is he, he hasn't the gold, and that damned viscount deceived us."

"I have gold!" cried Benvenuto, thrusting and parrying vigorously all the while. "I have no gold save a handful of gilded copper; but if you are ambitious to secure that, my children, you will pay dearer for it than if it were gold belonging to another, I promise you."

"Deuce take him!" said Procope, "he's really a soldier. Could any goldsmith fence so cleverly as he?

Expend all your wind on him, if you choose, you fellows; I don't fight for glory."

And Procope began to beat a retreat, grumbling to himself, while the attack of the others relaxed in vigor, by reason of their doubts, as well as of his absence. Benvenuto, with no such motive for weakening, seized the opportunity to drive them back, and to start for the château, backing before his assailants, but fighting all the time, and defending himself manfully. The savage boar was luring the hounds with him to his den.

"Come, my brave fellows, come with me," he said "bear me company as far as the entrance to the Pré-aux-Clercs, the Maison Rouge, where my sweetheart, whose father sells wine, is expecting me to-night. The road isn't very safe, so they say, and I should be glad to have an escort."

Upon that pleasantry, Fracasso also abandoned the chase, and went to join Procope.

"We are fools, Ferrante!" said Maledent; "this isn't your Benvenuto."

"Yes, yes, I say it is himself," cried Ferrante, who had at last discovered the basket bulging out with money under Benvenuto's arm, as a too sudden movement disarranged his cloak.

But it was too late: the château was within a hundred feet or less, and Benvenuto was shouting in his powerful voice: "Hôtel de Nesle ! ho ! help ! help !"

Fracasso had barely time to retrace his steps, Procope to hasten up, and Ferrante and Maledent to redouble their efforts; the workmen who were expecting their master, were on the alert. The door of the château was flung open at his first shout, and Hermann the colossus, little Jehan, Simon-le-Gaucher, and Jacques Aubry came running out armed with pikes.

At that sight the bravos turned and fled.

"Wait, wait, my dear young friends," Benvenuto shouted to the fugitives; "won't you escort me a little farther? O the bunglers! who could n't take from one lone man a thousand golden crowns which tired his arm!"

The brigands had in fact succeeded in inflicting no other injury than a slight scratch upon their opponent's hand, and they made their escape shamefaced, and Fracasso howling with pain. Poor Fracasso at the very last lost his right eye, and was one-eyed for the rest of his days, a circumstance which accentuated the tinge of melancholy which was the most prominent characteristic of his pensive countenance.

"Well, my children," said Benvenuto to his companions, when the footsteps of the bravos had died away in the distance, "we must have some supper after that exploit. Come all and drink to my escape, my dear rescuers. But God help me! I do not see Ascanio among you. Where is Ascanio?"

The reader will remember that Ascanio left the Louvre before his master.

"I know where he is?" said little Jehan.

"Where is he, my boy?" asked Benvenuto.

"Down at the end of the garden, where he has been walking for half an hour; the student and I went there to talk with him, but he begged us to leave him alone."

"Strange!" said Benevenuto. "How did he fail to hear my shout? How is it that he did not hasten to me with the others? Do not wait for me, but sup without me, my children. Ah, there you are, Scozzone!"

"O mon Dieu! what is this they tell me, — that some one tried to murder you, master?"

"Yes, yes, there was something like that."

"Mon Dieu!" cried Scozzone.

"It was nothing, my dear girl, nothing," said Benvenuto consolingly, for poor Catherine had become as pale as death. "Go now and bring wine, of the best, for these gallant fellows. Take the keys of the cellar from Dame Ruperta, Scozzone, and select it yourself."

"Why, you are not going out again?" said Scozzone.

"No, never fear: I am going to find Ascanio in the garden. I have important matters to discuss with him."

Scozzone and the others returned to the studio, and Benvenuto walked toward the gate leading to the garden.

The moon was just rising, and the master saw Ascanio very plainly; but, instead of walking, the young man was climbing a ladder set against the wall between the gardens of the Grand and Petit-Nesle. When he reached the top, he pulled the ladder up after him, lowered it on the other side, and disappeared.

Benvenuto passed his hand over his eyes like a man who cannot believe what he sees. Forming a sudden resolution, he went straight to the foundry and up into his cell, stepped to the window sill, and leaped to the wall of the Petit-Nesle; from there, with the aid of a stout vine, he dropped noiselessly into Colombe's garden; it had rained in the morning, and the ground was so damp that his footfalls were deadened.

He put his ear to the ground, and questioned the silence for some moments. At last he heard subdued voices in the distance, which guided his steps; he at once rose, and crept cautiously forward, feeling his way, and stopping from moment to moment. Soon the voices became more distinct.

Benvenuto walked toward them, and at last, when he reached the second path which crossed the garden, he recognized Colombe, or rather divined her presence in the shadow, dressed in white, and sitting beside Ascanio on the bench we already know. They were talking in low tones, but distinctly, and with animation.

Hidden from their observation by a clump of trees, Benvenuto drew near and listened.

III.

AN AUTUMN NIGHT'S DREAM.

It was a beautiful autumn evening, calm and clear. The moon had driven away almost all the clouds, and the few which remained were scattered here and there over the star-strewn sky. Around the group talking and listening in the garden of the Petit-Nesle, everything was calm and silent, but within their hearts all was sadness and agitation.

"My darling Colombe," said Ascanio, while Benvenuto, standing cold and pale behind him, seemed to be listening with his heart rather than with his ears, "my dearest love, why, alas! did our paths meet? When you know all that I have to tell you of misery and horror, you will curse me for being the bearer of such news."

"Nay, my dear," replied Colombe, "whatever you may have to tell me, I shall bless you, for in my eyes you are as one sent by God. I never heard my mother's voice, but I feel that I should have listened to her as I listen to you. Go on, Ascanio, and if you have terrible things to tell me, your voice will at least comfort me a little."

"Summon all your courage and all your strength," said Ascanio.

Thereupon he told her all that had taken place in his presence between Madame d'Etampes and Comte d'Orbec; he described the whole plot, a combination of treason against the kingdom and designs upon the honor of an innocent child; he subjected himself to the agony of explaining the infamous bargain made by the treasurer to that ingenuous soul, aghast at this revelation of wickedness; he must needs to make the maiden, whose heart was so pure that she did not blush at his words, understand the cruel refinements of torture and ignominy which hatred and baffled love suggested to the favorite. All that was perfectly clear to Colombe's mind was that her lover was filled with loathing and dismay, and, like the slender vine which has no other support than the sapling to which it clings, she trembled and shuddered with him.

"My dear," she said, "you must make known this fearful plot against my honor to my father. My father does not suspect our love, he owes you his life, and he will listen to you. Oh, never fear! he will rescue me from the clutches of Comte d'Orbec."

"Alas!" was Ascanio's only reply.

"O my love!" cried Colombe, who understood all the apprehension contained in her lover's exclamation. "Oh! can you suspect my father of complicity in so hateful a design? That would be too wicked, Ascanio. No, my father knows nothing, suspects nothing, I am sure, and although he has never shown me any great affection, he would never with his own hand plunge me into shame and misery."

"Forgive me, Colombe," rejoined Ascanio, "but your father is not accustomed to see misery in increased wealth. A title would conceal the shame, and in his courtier-like pride he would deem you happier as a king's mistress than as an artist's wife. It is my duty to hide nothing from you, Colombe: Comte d'Orbec told Madame la Duchesse d'Etampes that he would answer for your father."

"Just God, is it possible!" cried the poor girl. "Was such a thing ever seen, Ascanio, as a father who sold his daughter?"

"Such things are seen in all countries and at all times, my poor angel, and more than ever at this time and in this country. Do not picture to yourself the world as fashioned after the image of your heart, or society as taking pattern by your virtue. Yes, Colombe, the noblest names of France have shamelessly farmed out the youth and beauty of their wives and daughters to the royal lust: it is looked upon as a matter of course at court, and your father, if he cares to take the trouble to justify himself, will not lack illustrious precedents. I beg you to forgive me, my beloved, for bringing your chaste and spotless soul so abruptly in contact with this hideous reality; but I cannot avoid the necessity of showing you the snare that is laid for you."

"Ascanio, Ascanio!" cried Colombe, hiding her face against the young man's shoulder; "my father also turns against me. Oh, simply to repeat it kills me with shame! Where can I fly for shelter? Where but to your arms, Ascanio? Yes, it is for you to save me now. Have you spoken to your master, to Benvenuto, who is so strong and great and kindly, judging by your description of him, and whom I love because you love him?"

"Nay, do not love him, do not love him, Colombe!" cried Ascanio.

"Why not?" whispered the girl.

"Because he loves you, because, instead of the friend upon whom we thought we could rely, he is one enemy the more we have to contend against: an enemy, you understand, and the most formidable of all our enemies. Listen."

Thereupon he told her how, as he was on the point of making a confidant of Benvenuto, the goldsmith described to him his ideal love, and added that the favorite sculptor of François I. by virtue of the king's word of honor to which he had never proved false, could obtain whatever he chose to ask after the statue of Jupiter was cast. As we know, the boon that Benvenuto proposed to ask was Colombe's hand.

"O God! we have none to look to for succor but thee," said Colombe, raising her white hands and her lovely eyes to heaven. "All our friends are changed to enemies, every haven of refuge becomes a dangerous reef. Are you certain that we are so utterly abandoned?"

"Only too certain," replied Ascanio. "My master is as dangerous to us as your father, Colombe. Yes," he continued, wringing his hands, "I am almost driven to hate him, Benvenuto, my friend, my master, my protector, my father, my God! And yet I ask you, Colombe, why I should bear him ill will? Because he has fallen under the spell to which every exalted mind that comes in contact with yours must yield; because he loves you as I love you. His crime is my own, after all. But you love me, Colombe, and so I am absolved. What shall we do? For two days I have been asking myself the question, and I do not know whether I begin to detest him, or whether I love him still. He loves you, it is true; but he has loved me so dearly, too, that my poor heart wavers and trembles in its perplexity like a reed shaken in the wind. What will he do? First of all, I shall tell him of Comte d'Orbec's designs, and I hope that he will deliver us from them. But after that, when we find ourselves face to face as enemies, when I tell him that his pupil is his rival, Colombe, his will, which is omnipotent as fate, will perhaps be as blind; he will forget Ascanio to think only of Colombe; he will turn his eyes away from the man he once loved, to see only the woman he loves, for I feel myself that between him and you I should not hesitate. I feel that I would remorselessly sacrifice my heart's past for its future, earth for heaven ! And why should he act differently? he is a man, and to renounce his love would be more than human. We must therefore, fight it out, but how can I, feeble and alone as I am, resist him. But no matter, Colombe: even if I should come some day to hate him I have loved so long and so well, I tell you now that I would not for all the world subject him to the torture he inflicted upon me the other morning when he declared his love for you."

Meanwhile Benvenuto, standing like a statue behind his tree, felt the drops of icy sweat roll down his forehead, and his hand clutched convulsively at his heart.

"Poor Ascanio ! dear heart !" returned Colombe, "you have suffered bitterly already, and have much to suffer still. But let us face the future calmly. Let us not exaggerate our griefs, for the prospect is not altogether desperate. Including God there are three of us to make head against misfortune. You would rather see me Benvenuto's wife than Comte d'Orbec's, would you not? But you would also prefer to see me wedded to the Lord than to Benvenuto? Very well! if I am not yours, I will belong to none but the Lord, be sure of that, Ascanio. Your wife in this world, or your

betrothed in the other.   That is my promise to you,
Ascanio, and that promise I will keep: never fear."

"Thanks, thou angel from heaven, thanks!" said
Ascanio.   "Let us forget the great world around us,
and concentrate our lives upon this little thicket where
we now are.   Colombe, you have n't told me yet that
you love me.   Alas! it would almost seem that you are
mine because you could not do otherwise."

"Hush! Ascanio, hush! do you not see that I am
trying to sanctify my happiness by making it a duty?
I love you, Ascanio, I love you!"

Benvenuto could no longer find strength to stand; he
fell upon his knees with his head against a tree; his
haggard eyes were fixed vacantly on space, while, with
his ear turned toward the young people, he listened
with feverish intentness.

"Dear Colombe," echoed Ascanio, "I love you, and
something tells me that we shall be happy, and that the
Lord will not abandon the loveliest of all his angels.
Mon Dieu! Mon Dieu! in this atmosphere of joy
which surrounds me, I forget the circle of grief which
I must enter when I leave you."

"We must think of to-morrow," said Colombe: "let
us help ourselves, Ascanio, so that God may help us.
It would be disloyal, I think, to leave your master
Benvenuto in ignorance of our love, for he would
perhaps incur great risk in contending against Madame
d'Etampes and Comte d'Orbec.   It would not be fair:
you must tell him everything, Ascanio."

"I will obey you, dearest Colombe, for a word from
you, as you must know, is law to me.   My heart also
tells me that you are right, always right.   But it will
be a terrible blow for him.   Alas! I judge from my
own heart.   It is possible that his love for me may

turn to hatred, it is possible that he will turn me out of doors. In that case how can I, a stranger, without friends or shelter, resist such powerful enemies as the Duchesse d'Etampes and the king's treasurer. Who will help me to defeat the plans of that terrible couple? Who will fight on my side in this unequal struggle? Who will hold out a helping hand to me?"

"I!" said a deep, grave voice behind them.

"Benvenuto!" cried the apprentice, without even turning round.

Colombe shrieked and sprang to her feet. Ascanio gazed at his master, wavering between affection and wrath.

"Yes, it is I, Benvenuto Cellini," continued the goldsmith, — "I, whom you do not love, mademoiselle, — I, whom you no longer love, Ascanio, and who come to save you both, nevertheless."

"What do you say?" cried Ascanio.

"I say that you must come and sit down again, here by my side, for we must understand one another. You have no need to tell me aught. I have not lost a word of your conversation. Forgive me for listening after I came upon you by chance, but you understand: it is much better that I should know all. You have said some things very sad and terrible for me to hear; but some kind things too. Ascanio was sometimes right and sometimes wrong. It is very true, Mademoiselle, that I would have disputed you with him. But since you love him, that's the end of it, be happy; he has forbidden you to love me, but I will force you to it by giving you to him."

"Dear master!" cried Ascanio.

"You suffer, monsieur, do you not?" said Colombe clasping her hands.

"Ah, thanks, thanks!" said Benvenuto, as his eyes filled with tears, but restraining his feelings with a mighty effort. "You see that I suffer. He would not have noticed it, ungrateful boy! But nothing escapes a woman's eyes. Yes, I will not tell you a falsehood; I do suffer! and why not, since you are lost to me? But at the same time I am happy, because I am able to serve you; you will owe everything to me, and that thought comforts me a little. You were wrong, Ascanio; my Beatrice is jealous, and will brook no rival; you, Ascanio, must finish the statue of Hebe. Adieu, my sweetest dream, — the last!"

Benvenuto spoke with effort, in a broken voice. Colombe leaned gracefully toward him, and put her hand in his.

"Weep, my friend, weep," she said softly.

"Yes, yes," said Cellini, bursting into tears.

He stood for some time without speaking, weeping bitterly, and trembling with emotion from head to foot. His forceful nature gladly sought relief in tears too long held back. Ascanio and Colombe looked on in respectful silence at this exhibition of bitter grief.

"Except on the day when I wounded you, Ascanio, except at the moment when I saw your blood flow, I have not wept for twenty years," he said at last, recovering his self-control; "but it has been a hard blow to me. I was in such agony just now behind those trees that I was tempted for a moment to plunge my dagger in my heart, and end it all. The only thing that held my hand was your need of me, and so you saved my life. All is as it should be, after all. Ascanio has twenty years more of happiness to give you than I have, Colombe. And then he is my child: you will be very happy together, and it will rejoice my father's

heart. Benvenuto will succeed in triumphing over
Benvenuto himself, as well as over his enemies. It is
the lot of us creators to suffer, and perhaps each one of
my tears will cause some lovely statue to spring up, as
each of Dante's tears became a sublime strain. You see,
Colombe, I am already returning to my old love, my
cherished sculpture: that love will never forsake me.
You did well to bid me weep: all the bitterness has
been washed from my heart by my tears. I am sad
still, but I am kind once more, and I will forget my
pain in my efforts to save you."

Ascanio took one of the master's hands, and pressed
it warmly in his own. Colombe took the other, and put
it to her lips. Benvenuto breathed more heavily than
he had yet done. Shaking his head, he said with a
smile: —

"Do not make it harder for me, but spare me, my
children. It will be better never to speak of this again.
Henceforth, Colombe, I will be your friend, nothing
more; I will be your father. The rest is all a dream.
Now let us talk of the danger which threatens you, and
of what we are to do. I overheard you a moment since
discussing your plans. Mon Dieu! you are very young,
and neither of you has an idea of what life really is.
You offer yourselves, in the innocence of your heart,
to the cruel blows of destiny, unarmed, and you hope
to vanquish malignity, avarice, all the vile passions of
which man is capable with your kind hearts and your
smiles! Dear fools! I will be strong and cunning
and implacable in your stead. I am wonted to it, but
you, — God created you for happiness and tranquillity,
my lovely cherubs, and I will see to it that you fulfil
your destiny.

"Ascanio, anger shall not furrow thy calm brow:

grief, Colombe, shall not disturb the pure outlines of
thy face. I will take you in my arms, soft-eyed,
charming pair; I will bear you so through all the mire
and misery of life, and will not set you down until you
have arrived safe and sound at perfect joy; and then
I'll gaze at you, and be happy in your happiness. But
you must have blind confidence in me; I have my own
peculiar ways, abrupt and hard to understand, and
which may perhaps alarm you a little, Colombe. I
conduct myself somewhat after the manner of artillery,
and I go straight to my goal, heedless of what I may
meet on the road. Yes, I think more of the purity of
my intentions, I confess, than of the morality of the
means I use. When I set about modelling a beautiful figure I care but little whether the clay soils my
fingers. The figure finished, I wash my hands, and
that's the end of it. Do you then, mademoiselle, with
your refined and timorous heart, leave me to answer to
God for my acts. He and I understand each other. I
have a powerful combination to deal with. The count
is ambitious, the provost avaricious, and the duchess
very subtle. They are each and all very powerful.
You are in their power, and in their hands, and two of
them have rights over you: it may perhaps be necessary to resort to craft and violence. I shall arrange it,
however, so that you and Ascanio will have no part in a
contest in every way beneath you. Come, Colombe,
are you ready to close your eyes, and allow yourself to
be led? When I say, 'Do this,' will you do it? —
'Remain there,' will you remain? — 'Go,' will you go?"

"What does Ascanio say?" asked Colombe.

"Colombe," returned the apprentice, "Benvenuto is
great and good: he loves us and forgives the injury we
have done him. Let us obey him, I implore you."

"Command me, master," said Colombe, "and I will obey you as if you were sent by God himself.

"Very well, my child. I have but one thing more to ask you; it will cost you dear, perhaps, but you must make up your mind to it; thereafter your part will be confined to waiting, and allowing circumstances and myself to do our work. In order that both of you may have more perfect faith in me, and that you may confide unhesitatingly in one whose life may not be unspotted, but whose heart has remained pure, I am about to tell you the story of my youth. All stories resemble one another, alas! and sorrow lies at the heart of every one. Ascanio, I propose to tell you how my Beatrice, the angel of whom I have spoken to you, came to be associated with my existence; you shall know who she was, and you will wonder less no doubt at my determination to abandon Colombe to you, when you realize that by that sacrifice I am but beginning to pay to the child the debt I owe the mother. Your mother! a saint in paradise, Ascanio! Beatrice would say blessed; Stefana would say crowned."

"You have always told me, master, that you would tell me your whole story some day."

"Yes, and the moment has come to redeem my promise. You will have even more confidence in me, Colombe, when you know all the reasons I have for loving our Ascanio."

Thereupon Benvenuto took a hand of each of his children in his own, and told them what follows, in his grave, melodious voice, beneath the glimmering stars in the peaceful silence of the night.

IV.

STEFANA.

" TWENTY years since, I was twenty years old, as you
are now, Ascanio, and I was at work with a Florentine
goldsmith named Raphael del Moro. He was a good
workman and did not lack taste; but he cared more for
rest than for work, allowing himself to be inveigled
into attending parties with disheartening facility, and,
although he had little money, himself leading astray
those who were in his studio. Very often I was left
alone in the house, singing over some piece of work I
had in hand. In those days I sang as Scozzone does.
All the sluggards in the city came as a matter of course
to Master Raphael for employment, or rather in quest
of pleasure, for he had the reputation of being too weak
ever to quarrel. One grows rich slowly with such
habits as his; so he was always hard up, and soon came
to be the most discredited goldsmith in Florence.

" I am wrong. He had a confrère who had even less
custom than he, although he was of a noble family.
But it was not for irregularity in meeting his obligations that Gismondo Gaddi was cried down, but for his
notorious lack of talent and his sordid avarice. As
everything intrusted to him left his hands imperfect or
spoiled, and not a customer, unless he happened to be a
stranger, ventured into his shop, Gismondo undertook
to earn his living by usury, and to loan money at enor-

mous interest to young men desirous of discounting
their future prospects. This profession succeeded
better than the other, as Gaddi always demanded good
security, and went into nothing without reliable guaranties. With that exception, he was, as he himself
said, very considerate and long-suffering; he loaned to
everybody, compatriots and foreigners, Jews and Chris-
tians. He would have loaned to St. Peter upon the
keys of paradise, or to Satan upon his estates in hell.

"Need I say that he loaned to my poor Raphael del
Moro, who consumed every day his provision for the
morrow, but whose sterling integrity never wavered.
Their constant connection in business, and the social
ostracism to which both were subjected, tended to
bring the two goldsmiths together. Del Moro was
deeply grateful for his confrère's untiring amiability in
the matter of advancing money. Gaddi thoroughly
esteemed an honest and accommodating debtor. They
were, in a word, the best friends in the world, and
Gismondo would not have missed for an empire one of
the parties with which Del Moro regaled him.

"Del Moro was a widower, but he had a daughter of
sixteen, named Stefana. From a sculptor's point of
view Stefana was not beautiful, and yet her appearance
was most striking. Beneath her forehead, which was
almost too high and not smooth enough for a woman,
one could see her brain at work, so to speak. Her
great, moist eyes, of a velvety black hue, moved you to
respect and deep emotion as they rested upon you. An
ivory pallor overspread her face, which was lightened
by a melancholy yet charming expression, like the faint
sunshine of an autumn morning. I forget a crown of
luxurious raven locks, and hands a queen might have
envied.

"Stefana ordinarily stood bending slightly forward, like a lily swayed by the wind. You might at times have taken her for a statue of Melancholy. When she stood erect, when her lovely eyes sparkled, when her nostrils dilated, when her arm was outstretched to emphasize a command, you would have adored her as the Archangel Gabriel. She resembled you, Ascanio, but you have less weakness of resolution and capacity for suffering. The immortality of the soul was never more clearly revealed to my eyes than in that slender, graceful body. Del Moro, who feared his daughter almost as much as he loved her, was accustomed to say that he had consigned to the tomb only the body of his wife, that Stefana was her dead mother's soul.

"I was at this time an adventurous youth, an impulsive giddy-pated creature. I loved liberty before everything. I was bubbling over with life, and I expended my surplus energy in foolish quarrels and foolish love affairs. I worked nevertheless with no less passion than I put into my pleasures, and despite my vagaries I was Raphael's best workman, and the only one in the establishment who earned any money. But what I did well, I did by instinct, almost by chance. I had studied the ancients to good purpose. For whole days I had gazed upon the bas-reliefs and statues of Athens and Rome, making studies with pencil and chisel, and constant contact with these sublime artists of former days gave me purity and precision of outline; but I was simply a successful imitator; I did not create. Still, I say again, I was incontestably and easily the cleverest and most hardworking of Del Moro's comrades. I have since learned that the master's secret wish was that I should marry his daughter.

"But I was thinking little of settling down; i' faith,

I was enamored of independence, freedom from care, and an outdoor life. I was absent from the workshop whole days at a time. I would return completely overdone with fatigue, and yet in a few hours I would have overtaken and passed Raphael's other workmen. I would fight for a word, fall in love at a glance. A fine husband I should have made !

" Moreover, my feelings when I was with Stefana in no wise resembled those aroused by the pretty girls of Porta del Prato or Borgo Pinti. She almost overawed me ; if I had been told that I loved her otherwise than as an elder sister I should have laughed. When I returned from one of my escapades I dared not look Stefana in the face. She was more than stern, she was sad. On the other hand, when fatigue or a praiseworthy zealous impulse had detained me at home, I always sought Stefana's companionship, her sweet face, and her sweet voice; my affection for her had in it something serious and sacred, which I did not at the time fully understand, but which was very pleasant to me. Very often, amid my wildest excesses, the thought of Stefana would pass through my mind, and my companions would ask me why I had suddenly become thoughtful. Sometimes, when I was in the act of drawing my sword or my dagger, I would pronounce her name as it were that of my patron saint, and I noticed that whenever that occurred I retired from the contest unhurt. But this tender feeling for the dear child, innocent, lovely, and affectionate as she was, lay dormant at the bottom of my heart as in a sanctuary.

" For her part, it is certain, that she was as full of indulgence and kindly feeling for me as she was cold and dignified with my slothful comrades. She sometimes came to sit in the studio beside her father, and I would sometimes feel her eyes fixed on my face as she bent over my work. I was proud and happy in her preference, although I did not explain my feeling to myself. If one of my comrades indulged in a little vulgar flattery, and informed me that my master's daughter was in love with me, I received his insolence so wrathfully that he never repeated it.

"An accident which befell Stefana proved to me how deeply she had become rooted in my heart.

"One day when she was in the studio looking at a piece of work, she did not take away her little white hand quickly enough, and a bungling workman, who was tipsy, I think, struck the little finger and the finger beside it with his chisel. The poor child shrieked at first, then, as if ashamed of it, smiled to reassure us, but her hand as she held it up was covered with blood. I think I should have killed the fellow had my mind not been concentrated upon her.

"Gismondo Gaddi, who was present, said that he knew a surgeon in the neighborhood, and ran to fetch him. The villanous medicaster dressed the wound, and came every day to see Stefana; but he was so ignorant and careless that gangrene set in. Thereupon the ass pompously declared that, despite his efforts, Stefana's right arm would always be paralyzed.

"Raphael del Moro was in too straitened circumstances to be able to consult another physician; but when I heard the imbecile announce his decision, I refused to abide by it. I hurried to my room, emptied the purse which contained all my savings, and ran off to Giacomo Rastelli of Perouse, the Pope's surgeon, and the most eminent practitioner in all Italy. At my earnest entreaty, and as the sum I offered him was by no means contemptible, he came at once, exclaiming, 'O these

lovers !' After examining the wound, he announced
that he would answer for it that Stefana would be able
to use the right arm as well as the other within a
fortnight. I longed to embrace the worthy man. He
set about dressing the poor maimed fingers, and Stefana
was at once relieved. But a day or two later it was
necessary to remove the decayed bone.

"She asked me to be present at the operation to give
her courage, whereas I was entirely lacking in it myself, and my heart felt very small in my breast.
Master Giacomo made use of some great instrument
which caused Stefana terrible pain. She could not
restrain her groans, which echoed in my heart. My
temples were bathed in a cold perspiration.

"At last the torture exceeded my strength; the cruel
tool which tortured those poor, delicate fingers tortured
me no less. I rose, begging Master Giacomo to suspend
the operation, and to wait for me a quarter of an hour.

"I went down to the studio, and there, as if inspired
by my good genius, I made an instrument of thin, sharp
steel which would cut like a razor. I returned to the
surgeon, who with that operated so gently and easily
that the dear girl felt almost no pain. In five minutes
it was all over, and a fortnight later she gave me the
hand to kiss, which, as she said, I had preserved.

"But it would be impossible for me to describe the
poignant emotion I passed through when I saw the
suffering of my poor Résignée, as I sometimes called
her.

"Resignation was, in truth, the natural condition
of her mind. Stefana was not happy; her father's
improvidence and recklessness distressed her beyond
measure; her only consolation was religion; like all
unhappy women she was pious. Very often, as I

entered some church to pray, for I have always loved God, I would spy Stefana in a corner weeping and praying.

"Whenever, as too frequently happened, Master Del Moro's reckless extravagance left her penniless, she would appeal to me with a simple, trustful confidence, which went to my heart. She would say, dear girl, with the simplicity characteristic of noble hearts: ' Benvenuto, I beg you to pass the night at work, to finish that reliquary, or that ewer, for we have no money at all.'

"I soon adopted the habit of submitting to her every piece of work that I completed, and she would point out its imperfections and advise me with extraordinary sagacity. Solitude and sorrow had inspired and elevated her mind more than one would think possible. Her words, which were at once innocent and profound, taught me more than one secret of my art, and often opened new possibilities to my mind.

"I remember one day when I showed her a medal which I was engraving for a cardinal, and which had a representation of the cardinal's head on one side, and on the other Jesus walking on the sea, and holding out his hand to St. Peter, with this legend: *'Quare dubitasti?'* Wherefore didst thou doubt?

"Stefana was well pleased with the portrait, which was a very good likeness, and very well executed. She looked at the reverse in silence for a long while.

"' The face of Our Lord is very beautiful,' she said at last, 'and if it were intended for Apollo or Jupiter I should find nothing to criticise. But Jesus is something more than beautiful; Jesus is divine. The lines of this face are superb in their purity, but where is the soul? I admire the man, but I look in vain for the

God. Consider, Benvenuto, that you are not an artist simply, but a Christian as well. My heart, you know, has often bled; that is to say, alas! my heart has often doubted; and I, too, have shaken off my depression when I saw Jesus holding out his hand to me, and have heard the sublime words, "Wherefore hast thou doubted?" Ah, Benvenuto, your image of him is less beautiful than he. In his celestial countenance there was the sadness of the afflicted father, and the clemency of the king who pardons. His forehead shone, but his mouth smiled; he was more than great, he was good.'

"'Wait a moment, Stefana,' said I.

"I effaced what I had done, and in a few moments I once more began upon the Savior's face under her eyes.

"'Is that better?' I asked, as I handed it to her.

"'Oh yes!' she replied, with tears in her eyes; 'so our blessed Lord appeared to me when I was heavy-hearted. Yes, I recognize him now by his expression of compassion and majesty. Ah, Benvenuto! I advise you always henceforth to follow this course: before taking the wax in hand, be sure of the thought; you possess the instrument, master the expression; you have the material part, seek the spiritual part; let your fingers never be aught but the servants of your mind.'

"Such was the counsel given me by that child of sixteen, in her sublime good sense. When I was alone I reflected upon what she had said to me, and realized that she was right. Thus did she guide and enlighten my instinct. Having the form in my mind, I sought the idea, and to combine the form and the idea in such wise that they would issue from my hands a perfectly blended whole, as Minerva came forth all armed from the brain of Jupiter.

"Mon Dieu ! how lovely is youth, and how its memories do overpower one ! Ascanio, Colombe, this lovely evening we are passing together reminds me of all those I passed by Stefana's side sitting upon a bench outside her father's house. She would gaze up at the sky, and I would gaze at her. It was twenty years ago, but it seems only yesterday; I put out my hand and fancy that I can feel hers, but it is yours, my children; what God does is well done.

"Oh, simply to see her in her white dress was to feel tranquillity steal over my soul! Often when we parted we had not uttered a word, and yet I carried away from those silent interviews all sorts of fine and noble thoughts, which made me better and greater.

"But all this had an end, as all happiness in this world has.

"Raphael del Moro had but little farther to go to reach the lowest depths of destitution. He owed his kind neighbor Gismondo Gaddi two thousand ducats, which he knew not how to pay. The thought drove this honest man to desperation. He wished at least to save his daughter, and intrusted his purpose to give her to me to one of the workmen, doubtless that he might broach the subject to me. But he was one of the idiots whom I had lost my temper with when they threw Stefana's sisterly affection at my head as a reproach. The blockhead did not even allow Raphael to finish.

"'Abandon that scheme, Master Del Moro,' he said; 'the suggestion would not be favorably received, my word for it.'

"The goldsmith was proud: he believed that I despised him on account of his poverty, and he never referred to the subject again.

"Some time after, Gismondo Gaddi came to demand payment of his debt, and when Raphael asked for more time,

"'Hark ye,' said Gismondo, 'give me your daughter's hand, and I will give you a receipt in full.'

"Del Moro was transported with joy. To be sure Gaddi had the reputation of being a little covetous, a little high-tempered, and a little jealous, but he was rich, and what the poor esteem and envy most, alas! is wealth. When Raphael mentioned this unexpected proposition to his daughter, she made no reply; but that evening, as we left the bench where we had been sitting together, to return to the house, she said to me, 'Benvenuto, Gismondo Gaddi has asked my hand in marriage, and my father has given his consent.'

"With those simple words she left me. I leaped to my feet, and in a sort of frenzy I went out of the city and wandered about over the fields. Throughout the night, now running like a madman, and again lying at full length upon the grass and weeping, a myriad of mad, desperate, frenzied thoughts chased one another through my disordered brain.

"'She, Stefana, the wife of that odious Gismondo!' I said to myself, when I had in some degree recovered my self-control, and was seeking to collect my wits. 'The thought overpowers me and terrifies me as well, and as she would certainly prefer me, she makes a mute appeal to my friendship, to my jealousy. Ah, yes! I am jealous, furiously jealous; but have I the right to be? Gaddi is morose and violent tempered, but let us be just to one another. What woman would be happy with me? Am I not brutal, capricious, restless, forever involved in dangerous quarrels and unholy intrigues? Could I conquer myself? No, never; so long as the blood boils in my veins as at present, I shall always have my hand on my dagger, and my foot outside the house.

" 'Poor Stefana! I should make her weep and suffer, I should see her lose color and pine away. I should hate myself, and should soon come to hate her as well, as a living reproach. She would die, and I should have her death to answer for. No, I am not made — alas! I feel that I am not — for calm, peaceful family joys; I must have liberty, space, conflict, anything rather than the peace and monotony of happiness. I should break in my grasp that fragile, delicate flower. I should torture that dear, loving heart by my insults, and my own existence, my own heart would be blighted by remorse. But would she be happier with this Gismondo Gaddi? Why should she marry him? We were so happy together. After all, Stefana must know that an artist's instincts and temperament do not easily accommodate themselves to the rigid bonds, the commonplace necessities of family life. I must say farewell to all my dreams of glory, renounce the thought of making my name famous, and abandon art, which thrives on liberty and power. How can one create when held a prisoner at the domestic fireside? Say, O Dante Alighieri! O Michel-Angelo, my master, how you would laugh to see your pupil rocking his children to sleep, and asking his wife's pardon! No, I will be brave in my own behalf, and generous to Stefana: sad and alone I will dream out my dream and fulfil my destiny.'

" You see, my children, that I make myself no better than I am. There was some selfishness in my decision, but there was also much deep and sincere affection for Stefana, and my raving seemed to border closely on common sense.

" The next morning I returned to the workshop in a reasonably tranquil frame of mind. Stefana also seemed calm, but she was paler than usual. A month passed thus. One evening Stefana said, as we parted, —

" 'In a week, Benvenuto, I shall be Gismondo Gaddi's wife.'

" As she did not leave me at once, I had time to look at her. She stood with her hand on her heart, bending beneath her burden of sorrow, and her sweet smile was sad enough to make one weep. She gazed at me with a sorrowful expression, but without the least indication of reproach. It seemed to me as if my angel, ready to leave earth behind, was saying farewell to me. She stood thus, mute and motionless, for a moment, then entered the house.

" I was destined never to see her more in this world.

" This time again I left the city bareheaded and running like a madman; but I did not return the next day, or the next; I kept on until I reached Rome.

" I remained at Rome five years; I laid the foundation of my reputation, I won the friendship of the Pope, I had duels and love affairs and artistic success, but I was not contented, — something was lacking. Amid my engrossing occupations I never passed a day without turning my eyes toward Florence. There was no night when I did not see in my dreams Stefana, pale-faced and sad, standing in the doorway of her father's house, and gazing at me.

" After five years I received a letter from Florence, sealed with black. I read and reread it so many times that I know it now by heart.

" It ran thus : —

" 'Benvenuto, I am dying. Benvenuto, I loved you.

" 'Listen to the dreams I dreamed. I knew you as

well as I knew myself. I foresaw the power that is in
you, and that will make you great some day. Your
genius, which I read upon your broad forehead, in your
ardent glance and your passionate gestures, would
impose grave duties on her who should bear your name.
I was ready to undertake them. Happiness had for me
the solemnity of a divine mission. I would not have
been your wife, Benvenuto, I would have been your
friend, your sister, your mother. Your noble existence
belongs to all mankind, I know, and I would have
assumed no other right than that of diverting you in
your ennui, of uplifting you in your moments of depression. You would have been free, my friend, always
and everywhere. Alas! I had long since become
accustomed to your lamentable absences from home, to
all the exactions of your impulsive nature, to all the
whims of your tempest-loving heart. Every powerful
temperament has pressing needs. The longer the eagle
has soared aloft, the longer he is obliged to rest on
earth. But when you had torn yourself free from the
feverish dreams of your genius, I would have found
once more at the awakening my sublime Benvenuto,
whom I love so dearly, and who would have belonged
to me alone! I would never have reproached you for
the hours of neglect, for they would have contained no
insult for me. For my own part, knowing you to be
jealous, as is every noble heart, jealous as the God of
Holy Writ, I would have remained in seclusion when
you were away, in the solitude which I love, awaiting
your return and praying for you.

"'Such would my life have been.

"'But when I saw that you abandoned me, I bowed
submissively to God's will and yours, closed my eyes,
and placed my fate in the hands of duty. My father

ordered me to enter into a marriage which would save him from dishonor, and I obeyed. My husband has been harsh, stern, pitiless; he has not been content with my docile submission, but demanded a love beyond my power to give, and punished me brutally for my involuntary sadness. I resigned myself to endure everything. I have been, I trust, a pure and dignified spouse, but always very sad at heart, Benvenuto. God has rewarded me, however, even in this world, by giving me a son. My child's kisses have for four years past prevented me from feeling insults, blows, and last of all poverty ! for my husband ruined himself trying to gain too much, and he died last month from chagrin at his ruin. May God forgive him as I do !

" 'I shall be dead myself within the hour, dead from the effects of my accumulated suffering, and I bequeath my son to you, Benvenuto.

" 'Perhaps all is for the best. Who can say if my womanly weakness would have been equal to the task I would have undertaken with you. He, my Ascanio, — he is like me, — will be a stronger and more submissive companion for you; he will love you better, if not more dearly. I am not jealous of him.

" 'Do for my child what I would have done for you.

" 'Adieu, my friend. I loved you and I love you still, and I tell you without shame or remorse, at the very doors of eternity, for my love was holy. Adieu! be great, and I shall be happy: raise your eyes sometimes to heaven that I may see you.

" 'Your STEFANA.'

" Now, Colombe and Ascanio, will you have confidence in me, and are you ready to do what I advise ? "

The young people replied with a single exclamation.

V.

DOMICILIARY VISITS.

On the day following that on which this story was told in the garden of the Petit-Nesle, by the moon's pale light, Benvenuto's studio wore its accustomed aspect. The master was working at the gold salt dish, the mate-rial for which he had so valiantly defended against the four bravos, who strove to take it from him, and his life with it. Ascanio was chiselling Madame d'Etampes's lily; Jacques Aubry, reclining lazily on a lounging-chair, was putting question after question to Cellini, who paid no attention to him, and imposed upon the inquisitive student the necessity of framing his own replies. Pagolo was gazing at Catherine, who was busy with some woman's work. Hermann and the others were filing, welding, chiselling, and Scozzone's joyous singing furnished the element of cheerfulness in this tranquil, busy scene.

The Petit-Nesle was by no means so tranquil, for Colombe had disappeared.

There all was excitement and apprehension; they were seeking her everywhere, and calling her name. Dame Perrine was shrieking at the top of her voice, and the provost, who had been sent for in hot haste, was trying to lay hold upon something, in the midst of the good woman's lamentations, which might put him on the track of the absent one, who was in all prob-ability a fugitive.

"Look you, Dame Perrine; do you say that you last saw her a few moments after I went away last night?" demanded the provost.

"Alas! yes, messire. Jésus Dieu! what a misfortune! The poor, dear child seemed a bit cast down as she went to take off all her beautiful court fixings. She put on a simple white dress — saints in Paradise, have pity on us! — and then she said to me, 'Dame Perrine, it's a lovely evening, and I will go and take a turn or two in my path.' It might have been about seven o'clock. Madame here," added Perrine, pointing to Pulchérie, the woman who had been installed as her assistant or superior, — "Madame here had already gone to her room, doubtless to work at those lovely dresses which she makes so well, and I was at work sewing in the room below. I don't know how long I remained there, — it is possible that after a while my poor tired eyes closed in spite of me, and that I lost myself a moment."

"As usual," interposed Pulchérie sharply.

"At all events," continued Dame Perrine, not deigning to reply to this insidious slander, "about ten o'clock I left my chair and went to the garden to see if Colombe had not forgotten herself. I called and found no one: I supposed then that she had gone to her own room and to bed without disturbing me, as the dear child has done a thousand times. Merciful Heaven! who would have thought — Ah! Messire le Prévôt, I can safely say that she followed no lover, but some ravisher. I reared her in the way — "

"And this morning," the provost broke in impatiently, "this morning?"

"This morning when I found that she didn't come down — Holy Virgin help us!"

"To the devil with your litanies!" cried Messire d'Estourville. "Say what you have to say simply and without all these jeremiads. This morning?"

"Ah! Monsieur le Prévôt, you can't prevent my weeping until she is found. This morning, messire, being alarmed at not seeing her (she is always so early!) I knocked at her door to wake her, and, as she did not answer, I opened the door. No one. The bed was not even rumpled, messire. With that I called and cried, and lost my head, and you want me not to weep!"

"Dame Perrine," said the provost sternly; "have you admitted any one here during my absence?"

"I admit any one! the idea!" rejoined the governess with every indication of stupefaction, feeling a little conscience-stricken in that regard. "Didn't you forbid me, messire? Since when, pray, have I allowed myself to disobey your orders? Admit some one? Oh yes, of course!"

"This Benvenuto, for instance, who had the assurance to deem my daughter so fair; has he never tried to buy you?"

"Good lack! he would have been more likely to try to fly to the moon. I would have received him prettily, I promise you."

"I am to understand, then, that you have never admitted a man, a young man, to the Petit-Nesle?"

"A young man! Merciful Heaven! a young man! Why not the devil himself?"

"Pray who is the handsome boy," said Pulchérie, "who has knocked at the door at least ten times since I have been here, and in whose face I have shut the door as often?"

"A handsome boy? Your sight must be poor, my dear, unless it was Comte d'Orbec. Ah, bon Dieu!

I know: you may mean Ascanio. You know Ascanio,
Messire? the young fellow who saved your life. Yes,
I did give him my shoe-buckles to repair. But he,
that apprentice ! Wear glasses, my love! May these
walls and pavements speak, if they ever saw him
here ! "

" Enough," interposed the provost severely. " If you
have betrayed my confidence, Dame Perrine, I swear
that you shall pay me for it ! I am going now to this
Benvenuto; God knows how the clown will receive me,
but go I must."

Contrary to his expectation Benvenuto received the
provost with perfect civility. In the face of his cool
and easy manner and his good humor, Messire d'Estourville did not dare mention his suspicions. But
he said that his daughter, having been unnecessarily
alarmed the evening before, had fled in her panic terror
like a mad girl; that it was possible that she might
have taken refuge in the Grand-Nesle without Benvenuto's knowledge, — or else that she might have
fainted somewhere in the grounds as she was passing
through. In short, he lied in the most bungling way
imaginable.

But Cellini courteously accepted all his fables and all
his excuses; indeed, he was so obliging as to appear to
notice nothing out of the way. He did more, he sym-
pathized with the provost with all his heart, declaring
that he would be happy to assist in restoring his daughter to a father who had always hedged her around with
such touching affection. To hear him, one might suppose the fugitive was very much in the wrong, and
could not too soon return to so pleasant a home and so
loving a parent. Moreover, to prove the sincerity of
his interest in Messire d'Estourville's affliction, he

placed himself at his disposal to assist him in his search in the Grand-Nesle and elsewhere.

The provost, half convinced, and the more deeply affected by these eulogiums, in that he knew in his heart that he did not deserve them, began a careful search of his former property, of which he knew all the ins and outs. There was not a door that he did not open, not a wardrobe nor a chest into which he did not peer, as if by inadvertence. Having inspected every nook and corner of the hotel itself, he went into the garden, and searched the arsenal, foundry, stables and cellar, scrutinizing everything most rigorously. Benvenuto, faithful to his first offer, accompanied him throughout his investigations, and assisted him to the utmost of his ability, offering him all the keys, and calling his attention to this or that corridor or closet which the provost overlooked. He advised him to leave one of his people on guard in each spot as he left it, lest the fugitive should evade him by stealing from place to place.

Having continued his perquisitions for two hours to no purpose, Messire d'Estourville, feeling sure that he had omitted nothing, and overwhelmed by his host's politeness, left the Grand-Nesle, with profuse thanks and apologies to its master.

"Whenever it suits your pleasure to return," said the goldsmith, "and if you desire to renew your investigations here, my house is open to you at all times, as when it was your own. Indeed it is your right, messire; did we not sign a treaty whereby we agreed to live on neighborly terms?"

The provost thanked Benvenuto, and as he knew not how to return his courtesy, he loudly praised, as he went away, the colossal statue of Mars, which the artist was at work upon, as we have said. Benvenuto led him around it, and complacently called his attention to its amazing proportions; it was more than sixty feet high and nearly twenty in circumference at its base.

Messire d'Estourville withdrew much dejected. As he had failed to find his daughter in the precincts of the Grand-Nesle, he was convinced that she had found shelter somewhere in the city. But even at that time the city was sufficiently large to make his own task as chief officer of the police an embarrassing one. Then, too, there was this question to be solved. Had she been kidnapped, or had she fled? Was she the victim of some other person's violence, or had she yielded to her own impulse? There was nothing to set at rest his uncertainty upon this point. He hoped that in the first event she would succeed in escaping, and in the second would return of her own volition. He therefore waited with what patience he could muster, none the less questioning Dame Perrine twenty times a day, who passed her time calling upon the saints in paradise, and swearing by all the gods that she had admitted no one; and indeed she was no more suspicious than Messire d'Estourville himself of Ascanio.

That day and the next passed without news. The provost thereupon put all his agents in the field: a thing he had hitherto omitted to do, in order that the unfortunate occurrence, in which his reputation was so deeply interested, might not be noised abroad. To be sure he simply gave them Colombe's description, without giving them her name, and their investigations were made upon an entirely different pretext from the real one. But although he resorted to all his secret sources of information, all their searching was without result.

Surely he had never been an affectionate or gentle father, but if he was not in despair, he was in a bad

temper, and his pride suffered if his heart did not. He
thought indignantly of the fine match which the little
fool would perhaps miss by reason of this escapade, and
with furious rage of the witticisms and sarcasms with
which his misadventure would be greeted at court.

He had to make up his mind at last to confide his
woful tale to Comte d'Orbec.   Colombe's *fiancé* was
grieved by the news, in the same way as a merchant is
grieved who learns that part of his cargo has been jet-
tisoned, and not otherwise.   He was a philosopher, was
the dear count, and promised his worthy friend that, if
the affair did not make too much noise, the marriage
should come off none the less; and, as he was a man who
knew how to strike when the iron was hot, he seized the
opportunity to whisper to the provost a few words as to
the plans of Madame d'Etampes regarding Colombe.

The provost was dazzled at the honor which might
be in store for him: his anger redoubled, and he cursed
the ungrateful girl who was ruining her own chances of
such a noble destiny.   We spare our readers the details
of the conversation between the two old courtiers to
which this avowal of Comte d'Orbec led; we will say
simply that grief and hope were combined therein in a
curiously touching way.   As misfortune brings men
together, the prospective father-in-law and son-in-law
parted more closely united than ever, and without making up their minds to renounce the brilliant prospects
of which they had caught a glimpse.

They agreed to keep the occurrence secret from everybody; but the Duchesse d'Etampes was too intimate a
friend, and too deeply interested as an accomplice, not to
be let into their confidence.   It was a wise move on
their part, for she took the thing much more to heart
than the father and husband had done, and, as we know,

she was better qualified than any other to give the provost information and direct his search.

She knew of Ascanio's love for Colombe, and she had herself forced him, so to speak, to listen to the whole conspiracy. The young man, realizing that a blow was to be aimed at the honor of his beloved, had perhaps resolved upon some desperate act. But Ascanio had himself told her that Colombe did not love him, and not loving him she would be unlikely to lend herself to such a design. Now the Duchesse d'Etampes knew him upon whom her suspicion first fell sufficiently well to be sure that he would never have the courage to defy his mistress's scorn and her resistance; and yet, despite all her reasoning, and although in her eyes all the probabilities pointed to Ascanio's innocence, her jealous instinct told her that Colombe must be sought at the Hôtel de Nesle, and that they must make sure of Ascanio before everything.

But, on the other hand, Madame d'Etampes could not tell her friends the source of that conviction, for she must in that case confess her love for Ascanio, and that, in the imprudence of her passion, she had made known to him all her designs upon Colombe. She simply said to them that she would be very much mistaken if Benvenuto were not the culprit, Ascanio his accomplice, and the Grand-Nesle the place of concealment. To no purpose did the provost argue with her, and swear that he had inspected and searched every corner, she would not yield her point, saying that she had her reasons for the faith that was in her, and she was so obstinate in her opinion that she ended by arousing suspicion in the mind of Messire d'Estourville, who was certain nevertheless that he had made a thorough search.

"However," said the duchess, "I will send for Ascanio, I will see him and question him myself, never fear."

"O madame! you are too kind," said the provost.

"And you too stupid," muttered the duchess between her teeth. She dismissed them, and set about reflecting upon the method she should adopt to induce the young man to come to her; but before she had decided upon any, Ascanio was announced; it was as if he had anticipated her wish.

He was cold and calm. The gaze with which Madame d'Etampes received him was so piercing that you would have said she wished to read to the very bottom of his heart; but Ascanio did not seem to notice it.

"Madame," said he, as he saluted her, "I have come to show you your lily, which is almost finished; almost nothing is lacking to complete it save the two hundred thousand crown dewdrop you promised to furnish me."

"Very well! and your Colombe?" was the only reply vouchsafed by Madame d'Etampes.

"If you mean Mademoiselle d'Estourville, madame," rejoined Ascanio gravely, "I will beg you on my knees not to pronounce her name again before me. Yes, madame, I most humbly and earnestly implore you that this subject may never be mentioned between us, in pity's name!"

"Aha! spite!" said the duchess, who did not remove her penetrating gaze from Ascanio's face for an instant.

"Whatever the feeling which influences me, madame, and though I were to be disgraced in your eyes, I shall venture to decline hereafter to talk with you upon this subject. I have sworn a solemn oath that everything connected with that memory shall be dead and buried in my heart."

"Am I mistaken?" thought the duchess; "and has Ascanio no part in this transaction? Can it be that the child has followed some other adorer, voluntarily or perforce, and, although lost to my ambitious schemes, has served the interests of my passion by her flight?"

Having indulged in these reflections beneath her breath, she continued, aloud: —

"Ascanio, you beg me not to speak of her again, but you will at least allow me to speak of yourself. You see that in obedience to your entreaty I do not insist, but who knows if this second subject will not be even more disagreeable to you than the first? Who knows — "

"Forgive me for interrupting you, madame," said the young man, "but your kindness in granting me the favor I ask emboldens me to ask another. Although of noble birth, I am simply a poor, obscure youth, reared in the gloom of a goldsmith's workshop, and from that artistic cloister I am suddenly transported to a brilliant sphere, involved in the destiny of empires, and, weak creature that I am, having powerful noblemen for enemies, and a king for rival. And such a king, madame! François I., one of the most powerful princes in Christendom! I have suddenly found myself elbow to elbow with the most illustrious names of the age. I have loved hopelessly, I have been honored with a love I could not return! And with whose love? Great God! yours, madame, one of the loveliest and noblest women on earth! All this has sown confusion within me and without; it has bewildered and crushed me, madame.

"I am as terrified as a dwarf awaking to find himself among giants: I have n't an idea in its place, not a feeling which I can explain. I feel lost among all these

terrible animosities, all these implacable passions, all
these soaring ambitions. Madame, give me time to
breathe, I conjure you; permit the poor shipwrecked
wretch to collect his thoughts, the convalescent to recover his strength. Time, I hope, will restore order in
my mind and my life. Time, madame, give me time,
and in pity's name see in me to-day only the artist who
comes to ask if his lily is to your taste."

The duchess stared at Ascanio in doubt and amazement; she had not supposed that this young man, this
child, was capable of speaking in this grave, stern, poetic
fashion; she felt morally constrained to obey him, and
confined her conversation to the lily, praising and advising Ascanio, and promising to do her utmost to send
him very soon the large diamond to complete his work.
Ascanio thanked her, and took his leave with every
mark of gratitude and respect.

"Can that be Ascanio?" said Madame d'Etampes to
herself, when he had gone; "he seems ten years older.
What gives him this almost imposing gravity? Is it
suffering? is it happiness? Is he sincere, in short, or
acting under the influence of that accursed Benvenuto?
Is he playing a part with the talent of a consummate
artist, or is he simply following his own nature?"

Anne was perplexed. The strange vertigo which
gradually overpowered all those who contended with
Benvenuto Cellini began to steal over her, despite her
strength of mind. She set spies upon Ascanio, who
followed him on the rare occasions when he left the
studio, but that step led to no result. At last she sent
for the provost and Comte d'Orbec, and advised them,
as another would have ordered, to make a second and
unexpected domiciliary visit to the Grand-Nesle.

They followed her advice; but although surprised at

his work, Benvenuto received them even more cordially than he received the provost alone on the former occasion. One would have said, so courteous and expansive was he, that their presence implied no suspicions that were insulting to him. He told Comte d'Orbec good-humoredly of the ambush that he fell into as he left his house with his golden burden a few days before, — on the same day, he observed, on which Mademoiselle d'Estourville disappeared. This time as before he offered to accompany his visitors through the château, and to assist the provost in recovering his authority as a father, whose sacred duties he understood so well. He was very happy that he happened to be at home to do honor to his guests, for he was to start that same day within two hours for Romorantin, having been named by François I., in his condescension, as one of the artists who were to go to meet the Emperor.

For events in the world of politics had moved on as rapidly as those of our humble narrative. Charles V., emboldened by his rival's public promise, and by the secret undertaking of Madame d'Etampes, was within a few day's journey of Paris. A deputation had been selected to go out to receive him, and D'Orbec and the provost found Cellini in travelling costume.

"If he leaves Paris with the rest of the escort," D'Orbec whispered to the provost, "in all probability he did n't carry off Colombe, and we have no business here."

"I told you so before we came," retorted the provost.

However, they decided to go through with their perquisition, and set about it with painstaking minuteness. Benvenuto accompanied them at first, but as he saw that their investigations were likely to be very prolonged, he asked their permission to leave them, and return to the studio to give some orders to his workmen, as he was to take his leave very soon, and desired to find the preparations for casting his Jupiter finished at his return.

He did in fact return to the studio, and distributed the work among his men, bidding them obey Ascanio as if he were himself. He then said a few words in Italian in Ascanio's ear, bade them all adieu, and prepared to take his departure. A horse all saddled, and held by little Jehan, awaited him in the outer courtyard.

At that moment Scozzone went up to Benvenuto and took him aside.

" Do you know, master," she said with a sober face, " that your departure leaves me in a very difficult position ? "

" How so, my child ? "

" Pagolo is becoming fonder of me all the time."

" Ah ! is it so ? "

" And he is forever talking to me about his love."

" What do you reply ? "

" Dame ! as you bade me, master. I say that I will see, and that perhaps it may be arranged."

" Very well."

" How is it very well ? You don't understand, Benvenuto, that he takes everything that I say to him most seriously, and that I may be entering into a real engagement with him. It's a fortnight since you laid down a rule of conduct for me to adopt, is it not ? "

" Yes, I think so ; I hardly remember."

" But I have a better memory than you. During the first five days I replied by reasoning gently with him : I told him he must try to conquer his passion, and love me no more. The next five days I listened in silence, and that was a very compromising kind of an answer; but you bade me do it, so I did it. Since then I have been driven to talk of my duty to you, and yesterday, master, I reached a point where I besought him to be generous, while he pressed me to confess my love for him."

"If that is so, it puts a different face on the matter," said Benvenuto.

"Ah, at last!" said Scozzone.

"Yes, now listen, little one. During the first three days of my absence, you will let him think that you love him; during the next three, you will confess your love."

"What, you bid me do that, Benvenuto!" cried Scozzone, deeply wounded at the master's too great confidence in her.

"Never you fear. What have you to reproach yourself for when I authorize you to do it?"

"Mon Dieu! nothing, I know," said Scozzone; "but being placed as I am between your indifference and his love, I may end by falling in love with him outright."

"Nonsense! in six days? Are n't you strong enough to remain indifferent to him six days?"

"Yes, indeed! I give you six days; but don't remain away seven, I beg you."

"No fear, my child, I will return in time. Adieu, Scozzone."

"Adieu, master," returned Scozzone, sulking, smiling, and weeping all at once.

While Cellini was giving Catherine these instructions, the provost and D'Orbec returned to the studio.

When they were left to themselves, with unrestricted freedom of movement, they went about their search in a sort of frenzy; they explored the garrets and cellars, sounded all the walls, moved all the furniture; they

detained all the servants they met, and displayed the
ardor of creditors with the patience of hunters.   A
hundred times they retraced their steps, examining the
same thing again and again, like a sheriff's officer with
a writ to serve, and when they had finished they were
flushed and excited, but had discovered nothing.

"Well, messieurs," said Benvenuto, preparing to
mount his horse, "you found nothing, eh? So much the
worse! so much the worse! I understand what a painful thing it must be for two sensitive hearts like yours,
but notwithstanding my sympathy with your suffering
and my desire to assist in your search I must begone.
If you feel called upon to visit the Grand-Nesle in my
absence, do not hesitate, but make yourself perfectly at
home here.   I have given orders that the house be open
to you at all times.   My only consolation for leaving
you in so anxious a frame of mind is the hope that I
shall learn upon my return that you have found your
daughter, Monsieur le Prévôt, and you your fair *fiancée*,
Monsieur d'Orbec.   Adieu, messieurs."

Thereupon he turned to his companions, who were
standing in a group at the door, all save Ascanio, who
doubtless did not care to stand face to face with his
rival.

"Adieu, my children," he said.   "If during my
absence Monsieur le Prévôt desires to inspect my house
a third time, do not forget to receive him as its former
master."

With that little Jehan threw open the door, and
Benvenuto galloped away.

"You see that we are idiots, my dear fellow," said
Comte d'Orbec to the provost.   "When a man has kidnapped a girl, he doesn't go off to Romorantin with the
court."

VI.

CHARLES THE FIFTH AT FONTAINEBLEAU.

IT was not without grave doubts and a terrible sinking at the heart that Charles V. stepped foot upon French territory, where earth and air were, so to speak, his enemies, whose king he had treated unworthily when he was a prisoner in his hands, and whose Dauphin he had perhaps poisoned, — he was at least accused of it. Europe anticipated terrible reprisals on the part of François I. from the moment that his rival placed himself in his power. But Charles's audacity, great gambler in empires that he was, would not permit him to draw back; and as soon as he had skilfully felt the ground and paved the way, he boldly crossed the Pyrenees.

He counted upon finding devoted friends at the French court, and thought that he could safely trust to three guaranties: the ambition of Madame d'Etampes, the overweening conceit of the Connétable Anne de Montmorency, and the king's chivalrous nature.

We have seen how and for what reason the duchess chose to serve his interests. With the constable it was a different matter. The great stumbling-block in the way of statesmen of all lands and all periods is the question of alliances. Politics, which, in this matter and many others, is perforce conjectural only, is often mistaken, alas! like the science of medicine, in study-ing the symptoms of affinities between peoples, and in risking remedies for their animosities. Now the con-stable was a monomaniac on the subject of the Spanish alliance. He had got it into his head that France's salvation lay in that direction, and provided that he could satisfy Charles V., who had been at war with his master twenty years out of twenty-five, he cared but little how much he displeased his other allies, the Turks and the Protestants, or let slip the most magnifi-cent opportunities, like that which gave Flanders to François I.

The king had blind confidence in Montmorency. In truth the constable had in the last war against the Emperor displayed a hitherto unheard of resolution, and had checked the enemy's advance. To be sure he did it at the cost of the ruin of a province, by laying the country waste before him, by devastating a tenth part of France. But what especially impressed the king was his minister's haughty roughness of manner, his inflexible obstinacy, which to a superficial mind might seem cleverness and unswerving firmness of resolution. The result was that Francois listened to the "great suborner of men," as Brantôme calls him, with a def-erence equal to the fear inspired in his inferiors by this terrible reciter of *paternosters*, who alternated his prayers with hangings.

Charles V. could therefore safely rely upon the per-severing friendship of the constable.

He placed even more reliance upon his rival's gener-osity. Indeed, François I. carried magnanimity to an absurd point.

"My kingdom," he said, "has no toll-house, like a bridge, and I do not sell my hospitality." The astute

Charles knew that he could trust the word of the "knightly king."

Nevertheless, when the Emperor was fairly upon French territory, he could not overcome his apprehension and his doubts. He found the king's two sons awaiting him at the frontier, and throughout his journey they overwhelmed him with attentions and honors. But the crafty monarch shuddered as he thought that all this appearance of cordiality might conceal some deep-laid snare.

"I must say that I sleep very ill," he said, "in a foreign country."

He brought an anxious preoccupied face to the fêtes which were given him, and, as he advanced farther and farther toward the heart of the country, he became more and more sad and gloomy.

Whenever he rode into a city, he would ask himself, amid all the haranguing, as he passed beneath the triumphal arches, if that was the city where he was to be imprisoned; then he would murmur beneath his breath, "Not this or any other city, but all France, is my dungeon; all these assiduous courtiers are my jailers." And each hour as it passed added something to the apprehension of this tiger, who believed himself to be in a cage, and saw bars on all sides.

One day, as they were riding along, Charles d'Orléans, a fascinating, frolicsome child, — who was in great haste to be amiable and gallant, as a son of France, before dying of the plague like any peasant, — leaped lightly to the saddle behind the Emperor and threw his arms about his waist, crying gleefully, "Now you are my prisoner!" Charles became pale as death, and nearly fainted.

At Châtellerault, the poor imaginary captive was met

by François, who welcomed him fraternally, and on the
following day presented the whole court to him, — the
valorous, magnificent nobility, the glory of the country,
and the artists and men of letters, the glory of the king.
The fêtes and merry-makings began in good earnest.
The Emperor wore a brave face everywhere, but in his
heart he was afraid, and constantly reproached himself
for his imprudence. From time to time, as if to test
his liberty, he would go out at daybreak from the
château where he had lain at night, and he was
delighted to see that his movements were not interfered
with outside of the honors paid him. But could he be
sure that he was not watched from a distance? Sometimes, as if from mere caprice, he changed the itinerary
arranged for his journey, to the despair of François I.,
because part of the ceremonial prescribed by him went
for naught as a consequence.

When he was within two day's ride of Paris he
remembered with terror the French king's sojourn at
Madrid. For an emperor the capital would seem to be
the most honorable place of detention, and at the same
time the surest. He therefore begged the king to escort
him at once to Fontainebleau, of which he had heard so
much. This overturned all of François's plans, but
he was too hospitable to allow his disappointment to
appear, and at once sent word to the queen and all the
ladies to repair to Fontainebleau.

The presence of his sister Eleanora, and her confidence in her husband's good faith, allayed the Emperor's
anxiety to some extent. But, although reassured for
the moment, Charles V. was never able to feel at his
ease while he was within the dominions of the King of
France. François was the mirror of the past, Charles
the type of the future. The sovereign of modern times

never rightly understood the hero of the Middle Ages; it was impossible that there should be any real sympathy between the last of the chevaliers and the first of the diplomatists.

It is true Louis XI. might, strictly speaking, lay claim to this latter title, but in our opinion Louis XI. was not so much the scheming diplomatist as the grasping miser.

On the day of the Emperor's arrival there was a hunting party in the forest of Fontainebleau. Hunting was a favorite pastime of François I. It was not much better than a terrible bore to Charles V. Nevertheless he seized with avidity this further opportunity to see if he was not a prisoner; he let the hunt pass, took a by-road, and rode about at random until he was lost. But when he found that he was entirely alone in the middle of the forest, as free as the air that blew through the branches, or as the birds that flew through the air, he was almost wholly reassured, and began to recover his good humor in some measure. And yet the anxious expression returned to his face when, upon his making his appearance at the rendezvous, François came to him, flushed with the excitement of the chase, and still holding in his hand the bleeding boar-spear. The warrior of Marignano and Pavia was much in evidence in the king's pleasures.

"Come, my dear brother, let us enjoy ourselves!" said François, passing his arm through Charles's in a friendly way, when they had both alighted at the palace gate, and, leading him to the Galerie de Diane, resplendent with the paintings of Rosso and Primaticcio. "Vrai Dieu! you are as thoughtful as I was at Madrid. But you will agree, my dear brother, that I had some reason for being so, for I was your prisoner.

while you are my guest; you are free, you are on the
eve of a triumph. Rejoice therefore with us, if not
because of the fêtes, which are doubtless beneath the
notice of a great politician like yourself, at least in the
thought that you are on your way to humble all those
beer-drinking Flemings, who presume to talk of renew-
ing the Communes. Or, better still, forget the rebels,
and think only of enjoying yourself with friends.
Does not my court impress you pleasantly?"

"It is superb, my brother," said Charles, "and I
envy you. I too have a court — you have seen it — but
a stern, joyless court, a gloomy assemblage of statesmen
and generals like Lannoy, Peschiara, and Antonio de
Leyra. But you have, beside your warriors and statesmen, beside your Montmorencys and Dubellays, beside
your scholars, beside Budée, Duchâtel, and Lascaris, —
beside all these you have your poets and your artists,
Marot, Jean Goujon, Primaticcio, Benvenuto; and,
above all, your adorable women, — Marguerite de Navarre, Diane de Poitiers, Catherine de Medicis, and
so many others; and verily I begin to believe, my dear
brother, that I would willingly exchange my gold
mines for your flower-strewn fields."

"Ah! but you have not yet seen the fairest of all
these lovely flowers," said François naïvely to Eleanora's
brother.

"No, and I am dying with longing to see that marvellous pearl of loveliness," said the Emperor, who
understood that the king alluded to Madame d'Etampes;
"but even now I think that it is well said that yours is
the fairest realm on earth, my brother."

"But you have the fairest countship, Flanders; the
fairest duchy, Milan."

"You refused the first last month," said the Emperor,

smiling, " and I thank you for so doing; but you covet the other, do you not ? " he added with a sigh.

" Ah ! let us not talk of serious matters to-day, my cousin, I beg you," said François; " after the pleasures of war there is nothing, I confess, which I like less to disturb than the pleasures of a festal occasion like the present."

" It is the truth," rejoined Charles, with the grimace of a miser, who realizes that he must pay a debt, " it is the truth that the Milanese is very dear to my heart, and that it would be like tearing my heart out to give it to you."

" Say rather to return it to me, my brother; that word would be more accurate, and would perhaps soften your disappointment. But that is not the matter in hand now; we must enjoy ourselves. We will talk of the Milanese later."

" Gift or restitution, given or returned," said the Emperor, " you will none the less possess one of the finest lordships in the world; for you shall have it, my brother; it is decided, and I will keep my engagements with you as faithfully as you keep yours with me."

" Mon Dieu ! " cried François, beginning to be vexed at this everlasting recurrence to serious matters; " what do you regret, my brother? Are you not King of the Spains, Emperor of Germany, Count of Flanders, and lord, either by influence or by right of your sword, of all Italy, from the foot of the Alps to the farthest point of Calabria ? "

" But you have France! " rejoined Charles with a sigh.

" You have the Indies and their golden treasures; you have Peru and the mines! "

" But you have France! "

"You reign over an empire so vast that the sun never sets upon it."

"But you have France! What would your Majesty say, if I should cast an eye on this diamond among kingdoms, as fondly and gloatingly as you gaze upon that pearl of duchies, Milan?"

"Look, you, my brother," said François gravely, "I have instincts rather than ideas upon these momentous questions; but, as they say in your country, 'Do not touch the queen!' so I say to you, 'Do not touch France!'"

"Mon Dieu!" exclaimed Charles; "are we not cousins and allies?"

"Most certainly," was François's reply, "and I most earnestly hope that nothing will happen henceforth to embitter our relationship or disturb our alliance."

"I too hope so," said the Emperor. "But," he continued, with his cunning smile and hypocritical expression, "can I answer for the future, and prevent my son Philip, for instance, from falling out with your son Henri?"

"Such a quarrel would not be dangerous for France, if Augustus is succeeded by Tiberius."

"What matter who the master is?" said Charles, waxing warm; "the Empire will still be the Empire, and the Rome of the Cæsars was still Rome when the Cæsars had ceased to be Cæsars in everything save name."

"True, but the Empire of Charles V. is not the Empire of Octavius, my brother," said François, a little piqued. "Pavia was a glorious battle, but it was no Actium; then, too, Octavius was very wealthy, while, notwithstanding your Indian treasures and your Peruvian mines, you are well known to be in straitened circumstances financially; your unpaid troops were driven to sack Rome to procure means of subsistence, and now that Rome is sacked they are in revolt."

"And you, my brother," said Charles, "have alienated the royal domains, as I am informed, and are driven to treat Luther very tenderly, so that the German princes may consent to loan you money."

"Not to mention the fact," retorted François, "that your Cortes is very far from being so manageable as the Senate, while I can boast that I have freed the Kings of France from their dependence forever."

"Beware that your parliaments don't put you back into leading-strings some fine day."

The discussion was growing warm, both monarchs were getting excited, and the long standing antipathy which had kept them apart so long, was beginning to glow afresh. François was on the point of forgetting the duties of hospitality, and Charles the dictates of prudence, when the former suddenly remembered that he was beneath his own roof.

"On my word, my good brother," he exclaimed abruptly, laughing aloud, "I believe, by Mahomet's belly! that we were near losing our tempers. I told you that we must not talk of serious matters, but must leave such discussions to our ministers, and keep for ourselves only our good friendship. Come, let us agree, once for all, that you are to have the world, less France, and drop the subject."

"And less the Milanese, my brother," said Charles, realizing the imprudence he had been guilty of, and seeking at once to avoid its effects, "for the Milanese is yours. I have promised it to you, and I renew my promise."

As they exchanged these mutual assurances of con-

tinuing good will, the door of the gallery opened,
and Madame d'Etampes appeared. The king walked
quickly to meet her, took her hand, and led her to
where the Emperor stood, who, seeing her then for the
first time, and, being fully informed as to what had
taken place between her and Monsieur de Medina, fixed
his most penetrating gaze upon her as she approached.

"My brother," said the king smiling, "do you see
this fair dame?"

"Not only do I see her," replied Charles, "but I
admire her."

"Very well! you do not know what she wants?"

"Is it one of my Spains? I will give it her."

"No, no, brother, not that."

"What then?"

"She wants me to detain you at Paris until you have
destroyed the treaty of Madrid, and confirmed by acts
the promise you have given me."

"If the advice is good, you should follow it,"
rejoined the Emperor, bowing low before the duchess,
as much to hide the sudden pallor which these words
caused to overspread his face, as to perform an act of
courtesy.

He had no time to say more, nor could François see
the effect produced by the words he had laughingly
let fall, and which Charles was quite ready to take
seriously, for the door opened again and the whole
court poured into the gallery.

During the half-hour preceding dinner, when this
clever, cultivated, corrupt throng was assembled in the
salons of the palace, the scene we described apropos of
the reception at the Louvre was re-enacted in all its
essential details. There were the same men and the
same women, the same courtiers and the same valets.

Loving and malevolent glances were exchanged as usual, and sarcastic remarks and gallant speeches were indulged in with the customary freedom.

Charles V., spying Anne de Montmorency, whom he with good reason deemed to be his surest ally, went to him, and talked in a corner with him and the Duke of Medina, his ambassador.

"I will sign whatever you choose, constable," said the Emperor, who knew the old campaigner's loyalty; "prepare a deed of cession of the Duchy of Milan, and by Saint James, though it be one of the brightest jewels of my crown, I will sign an absolute surrender of it to you."

"A deed!" cried the constable, hotly putting aside the suggestion of a precaution which implied distrust. "A deed, Sire! what is your Majesty's meaning? No deed, Sire, no deed; your word, nothing more. Does your Majesty think that we shall have less confidence in you than you had in us, when you came to France with no written document to rely upon?"

"You will do as you should do, Monsieur de Montmorency," rejoined the Emperor, giving him his hand, "you will do what you should do."

The constable walked away.

"Poor dupe!" exclaimed the Emperor; "he plays at politics, Medina, as moles dig their holes, blindly."

"But the king, Sire?" queried Medina.

"The king is too proud of his own grandeur of soul not to be sure of ours. He will foolishly let us go, Medina, and we will prudently let him wait. To make him wait, my lord, is not to break my promise, but to postpone its fulfilment, that is all."

"But Madame d'Etampes?" suggested Medina.

"As to her we shall see," said the Emperor, moving

up and down a magnificent ring with a superb diamond, which he wore on his left thumb. " Ah ! I must have a long interview with her."

While these words were rapidly exchanged in low tones between the Emperor and his minister, the duchess was mercilessly making sport of Marmagne, apropos of his nocturnal exploits, all in presence of Messire d'Estourville.

" Can it be of your people, Monsieur de Marmagne," she was saying, " that Benvenuto tells every comer this extraordinary story ? Attacked by four bandits, and with but one arm free to defend himself, he simply made these gentry escort him home. Were you one of these gentlemanly bravos, viscount ? "

" Madame," replied poor Marmagne, in confusion, " it did not take place precisely in that way, and Benvenuto tells the story too favorably for himself."

" Yes, yes, I doubt not that he embroiders it a little, and adds a few details by way of ornament, but the main fact is true, viscount, the main fact is true; and in such matters the main fact is everything."

" Madame," returned Marmagne, " I promise you that I will have my revenge, and I shall be more fortunate next time."

" Pardon, viscount, pardon! it 's not a question of revenge, but of beginning another game. Cellini, I should say, has won the first two bouts."

" Yes, thanks to my absence," muttered Marmagne, with increasing embarrassment; " because my men took advantage of my not being there to run away, the miserable villains ! "

" Oh! " said the provost, " I advise you, Marmagne, to admit that you are beaten in that direction; you have no luck with Cellini."

"In that case it seems to me that we may console each other, my dear provost," retorted Marmagne, "for if we add known facts to the mysterious rumors which are in circulation, — the capture of the Grand-Nesle to the reported disappearance of one of its fair inmates, — Cellini would seem not to have brought you luck either, Messire d'Estourville. To be sure, he is said to be actively interested in the fortunes of your family, if not in your own, my dear provost."

"Monsieur de Marmagne," cried the provost fiercely, in a furious rage to learn that his paternal infelicity was beginning to be noised abroad, — "Monsieur de Marmagne, you will explain to me later what you mean by your words."

"Ah messieurs, messieurs!" exclaimed the duchess, "do not forget, I beg you, that I am here. You are both in the wrong. Monsieur le Prévôt, it is not for those who know so little about seeking to ridicule those who know so little about finding. Monsieur de Marmagne, in the hour of defeat we must unite against the common enemy, and not afford him the additional satisfaction of seeing the vanquished slashing at one another's throats. They are going to the *salle-à-manger;* your hand, Monsieur de Marmagne. Ah, well! since it seems that men, for all their strength, avail nothing against Cellini, we will see if a woman's wiles will find him equally invincible. I have always thought that allies were simply in the way, and have always loved to make war alone. The risk is greater, I know, but at least the honors of victory are not to be shared with any one."

"The impertinent varlet!" exclaimed Marmagne; "see how familiarly he is talking to our great king. Would not one say he was nobly born, whereas he is naught but a mere stone-cutter."

" What's that you say, viscount? Why, he is a nobleman, and of the most venerable nobility ! " said the duchess, with a laugh. " Do you know of many among our oldest families who descend from a lieutenant of Julius Cæsar, and who have the three *fleurs-de-lis* and the *lambel* of the house of Anjou in their crest? 'T is not the king who honors the sculptor by speaking to him, messieurs, as you see; the sculptor, on the other hand, confers honor upon the king by condescending to address him."

François I. and Cellini were in fact conversing at that moment with the familiarity to which the great ones of earth had accustomed the chosen artist of Heaven.

" Well, Benvenuto," the king was saying, " how do we come on with our Jupiter? "

" I am preparing to cast it, Sire."

" And when will that great work be performed? "

" Immediately upon my return to Paris, Sire."

" Take our best foundrymen, Cellini, and omit nothing to make the operation successful. If you need money, you know that I am ready."

" I know that you are the greatest, the noblest, and the most generous king on earth, Sire," replied Benvenuto; " but thanks to the salary which your Majesty orders paid to me, I am rich. As to the operation concerning which you are somewhat anxious, Sire, I will, with your gracious permission, rely upon my own resources to prepare and execute it. I distrust all your French foundrymen, not that they are unskilful, but because I am afraid that their national pride will make them disinclined to place their skill at the service of an artist from beyond the Alps. And I confess, Sire, that I attach too much importance to the success of my Jupiter to allow any other than myself to lay hand to it."

" Bravo, Cellini, bravo ! " cried the king; " spoken like a true artist. "

" Moreover, " added Benvenuto, " I wish to be entitled to remind your Majesty of the promise you made me. "

" That is right, my trusty friend.   If we are content with it, we are to grant you a boon.   We have not forgotten.   Indeed, if we should forget, we bound ourselves in the presence of witnesses.   Is it not so, Montmorency ? and Poyet ? · Our constable and our chancellor will remind us of our plighted word. "

" Ah ! your Majesty cannot conceive how precious that word has become to me since the day it was given. "

" Very well ! it shall be kept, Monsieur.   But the doors are open.   To table, messieurs, to table ! "

François thereupon joined the Emperor, and the two together walked at the head of the procession formed by the illustrious guests.   Both wings of the folding doors being thrown open, the two sovereigns entered side by side and took places facing each other, Charles between Eleanora and Madame d'Etampes, François between Catherine de Medicis and Marguerite de Navarre.

The banquet was exquisite and the guests in the best of spirits.   François was in his element, and enjoyed himself in kingly fashion, but laughed like a serf at all the tales told him by Marguerite de Navarre.   Charles overwhelmed Madame d'Etampes with compliments and attentions.   The others talked of art and politics, and so the time passed.

At dessert, as was customary, the pages brought water for the guests to wash their hands.   Thereupon Madame d'Etampes took the ewer and basin intended for Charles V. from the hands of the servitor, while

Marguerite did the same for François, poured water from
the ewer into the basin, and, kneeling upon one knee,
according to the Spanish etiquette, presented the basin
to the Emperor. He dipped the ends of his fingers, gazing at his noble and beautiful attendant the while, and
laughingly dropped the superb ring, of which we have
spoken, into the water.

"Your Majesty is losing your ring," said Anne,
dipping her own taper fingers into the water, and
daintily picking up the jewel, which she handed to the
Emperor.

"Keep the ring, madame," the Emperor replied, in a
low voice; "the hands in which it now is are too noble
and too beautiful for me to take it from them again.
It is to bind the bargain for the Duchy of Milan," he
added, in a still lower tone.

The duchess smiled and said no more. The pebble
had fallen at her feet, but the pebble was worth a
million.

As they returned from the *salle-à-manger* to the salon,
and passed thence to the ball-room, Madame d'Etampes
stopped Benvenuto, who was brought near to her by the
press.

"Messire Cellini," said she, handing him the ring
which constituted a pledge of the alliance between the
Emperor and herself, "here is a diamond which you
will hand, if you please, to your pupil Ascanio, for
the crown of my lily; it is the dewdrop I promised
him."

"And it has fallen from Aurora's fingers in very
truth, madame," rejoined the artist with a mocking
smile and affected gallantry.

He glanced at the ring, and started back in surprise,
for he recognized the diamond he had long ago set for

Pope Clement VII. and had himself carried to the sublime Emperor on the sovereign Pontiff's behalf.

To induce Charles V. to divest himself of such a priceless jewel, especially in favor of a woman, there must necessarily be some secret understanding, some occult treaty, between himself and the recipient.

While Charles continues to pass his days and nights at Fontainebleau, in the alternations of distrust and confidence, we have endeavored to describe, while he schemes, intrigues, burrows underground, promises, retracts, and promises anew, let us cast a glance upon the Grand-Nesle, and see if anything of interest is occurring among those of its occupants who have remained there.

VII.

THE GHOSTLY MONK.

The whole colony was in a state of intense excitement. The ghost of the monk, the unsubstantial guest of the convent, upon the ruins of which Amaury's palace was built, had returned within three or four days. Dame Perrine had seen him walking around at night in the gardens of the Grand-Nesle, clad in his long white frock, and treading so lightly that he left no footprints on the ground, and made no noise.

How happened it that Dame Perrine, whose domicile was the Petit-Nesle, had seen the ghostly visitor walking in the garden of the Grand-Nesle at three o'clock in the morning? We cannot tell except by committing a very grave indiscretion, but we are historians first of all, and our readers are entitled to know the most secret details of the lives of the characters we have brought upon the stage, especially when those details are calculated to throw a bright light upon the sequel of our narrative.

Dame Perrine, by virtue of Colombe's disappearance, by the retirement of Pulchérie, for whose presence there was no further pretext, and by the departure of the provost, was left absolute mistress of the Petit-Nesle; for the gardener Raimbault and his assistants were, for economical reasons, engaged in Messire

d'Estourville's service during the day only. Dame
Perrine found herself, therefore, queen of the Petit-
Nesle, but at the same time a solitary queen, so that
she nearly died of ennui during the day, and of fear at
night.

It occurred to her that there was a remedy for this
unfortunate condition of affairs, during the day at least;
her friendly relations with Dame Ruperta opened the
doors of the Grand-Nesle to her. She asked permission to visit her neighbors, and it was most cordially
granted.

But upon availing herself of this permission Dame
Perrine was naturally brought in contact with her
neighbors of the other sex. Dame Perrine was a
buxom creature of thirty-six years, who confessed to
twenty-nine of them. Plump and rosy still, and always
prepossessing, her coming was quite an event in the
studio, where ten or twelve worthy fellows were for-
ging, cutting, filing, hammering, chiselling, — good
livers all, fond of play on Sundays, of wine on Sundays
and holidays, and of the fair sex all the time. Three
of our old acquaintances, after three or four days had
passed, were all brought down with the same arrow.

They were little Jehan, Simon-le-Gaucher, and Hermann the German.

Ascanio, Jacques Aubry, and Pagolo escaped the
charm, having their minds on other things.

The other comrades may well have felt some sparks
of this Greek fire, but they realized their inferior position, no doubt, and poured the water of their humility
upon the first sparks before they became a conflagration.

Little Jehan loved after the manner of Cherubino,
that is to say, he was in love with loving. Dame

Perrine, as the reader will readily understand, had too much common sense to respond to such an *ignis fatuus* as that.

Simon-le-Gaucher could offer more reliable future prospects, and his flame promised to be more enduring, but Dame Perrine was a very superstitious person. She had seen Simon cross himself with his left hand, and she reflected that it would be necessary for him to sign the marriage contract with his left hand. Dame Perrine was convinced that the sign of the cross executed with the left hand was calculated to destroy rather than to save a soul, and in like manner no one could have persuaded her that a marriage contract signed with the left hand could have any other result than an unhappy menage. She therefore, but without disclosing the reasons for her repugnance, received Simon-le-Gaucher's first advances in a way to make him renounce all hope.

Hermann remained.   Ah, Hermann! that was a different matter.

Hermann was no coxcomb, like little Jehan, nor a man with the seal of Nature's displeasure upon him, like left-handed Simon; in Hermann's personality there was something honest and outspoken which appealed to Dame Perrine's heart. Moreover, Hermann, instead of having a left hand for the right and *vice versa*, made use of either or both so energetically that he seemed to have two right hands. He was a magnificent man too, according to all vulgar ideas. Dame Perrine therefore had fixed her choice upon Hermann.

But, as we know, Hermann was as innocent as Celadon. The result was that Dame Perrine's first broadsides, the pouting and sighs and sidelong glances, were utterly powerless against the naïve timidity of the honest German. He contented himself with staring at Dame Perrine out of his great round eyes; but, like the blind men of the Gospel, "eyes had he, but he saw not," or if he did see, he saw the buxom governess as a whole simply, without noting details. Dame Perrine repeatedly proposed that they should go for a walk on the Quai des Augustins, or in the gardens of the Grand- or Petit-Nesle, and on every occasion she selected Hermann for her cavalier. This made Hermann very happy internally. His great Teutonic heart beat five or six extra pulsations a minute when Dame Perrine was hanging upon his arm; but either because he found some difficulty in pronouncing the French language, or because it gave him greater pleasure to hear the object of his secret thoughts talk, Dame Perrine could rarely extract anything more from him than these two sacramental phrases, "Ponchour, matemoizelle," and "Atieu, matemoizelle," which Hermann generally pronounced at an interval of two hours; the first when Dame Perrine took his arm, the second when she let it go. Now, although this title of Mademoiselle was immensely flattering to Dame Perrine, and although there was something very agreeable in talking two hours without fear of interruption, she would have been glad to have her monologue broken in upon by an occasional interjection which might give her some idea of the progress she was making in the heart of her mute attendant.

Her progress, however, was none the less real for not being expressed in words or by play of feature; the fire was kindled in the honest German's heart, and, being fanned every day by Dame Perrine's presence, became a veritable volcano. Hermann began at last to be conscious of the preference Dame Perrine accorded him, and he was only waiting until he was a little more certain of it to declare himself. Dame Perrine understood his hesitation. One evening, as he parted from her at the door of the Petit-Nesle, she saw that he was so agitated that she thought it would be a real kindness on her part to press his hand. Hermann, transported with delight, responded by a similar demonstration; but to his great amazement Dame Perrine gave a piercing shriek. In his delirious bliss, Hermann did not measure his pressure. He thought that the tighter he squeezed her hand, the more accurate idea he would convey of the violence of his passion; and he very nearly crushed the poor governess's fingers.

Hermann was thunderstruck by her shriek; but Dame Perrine, fearing to discourage him just as he had summoned up courage to make his first advance, forced herself to smile, and said, as she separated her fingers, which were almost glued together for the moment: —

"It's nothing, nothing, dear Monsieur Hermann; it's nothing, absolutely nothing."

"Tausend pardons, Matemoizelle Perrine," said the German, "but I lofe you sehr viel, and I haf pressed your hant as I lofe you! Tausend pardons!"

"There's no need, Monsieur Hermann, there's no need. Your love is an honorable love, I trust, which a woman need not blush to win."

"O Tieu! O Tieu!" cried Hermann, "indeed, my lofe is honorable, Matemoizelle Perrine; put I haf not yet tared to speak to you of it; put since die wort haf escaped me, I lofe you, I lofe you, I lofe you sehr viel, Matemoizelle Perrine."

"And I, Monsieur Hermann," said Dame Perrine mincingly, "think I can say, for I believe you to be a gallant youth, incapable of compromising a poor woman, that — Mon Dieu ! how shall I say it ? "

" Oh say it ! say it ! " cried Hermann.

" Well ! that — ah, it is wrong of me to confess it ! "

" Nein, nein ! it is not wrong. Say it ! say it ! "

" Very well. I confess that I am not indifferent to your passion."

" Sacrement ! " cried the German, beside himself with joy.

Now one evening when, after a promenade, the Juliet of the Petit-Nesle had escorted her Romeo to the door of the Grand-Nesle, she espied as she was returning alone through the garden door, the white spectre we have mentioned, which, in the opinion of the worthy governess, could be no other than that of the monk. It is needless to say that Dame Perrine entered the house half dead with fear, and barricaded herself in her room.

The next morning the whole studio was acquainted with the story of the nocturnal apparition. Dame Perrine, however, contented herself with relating the simple fact without going into details. The ghostly monk had appeared. That was the whole of it. It was useless to question her, for she would say nothing more.

All that day the ghostly monk was the engrossing subject of conversation at the Grand-Nesle. Some believed in the appearance of the phantom, others laughed at it. It was noticed that Ascanio was the leader of the sceptics, the others being little Jehan, Simon-le-Gaucher, and Jacques Aubry. The faction of the believers included Dame Ruperta, Scozzone, Pagolo, and Hermann.

In the evening they all assembled in the second

courtyard of the Petit-Nesle. Dame Perrine, when questioned in the morning as to the origin of the legend of the ghostly monk, requested that she might have the day to refresh her memory, and when night came she announced that she was ready to relate the awful story. Dame Perrine was as knowing in the matter of stage effects as a modern dramatist, and she knew that a ghost story loses all its effect if told in the sunlight, while, on the other hand, that effect is doubled if it is told in the dark.

Her audience consisted of Hermann, who sat at her right, Dame Ruperta, who sat at her left, Pagolo and Scozzone, who sat side by side, and Jacques Aubry, who lay on the grass between his two friends, little Jehan and Simon-ie-Gaucher. Ascanio had declared that he held such old women's tales in utter contempt, and would not even listen to them.

" Unt zo, Matemoizelle Perrine," said Hermann after a moment of silence, while each one arranged his posture so as to listen at ease, " unt zo you are going to tell us the story of the monk's ghost? "

" Yes," said Dame Perrine, " yes; but I ought to warn you that it's a terrible story, and perhaps not a very comfortable one to listen to at this hour; but as we are all devout persons, although there may be some sceptics among us on the subject of ghosts, and as Monsieur Hermann is strong enough to put Satan himself to flight if he should make his appearance, I will venture to tell you the story."

" Pardon, pardon, Matemoizelle Perrine, put if Satan comes I must tell you not to count on me; I will fight mit men, ja, all you choose, put not mit der Teufel."

" Never mind ! I will fight him if he comes, Dame

Perrine," said Jacques Aubry. "Go on, and don't be afraid."

"Is there a charcoal-purner in your story, Matemoizelle Perrine?" queried Hermann.

"A charcoal-burner? No, Monsieur Hermann."

"All right; it's all the same."

"Why a charcoal-burner?"

"Because in all the Cherman stories there is a charcoal-purner. Put never mind, it must be a fine story all the same. Go on, Matemoizelle Perrine."

"You must know, then," began Dame Perrine, "that there was formerly on this spot where we now sit, and before the Hôtel de Nesle was built, a community of monks, composed of the handsomest men ever seen, the shortest of whom was as tall as Monsieur Hermann."

"Peste! what a community that must have been!" cried Jacques Aubry.

"Be quiet, babbler!" said Scozzone.

"Yes, be quiet, pappler!" echoed Hermann.

"I'll be quiet, I'll be quiet," said the student; "go on, Dame Perrine."

"The prior, whose name was Enguerrand, was a particularly fine specimen. They all had glossy black beards, with black and gleaming eyes; but the prior had the blackest beard and the brightest eyes of all. Moreover the worthy brethren were devout and austere in their devotion to an unparalleled degree, and their voices were so melodious and sweet that people came from leagues around simply to hear them sing the vesper service. At least so I have been told."

"Oh the poor monks!" said Ruperta.

"It's extremely interesting," said Jacques Aubry.

"Es ist sehr wunderbar," said Hermann.

"One day," pursued Dame Perrine, flattered by the

marks of appreciation evoked by her narrative, " a handsome young man was brought before the prior, who
requested to be admitted to the convent as a novice; he
had no beard as yet, but he had large eyes as black as
ebony, and long dark hair with a glossy shimmer like
jet, so that he was admitted without hesitation.   He
said that his name was Antonio, and requested to be
attached to the personal service of the prior, a request
which was granted without hesitation.   I spoke of
voices just now, but Antonio's was the fresh and melodious voice *par excellence*.   Everybody who heard
him sing on the following Sunday was carried away by
it, and yet there was a something in the voice which
distressed even while it fascinated you, a quality which
aroused worldly rather than celestial ideas in the hearts
of those who listened to it; but all the monks were so
pure of heart that none but strangers experienced this
singular emotion, and Don Enguerrand, who was utterly
unconscious of anything of the sort, was so enchanted
with Antonio's voice that he appointed him thenceforth
to sing the responses in the anthems alone, alternately
with the organ.

" The conduct of the young novice was most exem-
plary, and he waited upon the prior with incredible zeal
and earnestness.   The only thing for which he could
possibly be reproved was his constant fits of distraction
from his devotions; always and everywhere his glowing
eyes were fastened upon the prior.

" ' What are you looking at, Antonio ? ' Don Enguerrand would say to him.

" 'I am looking at you, my father,' would be the
reply.

" 'Look at your prayer-book, Antonio.   Now what
are you looking at ? '

" 'You, my father.'

" 'Antonio, look at the image of the Virgin. What are you looking at now ? '

" 'You, my father.'

" 'Antonio, look at the crucifix which we adore.'

" Don Enguerrand began to notice, after a time, upon searching his conscience, that since Antonio's reception into the community he had been more troubled than formerly by evil thoughts. Never before had he sinned more than seven times a day, which, as we all know, is the reckoning of the saints, — sometimes even he had examined his conduct for the day without being able to find more than five or six sins, an extraordinary thing. But now the total of his daily peccadillos mounted as high as ten, twelve, or even fifteen. He would try to make up for it on the following day; he would pray and fast and scourge himself, would the worthy man. Ah! but the farther he went, the greater became the reckoning, until at last it reached a full score. Poor Don Enguerrand knew not which way to turn; he felt that he was damned in spite of all he could do, and he noticed — an observation which might have comforted another, but which increased his consternation — that his most austere monks were under the same strange, incredible, incomprehensible influence; so that their confession, which formerly lasted twenty minutes, half an hour, or an hour at most, now occupied several hours.

" About this time, an occurrence which had been creating a great stir in the province for a month past at last became known at the convent. The lord of a castle near by had lost his daughter Antonia. Antonia had disappeared one fine evening exactly as my poor Colombe has disappeared. But there is this difference :

I am sure that Colombe is an angel, while it seems that
Antonia was possessed of the devil. The poor father
had sought the fugitive high and low, just as Monsieur
le Prévôt has sought Colombe. Only the convent remained to be visited, and as he knew that the evil spirit,
the better to elude search, sometimes conceals himself in
monasteries, he sent his chaplain to Don Enguerrand
to ask permission to make search in his. The prior
assented, with the best possible grace. Perhaps, he
thought, he might by means of this visit discover
something concerning the magic influence which had
been weighing upon him and his brethren for a month
past. But no! the search had no result whatever, and
the nobleman was about to retire more despairing than
ever, when all the monks passed in procession before
him and Don Enguerrand, on their way to the chapel
for the evening service. He looked at them mechanically, one after another, until the last one passed, when
he cried out: —

"'God in heaven! that is Antonia! that is my
daughter!'

"Antonia, for it was she, became as pale as a lily.

"'What are you doing in this sacred garb?' continued the father.

"'What am I doing, father?' said Antonia; 'I am
loving Don Enguerrand with all my heart.'

"'Leave this convent instantly, wretched girl!'
cried her father.

"'I will go out only as a corpse, father,' replied
Antonia.

"Thereupon, despite her father's outcries, she darted
into the chapel on the heels of the monks, and took
her place in her accustomed stall. The prior stood as
if turned to stone. The furious nobleman would have

pursued his daughter, but Don Enguerrand begged him not to profane the holy place by such a scandalous scene, and to wait until the service was at an end. The father consented, and followed Don Enguerrand into the chapel.

"The anthem was about to be chanted, and the majestic prelude upon the organ was like the voice of God. A wonderfully beautiful strain, but instinct with bitter irony, and awful to hear, responded to the sublime tones of the instrument; it was Antonia's voice, and every listening heart shuddered. The organ took up the chant, calm, grave, impressive, and seemed as if it were seeking to drown with its divine magnificence the bitter strains which insulted it from the stalls. Again, as if in acceptance of the challenge, Antonia's voice arose more wildly despairing, more impious, than before. Everybody awaited in speechless dismay the result of this awful dialogue, this alternation of blasphemy and prayer, this strange conflict between God and Satan, and it was amid the most intense and agonizing silence that the celestial music burst forth like a peal of thunder, when the blasphemous strain died away, and poured out upon the heads of the listeners, all bowed save one, the torrents of its wrath. It was something like the dread voice which the guilty will hear on the judgment day. Antonia tried to keep up the contest, but her song this time was nothing more than a shrill, heart-rending cry, like the laugh of the damned, and she fell pale and stiff upon the pavement of the chapel. When they raised her, she was dead."

"Jésus Maria !" cried Dame Ruperta.

"Poor Antonia !" said Hermann innocently.

"Little fool !" muttered Jacques Aubry.

The others kept silence, so great was the impression

produced even upon the sceptics by Dame Perrine's narrative, but Scozzone wiped away a tear, and Pagolo crossed himself.

"When the prior," resumed Dame Perrine, "saw the devil's messenger thus crushed by the wrath of God, he believed, poor dear man, that he was forever delivered from the snares of the tempter; but he reckoned without his host, a very appropriate expression, as he had been so imprudent as to extend his hospitality to one possessed of the devil. On the following night, just after he had dropped off to sleep, he was awakened by the clanking of chains; he opened his eyes, instinctively turned them toward the door, and saw that it swung open unaided, and at the same time a phantom clad in the white robe of a novice drew near the bed, took him by the arm, and cried, 'I am Antonia! Antonia, who loves thee! and God has given me full power over thee because thou hast sinned, in thought if not in act.' And every night at midnight the terrible apparition returned, implacably true to its word, until at last Don Enguerrand made a pilgrimage to the Holy Land, and died, by the special favor of God, just as he knelt before the Holy Sepulchre.

"But Antonia was not satisfied. She fell back upon all the monks in general, and, as there were very few who had not sinned as deeply as the poor prior, she visited them all one after another during the night, roughly awaking them, and crying in an awe-inspiring voice: 'I am Antonia! I am Antonia, who loves thee!'

"Hence the name of the ghostly monk.

"When you are walking through the streets at night, and a figure with a gray or white hood dogs your steps, hasten home; it is the ghostly monk in quest of prey.

" When the convent was demolished to make room for the château, they hoped to be rid of the spectre, but it seems that he is fond of the spot. At various times he has reappeared. And now, God forgive us our sins! the unhappy wretch has appeared again. May God preserve us from his wicked designs ! "

" Amen ! " said Dame Ruperta, crossing herself.

" Amen ! " said Hermann, with a shudder.

" Amen ! " said Jacques Aubry, laughing.

And each of the others repeated the word with an inflection corresponding to the impression produced upon him.

VIII.

WHAT ONE SEES AT NIGHT FROM THE TOP OF A POPLAR.

On the following day, which was that on which the whole court was to return from Fontainebleau, it was Dame Ruperta's turn to announce to the same auditory that she had a momentous revelation to make.

As may be imagined, after such an interesting announcement, the whole party assembled once more in the same spot at the same hour.

They were entirely at their case, because Benvenuto had written to Ascanio that he should stay behind for two or three days to prepare the hall where his Jupiter was to be displayed, which Jupiter was to be cast immediately upon his return.

The provost had simply made his appearance at the Hôtel de Nesle to ask if there was any news of Colombe; but upon being informed by Dame Perrine that everything was *in statu quo*, he at once returned to the Châtelet.

The occupants of the Grand and Petit-Nesle enjoyed entire freedom of action, therefore, both masters being absent.

In the case of Jacques Aubry, although he was to have met Gervaise that evening, curiosity carried the day over love, or rather he hoped that Dame Ruperta would be less diffuse than Dame Perrine, and that she would have finished so early that he might hear her story and still keep his appointment.

This is what Ruperta had to tell.

Dame Perrine's narrative ran in her head all night long, and from the moment that she entered her bedroom she trembled in every limb lest Antonia's spirit should pay her a visit, notwithstanding the blessed relics which hung about her bed.

She barricaded her door, but that was a very inadequate precaution; the old servant was too well versed in the ways of phantoms not to be aware that they know nothing of closed doors. Nevertheless she would have liked also to barricade the window looking upon the garden of the Grand-Nesle, but the original proprietor had neglected to provide the window with shutters, and the present proprietor deemed it useless to burden himself with that expense.

Ordinarily there were curtains at the window; but at this time, as luck would have it, they were at the laundry. The window offered no protection, therefore, save an unpretentious pane of glass, as transparent as the air that it excluded.

On entering the room Ruperta looked under the bed, felt in all the drawers and closets, and did not leave a single corner uninspected. She knew that the devil occupies but little space when he draws in his tail and claws and horns, and that Asmodeus was corked up in a bottle for nobody knows how many years.

The room was entirely untenanted, and there was not the slightest trace of the ghostly monk.

Ruperta went to bed therefore somewhat more at ease, but she left her lamp burning none the less. She was no sooner in bed than she looked toward the window, and saw outside the window a gigantic figure, whose outlines were just discernible in the darkness, and which intercepted the light of the stars. The moon was invisible as it was in its last quarter.

Good Ruperta shivered with fear; she was on the point of crying out or knocking, when she remembered the colossal statue of Mars which reared its head before her window. She immediately looked again in that direction, and recognized perfectly all the outlines of the god of war. This reassured Ruperta for the moment, and she determined positively to go to sleep.

But sleep, the poor man's treasure so often coveted by the rich, is at no man's orders. At night God opens heaven's gates for him, and the capricious rascal visits whom he pleases, turning aside disdainfully from him who calls, and knocking at their doors who least expect him. Ruperta invoked him long before he paid heed to her.

At last, toward midnight, fatigue won the day. Little by little, the good woman's faculties became confused, her thoughts which were in general but ill connected, broke the imperceptible thread which held them, and scattered like the beads of a rosary. Her heart alone, distraught by fear, was still awake; at last it too fell fast asleep, and all was said; the lamp alone kept vigil.

But, like all things of earth, the lamp found rest two hours after Ruperta had closed her eyes in the sleep of the just. Upon the pretext that it had no oil to burn, it began to grow dim, sputtered, blazed up for an instant, and then died.

Just at that time Ruperta had a fearful dream; she dreamed that, as she was returning home from visiting Perrine, the ghostly monk pursued her; but happily, against all precedents of those who dream, Ruperta to her joy found that she had the legs of fifteen years, and fled so swiftly that the ghostly monk, although he seemed to glide and not to run over the ground, only arrived in time to have the door slammed in his face. Ruperta thought, still dreaming, that she heard him snarl and pound upon the door. But, as may be imagined, she was in no haste to let him in. She lit her lamp, ran up the stairs four at a time, jumped into bed, and put out the light.

But, just as she put out the light, she saw the monk's head outside her window; he had crawled up the wall like a lizard, and was trying to come through the glass. In her dream, she heard the grinding of his nails against it.

No sleep can be so sound as to hold out against a dream of that sort. Ruperta awoke with her hair standing on end, and dripping with icy perspiration. Her eyes were open, staring wildly around, and in spite of her they sought the window. With that she uttered a fearful shriek, for this is what she saw.

She saw the head of the colossal Mars shooting forth flame from its eyes and nose and mouth and ears.

She thought at first that she was still asleep, and that it was a continuation of her dream; but she pinched herself till the blood came to make sure that she was really awake; she crossed herself, and repeated mentally three *Paters* and two *Aves*, and the extraordinary phenomena did not disappear.

Ruperta summoned strength enough to put out her hand, seize her broom, and pound against the ceiling with the handle thereof. Hermann slept in the room above hers, and she hoped that the sturdy Teuton would be aroused and hurry to her assistance. But in vain did Ruperta knock: Hermann gave no sign of life

Thereupon she changed the direction of her blows, and, instead of knocking on the ceiling to arouse Hermann, began to knock on the floor to arouse Pagolo, who slept in the room below.

But Pagolo was as deaf as Hermann, and Ruperta pounded to no purpose.

She then abandoned the vertical for the horizontal line. Ascanio was her neighbor, and she knocked on the partition with her broom-handle.

But all was silence in Ascanio's quarters, as in those of Hermann and Pagolo. It was evident that neither of the three was at home. In an instant it occurred to Ruperta that the monk had carried off all three of them.

As there was little consolation in this idea, Ruperta's terror waxed greater and greater, and, as she was certain that no one would come to her assistance, she thrust her head beneath the bedclothes and waited.

She waited an hour, an hour and a half, two hours perhaps, and as she heard no noise, she regained her courage in a measure, softly removed the sheet from her head, and ventured to look with one eye, then with both. The vision had disappeared. The head of Mars had gone out, and all was dark once more.

Although the silence and darkness were calculated to set her mind at rest, it will readily be understood that Dame Ruperta and slumber were at odds for the balance of the night. The poor woman lay, with her ear on the alert and both eyes wide open, until the first rays of dawn reflected on her window announced that the time for ghosts to walk had passed.

Now this is what Ruperta had to tell, and it must be said in her honor that her narrative produced an even deeper impression than that of the preceding night; its effect upon Dame Perrine and Hermann, Scozzone and Pagolo, was particularly noticeable. The two men essayed to make excuses for not hearing Ruperta, but their voices trembled so, and their embarrassment was so great, that Jacques Aubry roared with laughter. Dame Perrine and Scozzone, on the other hand, did not breathe a word. They turned red and pale by turns, so that, if it had been daylight and you could have followed upon their faces the reflection of what was taking place in their minds, you would have believed them at the point of death from apoplexy, and again from inanition, all within ten seconds.

"And so, Dame Perrrine," said Scozzone, who was the first to recover her self-possession, "you claim to have seen the monk's ghost walking in the garden of the Grand-Nesle?"

"As plainly as I see you, my child," was Dame Perrrine's reply.

"And you, Ruperta, saw the head of the Mars on fire?"

"I can see it still."

"Look you," said Dame Perrine, "the accursed ghost must have chosen the head of the statue for his domicile; and as a ghost must of course take a little exercise now and then like a natural being, he comes down at certain hours, walks hither and thither, and when he's tired goes back into the head. Idols and spirits, you see, understand one another, like thieves on market day; they live in hell together, and this horrible false god Mars naturally enough offers his hospitality to the infernal monk."

"Pelieve you zo, Dame Perrine?" queried the innocent German.

"I am sure of it, Monsieur Hermann, sure of it."

" It makes my flesh to greep, on my vord ! " muttered
Hermann with a shudder.

" So you believe in ghosts, Hermann ? " asked Aubry.

" Ja, I do pelieve in tem."

Jacques Aubry shrugged his shoulders, but as he did
so he determined to solve the mystery. It was the
easiest thing in the world for one who, like himself,
went in and out of the house as familiarly as if he were
one of the family. He made up his mind, therefore,
that he would go and see Gervaise the next day, but
that on this evening he would remain at the Grand-
Nesle until ten o'clock; at ten o'clock he would say
good night to everybody and pretend to go away, but
that he would remain within the precincts, climb a
poplar, and make the acquaintance of the phantom from
a hiding place among the branches.

Everything fell out as the student planned. He left
the studio alone as usual, shut the door leading into the
quay with a great noise to indicate that he had gone
out, then ran rapidly to the foot of the poplar, seized
the lowest branch, drew himself up to it by his wrists,
and in an instant was at the top of the tree. There he
was just on a level with the head of the statue, and
overlooked both the Grand and Petit-Nesle, so that
nothing could take place in the courtyard or garden of
either unseen by him.

While Jacques Aubry was taking up his position on
his lofty perch, a grand soirée was in progress at the
Louvre, and all the windows were ablaze with light.
Charles V. had finally decided to leave Fontainebleau,
and venture within the walls of the capital, and the
two sovereigns had entered Paris that same evening.

A gorgeous welcoming fête awaited the Emperor there.
There was a banquet, gaming, and a ball. Gondolas

lighted by colored lanterns glided up and down the
Seine, laden with musicians, and made melodious
pauses in front of the famous balcony, from which,
thirty years later, Charles IX. was to fire upon his
people, while boats gayly decked with flowers con-
veyed from one bank of the river to the other those
guests who were on their way from the Faubourg Saint-
Germain to the Louvre, or who were returning to the
Faubourg Saint-Germain.

Among the guests the Vicomte de Marmagne was
naturally included.

As we have said, the Vicomte de Marmagne, a tall,
pink-cheeked, insipid dandy, claimed to be a great
destroyer of hearts.   On this occasion he thought that
a certain pretty little countess, whose husband happened to be with the army in Savoy, cast meaning
glances at him ; thereupon he danced with her, and
fancied that her hand was not insensible to the pressure
he ventured to bestow upon it.   And so, when he saw
the fair object of his thoughts leave the ball-room, he
imagined, from the glance she gave him as she departed,
that, like Galatea, she was flying toward the willows
in the hope of being pursued.   Marmagne therefore set
out in pursuit, and as she lived in the vicinity of Rue
Hautefeuille his course lay from the Louvre to the
Tour de Nesle, and thence along the quay and through
Rue des Grands-Augustins to Rue Saint-André.   He
was walking along the quay when he heard steps behind
him.

It was about one o'clock in the morning.   The moon,
as we have said, was entering her last quarter, so that
the night was quite dark.   Among the rare moral quali-
ties with which nature had endowed Marmagne, courage
did not hold a prominent position.   He began there-

fore after a while to be somewhat disturbed by these footsteps, which seemed to be following his own, and quickened his gait, wrapping himself more closely than ever in his cloak, and instinctively grasping the hilt of his sword.

But the acceleration of speed profited him not; the steps behind governed themselves by his, and even seemed to gain upon him, so that, just as he passed the doorway of the church of the Augustins he realized that he should very soon be overtaken by his fellow traveller unless he quickened his pace still more to a racing speed. He was just about to adopt that extreme course when the sound of a voice mingled with the sound of the footsteps.

"Pardieu! my fine sir, you do well to walk fast," said the voice, "for this isn't a very safe place, especially at this hour; right here, you know of course, is where my worthy friend Benvenuto was attacked, — Benvenuto, the sublime artist, who is at Fontainebleau at this moment, and has no suspicion of what is going on under his roof. But as we are going in the same direction apparently, we can walk along together, and if we meet any cut-throats they will look twice before they attack us. I offer you therefore the safeguard of my companionship, if you will give me the honor of yours."

At the first word our student uttered, Marmagne knew that it was the voice of one who wished him no ill, and at the name of Benvenuto he remembered and recognized the garrulous law student, who had on a previous occasion given him so much useful information concerning the interior of the Grand-Nesle. He at once halted, and waited for master Jacques Aubry to come up, for his society would be of advantage to him in two ways. In the first place, he would serve as a sort of body guard, and might in the mean while give him some fresh information concerning his enemy, which his hatred would enable him to turn to advantage. He therefore welcomed the student with his most agreeable manner.

"Good evening, my young friend," he said, in reply to the familiar harangue addressed to him by Jacques Aubry in the darkness. "What were you saying of our good Benvenuto, whom I hoped to meet at the Louvre, but who has remained at Fontainebleau, like the fox that he is !"

"Well, by my soul, here 's luck !" cried Jacques Aubry. "What, is it you, my dear vicomte — de — You forgot to tell me your name, or I forgot to remember it. You come from the Louvre ? Was it very lovely, very lively, with love-making galore ? We are in good luck, my gentleman, are n't we ? O you heart-breaker !"

"Faith !" said Marmagne with a simper, "you 're a sorcerer, my dear fellow; yes, I come from the Louvre, where the king said some very gracious things to me, and where I should still be if a certain fascinating little countess had not signified to me that she preferred a solitude *à deux* to all that crush. But whence come you ?"

"Whence come I ?" rejoined Aubry, with a hearty laugh. "Faith ! you remind me ! Poor Benvenuto ! On my word, he does n't deserve it !"

"Pray what has happened to our dear friend ?"

"In the first place, you must know that I come from the Grand-Nesle, where I have passed two hours clinging to the branch of a tree like any parrot."

"The devil ! that was no very comfortable position !"

"Never mind, never mind! I don't regret the cramp I got there, for I saw things, my friend, I saw things — Why, simply in thinking of them I suffocate with laughter."

As he spoke Jacques Aubry did laugh, so joyously and frankly that, although Marmagne had as yet no idea what he was laughing at, he could not forbear joining in the chorus. But his ignorance of the cause of the student's amusement naturally made him the first to cease.

"Now, my young friend, that I have been drawn on by your hilarity to laugh in confidence," said Marmagne, "may I not know what wonderful things they were to amuse you so? You know that I am one of Benvenuto's faithful friends, although I have never met you at his house, as my occupation leaves me very little time to devote to society, and that little I prefer to devote to my mistresses rather than my friends, I confess. But it is none the less true that whatever affects him affects me. Dear Benvenuto! Tell me what is going on at the Grand-Nesle in his absence? That interests me more than I can explain to you."

"What is going on?" said Aubry. "No, no, that's a secret."

"A secret to me!" said Marmagne. "A secret to me, who love Benvenuto so dearly, and who this very evening outdid King François I. in eulogizing him! Ah! that is too bad," added the viscount, with an injured expression.

"If I were only sure that you would mention it to nobody, my dear — What the devil is your name, my dear friend? — I would tell you about it, for I confess that I am as anxious to tell my story as King Midas's reeds were to tell theirs."

" Tell it then, tell it," said Marmagne.

" You won't repeat it to anybody? "

" To nobody, I swear ! "

" On your word of honor ? "

" On the faith of a nobleman."

" Fancy then — But, in the first place, my dear friend, you know the story of the monk's ghost, don't you ? "

" Yes, I 've heard of it. A phantom that is said to haunt the Grand-Nesle."

" Just so. Very well ! if you know that, I can tell you the rest. Fancy that Dame Perrine — "

" Colombe's governess ? "

" Just so. Well, well, it 's easy to see that you 're a friend of the family. Fancy then that Dame Perrine, in a nocturnal walk which she was taking for her health, thought that she saw the ghostly monk also taking a walk in the garden of the Grand-Nesle, while at the same time Dame Ruperta — You know Dame Ruperta ? "

" Is n't she Cellini's old servant ? "

" Just so. While Dame Ruperta, during one of her fits of sleeplessness, saw flames darting from the eyes, nose, and mouth of the great statue of Mars which you have seen in the gardens of the Grand-Nesle."

"Yes, a veritable *chef-d'œuvre !* " said Marmagne.

" *Chef-d'œuvre* is the word. Cellini makes nothing else. Now, these two respectable ladies — I speak of Dame Perrine and Dame Ruperta — agreed between themselves that the two apparitions had the same cause, and that the demon, who stalked abroad at night in the guise of the ghostly monk, ascended at cock-crow into the head of the god Mars, a fitting retreat for a lost soul like him, and was there consumed by such fierce flames that they came out through the statue's eyes, nose, and ears."

"What sort of a fairy tale is this, my dear man?" said Marmagne, unable to tell whether the student was joking or talking seriously.

"The tale of a ghost, my friend, nothing more nor less."

"Can it be that an intelligent fellow like you believes in such stuff?"

"Why no, I don't believe in it," said Jacques Aubry. "That is just why I concluded to pass the night in a poplar tree to clear up the mystery, and find out who the demon really is who is upsetting the whole household. So I pretended to come out, but instead of closing the door of the Grand-Nesle behind me I closed it in front of me, glided back in the darkness without being seen, and got safely to the poplar upon which I had my eye: five minutes later I was snugly ensconced among the branches on a level with Mars's head. Now guess what I saw."

"How can I guess, pray?"

"To be sure, one must be a sorcerer to guess such things. In the first place I saw the great door open; the door at the top of the steps, you know?"

"Yes, yes, I know it," said Marmagne.

"I saw the door open and a man put his nose out to see if there was any one in the courtyard. It was Hermann, the fat German."

"Yes, Hermann, the fat German," echoed Marmagne.

"When he was fully assured that the courtyard was deserted, having looked about everywhere, except in the tree, where, as you can imagine, he was very far from suspecting my presence, he came out, closed the door behind him, descended the five or six steps, and went straight to the door of the Petit-Nesle, where he knocked three times. At that signal a woman came out of the Petit-Nesle and opened the door. This woman was our friend Dame Perrine, who apparently has a weakness for walking about at night with our Goliath."

"No, really?   Oh the poor provost!"

"Wait a moment, wait, that's not all!   I was looking after them as they went into the Petit-Nesle, when suddenly I heard the grating of a window-sash at my left.   I turned; the window opened and out came Pagolo, — that brigand of a Pagolo! — who would have believed it of him with all his protestations, and his Paters and Aves? — out came Pagolo, and, after looking about as cautiously as Hermann, straddled the window-sill, slid down the gutter, and went from balcony to balcony until he reached the window — guess of whose room, viscount!"

"How can I tell? was it Dame Ruperta's?"

"Oh no! Scozzone's, nothing less! Scozzone, Benvenuto's beloved model, — a lovely brunette, my word for it.   Can you believe it of the rascal, viscount?"

"Indeed, it's most diverting," said Marmagne.   "Is that all you saw?"

"Wait a bit, wait a bit, my dear fellow!   I have kept the best till the last, the best morsel for the *bonne bouche*; wait a bit, we aren't there yet, but we soon shall be, never fear!"

"I am listening," said Marmagne.   "On my honor, my dear fellow, it couldn't be more diverting."

"Wait a bit, I say, wait a bit.   I was watching my Pagolo running from balcony to balcony at the risk of breaking his neck, when I heard another noise, which came almost from the foot of the tree in which I was sitting. I looked down and saw Ascanio creeping stealthily along from the foundry."

" Ascanio, Benvenuto's beloved pupil ? "

" Himself, my friend, himself. A sort of choir-boy, to whom one would give absolution without confession. Oh yes ! that comes of trusting to appearances."

" Why had Ascanio come out ? "

" Ah, that's just it! Why had he ? that's what I asked myself at first, but soon I had no occasion to ask it; for Ascanio, after having made sure, as Hermann and Pagolo had done, that nobody could see him, took from the foundry a long ladder, which he rested against the shoulders of Mars, and up he climbed. As the ladder was on the opposite side from myself, I lost sight of him as he went up, and was just wondering what had become of him when I saw a light in the eyes of the statue."

" What's that you say ? " cried Marmagne.

" The exact truth, my friend, and I confess that, if it had happened without any knowledge on my part of what had happened previously, I should not have been altogether at my ease. But I had seen Ascanio disappear, and I suspected that the light was caused by him."

" But what was Ascanio doing at that hour in the head of the god Mars ? "

" Ah ! that is just the question I asked myself, and as there was no one to answer me I determined to find out for myself. I gazed with all my eyes, and succeeded in discovering, through those of the statue, a ghost, i' faith ! yes, dressed all in white; the ghost of a woman, at whose feet Ascanio was kneeling as respectfully as before a Madonna. Unfortunately, the Madonna's back was turned to me, and I could not see her face, but I saw her neck. Oh what lovely necks ghosts have, my dear viscount! Imagine a perfect swan's neck, white as snow. And Ascanio was gazing at it, the impious varlet! with a degree of adoration which convinced me that the ghost was a woman. What do you say to that, my dear fellow? Gad! it's a neat trick, eh? to conceal one's mistress in the head of a statue."

"Yes, yes, it's most ingenious," rejoined Marmagne, laughing and reflecting at the same time; "very ingenious, in good sooth. And you have no suspicion who the woman can be?"

"Upon my honor, I have no idea. And you?"

"No more than you. What did you do, pray, when you saw all this?"

"What did I do? I laughed so that I lost my balance, and if I hadn't caught on a branch I should have broken my neck. As there was nothing more to see, and I had fallen half-way to the ground, I climbed down the rest of the way, crept to the door, and was on my way home, still laughing all by myself, when I met you, and you compelled me to tell you the story. Now, give me your advice, as you are of Benvenuto's friends. What must I do about telling him? As for Dame Perrine, that doesn't concern him; the dear woman is of age, and consequently mistress of her actions; but as to Scozzone, and the Venus who lodges in the head of Mars, it's a different matter."

"And you want me to advise you as to what you ought to do?"

"Yes, I do indeed! I am much perplexed, my dear — my dear — I always forget your name."

"My advice is to say nothing to him. So much the worse for those who are foolish enough to allow themselves to be deceived. I am obliged to you, Master Jacques Aubry, for your company and your agreeable conversation; but here we are at Rue Hautefeuille, and to return confidence for confidence, this is where my charmer dwells."

" Adieu, my dear, my excellent friend," said Jacques Aubry, pressing the viscount's hand. " Your advice is good and I will follow it. Good luck, and may Cupid watch over you ! "

Thereupon they parted, Marmagne taking Rue Hautefeuille, and Jacques Aubry Rue Poupée, on his way to Rue de la Harpe, at the far end of which he had taken up his abode.

The viscount lied to the unlucky student when he declared that he had no suspicion as to the identity of the female demon whom Ascanio adored on his knees. His first thought was that the inhabitant of Mars was no other than Colombe, and the more he reflected upon it, the more firmly convinced he became. As we have said, Marmagne was equally ill disposed toward the provost, D'Orbec, and Cellini, and he found himself in a very awkward position as regarded the gratification of his ill will, for he could not inflict suffering upon one without giving pleasure to the others. If he held his peace, D'Orbec and the provost would remain in their present embarrassed plight; but Benvenuto would likewise continue in his present joyous frame of mind. If, on the other hand, he disclosed what he had learned, Benvenuto would be in despair, but the provost would recover his child, D'Orbec his betrothed. He determined, therefore, to turn the thing over in his mind until it should be made clear to him what was the most advantageous course for him to follow.

His indecision did not long endure; without know-

ing the real motive for her interest, he was aware that
Madame d'Etampes was deeply interested in the marriage of Comte d'Orbec with Colombe. He thought
that, by revealing his secret to the duchess, he might
gain sufficient credit for perspicacity to make up for
what he had lost in the matter of courage; he resolved,
therefore, to appear at her morning reception on the
following day, and tell her everything. Having formed
that resolution, he punctually put it in execution.

By one of those fortunate chances which sometimes
serve the purpose of evil deeds so well, all the courtiers
were at the Louvre, paying court to François I. and the
Emperor, and there was nobody at Madame d'Etampes's
reception save her two faithful servants, the provost
and Comte d'Orbec, when the Vicomte de Marmagne
was announced.

The viscount respectfully saluted the duchess, who
acknowledged his salutation with one of those smiles
which belonged to her alone, and in which she could
express pride, condescension, and disdain all at the same
time. But Marmagne did not worry about this smile,
with which he was well acquainted from having seen it
upon the duchess's lips not only for his own benefit,
but for the benefit of many another. He knew moreover that he possessed a certain means of transforming
that smile of contempt into a smile of good will by a
single word. ·

"Aha ! Messire d'Estourville," he said, turning to
the provost, " so the prodigal child has returned ? "

" Still the same pleasantry, Viscount ! " cried Messire d'Estourville with a threatening gesture, and flush-
ing with anger.

" Oh don't lose your temper, my good friend, don't
lose your temper! " returned Marmagne; "I tell you

this, because, if you have n't yet found your vanished
dove, I know where she has built her nest."

"You do?" cried the duchess, in the most charmingly
friendly way.   "Where is it, pray?   Tell me quickly,
I beg, my dear Marmagne?"

"In the head of the statue of Mars, which Benvenuto
has modelled in the garden of the Grand-Nesle."

IX.

MARS AND VENUS.

THE reader will doubtless have guessed the truth, no less accurately than Marmagne, strange as it may have appeared at first glance. The head of the colossus was Colombe's place of retreat. Mars furnished apartments for Venus, as Jacques Aubry said. For the second time Benvenuto gave his handiwork a part to play in his life, summoned the artist to the assistance of the man, and embodied his fate in his statues as well as his thought and his genius. He had on an earlier occasion concealed his means of escape in one of his figures; he was now concealing Colombe's freedom and Ascanio's happiness in another.

But, having reached this point in our narrative, it becomes necessary for greater clearness to retrace our steps a moment.

When Cellini finished the story of Stefana, there was a brief pause. Benvenuto saw, among the phantoms which stood out vividly in his painful, obtrusive memories of the past, the melancholy, but serene features of Stefana, twenty years dead. Ascanio, with head bent forward, was trying to recall the pale face of the woman who had leaned over his cradle and often awoke him in his infancy, while the tears fell from her sad eyes upon his chubby cheeks. Colombe was gazing with deep emotion at Benvenuto, whom another woman, young and pure like herself, had loved so dearly: at that moment his voice seemed to her almost as soft as Ascanio's, and between the two, both of whom loved her devotedly, she felt instinctively that she was as safe as a child could be upon its mother's knee.

Benvenuto was the first to break the silence.

" Well !" he said, " will Colombe trust herself to the man to whom Stefana intrusted Ascanio? "

" You are my father, he my brother," replied Colombe, giving a hand to each of them with modest grace and dignity, " and I place myself blindly in your hands to keep me for my husband."

" Thanks," said Ascanio, " thanks, my beloved, for your trust in him."

" You promise to obey me in everything, Colombe? " said Benvenuto.

" In everything."

" Then listen, my children. I have always been convinced that man could do what he would, but only with the assistance of God on high and time here below. To save you from Comte d'Orbec and infamy, and to give you to my Ascanio, I must have time, Colombe, and in a very few days you are to be the count's wife. First of all then the essential thing is to delay this unholy union, is it not, Colombe, my sister, my child, my daughter? There are times in this sad life when it is necessary to do wrong in order to prevent a crime. Will you be courageous and resolute? Will your love, which is so pure and devoted, be brave and strong as well? Tell me."

" Ascanio will answer for me," said Colombe, with a smile, turning to the youth. " It is his right to dispose of me."

" Have no fear, master: Colombe will be brave, " said
Ascanio.

" In that case, Colombe, will you, trusting in our
loyalty and your own innocence, boldly leave this house
and go with us ? "

Ascanio started in surprise. Colombe looked at them
both for a moment without speaking, then rose to her
feet, and said simply, —

" Where am I to go ? "

" O Colombe, Colombe ! " cried Benvenuto, deeply
moved by such absolute trust, " you are a noble, saintly
creature, and yet Stefana made me very exacting in my
ideal. Everything depended upon your reply. We
are saved now, but there is n't a moment to lose. This
is the decisive hour. God places it at our disposal, let
us avail ourselves of it. Give me your hand, Colombe,
and follow me. "

The maiden lowered her veil as if to hide her blush
from itself, then followed the master and Ascanio. The
door between the Grand and Petit-Nesle was locked,
but the key was in the lock. Benvenuto opened it
noiselessly.

When they were passing through, Colombe stopped.

" Wait a moment, " she said in a voice trembling
with emotion; and upon the threshold of the house
which she was leaving because it had ceased to be a
sanctuary for her, the child knelt and prayed. Her
prayer remained a secret between God and herself; but
doubtless she prayed that he would forgive her father
for what she was driven to do. Then she rose, calm
and strong, and went on under the guidance of Cellini.
Ascanio with troubled heart followed them in silence,
gazing fondly at the white dress which fled before him
in the shadow. They walked in this way across the

garden of the Grand-Nesle; the songs and heedless, joyous laughter of the workmen at their supper, for it will be remembered that it was a holiday at the château, reached the ears of our friends, who were anxious and nervous as people ordinarily are at supreme moments.

When they reached the foot of the statue, Benevenuto left Colombe a moment, went to the foundry, and reappeared, laden with a long ladder which he leaned against the colossus. The moon, the celestial watcher, cast her pale light upon the scene. Having made sure that the ladder was firmly fixed in its place, the master knelt upon one knee in front of Colombe. The most touching respect softened the sternness of his expression.

" My child," said he, " put your arms around me, and hold fast."

Colombe obeyed without a word, and Benvenuto lifted her as if she had been a feather.

" The brother," he said to Ascanio as he drew near, " must allow the father to carry his beloved daughter."

The powerful goldsmith, laden with the most precious of all burdens, started up the ladder as lightly as if he were carrying nothing heavier than a bird. As her head lay upon the master's shoulder, Colombe could watch his manly, good-humored face, and felt a degree of filial trust in him which was unlike anything she had ever experienced. As to Cellini, so powerful was the will of this man of iron, that he was able to hold her in his arms, for whom he would have given his life two hours earlier, with a hand that did not tremble, nor did his heart beat more rapidly or a single one of his muscles of steel weaken for an instant. He had ordered his heart to be calm, and his heart had obeyed.

When he reached the neck of the statue he opened a

small door, entered the head, and deposited Colombe therein.

The interior of this colossal head of a statue nearly sixty feet high formed a small round room some eight feet in diameter, and ten feet high; air and light made their way in through the openings for the eyes, nose, mouth, and ears. This miniature apartment Benvenuto made when he was working at the head; he used it as a receptacle for the tools he was using, so that he need not be at the trouble of taking them up and down five or six times a day; often too he carried up his lunch with him and set it out upon a table which stood in the centre of this unqiue dining-room, so that he had not to leave his scaffolding to take his morning meal. This innovation which was so convenient for him, made the place attractive to him; he followed up the table with a cot-bed, and latterly he had formed the habit of taking his noon-day siesta in the head of his Mars, as well as of breakfasting there. It was quite natural, therefore, that it should occur to him to ensconce Colombe in what was clearly the most secure hiding-place of all he could offer her.

"This is where you must remain, Colombe," said Benvenuto, "and you must make up your mind to go down only after dark. Await here in this retreat, under God's eye and our watchful care, the result of my efforts. Jupiter," he added with a smile, alluding to the king's promise, "will finish, I trust, what Mars has begun. You don't understand, but I know what I mean. We have Olympus on our side, and you have Paradise. How can we not succeed? Come, smile a little, Colombe, for the future at least, if not for the present. I tell you in all seriousness that we have ground for hope. Hope therefore with confidence, —

in God, if not in me. I have been in a sterner prison
than yours, believe me, and my hope made me indifferent to my captivity. From now until the day that
success crowns my efforts, Colombe, you will see me no
more. Your brother Ascanio, who is less suspected
and less closely watched than I am, will come to see
you, and will stand guard over you. I rely upon him
to transform this workman's chamber into a nun's cell.
Now that I am about to leave you, mark well and
remember my words: you have done all that you had
to do, trustful and courageous child; the rest concerns
me. We have now only to allow Providence time to
do its part, Colombe. Now listen. Whatever happens
remember this: however desperate your situation may
seem to be or may really be, even though you stand
at the altar and have naught left to say but the terrible
Yes which would unite you forever to Comte d'Orbec,
do not doubt your friend, Colombe; do not doubt your
father, my child; rely upon God and upon us; I will
arrive in time, I promise you. Will you have the
requisite faith and resolution? Tell me."

"Yes," said the girl confidently.

"'T is well," said Cellini. "Adieu. I leave you
now in your solitude; when everybody is asleep, Ascanio will come and bring you what you need. Adieu,
Colombe."

He held out his hand, but Colombe gave him her
forehead to kiss as she was accustomed to do with her
father. Benvenuto started, but, passing his hand over
his eyes, he mastered the thoughts which came to his
mind and the passions which raged in his heart, and
deposited upon that spotless forehead the most paternal
of kisses.

"Adieu, dear child of Stefana," he whispered, and

went quickly down the ladder to Ascanio, with whom he joined the workmen, who had finished eating, but were drinking still.

A new life, a strange, dream-like life, thereupon began for Colombe, and she accommodated herself to it as she would have done to the life of a queen.

Let us see how the aerial chamber was furnished. It had already, as we know, a bed and a table. Ascanio added a low velvet chair, a Venetian mirror, a collection of religious books selected by Colombe herself, a crucifix,— a marvellous piece of carving,— and a silver vase, also from the master's hand, which was filled every night with fresh flowers. There was room for nothing more in the white shell, which contained so much of innocence and charm.

Colombe ordinarily slept during the day. Ascanio had advised that course for fear that, if she were awake, she might thoughtlessly do something that would betray her presence. She awoke with the stars and the nightingale's song, knelt upon her bed, in front of her crucifix, and remained for some time absorbed in fervent prayer; then she made her toilet, dressed her lovely, luxuriant hair, and sat and mused. Erelong a ladder would be placed against the statue and Ascanio would knock at the little door. If Colombe's toilet was completed, she would admit him and he would remain with her until midnight. At midnight, if the weather was fine, she would go down into the garden, and Ascanio would return to the Grand-Nesle for a few hours' sleep, while Colombe took her nightly walk, beginning once more the old dreams she used to dream in her favorite path, and which seemed now more likely to be fulfilled. After about two hours the white apparition would return to her snug retreat, where she would wait for daylight and her bedtime, inhaling the sweet odor of the flowers she had collected for her little nest, and listening to the singing of the nightingales in the Petit-Nesle, and the crowing of the cocks in the Pré-aux-Clercs.

Just before dawn Ascanio would return to his beloved once more, bringing her daily supply of provisions, adroitly subtracted from Dame Ruperta's larder by virtue of Cellini's complicity. Then they would sit for a while, conversing as only lovers can converse, evoking memories of the past, and forming plans for the future when they should be man and wife. Sometimes Ascanio would sit silently contemplating Colombe, and Colombe would meet his earnest gaze with her sweet smile. Often when they parted they had not exchanged a single word, but those were the occcasions on which they said most. Had not each of them in his or her heart all that the other could have said, in addition to what the heart cannot say, but God reads?

Grief and solitude have this advantage in youth, that, while they make the heart nobler and greater, they preserve its freshness. Colombe, a proud, dignified maiden, was at the same time a light-hearted young madcap: so there were days when they laughed as well as days when they dreamed, — days when they played together like children; and, most astonishing thing of all, those days — or nights, for, as we have seen, the young people had inverted the order of nature — were not the ones that passed most quickly. Love, like every other shining thing, needs a little darkness to make its light shine the brighter.

Never did Ascanio utter a word that could alarm the timid, innocent child who called him brother. They were alone, and they loved each other; but for the very reason that they were alone they were the more conscious of the presence of God, whose heaven they saw nearer at hand, and for the very reason that they loved each other, they respected their love as a divinity.

As soon as the first rays of dawn began to cast a feeble light upon the roofs of the houses, Colombe regretfully sent her friend away, but called him back as many times as Juliet did Romeo. One or the other had always forgotten something of the greatest importance; however, they had to part at last, and Colombe, up to the moment, toward noon, when she committed her heart to God, and slept the sleep of the angels, would sit alone, and dream, listening to the voices whispering in her heart, and to the little birds singing under the lindens in her old garden. It goes without saying that Ascanio always carried the ladder away with him.

Every morning she strewed bread around the mouth of the statue for the little birds; the bold-faced little fellows would come and seize it, and fly quickly away again at first; but they gradually grew tame. Birds seem to understand the hearts of young girls, who are winged like themselves. They finally would remain for a long while, and would pay in song for the banquet with which Colombe regaled them. There was one audacious goldfinch who ventured within the room, and finally acquired the habit of eating from Colombe's hand at morning and evening. When the nights began to be a little cool, one night he allowed himself to be taken captive by the young prisoner, who put him in her bosom, and there he slept until morning, notwithstanding Ascanio's visit and Colombe's nightly promenade. After that the willing captive never failed to return at night. At daybreak he would begin to sing:

Colombe would then hold him for Ascanio to kiss, and set him at liberty.

Thus did Colombe's days glide by in the head of the statue. Only two things occurred to disturb the tranquillity of her existence; those two things were the provost's domiciliary visits. Once Colombe awoke with a start at the sound of her father's voice. It was no dream; he was down in the garden beneath her, and Benvenuto was saying to him: "You ask what this colossal figure is, Monsieur d'Estourville? It is the statue of Mars, which his Majesty condescended to order for Fontainebleau. A little bauble sixty feet high, as you see!"

"It is of noble proportions, and very beautiful," replied D'Estourville; "but let us go on, this is not what I am in search of."

"No, it would be too easy to find."

And they passed on.

Colombe, kneeling with outstretched arms, felt an intense longing to cry out, "Father, father, I am here!" The old man was seeking his child, weeping for her perhaps; but the thought of Comte d'Orbec, the hateful schemes of Madame d'Etampes, and the memory of the conversation Ascanio overheard, paralyzed her impulse. And on the second visit the same impulse did not come to her when the voice of the odious count was mingled with the provost's.

"There's a curious statue built just like a house," said D'Orbec, as he halted at the foot of the colossus. "If it stands through the winter, the swallows will build their nests in it in the spring."

On the morning of the day when the mere voice of her *fiancé* so alarmed Colombe, Ascanio had brought her a letter from Cellini.

"My child," so ran the letter, "I am obliged to go away, but have no fear. I leave everything prepared for your deliverance and your happiness. The king's word guarantees my success, and the king you know has never been false to his word. From to-day your father also will be absent. Do not despair. I have now had all the time that I needed. Therefore I say to you again, dear girl, though you should be at the church door, though you should be kneeling at the altar, and on the point of uttering the words which bind you for life, let things take their course. Providence will intervene in time, I swear to you. Adieu.

"Your father,

"BENVENUTO CELLINI."

This letter, which filled Colombe's heart with joy by reviving her hopes, had the unfortunate result of causing the poor children to feel a dangerous sense of security. Youth is incapable of moderate feelings: it leaps at one bound from despair to the fullest confidence; in its eyes the sky is always black with tempests or resplendently clear. Being rendered doubly confident by the provost's absence and Cellini's letter, they neglected their precautions, and thought more of their love and less of prudence. Colombe was not so guarded in her movements, and Dame Perrine saw her, but luckily mistook her for the monk's ghost. Ascanio lighted the lamp without drawing the curtains, and the light was seen by Dame Ruperta. The tales of the two gossips taken in conjunction aroused the curiosity of Jacques Aubry, and the indiscreet student, like Horace in the "Ecole des Femmes," revealed everything to the very person to whom he should have revealed absolutely nothing. We know the result of his disclosures.

Let us now return to the Hôtel d'Etampes.

When Marmagne was asked how he had stumbled upon his valuable discovery, he assumed an air of mystery and refused to tell. The truth was too simple, and did not reflect sufficient credit upon his penetration; he preferred to let it be understood that he had arrived at the magnificent results which aroused their wonder by dint of strategy and perseverance. The duchess was radiant; she went and came, and plied the viscount with questions. So they had her at last, the little rebel who had terrified them all! Madame d'Etampes determined to go in person to the Hôtel de Nesle to make sure of her friend's good fortune. Moreover, after what had happened after the flight, or rather the abduction, of Colombe, the girl must not be left at the Petit-Nesle. The duchess would take charge of her: she would take her to the Hôtel d'Etampes, and would keep a closer watch upon her than duenna and *fiancé* together had done; she would keep watch upon her as a rival, so that Colombe would surely be well guarded.

The duchess ordered her litter.

" The affair has been kept very secret," said she to the provost. " You, D'Orbec, are not the man to worry about a childish escapade of this sort? I don't see, then, what is to prevent the marriage from taking place, and our plans from being carried out."

" On the same conditions, of course, duchess?" said D'Orbec.

" To be sure, on the same conditions, my dear count. As to Benvenuto," continued the duchess, " who is guilty, either as principal or accessory, of an infamous abduction, — never fear, dear viscount, we will avenge you, while avenging ourselves."

" But I understand, madame," rejoined Marmagne,

"that the king in his artistic enthusiasm had made him a solemn promise, in case the statue of his Jupiter should be cast successfully, so that he will simply have to breathe a wish to see his wish gratified."

"Never fear, that's just where I will watch," rejoined the duchess; "I will prepare a surprise for him on that day that will be a surprise indeed. So rely upon me, and let me manage everything."

That was in truth the best thing they could do: not for a long while had the duchess seemed so eager, so animated, so charming. Her joy overflowed in spite of her. She sent the provost away in hot haste to summon his archers, and erelong that functionary, accompanied by D'Orbec and Marmagne, and preceded by a number of subordinates, arrived at the door of the Hôtel de Nesle, followed at a short distance by Madame d'Etampes, who waited upon the quay, trembling with impatience, and constantly thrusting her head out of the litter.

It was the dinner hour of the workmen, and Ascanio, Pagolo, little Jehan, and the women were the only occupants of the Grand-Nesle at the moment. Benvenuto was not expected until the evening of the following day, or the morning of the day following that. Ascanio, who received the visitors, supposed that it was a third domciliary visit, and, as he had very positive orders from the master on that subject, he offered no resistance, but welcomed them, on the other hand, most courteously.

The provost, his friends and his retainers, went straight to the foundry.

"Open this door for us," said D'Estourville to Ascanio.

The young man's heart was oppressed with a terrible

presentiment. However he might be mistaken, and as the least hesitation might awaken suspicion, he handed the provost the key without moving a muscle.

"Take that long ladder," said the provost to his archers.

They obeyed, and under Messire d'Estourville's guidance marched straight to the statue. There the provost himself put the ladder in place, and prepared to ascend, but Ascanio, pale with terror and wrath placed his foot on the first round.

"What is your purpose, messieurs?" he cried; "this statue is the master's masterpiece. It has been placed in my charge, and the first man who lays hand upon it for any purpose whatsoever is a dead man, I warn you!"

He drew from his belt a keen-edged, slender dagger, of such marvellous temper that it would cut through a gold crown at a single blow.

The provost gave a signal and his archers advanced upon Ascanio pike in hand. He made a desperate resistance and wounded two men; but he could do nothing alone against eight, leaving the provost, Marmagne, and D'Orbec out of the reckoning. He was forced to yield to superior numbers: he was thrown down, bound and gagged, and the provost started up the ladder, followed by two sergeants for fear of a surprise.

Colombe had heard and seen everything; her father found her in a swoon, for when she saw Ascanio fall she believed him to be dead.

Aroused to anger rather than anxiety by this sight, the provost threw Colombe roughly over his broad shoulders, and descended the ladder. The whole party then returned to the quay, the archers escorting Ascanio, at whom D'Orbec gazed most earnestly. Pagolo saw his comrade pass and did not stir. Little Jehan had disappeared. Scozzone alone, understanding nothing of what had taken place, tried to bar the door, crying, —

"What means this violence, messieurs? Why are you taking Ascanio away? Who is this woman?"

But at that moment the veil which covered Colombe's face fell off, and Scozzone recognized the model for the statue of Hebe.

Thereupon she stood aside, pale with jealousy, and allowed the provost and his people, as well as their prisoners, to pass without another word.

"What does this mean, and why have you abused this boy so?" demanded Madame d'Etampes, when she saw Ascanio bound, and pale and covered with blood. "Unbind him! unbind him!"

"Madame," said the provost, "this same boy resisted us desperately; he wounded two of my men; he is his master's accomplice without doubt, and it seems to me advisable to take him to some safe place."

"And furthermore," said D'Orbec in an undertone to the duchess, "he so strongly resembles the Italian page I saw at your reception, and who was present throughout our conversation, that, if he were not dressed differently, and if I had not heard him speak the language which you assured me the page could not understand, upon my honor, Madame la Duchesse, I would swear it was he!"

"You are right, Monsieur le Prévôt," said Madame d'Etampes hastily, thinking better of the order she had given to set Ascanio at liberty; "you are right, this young man may be dangerous. Make sure of his person."

"To the Châtelet with the prisoner," said the provost.

"And we," said the duchess, at whose side Colombe,
still unconscious, had been placed, — "we, messieurs,
will return to the Hôtel d'Etampes!"

A moment later the hoof-beats of a galloping horse
rang out upon the pavement.   It was little Jehan,
riding off at full speed to tell Cellini what had taken
place at the Hôtel de Nesle.

Ascanio, meanwhile, was committed to the Châtelet
without having seen the duchess, and in ignorance of
the part played by her in the event which destroyed his
hopes.

X.

THE RIVALS.

MADAME D'ETAMPES, who had been so desirous to see Colombe at close quarters ever since she had first heard of her, had her heart's desire at last: the poor child lay there before her in a swoon.

The jealous duchess did not once cease to gaze at her throughout the whole journey to the Hôtel d'Etampes. Her eyes, blazing with anger when she saw how beautiful she was, scrutinized each of her charms, analyzed each feature, and passed in review one after another all the elements which went to make up the perfect beauty of the pale-cheeked girl who was at last in her power and under her hand. The two women, who were inspired with the same passion and disputing possession of the same heart, were face to face at last. One all-powerful and malevolent, the other weak, but beloved; one with her splendor, the other with her youth; one with her passion, the other with her innocence. Separated by so many obstacles, they had finally come roughly in contact, and the duchess's velvet robe brushed against Colombe's simple white gown.

Though Colombe was in a swoon, Anne was not the least pale of the two. Doubtless her mute contemplation of her companion's loveliness caused her pride to despair, and destroyed her hopes; for while, in her own despite, she murmured, " They told me truly, she is lovely, very lovely ! " her hand, which held Colombe's, pressed it so convulsively that the young girl was brought to her senses by the pain, and opened her great eyes, saying, —

" Oh, madame, you hurt me ! "

As soon as the duchess saw that Colombe's eyes were open, she let her hand fall. But the consciousness of pain preceded the return of the faculty of thought. For some seconds after she uttered the words, she continued to gaze wonderingly at the duchess, as if she could not collect her thoughts.

" Who are you, madame," she said at last, " and whither are you taking me ? " Then she suddenly drew away from her, crying, —

" Ah ! you are the Duchesse d'Etampes. I remember, I remember ! "

" Hush ! " returned Anne imperiously. " Hush ! Soon we shall be alone, and you can wonder and cry out at your ease."

These words were accompanied by a stern, haughty glance ; but it was a sense of her own dignity, and not the glance, which imposed silence upon Colombe. She said not another word until they reached the Hôtel d'Etampes, where, at a sign from the duchess, she followed her to her oratory.

When the rivals were at last alone and face to face, they eyed each other for one or two minutes without speaking, but with very different expressions. Colombe was calm, for her trust in Providence and in Benvenuto sustained her. Anne was furious at her calmness, but although her fury was clearly evidenced by the contortion of her features, she did not give expression to it, for she relied upon her imperious will, and her unbounded power to crush the feeble creature before her. She was the first to break the silence.

"Well, my young friend," she said, in a tone which left no doubt as to the bitterness of the thought, although the words were soft, "you are restored to your father, at last. It is well, but allow me first of all to compliment you upon your courage; you are — bold for your age, my child."

"I have God on my side, madame," rejoined Colombe simply.

"What god do you refer to, mademoiselle? Oh, the god Mars, of course!" returned the duchess with one of those impertinent winks which she so often had occasion to resort to at court.

"I know but one God, madame; the Eternal God, merciful and protecting, who teaches charity in prosperity, and humility in grandeur. Woe to them who know not the God of whom I speak, for there will come a day when He will not know them."

"Very good, mademoiselle, very good!" said the duchess. "The situation is admirably adapted for a moral lecture, and I would congratulate you upon your happy choice of a subject if I did not prefer to think that you are trying to excuse your wantonness by impudence."

"In truth, madame," replied Colombe, without bitterness, but with a slight shrug of the shoulders, "I do not seek to excuse myself to you, because I am as yet ignorant of any right on your part to accuse me. When my father chooses to question me, I shall reply with respect and sorrow. If he reproves me I will try to justify myself; but until then, Madame la Duchesse, permit me to hold my peace."

"I understand that my voice annoys you, and you

would prefer, would you not, to remain alone with your thoughts and think at leisure of the man you love ? "

"No noise, however annoying it may be, can prevent me from thinking of him, madame, especially when he is unhappy."

"You dare confess that you love him ? "

"That is the difference between us, madame; you love him, and dare not confess it."

"Impudent hussy ! " cried the duchess, "upon my word I believe she defies me."

"Alas ! no," replied Colombe softly, "I do not defy you, I reply, simply because you force me to reply. Leave me alone with my thoughts, and I will leave you alone with your schemes."

"Very good ! since you drive me to it, child, since you imagine that you are strong enough to contend with me, since you confess your love, I will confess mine; but at the same time I will confess my hatred. Yes, I love Ascanio, and I hate you ! After all, why should I dissemble with you, the only person to whom I may say whatever I choose ? for you are the only one who, whatever you say, will not be believed. Yes, I love Ascanio."

"In that case I pity you, madame," rejoined Colombe softly, "for Ascanio loves me."

"Yes, it is true, Ascanio does love you; but by seduction if I can, by falsehood if I must, by a crime if it becomes necessary, I will steal his love away from you, mark that! I am Anne d'Heilly, Duchesse d'Etampes ! "

"Ascanio, madame, will love the one who loves him best."

"In God's name hear her ! " cried the duchess, exasperated by such sublime confidence. "Would not one think that her love is unique, and that no other love can be compared to it ? "

" I do not say that, madame. For the reason that I love, I know that other hearts may love as I do, but I doubt if yours is one of them. "

" What would you do for him ? Come, let us see, you who boast of this love of yours which mine can never equal. What have you sacrificed for him thus far ? an obscure life and wearisome solitude ? "

" No, madame, but my peace of mind. "

" You have given him preference over what ? Comte d'Orbec's absurd love ? "

"No, madame, but my filial obedience. "

" What have you to give him ? Can you make him rich, powerful, feared ? "

" No, madame, but I hope to make him happy. "

" Ah ! " exclaimed the duchess; " it's a very different matter with me, and I do much more for him: I sacrifice a king's affection; I lay wealth, titles, and honors at his feet; I bring him a kingdom to govern. "

" Yes, " said Colombe with a smile, " it's true that your love gives him everything that is not love. "

" Enough, enough of this insulting comparison! " cried the duchess violently, feeling that she was losing ground step by step.

Thereupon ensued a momentary pause, during which Colombe seemed to feel no embarrassment, while Madame d'Etampes succeeded in concealing hers only by revealing her anger. However, her features gradually relaxed, her face assumed a milder expression, lightened by a gleam of real or feigned benevolence. She was the first to reopen the conflict which she did not propose should end otherwise than in a triumph.

" Let us see, Colombe, " said she in a tone that was

almost affectionate, " if some one should bid you sacrifice
your life for him, what would you do ? "

" Ah ! I would give it to him blissfully ! "

" And so would I ! " cried the duchess with an accent
which proved the violence of her passion, if not the sincerity of the sacrifice.

" But your honor," she continued, " would you sacrifice that as well as your life ? "

" If by my honor you mean my reputation, yes; if by
my honor you mean my virtue, no. "

" What ! you do not belong to him? is he not your
lover ? "

" He is my *fiancé*, madame; that is all. "

" Oh, she does n't love him ! " rejoined the duchess,
" she does n't love him ! She prefers her honor, a mere
empty word, to him. "

" If some one were to say to you, madame," retorted
Colombe, angered in spite of her sweet disposition, " if
some one were to say to you, 'Renounce for his sake
your titles and your grandeur; abandon the king for
him, — not in secret, that would be too easy, — but
publicly.' If some one were to say to you, 'Anne
d'Heilly, Duchesse d'Etampes, leave your palace, your
luxurious surroundings, and your courtiers for his humble artist's studio' ? "

" I would refuse in his own interest," replied the
duchess, as if it were impossible to say what was false
beneath the profound, penetrating gaze of her rival.

" You would refuse ? "

" Yes. "

" Ah ! she does n't love him ! " cried Colombe; " she
prefers honors, mere chimeras, to him. "

" But when I tell you that I wish to retain my position for his sake," returned the duchess, exasperated

anew by this fresh triumph of her rival, — "when I tell
you that I wish to retain my honors so that he may
share them? All men care for them sooner or later."

"Yes," replied Colombe, smiling; "but Ascanio is
not one of them."

"Hush!" cried Anne, stamping her foot in passion.

Thus had the cunning and powerful duchess signally
failed to gain the upper hand over a mere girl, whom she
expected to intimidate simply by raising her voice. To
her questions, angry or satirical, Colombe had made
answer with a modest tranquillity which disconcerted
her. She realized that the blind impulsion of her
hatred had led her astray, so she changed her tactics.
To tell the truth, she had not reckoned upon the possession of so much beauty or so much wit by her rival,
and, finding that she could not bend her, she determined
to take her by surprise.

Colombe as we have seen, was not alarmed by the
double explosion of Madame d'Etampes's wrath, but
simply took refuge in cold and dignified silence. The
duchess, however, following out the new plan she had
adopted, now approached her with her most fascinating
smile, and took her affectionately by the hand.

"Forgive me, my child," she said, "but I fear I
lost my temper; you must not bear me ill will for it;
you have the advantage of me in so many ways, that
it's natural that I should be jealous. Alas! you, no
doubt, like everybody else, consider me a wicked
woman. But, in truth, my destiny is at fault, not I.
Forgive me, therefore; because we both happen to love
Ascanio is no reason why we should hate each other.
And then he loves you alone, so 't is your duty to be
indulgent. Let us be sisters, what say you? Let us
talk frankly together, and I will try to efface from your

mind the unfortunate impression which my foolish anger may have left there."

"Madame!" said Colombe, with reserve, and withdrawing her hand with an instinctive movement of repulsion; but she added at once, "Speak, I am listening."

"Oh," said Madame d'Etampes playfully, and as if she understood perfectly her companion's reserve, "have no fear, little savage, I do not ask for your friendship without a guaranty. In order that you may know what manner of woman I am, that you may know me as I know myself, I propose to tell you in two words the story of my life. My heart has little to do with my story, and we poor women, who are called great ladies, are so often slandered! Ah! envy does very wrong to speak ill of us when we are fitter subjects for compassion. For instance, what is your judgment of me, my child? Be frank. You look upon me as a lost woman, do you not?"

Colombe made a gesture indicative of the embarrassment she felt at the idea of replying to such a question.

"But if I am a lost woman, is it my fault? You in your happiness, Colombe, must not be too hard upon those who have suffered, — you who have lived hitherto in innocent solitude, and do not know what it is to be reared upon ambitious dreams: for they who are destined to that torture, like victims decked out with flowers, see only the bright side of life. There is no question of love, simply of pleasing. So it was that from my earliest youth my thoughts were all bent upon fascinating the king; the beauty which God gives to woman to be exchanged for true love, I was forced to exchange for a title; they made of my charms a snare. Tell me now, Colombe, what could be the fate of a poor child, taken in hand before she has learned to know the difference between good and evil, and who is told, ' The good is evil, the evil is good ' ? And so, you see, although others despair of me, I do not despair of myself. Perhaps God will forgive me, for no one stood beside me to tell me of him. What was there for me to do, alone as I was, and weak and defenceless ? Craft and deceit have made up my whole life from that time on. And yet I was not made to play such a hideous *rôle;* the proof is that I love Ascanio, and that when I found that I loved him I was happy and ashamed at the same time. Now tell me, my pure, darling child, do you understand me ? "

" Yes, " innocently replied Colombe, deceived by this false good faith, this lie masquerading in the guise of truth.

" Then you will have pity on me, " cried the duchess; " you will let me love Ascanio from a distance, all by myself, hopelessly; and in that way I shall not be your rival, for he will not care for me; and, in return, I, who know the world and its snares, its pitfalls and deceit, will take the place of the mother you have lost. I will guide you, I will save you. Now you see that you can trust me, for you save my life. A child in whose heart the passions of a woman were sown, that in brief is my past. My present you see for yourself; it is the shame of being the declared mistress of a king. My future is my love for Ascanio, — not his for me, because, as you have said, and as I have very often told myself, Ascanio will never love me; but for the very reason that that love will remain pure it will purify me. Now it is your turn, to speak, to open your heart, to tell me everything. Tell me your story, dear girl. "

" My story, madame, is very brief and very simple, "

said Colombe; "it may all be summed up in three
loves. I have loved, I love, and I shall love, — God,
my father, and Ascanio. But in the past my love for
Ascanio, whom I had not then met, was a dream; at
present it is a cause of suffering; in the future, it is
a hope."

"Very good," said the duchess, restraining her jealousy, and forcing back her tears; "but do not half
confide in me, Colombe. What do you mean to do
now? How can you, poor child, contend with two such
powerful wills as your father's and Comte d'Orbec's?
To say nothing of the king's having seen you and fallen
in love with you."

"O mon Dieu!" murmured Colombe.

"But as this passion on the king's part was the work
of the Duchesse d'Etampes, your rival, your friend,
Anne d'Heilly will deliver you from it. So we won't
disturb ourselves about the king: but your father and
the count must be reckoned with. Their ambition is
less easy to balk than the commonplace fancy of the
king."

"Oh, do not be half kind!" cried Colombe; "save
me from the others as well as from the king."

"I know but one way," said Madame d'Etampes,
seeming to reflect.

"What is that?"

"You will take fright, and refuse to adopt it."

"Oh, if only courage is required, tell me what it is."

"Come here, and listen to me," said the duchess,
affectionately drawing Colombe to a seat upon a stool
beside her arm-chair, and passing her arm around her
waist. "Don't be alarmed, I beg, at the first words
I say."

"Is it very terrifying?" Colombe asked.

" Your virtue is unbending, and unspotted, my dear little one, but we live, alas! at a time and in a society where such fascinating innocence is but a danger the more, for it places you, without means of defence, at the mercy of your enemies, whom you cannot fight with the weapons they use to attack you. So make an effort, descend from the heights to which your dreams have transported you, to the lower level of reality. You said just now that you would sacrifice your reputation for Ascanio. I do not ask so much as that, but simply that you sacrifice the appearance of fidelity to him. It is pure madness for you, alone and helpless, to struggle against your destiny: for you, the daughter of a gentleman, to dream of marriage with a goldsmith's apprentice! Come, trust the advice of a sincere friend; do not resist them, but let them have their way: remain at heart the spotless *fiancé*, the wife of Ascanio, and give your hand to Comte d'Orbec. His ambitious schemes require that you should bear his name; but once you are Comtesse d'Orbec, you can easily overturn his detestable schemes, for you have only to raise your voice and complain. Whereas now, who would take your part in the contest? No one: even I cannot assist you against the legitimate authority of a father, while, if it were a question of foiling your husband's combinations, you would soon see me at work. Reflect upon what I say. To remain your own mistress, obey; to become independent, pretend to abandon your liberty. Strong in the thought that Ascanio is your lawful husband, and that union with any other is mere sacrilege, you may do what your heart bids you, and your conscience will be at rest, while the world, in whose eyes appearances will be preserved, will take your part."

" Madame! madame!" murmured Colombe, rising and

straightening herself against the duchess's arm, as she
sought to detain her, "I am not sure that I understand
you aright, but it seems to me that you are advising me
to do an infamous thing!"

"What do you say?" cried the duchess.

"I say that virtue is not so subtle as all that,
madame; I say that your sophistries make me blush for
you; I say that beneath the cloak of friendship with
which you conceal your hatred, I see the net you have
spread for me. You wish to dishonor me in Ascanio's
eyes, do you not, because you know that Ascanio will
never love or will cease to love the woman he despises?"

"Well, yes!" said the duchess, bursting forth at last;
"I am weary of wearing a mask. Ah! you will not fall
into the net I have spread, you say? Very good, then
you will fall into the abyss I will push you into.
Hear this: Whether you will or no, you shall marry
D'Orbec!"

"In that case the force put upon me will be my
excuse, and by yielding, if I do yield, I shall not have
profaned my heart's religion."

"Pray, do you mean to resist?"

"By every means in the power of a poor girl. I
warn you that I will say No! to the end. You may put
my hand in that man's, I will say No! You may drag
me before the altar, I will say No! You may force me
to kneel at the priest's feet, and to the priest's face
I will say No!"

"What matters it? Ascanio will believe that you
have consented to the marriage that is forced upon
you."

"For that reason I hope I may not have to submit to
it, madame."

"Upon whom do you rely to come to your assistance?"

"Upon God above, and upon a man on earth."

"But the man is a prisoner."

"The man is free, madame."

"Why, who is the man, I pray to know?"

"Benvenuto Cellini."

The duchess ground her teeth when she heard the name of the man she considered her deadliest foe. But as she was on the point of repeating the name, accompanied by some terrible imprecation, a page raised the portière and announced the king.

At that announcement she darted from the room to meet François I. with a smile upon her lips, and led him to her own apartments, motioning to her people to keep watch upon Colombe.

VOL. II. — 11

XI.

BENVENUTO AT BAY.

AN hour after the imprisonment of Ascanio and the abduction of Colombe, Benvenuto Cellini rode along the Quai des Augustins at a footpace. He had just parted from the king and the court, whom he had amused throughout the journey by innumerable tales, told as he only could tell them, mingled with anecdotes of his own adventures. But when he was once more alone he became thoughtful and abstracted; the frivolous talker gave place to the profound dreamer. While his hand shook the rein, his brain was busily at work; he dreamed of the casting of his Jupiter, upon which depended his dear Ascanio's happiness as well as his artistic fame; the bronze was fermenting in his brain before being melted in the furnace. Outwardly he was calm.

When he reached the door of the Hôtel de Nesle he stopped for a moment, amazed not to hear the sound of hammering; the blackened walls of the château were mute and gloomy, as if no living thing were within. Twice the master rapped without obtaining a reply; at the third summons Scozzone opened the door.

" Ah, there you are, master! " she cried when she saw that it was Benvenuto. " Alas! why did you not return two hours earlier? "

" What has happened, in God's name ? " demanded Cellini.

" The provost, Comte d'Orbec, and the Duchesse d'Etampes have been here."

" Well ? "

" They made a search."

" And then ? "

" They found Colombe in the head of the statue of Mars."

" Impossible ! "

" The Duchesse d'Etampes carried Colombe home with her, and the provost ordered Ascanio to be taken to the Châtelet."

" Ah ! we have been betrayed ! " cried Benvenuto striking his hand against his forehead and stamping upon the ground. As his first thought on every occasion was of vengeance, he left his horse to find his own way to the stable, and darted into the studio.

" Come hither, all of you," he cried, — " all ! "

Thereupon each one had to undergo an examination in due form, but they were all equally ignorant, not only of Colombe's hiding place, but of the means by which her enemies had succeeded in discovering it. There was not a single one, including Pagolo, upon whom the master's suspicion fell first of all, who did not exculpate himself in a way that left no doubt in Benvenuto's mind. It is needless to say that he did not for an instant suspect Hermann, and Simon-le-Gaucher for no more than an instant.

When he became convinced that he could learn nothing in that direction, Benvenuto, with the rapidity of decision which was usual with him, made up his mind what course to pursue; and having made sure that his sword was at his side and that his dagger moved easily in its sheath, he ordered everybody to remain at home in order to be at hand in case of need. He then left the studio, and hurried across the courtyard into the street.

His features, his gait, and his every movement, bore the stamp of intense excitement. A thousand thoughts, a thousand schemes, a thousand painful reflections, were jostling one another confusedly in his head. Ascanio failed him at the moment when his presence was most essential, for all his apprentices, with the most intelligent of them all at their head, were none too many for the casting of his Jupiter. Colombe was abducted; and Colombe in the midst of her foes might lose heart. The serene, sublime confidence which served the poor child as a bulwark against evil thoughts and perverse designs would perhaps grow weaker, or abandon her altogether, in such a maze of plots and threats. With all the rest, he remembered that one day he had spoken to Ascanio of the possibility of some cruel vengeance on the part of the Duchesse d'Etampes, whereupon Ascanio replied with a smile, —

"She will not dare to ruin me, for with a word I could ruin her."

Benvenuto sought to learn the secret, but Ascanio would make no other reply to his questions than this: —

"To-day it would be treachery, master. Wait until the day comes when it will be only a legitimate means of defence."

Benvenuto understood the delicacy which closed his mouth, and waited. Now it was necessary that he should see Ascanio, and his first endeavors should be directed to that end.

With Benvenuto the wish led at once to the decision

necessarily to gratify it. He had hardly said to himself that he must see Ascanio, before he was knocking at the door of the Châtelet. The wicket opened, and one of the provost's people asked Cellini who he was. Another man was standing behind him in the shadow.

"My name is Benvenuto Cellini," replied the goldsmith.

"What do you wish?"

"To see a prisoner who is confined herein."

"What is his name?"

"Ascanio."

"Ascanio is in secret and can see no one."

"Why is he in secret?"

"Because he is charged with a crime punishable with death."

"An additional reason why I should see him," cried Benvenuto.

"Your logic is most extraordinary, Signor Cellini," said the man who was standing in the background, in a jeering tone, "and does n't pass current at the Châtelet."

"Who laughs when I proffer a request? Who jeers when I implore a favor?" cried Benvenuto.

"I," said the voice, — "I, Robert d'Estourville, Provost of Paris. To each his turn, Signor Cellini. Every contest consists of a game and revenge. You won the first bout, and the second is mine. You illegally took my property, I legally take your apprentice. You refused to return the one to me, so never fear, I will not return the other to you. You are gallant and enterprising; you have an army of devoted retainers. Come on, my stormer of citadels! Come on, my scaler of walls! Come on, my burster in of doors! Come and take the Châtelet! I am waiting for you."

With that the wicket was closed.

Benvenuto, with a roar, darted at the massive iron door, but could make no impression upon it with the united efforts of his feet and hands.

" Come on, my friend, come on, strike, strike! " cried the provost from the other side of the door; " you will only succeed in making a noise, and if you make too much, beware the watch, beware the archers! Ah! the Châtelet is n't like the Hôtel de Nesle, you 'll find; it belongs to our lord the king, and we shall see if you are more powerful in France than the king."

Benvenuto cast his eyes about and saw upon the quay an uprooted mile-stone which two ordinary men would have found difficulty in lifting. He walked to where it lay picked it up and put it on his shoulder as easily as a child could do the same with a pebble. He had taken but a step or two, however, when he reflected that, when the door was broken in, he should find the guard waiting for him, and the result would be that he should himself be imprisoned, — imprisoned when Ascanio's liberty was dependent upon his own. He therefore dropped the stone, which was driven some inches into the ground by its own weight.

Doubtless the provost was watching him from some invisible loophole, for he heard a burst of laughter.

Benvenuto hurried away at full speed, lest he should yield to the desire to dash his head against the accursed door.

He went directly to the Hôtel d'Etampes.

All was not lost, if, failing to see Ascanio, he could see Colombe. Perhaps Ascanio, in the overflowing of his heart, had confided to his beloved the secret he had refused to confide to his master.

All went well at first. The gateway of the mansion

was open; he crossed the courtyard and entered the reception-room, where stood a tall footman with lace on all the seams of his livery, — a sort of colossus four feet wide and six high.

"Who are you?" he demanded, eying the goldsmith from head to foot.

At another time Benvenuto would have answered his insolent stare by one of his customary violent outbursts, but it was essential that he should see Colombe. Ascanio's welfare was at stake: so he restrained himself.

"I am Benvenuto Cellini, the Florentine goldsmith," he replied.

"What do you wish?"

"To see Mademoiselle Colombe."

"Mademoiselle Colombe is not visible."

"Why is she not visible?"

"Because her father, Messire d'Estourville, Provost of Paris, gave her in charge to Madame d'Etampes, and requested her to keep an eye upon her."

"But I am a friend."

"An additional reason for suspecting you."

"I tell you that I must see her," said Benvenuto, beginning to get warm.

"And I tell you that you shall not see her," retorted the servant.

"Is Madame d'Etampes visible?"

"No more than Mademoiselle Colombe."

"Not even to me, her jeweller?"

"Less to you than to any other person."

"Do you mean that orders have been given not to admit me?"

"Just so," replied the servant; "you have put your finger on the spot."

" Do you know that I am a strange man, my friend,"
said Benvenuto, with the terrible laugh which ordinarily preceded his outbursts of wrath; " and that
the place I am forbidden to enter is the place I am
accustomed to enter ? "

" How will you do it, eh ? You amuse me."

" When there is a door, and a blackguard like you in
front of it, for instance — "

" Well ? " said the valet.

" Well! " retorted Benvenuto, suiting the action to
the word, " I overturn the blackguard, and break in the
door."

And with a blow of his fist he laid the valet sprawl-
ing on the floor, and burst in the door with a blow of
his foot.

" Help! " cried the servant; " help! "

But the poor devil's cry of distress was not needed;
as Benvenuto passed into the reception-room he found
himself confronted by six others, evidently stationed
there to receive him. He at once divined that Madame
d'Etampes had been informed of his return, and had
taken measures accordingly.

Under any other circumstances, armed as he was with
dagger and sword, Benvenuto would have fallen upon
them, and would probably have given a good account
of himself, but such an act of violence in the abode of
the king's mistress might have deplorable results. For
the second time, contrary to his custom, common sense
carried the day over wrath, and, being certain that he
could at all events have audience of the king, to whose
presence, as we know, he had the privilege of being
admitted at any hour, he replaced his sword, already
half drawn, in its scabbard, retraced his steps, pausing
at every movement in his rear, like a lion in retreat,

walked slowly across the courtyard, and bent his steps toward the Louvre.

Benvenuto once more assumed a calm demeanor, and walked with measured step, but his tranquillity was only apparent. Great drops of perspiration were rolling down his cheeks, and his wrath was rising mountain high within his breast, his superhuman efforts to master it making him suffer the more. Indeed, nothing could be more utterly antipathetic to his impulsive nature than delay, than the wretched obstacle of a closed door, or the vulgar insolence of a lackey. Strong men who command their thoughts are never so near despair as when they come in collision with some material obstacle and struggle to no purpose to surmount it. Benvenuto would have given ten years of his life to have some man jostle him, and as he walked along he raised his head from time to time and gazed threateningly at those who passed, as if he would say : —

"Isn't there some unfortunate wretch among you who is tired of life? If so, let him apply to me, I'm his man!"

A quarter of an hour later he reached the Louvre and went at once to the apartment set apart for the pages, requesting immediate speech of his Majesty. It was his purpose to tell François the whole story, and make an appeal to his loyalty, and, if he could not obtain Ascanio's release, to solicit permission to see him. As he came through the streets he considered what language he would use to the king, and as he had some pretensions to eloquence he was well content with the little speech he had prepared. The excitement, the terrible news he had learned so suddenly, the insults heaped upon him, the obstacles he could not overcome, all these had combined to set the blood on fire in the irascible artist's veins: his temples throbbed, his heart beat quickly, his hands shook. He did not himself know the extent of the feverish agitation which multiplied the energy of his body and his heart. A whole day is sometimes concentrated in one minute.

In such a frame of mind was Benvenuto when he appealed to a page for admission to the king's apartments.

"The king is not visible," was the young man's reply.

"Do you not recognize me?" asked Benvenuto in surprise.

"Perfectly."

"I am Benvenuto Cellini, and his Majesty is always visible to me."

"It is precisely because you are Benvenuto Cellini," returned the page, "that you cannot enter."

Benvenuto was thunderstruck.

"Ah! is it you, M. de Termes?" continued the page, addressing a courtier who arrived just behind the goldsmith. "Pass in, pass in, Comte de la Faye; pass in, Marquis des Prés."

"And what of me! what of me, pray?" cried Benvenuto, turning white with anger.

"You? The king, when he returned ten minutes since, said, 'If that insolent Florentine makes his appearance, let him know that I do not choose to receive him, and advise him to be submissive unless he desires to make a comparison between the Castle of San Angelo and the Châtelet."

"Help me, patience! Oh help me!" muttered Benvenuto in a hollow voice: "Vrai Dieu! I am not accustomed to being made to wait by kings. The Vatican's no less a place than the Louvre, and Leo X. is no less great a man than François I., and yet I was not kept waiting at the door of the Vatican, nor at that of Leo X. But I understand; it's like this: the king was with Madame d'Etampes, — yes, the king has just come from his mistress and has been put on his guard by her against me. Yes, that's the way it is: patience for Ascanio! patience for Colombe!"

Notwithstanding his praiseworthy resolution to be patient, however, Benvenuto was obliged to lean against a pillar for support: his heart was swollen to bursting, and his legs trembled under him. This last insult not only wounded him in his pride, but in his friendship. His soul was filled with bitterness and despair, and his clenched hands, his frown, and his tightly closed lips bore witness to the violence of his suffering.

However, in a moment or two he recovered himself, tossed back the hair which was falling over his brow, and left the palace with firm and resolute step. All who were present watched him with something very like respect as he walked away.

Benvenuto's apparent tranquillity was due to the marvellous power he possessed over himself, for he was in reality more confused and desperate than a stag at bay. He wandered through the streets for some time, heedless as to where he might be, hearing nothing but the buzzing of the blood in his ears, and vaguely wondering, as one does in intoxication, whether he was awake or asleep. It was the third time he had been shown the door within an hour. It was the third time that doors had been shut in his face, — in his face, Benvenuto's, the favorite of princes, popes, and kings, before whom all doors were thrown open to their fullest extent when his footsteps were heard approaching! And yet, notwithstanding this threefold affront, he had not the right to give way to his anger; he must dissemble, and hide

his humiliation until he had rescued Colombe and
Ascanio. The throng through which he passed, thought-
less or full of business, seemed to him to read upon his
brow the story of the repeated insults he had under-
gone. It was perhaps the only moment in his whole
life when his great heart lost faith in itself. But after
ten or fifteen minutes of this aimless, blind wandering,
his will reasserted itself, and he raised his head: his
depression left him, and the fever returned.

"Go to!" he cried aloud, to such a degree did his
mind dominate his body; "go to! in vain do they
crowd the man, they cannot throw down the artist!
Come, sculptor, and make them repent of their base
deeds when they admire thy handiwork! Come, Jupiter, and prove that thou art still, not the king of the
gods alone, but the master of mankind!"

As he spoke, Benvenuto, acting upon an impulse
stronger than himself, bent his step toward the Tour-
nelles, that former royal residence, where the old constable, Anne de Montmorency, still dwelt.

The effervescent artist was required to await his turn
for an hour before he was admitted to the presence of
the warrior minister of François I., who was besieged
by a mob of courtiers and petitioners. At last he was
introduced.

Anne de Montmorency was a man of great height,
little if any bent by age, cold, stiff, and spare, with a
piercing glance and an abrupt manner of speaking; he
was forever scolding, and no one ever saw him in good
humor. He would have looked upon it as a humiliation to be surprised with a laugh upon his face. How
had this morose old man succeeded in making himself
agreeable to the amiable and gracious prince, who then
governed France? It is something that can be explained

in no other way than by the law of contrasts. François I. had a way of sending away satisfied those whose petitions he refused; the constable, on the other hand, arranged matters in such a way that those whom he gratified went away in a rage. He was only moderately endowed in the way of genius, but he won the king's confidence by his military inflexibility and his dictatorial gravity.

When Benvenuto entered, Montmorency was, as usual, striding back and forth in his apartment. He nodded in response to the goldsmith's salutation; then paused in his walk, and, fixing his piercing gaze upon him, inquired, —

" Who are you ? "

" Benvenuto Cellini."

" Your profession ? "

" Goldsmith to the king," replied the artist, wondering to find that his first reply did not make the second question unnecessary.

" Ah! yes, yes," growled the constable. " I recognize you. Well, what do you want, what have you to ask, my friend? That I give you an order? If you have counted on that, your time is thrown away, I give you warning. Upon my word, I have no patience with this mania for art which is raging so everywhere to-day. One would say it was an epidemic that has attacked every one except myself. No, sculpture does n't interest me in the very least, Master Goldsmith, do you hear? So apply to others, and good night."

Benvenuto made a gesture, but before he could speak, the constable continued: —

" Mon Dieu! don't let that discourage you. You will find plenty of courtiers who like to ape the king, and noodles who pose as connoisseurs. As for me, hark ye?

I stick to my trade, which is to wage war, and I tell you frankly that I much prefer a good, healthy peasant-woman, who gives me a child, that is to say, a soldier, every ten months, than a wretched sculptor, who wastes his time turning out a crowd of men of bronze who are good for nothing but to raise the price of cannon."

"Monseigneur," said Benvenuto, who had listened to this long heretical harangue with a degree of patience which amazed himself, "I am not here to speak upon artistic subjects, but upon a matter of honor."

"Ah! that's a different matter. What do you desire of me? Tell me quickly."

"Do you remember, monseigneur, that his Majesty once said to me in your presence that, on the day when I should bring him the statue of Jupiter cast in bronze, he would grant whatever favor I might ask, and that he bade you, monseigneur, and Chancelier Poyet remind him of his promise in the event of his forgetting it?"

"I remember. What then?"

"The moment is at hand, monseigneur, when I shall implore you to provide a memory for the king. Will you do it?"

"Is that what you come here to ask me, monsieur?" cried the constable; "have you intruded upon me to beg me to do something I am bound to do?"

"Monseigneur!"

"You're an impertinent fellow, Master Goldsmith. Understand that the Connétable Anne de Montmorency does not need to be reminded to be an honorable man. The king bade me remember for him, and that is a precaution he might well take more frequently, with all due respect; I shall do as he bade me, even though the reminder be annoying to him. Adieu, Master Cellini, and make room for others."

With that the constable turned his back on Benvenuto, and gave the signal for another petitioner to be introduced.

Benvenuto saluted the constable, whose somewhat brutal frankness was not displeasing to him, and took his leave. Still agitated, and impelled by the same feverish excitement and the same burning thoughts, he betook himself to the abode of Chancelier Poyet, near Porte Saint-Antoine, only a short distance away.

Chancelier Poyet formed a most striking and complete contrast, moral and physical, to Anne de Montmorency, who was always crabbed and always incased in armor from head to foot. He was polished, shrewd, crafty, buried in his furs, lost, so to speak, in the ermine. Naught could be seen of him save a bald head surrounded by a grizzly fringe of hair, intelligent, restless eyes, thin lips, and a white hand. He was quite as honest perhaps as the constable, but much less outspoken.

There again Benvenuto was forced to wait for half an hour. But his friends would not have recognized him; he had accustomed himself to waiting.

"Monseigneur," he said, when he was at last ushered into the chancellor's presence, "I have come to remind you of a promise the king made me in your presence, and constituted you not only the witness thereof but the guarantor."

"I know what you refer to, Messire Benvenuto," said Poyet, "and I am ready, if you wish, to bring his Majesty's promise to his mind; but it is my duty to inform you that, from a legal standpoint, you have no claim upon him, for an undertaking indefinite in form, and left to your discretion, cannot be enforced before the courts, and never affords a cause of action; where-

fore, if the king satisfies your demand, he will do so
purely as a matter of generosity and good faith."

"That is as I understand it, monseigneur," said
Benvenuto, "and I simply have to request you when
the occasion arises to fulfil the duty his Majesty intrusted
to you, leaving the rest to his good will."

"Very well," said Poyet, "I am at your service, my
dear monsieur, to that extent."

Benvenuto thereupon took his leave of the chancellor,
with his mind more at ease, but his blood was still
boiling, and his hands were trembling with fever. His
thoughts, excited by the annoyance and irritation and
insults to which he had been subjected, burst forth at
last in full freedom, after their long restraint. Space
and time no longer existed for the mind which they
overflowed, and as Benvenuto strode along toward his
home he saw in a sort of luminous dream Del Moro's
house, Stefana, the Castle of San Angelo, and Colombe's
garden. At the same time, he felt that his strength
became more than human, and he seemed to be living
in another world.

He was still laboring under this intense exaltation of
feeling when he entered the Hôtel de Nesle. All the
apprentices were awaiting his return, in accordance with
his commands.

"Now for the casting of the Jupiter, my children!"
he cried from the doorway, and darted into the studio.

"Good morning, master," said Jacques Aubry, who
had come in behind Cellini, singing joyously as his
wont was. "You neither saw nor heard me, did you?
For five minutes I have been following you along the
quay, calling you; you walked so fast that I am quite
out of breath. In God's name, what's the matter with
you all? You are as sober as judges."

"To the casting!" continued Benvenuto, without answering Aubry, although he had seen him out of the corner of his eye, and listened to him with one ear. "To the casting! Everything depends upon that. Merciful God, shall we be successful? Ah! my friend," he continued, abruptly, addressing Aubry, — "ah, my dear Jacques, what sad news awaited me on my return, and what a cruel advantage they took of my absence!"

"What is the matter, master?" cried Aubry, really disturbed by Cellini's excitement and the dejection of the apprentices.

"Above all things, boys, throw in plenty of dry spruce. You know that I have been laying in a stock of it for six months. The matter, my good Jacques, is that Ascanio is under lock and key at the Châtelet; and that Colombe, the provost's daughter, that lovely girl whom Ascanio loves, as you know, is in the hands of the Duchesse d'Etampes, her enemy: they found her in the statue of Mars where I had hidden her. But we will rescue them. Well, well, where are you going, Hermann? the wood's in the yard, not in the cellar."

"Ascanio arrested!" cried Aubry; "Colombe carried off!"

"Yes, yes, some villanous spy must have watched them, poor children, and surprised a secret which I had kept even from you, dear Jacques. But if I discover the knave! — To the casting, boys, to the casting! — That isn't all. The king refuses to see me, whom he called his friend. So much for the friendship of men: to be sure kings are not men, but kings. The result was that I went to the Louvre to no purpose; I could not get speech of him. Ah! but my statue shall speak for me. Prepare the mould, my friends, and let us not lose a moment. That woman insulting poor Colombe! that infamous provost jeering at me! that jailer torturing Ascanio! Oh, I have had some fearful visions to-day, dear Jacques! I would give ten years of my life to the man who could gain admission to the prisoner, speak to him, and learn the secret by means of which I may subdue that arrogant duchess: for Ascanio knows a secret which possesses that power, Jacques, and refused to divulge it to me, noble heart! But no matter: have no fear for thy child, Stefana; I will defend him to my latest breath, and I will save him! Yes, I will save him! Ah! where is the vile traitor who betrayed us, that I may strangle him with my own hands! Let me live but three days, Stefana, for it seems to me that the fire which consumes me is burning my life away. Oh if I should die before my Jupiter is finished! To the casting, children! to the casting!"

At Benvenuto's first words Jacques Aubry became pale as death, for he suspected that he was the cause of it all. As the master proceeded, his suspicion was changed to certainty. Thereupon some plan doubtless suggested itself to him, for he stole silently away while Cellini hurried away to the foundry, followed by his workmen, and shouting like a madman, —

"To the casting, children! to the casting!"

XII.

OF THE DIFFICULTY WHICH AN HONEST MAN EX-PERIENCES IN PROCURING HIS OWN COMMITTAL TO PRISON.

Poor Jacques Aubry was in a frame of mind bordering on despair when he left the Grand-Nesle; there could be no doubt that it was he who, involuntarily to be sure, had betrayed Ascanio's secret. But who was the man who had betrayed him? Surely not that gallant noble-man whose name he did not know: ah, no! he was a gentleman. It must have been that knave of a Henriot, unless it was Robin, or Charlot, or Guillaume. To tell the truth, poor Aubry rather lost himself in his conjec-tures; for the fact was that he had intrusted the secret to a dozen or more intimate friends, among whom it was no easy matter to find the culprit. But no matter! the first, the real traitor was himself, Jacques Aubry, — the infamous spy so roundly denounced by Benvenuto was himself. Instead of locking away in his heart his friend's secret which he had surprised, he had spread it broadcast in a score of- places, and had brought disaster upon his brother Ascanio with his infernal tongue. Jacques tore his hair; Jacques beat himself with his fists; Jacques heaped mortal insults upon himself, and could find no invectives sufficiently bitter to qualify his conduct as it deserved.

His remorse became so keen, and threw him into such a state of exasperation with himself, that, for the first

time in his life perhaps, Jacques Aubry indulged in reflection.   After all, when his head should be bald. his
chest black and blue, and his conscience torn to rags,
Ascanio would be no nearer freedom.   At any cost, he
must repair the evil he had done, instead of wasting his
time in despairing.

Honest Jacques had retained these words of Benvenuto: "I would give ten years of my life to the man
who would gain admission to the prisoner, speak to him,
and learn the secret by means of which I may subdue
that arrogant duchess."   And, as we have said, he began
to reflect, contrary to his wont.   The result of his reflections was that he must gain admission to the Châtelet.
Once there, he would find a way to reach Ascanio.

But Benvenuto had sought in vain to gain admission
as a visitor; and surely Jacques Aubry could never be
so audacious as to think of attempting a thing in which
the master had failed.   However, although it might be
impossible to effect an entrance as a visitor, it certainly
should be much easier, at least so the student thought,
to be admitted as a prisoner.   He determined, therefore,
to enter the Châtelet in that character; then, when he
had seen Ascanio, and Ascanio had told him all, so that
he had no further business at the Châtelet, he would take
his leave, rich in the possession of the precious secret,
and would go to Benvenuto, not to demand the ten years
of his life that he offered, but to confess his crime, and
implore forgiveness.

Delighted with the fecundity of his imagination, and
proud of his unexampled devotion, he bent his steps
toward the Châtelet.

"Let us see," he ruminated, as he walked with de-
liberate step toward the prison where all his hopes were
centred, — "let us see, in order to avoid any more idiotic

mistakes, how matters stand, — no easy task, considering that the whole business seems to me as tangled as Gervaise's skein when she gives it to me to hold, and I try to kiss her. Let's begin at the beginning. Ascanio loved Colombe, the provost's daughter: so far, so good. As the provost proposed to marry her to Comte d'Orbec, Ascanio carried her off: very good. Not knowing what to do with the sweet child when he had abducted her, he hid her in the head of the statue of Mars: best of all. Faith, it was a wonderfully ingenious hiding place, and nothing less than a beast — but let us pass over that: I shall find myself again later. Thereupon it would seem that the provost, acting upon my information, got his daughter into his clutches once more, and imprisoned Ascanio. Triple brute that I am! But here is where the skein begins to be tangled. What interest has the Duchesse d'Etampes in all this? She detests Colombe, whom everybody else loves. Why? Ah! I know. I remember certain jocose remarks of the apprentices, Ascanio's embarrassment when the duchess was mentioned, — Madame d'Etampes has her eye on Ascanio, and naturally abominates her rival. Jacques, my friend, you are a miserable wretch, but you are a clever dog all the same. Ah, yes! but now how does it happen that Ascanio has in his hands the means of ruining the duchess? Why does the king appear at intervals in the affair, with one Stefana? Why did Benvenuto constantly invoke Jupiter, rather a heathenish invocation for a Catholic? Deuce take me if I can see through all that. But it isn't absolutely necessary that I should understand. Light is to be found in Ascanio's cell; therefore the most essential thing is to get myself cast into the cell with him. I will manage the rest afterward."

As he thus communed with himself he reached his

destination, and struck a violent blow upon the great door of the Châtelet. The wicket opened, and a harsh voice demanded to know his business: it was the jailer's.

"I wish for a cell in your prison," replied Aubry in a hollow voice.

"A cell!" exclaimed the astonished jailer.

"Yes, a cell: the blackest and deepest; even that will be better than I deserve."

"Why so?"

"Because I am a great criminal."

"What crime have you committed?"

"Ah! indeed, what crime have I committed?" Jacques asked himself, for he had not thought of preparing a crime suited to the occasion. As a fertile, lively imagination was not his most prominent characteristic, notwithstanding the compliments he had addressed to himself just before, he repeated, stupidly, —

"What crime?"

"Yes, what crime?"

"Guess," said Jacques. "This fellow ought to know more about crimes than I do," he added to himself, "so I will let him give me a list, and then make my selection."

"Have you murdered anybody?" asked the jailer.

"Great God! what do you take me for, my friend?" cried the student, whose conscience rose in revolt at the thought of being taken for a murderer.

"Have you stolen anything?" continued the jailer.

"Stolen? the idea!"

"What in Heaven's name have you done then?" cried the jailer testily. "To give yourself up as a criminal isn't all that is necessary: you must say what crime you've committed."

"But I tell you that I'm a villain, a vile wretch, and that I deserve the wheel or the gallows!"

"The crime? the crime?" the jailer repeated.

"The crime? Well! I have betrayed my friend."

"That's no crime," said the jailer. "Good night."
And he closed the wicket.

"That's not a crime, you say? that's not a crime?
What is it then, pray?"

And Jacques grasped the knocker with both hands,
and knocked with all his strength.

"What's the matter? what's the matter?" said a
different voice from within the Châtelet.

"It's a madman, who wants to be admitted into the
prison," replied the jailer.

"If he's a madman, his place is not at the Châtelet,
but at the asylum."

"At the asylum!" cried Aubry, scampering away as
fast as his legs would carry him, "at the asylum! Peste!
that's not what I want. I want to get into the Châtelet,
not the asylum! Besides, paupers and beggars are sent
to the asylum, and not people who have twenty Paris
sous in their pocket as I have. The asylum! Why,
that wretched jailer claims that to betray one's friend
is no crime! So it seems that, in order to have the
honor of being committed to prison one must have murdered or stolen. But now I think of it, — why might I
not have led some young girl astray? There's nothing
dishonorable about that. Very good, but what girl?
Gervaise?"

Despite his preoccupation, the student roared with
laughter.

"But, after all," he said, "though it is n't so, it might
have been. Good! good! I have discovered my crime:
I seduced Gervaise!"

On the instant he set off for the young working-girl's
home, ran up the sixty stairs which led to her lodgings,

and burst into the room where the lovely grisette in a coquettish *négligé* was ironing her linen.

"Ah!" exclaimed Gervaise, with a fascinating little shriek; "ah! monsieur, you frightened me!"

"Gervaise, my dear Gervaise," cried Aubry, rushing toward her with open arms: "you must save my life, my child."

"One moment, one moment," said Gervaise, using the hot flat-iron as a shield; "what do you want, master gadabout? for three days I haven't seen you."

"I have done wrong, Gervaise, I am an unfortunate wretch. But a sure proof that I love you is that I run to you in my distress. I repeat it, Gervaise, you must save my life."

"Yes. I understand, you have been getting tipsy in some wine shop, and have had a dispute with some one. The archers are after you to put you in prison, and you come to poor Gervaise to give you shelter. Go to prison, monsieur, go to prison, and leave me in peace."

"That is just what I ask and all I ask, my little Gervaise, — to go to prison. But the villains refuse to commit me."

"O mon Dieu! Jacques," said the young woman compassionately, "have you gone mad?"

"There you are! they say that I am mad, and propose to send me to the asylum, while the Châtelet is where I want to go."

"You want to go to the Châtelet? What for, Aubry? The Châtelet's a frightful prison; they say that when one gets in there, it's impossible to say when one will come out."

"I *must* get in there, however, I must!" cried the student. "There is no other way to save him."

"To save whom?"

"Ascanio."

"Ascanio? what, that handsome young fellow, your Benvenuto's pupil?"

"Himself, Gervaise.   He is in the Châtelet, and he's there by my fault."

"Great God!"

"So that I must join him there," said Jacques, "and save him."

"Why is he in the Châtelet?"

"Because he loved the provost's daughter, and seduced her."

"Poor boy!   Why, do they imprison men for that?"

"Yes, Gervaise.   Now you see it was like this: he had her in hiding.   I discovered the hiding place, and, like an idiot, like an infamous villain, I told the whole story to everybody."

"Except me!" cried Gervaise.   "That was just like you!"

"Did n't I tell it to you, Gervaise?"

"You did n't mention it.   You 're a great babbler with others, but not with me.   When you come here it 's to kiss me, to drink, or to sleep, — never to talk.   Understand, monsieur, that a woman loves to talk."

"Well, what are we doing at this moment, my little Gervaise?" said Jacques.   "We are talking, I should say."

"Yes, because you need me."

"It is true that you could do me a great service."

"What is it?"

"You could say that I seduced you."

"Why, of course you seduced me, you wretch."

"I!" cried Jacques in amazement.   "I seduced you, Gervaise?"

"Alas! yes, that is the word: seduced, monsieur, shamelessly seduced by your fine words, by your false promises."

" By my fine words and false promises? "

" Yes.   Did n't you tell me I was the prettiest girl in the whole quarter of Saint-Germain des Prés? "

" I tell you that now."

" Did n't you say that, if I did n't love you, you should die of love? "

" Do you think I said that?   It 's strange I don't remember it."

" While, on the contrary, if I did love you, you would marry me."

" Gervaise, I did n't say that.   Never! "

" You did say it, monsieur."

" Never, never, never, Gervaise.   My father made me take an oath like Hannibal's to Hamilcar."

" What was that? "

" He made me swear to die a bachelor, like himself."

" Oh! " cried Gervaise, summoning tears to the assistance of her words with a woman's marvellous power of weeping to order, " oh! you 're like all the rest.   Promises cost nothing, and when the poor girl is seduced they forget what they promised.   I will take my turn at swearing now, and swear that I will never be caught again."

" And you will do well, Gervaise, " said the student.

" When one thinks, " cried the grisette, " that there are laws for robbers and cut-purses, and none for the scoundrels who ruin poor girls! "

" But there are, Gervaise."

" There are? "

" Why, of course.   Did n't I tell you that they sent poor Ascanio to the Châtelet for seducing Colombe."

" They did well, too, " said Gervaise, to whom the loss of her honor had never presented itself so forcibly until she was fully convinced that Jacques Aubry was determined not to give her his name by way of compensation.

"Yes. they did well, and I wish you were in the Châtelet with him!"

"Mon Dieu! that's all I ask," cried the student; "and as I told you, my little Gervaise, I rely upon you to put me there."

"You rely upon me."

"Yes."

"Make sport of me, ingrate!"

"I'm not making sport of you, Gervaise. I say that if you had the courage — "

"To do what?"

"Accuse me before the judge."

"Of what?"

"Of having seduced you; but you would never dare."

"What's that? I wouldn't dare," cried Gervaise in an injured tone, — "I wouldn't dare to tell the truth!"

"Consider that you would have to make oath to it, Gervaise."

"I'll do it."

"You will make oath that I seduced you?"

"Yes, yes, — a hundred times yes!"

"Then all goes well," said the student joyfully. "I confess I was afraid: an oath is a serious matter."

"I'll take my oath to it this instant, and send you to the Châtelet, monsieur."

"Good!"

"And you will find your Ascanio there."

"Splendid!"

"And you will have all the time you need to do penance together."

"It's all that I ask."

"Where is the lieutenant criminal?"

"At the Palais de Justice."

"I will go there at once."

" Let us go together, Gervaise."

" Yes, together. In that way the punishment will follow at once."

" Take my arm, Gervaise."

" Come, monsieur."

They set off toward the Palais de Justice at the same
gait at which they were accustomed to repair on Sundays
to the Pré-aux-Clercs or the Butte Montmartre.

As they drew near the Temple of Themis, as Jacques
Aubry poetically called the edifice in question, Gervaise's
pace slackened perceptibly. When they reached the foot
of the staircase, she had some difficulty in ascending ; and
finally, at the door of the lieutenant criminal's sanctum,
her legs failed her altogether, and the student felt her
whole weight hanging upon his arm.

" Well, Gervaise," said he, " is your courage giving
out ? "

" No," said Gervaise, " but a lieutenant criminal is an
appalling creature."

" Pardieu! he 's a man like other men ! "

" True, but one must tell him things — "

" Very well; tell them."

" But I must swear."

" Then swear."

" Jacques," said Gervaise, " are you quite sure that
you seduced me ? "

" Am I sure of it! " said Jacques. " Pardieu ! Besides, did n't you just insist upon it yourself that I
did ? "

" Yes, that is true; but, strangely enough, I don't
seem to see things now in just the same light that I did
a short time ago."

" Come, come," said Jacques, " you are weakening
already : I knew you would."

" Jacques, my dear, " cried Gervaise, " take me back to the house. "

" Gervaise, Gervaise, " said the student, " this isn't what you promised me. "

" Jacques, I will never reproach you again, or say a word about it. I loved you because you took my fancy, that 's all. "

" Alas! " said the student, " this is what I feared; but it 's too late. "

" How too late ? "

" You came here to accuse me, and accuse me you must. "

" Never, Jacques, never: you didn't seduce me, Jacques; I was a flirt. "

" Nonsense! " cried the student.

" Besides, " added Gervaise, lowering her eyes, " one can be seduced but once. "

" What do you mean ? "

" The first time one loves. "

" Hoity-toity ! and you made me believe that you had never loved! "

" Jacques, take me back to the house. "

" Oh indeed I won't! " said Jacques, exasperated by her refusal, and by the reason she gave for it. " No! no! no! "

And he knocked at the magistrate's door.

" What are you doing? " cried Gervaise.

" You see! I am knocking. "

" Come in ! " cried a nasal voice.

" I will not go in, " exclaimed Gervaise, doing her utmost to release her arm from the student's. " I will not go in ! "

" Come in, " said the same voice a second time, a little more emphatically.

"Jacques, I will shriek, I will call for help," said Gervaise.

"Come in, I say!" said the voice a third time, nearer at hand, and at the same moment the door opened.

'Well! what do you want?" said a tall thin man dressed in black, the mere sight of whom made Gervaise tremble from head to foot.

"Mademoiselle here," said Aubry, "has come to enter complaint against a knave who has seduced her."

With that he pushed Gervaise into the black, filthy closet, which served as an anteroom to the lieutenant criminal's office. The door closed behind her as if by a spring.

Gervaise gave a feeble shriek, half terror, half surprise, and sat down, or rather fell, upon a stool which stood against the wall.

Jacques Aubry, meanwhile, lest she should call him back, or run after him, hurried away through corridors known only to law students and advocates, until he reached the courtyard of Sainte-Chapelle; thence he tranquilly pursued his way to Pont Saint-Michel, which it was absolutely certain that Gervaise must cross.

Half an hour later she appeared.

"Well!" said he, running to meet her, "what happened?"

"Alas!" said Gervaise, "you made me tell a monstrous lie; but I hope God will forgive me for it in view of my good intention."

"I'll take it upon myself," said Aubry. "Tell me what happened."

"Do you fancy that I know?" said Gervaise. "I was so ashamed that I hardly remember what it was all about. All I know is that the lieutenant criminal questioned me, and that I answered his questions sometimes yes, sometimes no : but I am not sure that I answered as I should."

" Wretched girl ! " cried Aubry, " I believe it will turn out that she accused herself of seducing me."

" Oh, no ! I don't think I went as far as that."

" At least they have my address, have n't they, so that they can summon me ? "

" Yes, " murmured Gervaise, " I gave it to them."

" It 's all right then, " said Aubry, " and now let us hope that God will do the rest."

Having escorted Gervaise to her abode and comforted her as best he could for the false testimony she had been compelled to give, Jacques Aubry returned home, over-flowing with faith in Providence.

In fact, whether Providence took a hand in it, or chance did it all, Jacques Aubry received the next morning a summons to appear before the lieutenant criminal that same day.

This summons fulfilled Aubry's dearest hopes, and yet a court of justice is so redoubtable a place that he felt a shiver run through his veins as he read it. But we hasten to say that the certainty of seeing Ascanio again, and the longing to save the friend upon whom he had brought disaster, soon put an end to this demonstration of weakness on our student's part.

The summons fixed the hour of noon, and it was only nine o'clock : so he called upon Gervaise, whom he found no less agitated than on the previous day.

" Well ? " said she, inquiringly.

" Well ! " repeated Jacques triumphantly, exhibiting the paper covered with hieroglyphics which he held in his hand. " Here it is."

" For what hour ? "

" Noon.   That 's all I was able to read."

" Then you don't know what you 're accused of ? "

" Why, of seducing you, my little Gervaise, I presume."

" You won't forget that you yourself insisted upon my doing it ? "

" Why no; I am ready to give you a certificate that you utterly refused to do it."

" Then you bear me no ill will for obeying you."

" On the contrary, I could n't be more grateful to you."

" Whatever happens ? "

" Whatever happens."

" If I did say all that, it was because I was obliged to."

" Of course."

" And if, in my confusion, I said more than I meant to say, you will forgive me ? "

" Not only will I forgive you, my dear, my divine Gervaise, but I do forgive you now in advance."

" Ah!" said Gervaise, with a sigh; " ah! bad boy, with such words as those you turned my head! "

From which it is easy to see that Gervaise had really been seduced.

At a quarter before twelve Jacques Aubry remembered that his summons bade him appear at twelve. He took leave of Gervaise, and as he had a long distance to go he ran all the way. Twelve o'clock was striking as he knocked at the lieutenant criminal's door.

" Come in! " cried the same nasal voice.

He was not called upon to repeat the invitation, for Jacques Aubry, with a smile on his lips, his nose in the air, and his cap over his ear, at once stood in the tall black-coated man's presence.

" What is your name ? " asked the tall man.

" Jacques Aubry," replied the student.

" What are you ? "

" Law student."

" What have you been doing ? "

" Seducing girls."

" Aha! you 're the man against whom a complaint was lodged yesterday by — by — "

" By Gervaise-Perrette Popinot."

" Very good ; sit down yonder and await your turn."

Jacques sat down as the man in black bade him do, and waited.

Five or six persons of varying age, sex, and feature were waiting like himself, and as they had arrived before him their turns naturally came before his.   Some of them went out alone, — they were the ones, doubtless, against whom no sufficient evidence was adduced, — while others went out accompanied by an exempt, or by two of the provost's guards.   Jacques Aubry envied the fortune of these latter, for they were being taken to the Châtelet, to which he was so anxious to be admitted.

At last the name of Jacques Aubry, student, was called.

Jacques Aubry instantly rose and rushed into the magistrate's office as joyously as if he were on his way to the most agreeable of entertainments.

There were two men in the lieutenant criminal's sanctum ; one taller, thinner, and more forbidding than he in the antechamber, which Jacques Aubry would have deemed impossible five minutes earlier: this was the clerk.   The other was short, fat, coarse, with a cheerful eye, a smiling mouth, and a jovial expression generally : this was the magistrate.

Aubry's smile and his met, and the student was quite ready to grasp his hand, so strongly conscious was he of the existence of a bond of sympathy between them.

"Ha! ha! ha!" laughed the lieutenant criminal, as he caught the student's eye.

"Faith, that is true, messire," the student rejoined.

"You seem a jolly dog," said the magistrate. "Come, master knave, take a chair and sit you down."

Jacques Aubry took a chair, sat down, threw one leg over the other and swung it in high glee.

"Ah!" exclaimed the lieutenant, rubbing his hands. "Master Clerk, let us look over the complainant's deposition."

The clerk rose, and, by virtue of his great height, reached over to the other side of the table, and selected the documents concerning Jacques Aubry from a pile of papers.

"Here it is," he said.

"Who lodges the complaint?" inquired the magistrate.

"Gervaise-Perrette Popinot," said the clerk.

"That's it," said the student, nodding his head violently; "that's the one."

"A minor," said the clerk; "nineteen years of age."

"Oho! a minor!" exclaimed Aubry.

"So it appears from her declaration."

"Poor Gervaise!" muttered Aubry. "She was quite right when she said that she was so confused she didn't know what answers she made; she has confessed to twenty-two. However, nineteen it is."

"And so," said the lieutenant criminal, "and so, my buck, you are charged with seducing a minor child. Ha! ha! ha!"

"Ha! ha! ha!" echoed Aubry, joining in the judge's hilarity.

"With aggravating circumstances," continued the clerk, mingling his yelping tones with the jovial voices of the magistrate and the student.

"With aggravating circumstances," repeated the former.

"The devil!" exclaimed Jacques. "I should like very much to know what they were."

"As the complainant remained deaf to all the entreaties and wiles of the accused for six months —"

"For six months?" Jacques interposed. "Pardon, monsieur, I think there's a mistake there."

"For six months, monsieur, so it is written," replied the man in black, in a tone which admitted no rejoinder.

"So be it! six months it is," said Jacques; "but in truth Gervaise was quite right when she said — "

"The said Jacques Aubry, angered by her coldness, threatened her — "

"Oh! oh!" exclaimed Jacques.

"Oh! oh!" echoed the judge.

"But," the clerk read on, "the said Gervaise-Perrette Popinot held out so stubbornly and courageously that the insolent fellow begged her forgiveness in view of his sincere repentance."

"Ah! ah!" muttered Aubry.

"Ah! ah!" exclaimed the magistrate.

"Poor Gervaise!" Aubry continued, speaking to himself, with a shrug; "what was the matter with her head?"

"But," continued the clerk, "his repentance was only feigned; unfortunately, the complainant, in her innocence and purity, allowed herself to be deceived by it, and one evening, when she was imprudent enough to accept refreshments of which the accused invited her to partake, the said Jacques Aubry mixed with her water — "

"With her water?" the student interrupted.

"The complainant declared that she never drinks wine," said the clerk. — "The said Jacques Aubry mixed an intoxicating decoction with her water."

"Look you, Master Clerk," cried Aubry; "what the deuce are you reading from?"

"The complainant's deposition."

"Impossible!"

"Is it so written?" inquired the magistrate.

"It is written."

"Go on."

"After all," said Aubry aside, "the more guilty I am, the surer I shall be of being sent to join Ascanio at the Châtelet. Intoxicating decoction it is. Go on, Master Clerk."

"You confess, do you?" queried the judge.

"I confess," said the student.

"Ah, gallows-bird!" exclaimed the judge, roaring with laughter, and rubbing his hands.

"So that," continued the clerk, "poor Gervaise, bereft of her reason, ended by confessing to her seducer that she loved him."

"Aha!" said Jacques.

"Lucky knave!" murmured the lieutenant criminal, whose little eyes shone.

"Why!" cried Aubry; "why, there isn't a word of truth in the whole of it!"

"You deny the charge?"

"Absolutely."

"Write," said the magistrate, "that the accused declares that he is not guilty of any of the charges brought against him."

"Wait a moment! wait a moment!" cried the student, who reflected that if he denied his guilt, they would not send him to prison.

"So you don't deny it altogether?" queried the judge.

"I confess that there is some little truth, not in the form, but in the substance."

"Oh! as you have confessed to the decoction," said the judge, "you may as well admit the results."

"True," said Jacques, "as I 've confessed to the decoction, I admit the rest, Master Clerk. But, upon my word," he added in an undertone, "Gervaise was quite right in saying — "

"But that 's not all," the clerk interrupted him.

"What! that 's not all!"

"The crime of which the accused was guilty had terrible results. The unhappy Gervaise discovered that she was about to become a mother."

"Ah! that is too much!" cried Jacques.

"Do you deny the paternity?" asked the judge.

"Not only do I deny the paternity, but I deny the condition."

"Write," said the judge, "that the accused denies the paternity, and also denies the condition; an inquiry will be ordered on that point."

"One moment, one moment!" cried Aubry, realizing that if Gervaise were convicted of falsehood on a single point the whole structure would fall to the ground: "did Gervaise really say what the clerk has read?"

"She said it word for word," replied the clerk.

"Then if she said it," continued Aubry, "if she said it — why — "

"Well?" queried the lieutenant criminal.

"Why, it must be so."

"Write that the accused pleads guilty to all the charges."

The clerk wrote as directed.

"Pardieu!" said the student to himself, "if Ascanio deserves a week in the Châtelet for simply paying court to Colombe, I, who have deceived Gervaise, drugged her, and seduced her, can count upon three months' incarcera-

tion at the very least. But, faith, I would like to be
sure of my facts. However, I must congratulate Gervaise. Peste! she kept to her word, and Jeanne d'Arc
was nowhere beside her."

"So you confess to all the crimes you're accused of?"
said the judge.

"I do, messire," replied Jacques unhesitatingly; "I
do: all of them and more too, if you choose. I am a
great sinner, Monsieur le Lieutenant Criminel, don't spare
me."

"Impudent varlet!" muttered the magistrate, in the
tone in which the uncle of comedy speaks to his nephew,
"impudent varlet, out upon you!"

With that he let his great round head, with his bloated,
purple face, fall upon his breast, and reflected magis-
terially.

"Whereas," he began, after meditating a few moments,
raising his head, and lifting the index finger of his right
hand, — "write, Master Clerk, — whereas Jacques Aubry,
clerk of the Basoche, has pleaded guilty to the charge
of seducing one Gervaise-Perrette Popinot by fine promises and simulated affection, we sentence said Jacques
Aubry to pay a fine of twenty Paris sous, to support the
child, if it is a boy, and to pay the costs."

"And the imprisonment?" cried Aubry.

"Imprisonment! what do you mean?" asked the judge.

"Why, I mean the imprisonment. For Heaven's sake,
aren't you going to sentence me to prison?"

"No."

"You're not going to order me committed to the
Châtelet as Ascanio was?"

"Who's Ascanio?"

"Ascanio is a pupil of Master Benvenuto Cellini."

"What did he do?"

" He seduced a maid."

" Who was she ? "

" Mademoiselle Colombe d'Estourville, daughter of the Provost of Paris."

" What then ? "

" What then ! why I say that it 's unjust, when we both committed the same crime, to make a distinction in the punishment. What! you send him to prison and fine me twenty Paris sous ! In God's name, is there no justice in this world ? "

" On the contrary," rejoined the magistrate, " it is because there is justice in this world, and enlightened justice too, that this is as it is."

" How so ? "

" There are honors and honors, my young rascal; the honor of a noble maiden is valued at imprisonment; the honor of a grisette is worth twenty Paris sous. If you want to go to the Châtelet, you must try your arts on a duchess, and then the affair will take care of itself."

" But this is frightful! immoral! outrageous! " cried the student.

" My dear friend," said the judge, " pay your fine and begone ! "

" I won't pay my fine, and I won't go."

" Then I shall call a couple of archers and commit you to prison until you do pay it."

" That 's all I ask."

The judge summoned two guards: —

" Take this scoundrel to the Grands-Carmes ! "

" The Grands-Carmes ! " cried Jacques; " why not the Châtelet, pray ? "

" Because the Châtelet is not a debtor's prison, my friend; because the Châtelet is a royal fortress, and one must have committed some heinous crime to be sent

there.   The Châtelet!   Ah! yes, my little fellow, you 'll
get to the Châtelet soon enough, just wait!"

"One moment," said Aubry, "one moment."

"What is it?"

"If I am not to be sent to the Châtelet, I will pay."

"Very well; if you pay, there's nothing more to be
said.   You may go, you fellows, the young man will
pay."

The archers went out and Jacques Aubry took from
his wallet twenty Paris sous, which he spread out in a
line on the judge's desk.

"See if that is right," said the lieutenant criminal.

The clerk rose, and to execute the order bent his back
like a bow, embracing in the half-circle described by his
body, which seemed to possess the power of lengthening
itself out indefinitely, his table and the papers which lay
upon it.   As he stood with his feet on the floor and his
hands on the judge's desk, he reminded one of a sombre-
hued rainbow.

"It is right," he said.

"Then off with you, my young rascal," said the
magistrate, "and give place to others; the court has no
more time to waste on you.   Go."

Jacques saw that he had nothing to gain by remaining
there, and withdrew in despair.

XIII.

IN WHICH JACQUES AUBRY RISES TO EPIC PROPORTIONS.

"WELL, upon my word," said the student to himself as he left the Palais de Justice, and mechanically crossed the Pont aux Moulins, which brought him out almost opposite the Châtelet; "upon my word, I am curious to know what Gervaise will say when she learns that her honor is valued at twenty Paris sous! She will say that I have been indiscreet, and told things I should n't have told, and she 'll tear my eyes out. But what do I see yonder?"

What the student saw was a page belonging to the amiable nobleman to whom he was accustomed to confide his secrets, and whom he looked upon as one of his dearest friends. The boy was leaning up against the parapet of the bridge and amusing himself by performing sleight-of-hand tricks with pebbles.

"Pardieu!" said the student, "this happens very fortunately. My friend, whose name I don't know, and who seems to stand extremely well at court, may have influence enough to have me committed to prison: Providence sends his page to me to tell me where I can find him, as I know neither his name nor his address."

In order to avail himself of what he considered a direct interposition of Providence in his behalf, Jacques Aubry advanced toward the young page, who likewise recognized him, and, letting his three pebbles fall into the same hand, crossed his legs and awaited the student with that knowing look which is especially characteristic of the profession to which he had the honor to belong.

"*Bon jour*, Monsieur le Page," cried Aubry from the most distant point at which he thought the boy could hear his voice.

"*Bon jour*, Seigneur Student," was the reply; "what are you doing in this quarter?"

"Faith! if I must tell you, I was looking for something which I think I have found, now that I see you; I was seeking the address of my excellent friend, the comte — the baron — the vicomte — your master's address."

"Do you wish to see him?" asked the page.

"Instantly, if possible."

"In that case you will have your wish in a moment, for he is calling on the provost."

"At the Châtelet."

"Yes, he will come out directly."

"He's very lucky to be admitted to the Châtelet when he wishes; but is my friend the vicomte — the comte — the baron — "

"Vicomte."

"On intimate terms with Messire Robert d'Estourville? The Vicomte de — Tell me," continued Aubry, anxious to avail himself of the opportunity to learn his friend's name at last; "the Vicomte de — "

"The Vicomte de Mar— "

"Ah!" cried the student, interrupting the page in the middle of the word, as he saw the man he sought appear at the door. "Ah! my dear viscount, there you are. I was looking for you and waiting for you."

"*Bon jour*," said Marmagne, evidently but little pleased at the meeting. "*Bon jour*, my dear fellow. I would be glad to talk with you, but unfortunately I am very hurried. So adieu."

"One moment, one moment," cried Jacques, clinging to his friend's arm; "deuce take me! you won't leave me like this. In the first place I have a very great favor to ask of you."

"You?"

"Yes, I; and God's law, you know, bids friends to succor one another."

"Friends?"

"To be sure; are n't you my friend? What constitutes friendship? Confidence. Now I am full of confidence in you. I tell you all my own business, and other people's too."

"Have you ever had occasion to repent of your confidence."

"Never, so far as you are concerned at least; but it's not so with everybody. There is one man in Paris that I am looking for, and with God's help I shall meet him some day."

"My dear fellow," interrupted Marmagne, who had a shrewd suspicion who the man was, "I told you that I was much hurried."

"But wait a moment, pray, when I tell you that you can do me a great service."

"Well, speak quickly."

"You stand well at court, do you not?"

"My friends say so."

"You have some influence then?"

"My enemies may discover it to their cost."

"Very good! Now my dear comte — my dear baron — my dear — "

" Vicomte."

" Help me to get into the Châtelet."

" In what capacity ? "

" As a prisoner."

" As a prisoner? That's a singular ambition, on my word."

" As you please, but it's my ambition."

" For what purpose do you wish to be committed to the Châtelet ? " queried Marmagne, who suspected that this strange desire on the part of the student indicated some new secret which it might be to his advantage to know.

" To any other than you I wouldn't tell it, my good friend," replied Jacques; " for I have learned to my cost, or rather to poor Ascanio's, that I must learn to hold my tongue. But with you it's a different matter. You know that I have no secrets from you."

" In that case tell me quickly."

" Will you have me committed to the Châtelet if I tell you ? "

" Instantly."

" Well, my friend, imagine that I was idiot enough to confide to others than yourself the fact that I had seen a lovely girl in the head of the statue of Mars."

" What then ? "

" The crack-brained fools! would you believe that they spread the story so that it came to the provost's ears; and as the provost had lost his daughter some days before, he suspected that it was she who had selected that hiding place. He notified D'Orbec and the Duchesse d'Etampes: they came to the Hôtel de Nesle to make a domiciliary visit while Benvenuto Cellini was at Fontainebleau. They carried off Colombe and imprisoned Ascanio."

" Nonsense ! "

"It's as I tell you, my dear viscount. And who managed it all? A certain Vicomte de Marmagne."

"But," interposed the viscount, not at all pleased to hear his name upon the student's lips, "you don't tell me why you want to be committed to the Châtelet."

"You don't understand?"

"No."

"They arrested Ascanio."

"Yes."

"And took him to the Châtelet."

"Very good."

"But what they don't know, and what nobody knows save the Duchesse d'Etampes, Benvenuto, and myself, is that Ascanio possesses a certain letter, a certain secret, which places the duchess in his power. Now do you understand?"

"Yes I begin to see light. But do you help me, my dear friend."

"You see, viscount," continued Aubry, assuming a more and more aristocratic air, "I want to be admitted to the Châtelet, get to Ascanio's cell, take the letter or learn the secret, leave the prison again, go to Benvenuto and arrange with him some method whereby Colombe's virtue and Ascanio's love may triumph, to the confusion of the Marmagnes and D'Orbecs, the provost, the Duchesse d'Etampes, and the whole clique."

"That's a very ingenious plan," said Marmagne. "Thanks for your confidence, my dear student. You shall have no reason to regret it."

"Do you promise me your assistance?"

"To what end?"

"Why, to help me get committed to the Châtelet, as I asked you."

"Rely upon me."

" Immediately ? "

" Wait here for me."

" Where I am ? "

" In this same spot."

" And you ? "

" I am going to get the order for your arrest."

" Ah, my friend, my dear baron, my dear count! But you must tell me your name and address in case I may need you."

" Useless.   I will return at once."

" Yes, return as soon as possible; and if you chance to meet that accursed Marmagne on the road, tell him — "

" What ? "

" Tell him that I have sworn an oath that he shall die by no hand but mine."

" Adieu! " cried the viscount; " adieu, and wait here for me."

" *Au revoir!* " said Aubry.   " I will expect you soon. Ah! you are a friend indeed, a man one can trust, and I would be glad to know — "

" Adieu, Seigneur Student," said the page, who had stood aloof during this conversation, and was now about to follow his master.

" Adieu, my pretty page," said Aubry; " but before you leave me do me a favor."

" What is it ? "

" Who is this gallant nobleman to whom you have the honor to belong ? "

" He whom you 've been talking with for the last fifteen minutes ? "

" The same."

" And whom you call friend ? "

" Yes."

" You don't know his name ? "

" No."

" Why, he is — "

" A very well known nobleman, is he not ? "

" To be sure."

" And influential ? "

" Next to the king and the Duchesse d'Etampes, he 's the man."

" Ah ! and his name you say is — "

" He is the Vicomte de —   But he is turning back and calling me.   Pardon — "

" The Vicomte de — "

" The Vicomte de Marmagne."

" Marmagne ! " cried Aubry, " Vicomte de Marmagne ! That young gentleman is the Vicomte de Marmagne ! "

" Himself."

" Marmagne ! the friend of the provost and D'Orbec and Madame d'Etampes ? "

" In person."

" And the enemy of Benvenuto Cellini ? "

" Just so."

" Ah ! " exclaimed Aubry, to whom the whole past was revealed as by a flash of lightning.   " Ah ! I understand now.   O Marmagne, Marmagne ! "

As the student was unarmed, with a movement as swift as thought, he seized the page's short sword by the hilt, drew it from its sheath, and darted in pursuit of Marmagne, shouting, " Halt ! "

At his first shout, Marmagne, decidedly ill at ease, looked around, and, seeing Aubry rushing after him sword in hand, suspected that he was discovered.   To stand his ground or fly was therefore the only alternative. Marmagne was not quite courageous enough to stand his ground, nor was he quite enough of a coward to fly ; he therefore adopted the intermediate course of darting into

a house, the door of which stood open, hoping to close
the door behind him. But unluckily for him it was held
fast to the wall by a chain which he could not detach, so
that Aubry, who was some little distance behind him,
was in the little courtyard before he had time to reach
the staircase.

"Ah! Marmagne! you damned viscount! you infernal spy! you filcher of secrets! it 's you, is it?   At last
I know you, and have my hand on you! On guard,
villain! on guard!"

"Monsieur," replied Marmagne, trying to assume a
lordly bearing, "do you imagine that the Vicomte de
Marmagne will honor the student Jacques Aubry by
crossing swords with him?"

"If the Vicomte de Marmagne will not honor Jacques
Aubry by crossing swords with him, Jacques Aubry will
have the honor of passing his sword through the Vicomte
de Marmagne's body."

To leave no doubt in the mind of him to whom this
threat was addressed, Jacques Aubry placed the point of
his sword against the viscount's breast, and let him feel
the touch of the cold steel through his doublet.

"Murder!" cried Marmagne.   "Help! help!"

"Oh, shout as much as you choose," retorted Jacques;
"you will have done shouting before any one comes.
And so the best thing you can do, viscount, is to defend
yourself. On guard, viscount! on guard!"

"If you will have it so," cried the viscount, "wait a
bit, and you will see!"

Marmagne, as the reader will have discovered ere this,
was not naturally brave; but like all noblemen of that
chivalrous epoch he had received a military education; furthermore, he was reputed to have some skill in fencing.
It is true that this reputation was said to result rather in

enabling him to avoid unpleasant encounters which he might have had, than in bringing to a fortunate conclusion those which he did have. It is none the less true that, being closely pressed by Jacques, he drew his sword and stood on guard in the most approved style of the art.

But if Marmagne's skill was recognized among the noblemen at court, Jacques Aubry's address was accepted as an incontestable fact among the students at the University and the clerks of the Basoche. The result was, that the moment their swords crossed each of the combatants saw that he had to do with no despicable opponent. But Marmagne had one great advantage; the page's sword, which Aubry had taken, was six inches shorter than the viscount's; this was no great disadvantage in defensive work, but became a serious matter when he wished to assume the offensive. Furthermore, Marmagne was six inches taller than the student, and being armed with a sword as much longer he had simply to present the point at his face to keep him at a distance, while Jacques cut and thrust and feinted to no purpose. Marmagne, without retreating a step, got out of reach simply by drawing his right leg back beside the left. The consequence was that, despite Aubry's agility, the viscount's long sword grazed his chest several times, while he could succeed in cutting nothing more substantial than the air, try as hard as he would.

Aubry realized that he was lost if he continued to play the same game, but in order to give his opponent no idea of the plan he proposed to adopt, he continued to thrust and parry in the ordinary way, gaining ground imperceptibly inch by inch; when he thought he was sufficiently near he allowed himself to be caught off guard as if through awkwardness. Marmagne, seeing an opening, made a lunge, but Aubry was ready for him; he parried the blow, and, taking advantage of the position of his opponent's sword, two inches above his head, darted under it, leaped upon him, and thrust as he leaped, so cleverly and so vigorously that the page's short sword disappeared up to the hilt in the viscount's breast.

Marmagne uttered one of those shrill cries, which indicate a severe wound; his hand fell to his side, the blood left his cheeks, and he fell headlong to the ground.

At that moment the patrol came running up, attracted by Marmagne's shrieks, the gestures of the page, and the sight of the crowd in front of the door. As Aubry still held his bloody sword in his hand, they arrested him.

Aubry undertook at first to make some resistance; but as the leader of the patrol shouted, " Disarm the villain and take him to the Châtelet," he gave up his sword, and followed the guards to the prison to which he was so anxious to gain admission, marvelling at the merciful decrees of Providence, which accorded him at the same time the two things he most desired, — vengeance upon Marmagne, and access to Ascanio.

This time no objection was made to his reception within the walls of the royal fortress; but as it seemed that it was at the moment somewhat overburdened with guests, there was a long discussion between the jailer and the warden of the prison, as to where the new comer should be lodged. At last the two worthies seemed to agree upon the point; the jailer motioned to Aubry to follow him, led him down thirty-two steps, opened a door, pushed him into a very dark dungeon, and closed the door behind him.

XIV.

OF THE DIFFICULTY WHICH AN HONEST MAN EXPERI- ENCES IN SECURING HIS RELEASE FROM PRISON.

THE student stood for an instant blinded by the ab- rupt transition from light to darkness.   Where was he? He had no idea.   Was he near Ascanio or far from him? He knew not.   In the corridor through which he had passed, he had noticed but two other doors beside the one which was opened for him.   But his primary object was gained; he was under the same roof as his friend.

Meanwhile, as he could not spend the rest of his life in that one spot, and as he could see at the other end of the dungeon, about fifteen feet away, a faint ray of light struggling in through an air hole, he cautiously put forth his leg, with the instinctive purpose of walking to that spot; but at the second step that he took the floor seemed suddenly to give way under his feet; he plunged down three or four stairs, and would doubtless have gone head foremost against the wall had not his feet come in contact with some object which tripped him up.   The result was that he escaped with nothing worse than a few bruises.

The object which had unwittingly rendered him so important a service, uttered a hollow groan.

" I beg your pardon, " said Jacques, rising and politely removing his cap.   " It seems that I stepped upon some person or some thing, a rudeness of which I should never have been guilty, if I had been able to see clearly. "

"You stepped," said a voice, "upon what was for sixty years a man, but is soon to become a corpse for all eternity."

"In that case," said Jacques, "my regret is all the greater for having disturbed you at a moment when you were engaged doubtless, as every good Christian should be at such a time, in settling your accounts with God."

"My accounts are all settled, Master Student: I have sinned like a man, but I have suffered like a martyr; and I hope that God, when weighing my sins and my sorrows, will find that the sum of the latter exceeds that of the former."

"Amen!" said Aubry, "I hope so too with all my heart. But if it will not fatigue you too much, my dear companion in adversity, — I say my dear companion, because I presume you bear no malice on account of the little accident which procured me the honor of your acquaintance a short time since, — if it will not fatigue you too much, I say, pray tell me how you succeeded in ascertaining that I am a student."

"I knew it by your costume, and by the inkhorn hanging at your belt, in the place where a gentleman carries his dagger."

"You say you knew it by my costume, — by the inkhorn? Ah! my dear companion, you told me, if I mistake not, that you are at the point of death?"

"I hope that I have at last reached the end of my sufferings: yes, I hope to fall asleep to-day on earth, to wake to-morrow in heaven."

"I in no wise dispute what you say," replied Jacques, "but I will venture to remind you that your present situation is not one in which it is customary to joke."

"Who says that I am joking?" murmured the dying man with a deep sigh.

"What! you say that you recognized me by my costume, by the inkhorn at my belt, and I, look as hard as I may, cannot see my hands before my face."

"Possibly," rejoined the prisoner, "but when you have been fifteen years in a dungeon as I have, you will be able to see in the darkness, as well as you could see formerly in broad daylight."

"May the devil tear my eyes out rather than make them serve such an apprenticeship!" cried the student. "Fifteen years! you have been fifteen years in prison?"

"Fifteen or sixteen years, perhaps more, perhaps less. I long since ceased to count days or to measure time."

"You must have committed some abominable crime," cried the student, "to have been punished so pitilessly."

"I am innocent," replied the prisoner.

"Innocent!" cried Jacques aghast. "Ah! my dear comrade, I have already reminded you that this is no time for joking."

"And I replied that I was not joking."

"But still less is it a time for lying, for a joke is simply a relaxation of the mind, which offends neither heaven nor earth, while lying is a deadly sin, which compromises the soul's wellbeing."

"I have never lied."

"Why you say that you are innocent, and yet you have been fifteen years in prison?"

"Fifteen years more or less, I said."

"Ah!" cried Jacques, "and I also am innocent!"

"May God protect you then!" rejoined the dying man.

"Why do you say that?"

"Because a guilty man may hope for pardon; an innocent man, never!"

"What you say is very profound, my friend; but it's not consoling at all, do you know?"

"I tell you the truth."

"Come," said Jacques, "come, you have some little peccadillo or other to reproach yourself with, have n't you? Between ourselves, tell me about it."

With that Jacques, who was really beginning to distinguish objects in the darkness, took a stool, carried it to the dying man's bedside, and, selecting a spot where there was a recess in the wall, placed the stool there and made himself as comfortable as possible in his improvised armchair.

"Ah! you say nothing, my friend; you have no confidence in me. Oh, well! I can understand that: fifteen years in prison may well have made you suspicious. My name is Jacques Aubry. I am twenty-two years old, and a student, as you have discovered, — according to what you say, at least. I had certain reasons which concern myself alone, for getting myself committed to the Châtelet; I have been here ten minutes; I have had the honor of making your acquaintance. There's my whole life in a word, and you know me now as well as I know myself. Now, my dear companion, I will listen to you."

"I am Etienne Raymond," said the prisoner.

"Etienne Raymond," the student repeated; "I don't know that name."

"In the first place," said the prisoner, "you were a child when it pleased God to have me disappear from the world: in the next place, I was of little consequence in the world, so that no one noticed my absence."

"But what did you do? Who were you?"

"I was the Connétable de Bourbon's confidential servant."

"Oho! and you had a share with him in betraying the state. In that case I am no longer surprised."

"No; I refused to betray my master, that was all."

"Tell me about it; how did it happen?"

"I was at the constable's hôtel in Paris, while he was living at his château of Bourbon-l'Archambault. One day the captain of his guards arrived with a letter from monseigneur. The letter bade me instantly hand to the messenger a small sealed package which I would find in the duke's bedroom in a small closet near the head of his bed. I went with the captain to the bedroom, opened the closet, found the package in the place described, and handed it to the messenger, who immediately took his leave. An hour later an officer with a squad of soldiers came from the Louvre, and bade me throw open the duke's bedroom and show them a small closet near the head of the bed. I obeyed: they opened the closet, but failed to find what they sought, which was nothing less than the package the duke's messenger had carried away."

"The devil! the devil!" muttered Aubry, beginning to take a deep interest in the situation of his companion in misfortune.

"The officer made some terrible threats, to which I made no other reply than that I knew nothing about what he asked me; for if I had said that I had just handed the package to the duke's messenger, they could have pursued him and taken it from him."

"Peste!" Aubry interrupted; "that was clever of you, and you acted like a faithful and trusty retainer."

"Thereupon the officer gave me in charge to two guards, and returned to the Louvre with the others. In half an hour he returned with orders to take me to the château of Pierre-Encise at Lyons. They put irons on my feet, bound my hands, and tossed me into a carriage with a soldier on either side. Five days later I was confined in a prison, which, I ought to say, was far from being as dark and severe as this. But what does that matter?" muttered the dying man; "a prison's a prison, and I have ended by becoming accustomed to this, as to all the others."

"Hum!" said Jacques Aubry; "that proves you to be a philosopher."

"Three days and three nights passed," continued Etienne Raymond; "at last, during the fourth night, I was awakened by a slight noise. I opened my eyes; my door turned upon its hinges; a woman closely veiled entered with the jailer. The jailer placed a lamp upon the table, and, at a sign from my nocturnal visitor, left the cell; thereupon she drew near my bed and raised her veil. I cried aloud."

"*Hein?* who was it, pray?" Aubry asked, edging closer to the narrator.

"It was Louise of Savoy herself, the Duchesse d'Angoulême in person; it was the Regent of France, the king's mother."

"Oho!" said Aubry; "and what was she doing with a poor devil like you?"

"She was in quest of the same sealed package which I had delivered to the duke's messenger, and which contained love letters written by the imprudent princess to the man she was now persecuting."

"Well, upon my word!" muttered Jacques between his teeth, "here's a story most devilishly like the story of the Duchesse d'Etampes and Ascanio."

"Alas! the stories of all frivolous, love-sick princesses resemble one another," replied the prisoner, whose ears seemed to be as quick as his eyes were piercing; "but woe to the poor devils who happen to be involved in them!"

"Stay a moment! stay a moment, prophet of evil!"

cried Aubry; " what the devil's that you're saying? I
too am involved in the story of a frivolous, love-sick
princess."

" Very well; if that is so, say farewell to the light of
day, say farewell to life."

" Go to the devil with your predictions of the other
world! What 's all that to me? I 'm not the one she
loves, but Ascanio."

" Was it I that the regent loved?" retorted the prisoner. " Was it I, whose very existence they had never
heard of? No, but I was placed between a barren love
and a fruitful vengeance, and when they came together
I was the one to be crushed."

" By Mahomet's belly! you are not very encouraging,
my good man!" cried Aubry. " But let us return to the
princess, for your narrative interests me beyond measure,
just because it makes me tremble."

" The packet contained letters which she wanted, as I
have told you. In exchange for them she promised me
honors, dignities, titles; to see those letters again she
would have extorted four hundred thousand crowns anew
from another Semblançay, though he should pay for his
complaisance on the scaffold.

" I replied that I hadn't the letters, that I knew
nothing about them, that I had no idea what she
meant.

" Thereupon her munificent offers were succeeded by
threats; but she found it no easier to intimidate than to
bribe me, for I had told the truth. I had delivered the
letters to my noble master's messenger.

" She left my cell in a furious rage, and for a year I
heard nothing more. At the end of a year she returned,
and the same scene was repeated.

" At that time I begged, I implored her to let me go

free. I adjured her in the name of my wife and children; but to no purpose. I must give up the letters or die in prison.

"One day I found a file in my bread.

"My noble master had remembered me; absent, exiled, a fugitive as he was, of course he could not set me free by entreaty or by force. He sent one of his servants to France, who induced the jailer to hand me the file, telling me whence it came.

"I filed through one of the bars at my window. I made myself a rope with my sheets. I descended by the rope, but when I came to the end of it I felt in vain for the ground with my feet. I dropped, with God's name upon my lips, and broke my leg in the fall; a night patrol found me unconscious.

"I was thereupon transferred to the château of Chalons-sur-Saône. I remained there about two years, at the end of which time my persecutress made her appearance again. It was still the letters that brought her thither. This time she was accompanied by the torturer, and I was put to the question. This was useless barbarity, as she obtained no information, — indeed, she could obtain none. I knew nothing save that I had delivered the letters to the duke's messenger.

"One day at the bottom of my jug of water I found a bag filled with gold; once more my noble master bethought himself of his poor servant.

"I bribed a turnkey, or rather the miserable creature pretended to be bribed. At midnight he opened the door of my cell, and I went out. I followed him through several corridors; I could already feel the air that living men breathe, and thought that I was free, when guards rushed out upon us and bound us both. My guide had pretended to yield to my entreaties in order to get possession of the gold he had seen in my hands, and then betrayed me to earn the reward offered to informers.

" They brought me to the Châtelet, to this cell.

" Here, for the last time, Louise of Savoy appeared; she was accompanied by the executioner.

" The prospect of death could have no other effect than the promises, threats, and torture. My hands were bound; a rope was passed through a ring and placed around my neck. I made the same reply as always to her demands, adding that she would fulfil my dearest wish by putting me to death, for I was driven to despair by my life of captivity.

" It was that feeling, doubtless, which made her hold her hand. She went out and the executioner followed her.

" Since then I have never seen her. What has become of my noble master? What has become of the cruel duchess? I have no idea, for since that time, some fifteen years perhaps, I have not exchanged a single word with a single living being."

" They are both dead," said Aubry.

" Both dead! the noble-hearted duke is dead! Why, he would still be a young man, not more than fifty-two. How did he die?"

" He was killed at the siege of Rome, and probably — "

Jacques was about to add, " by one of my friends," but he refrained, thinking that that might cause a coolness between the old man and himself. Jacques, as we know, was becoming very discreet.

" Probably?" the prisoner repeated.

" By a goldsmith named Benvenuto Cellini."

" Twenty years ago I would have cursed the murderer: to-day I say from the bottom of my heart, 'May his murderer be blessed!' Did they give my noble lord a burial worthy of the man?"

"I think so: they built a tomb for him in the cathedral of Gaeta, and upon the tomb is an epitaph wherein it is said that, beside him who sleeps there, Alexander the Great was a sorry knave, and Cæsar an idle blackguard."

"And the other?"

"What other?"

"The woman who persecuted me?"

"Dead also: dead nine years since."

"Just so. One night, here in my cell, I saw a phantom kneeling and praying. I cried out and it disappeared. It was she asking my forgiveness."

"Do you think, then, that when death came upon her she relented?"

"I trust so, for her soul's sake."

"But in that case they should have set you free."

"She may have requested it, but I am of so little importance that I was probably forgotten in the excitement of that great catastrophe."

"And so you would likewise forgive her, as you are about to die?"

"Lift me up, young man, that I may pray for both of them." And the dying man, resting in Jacques Aubry's arms, coupled the names of his protector and persecutress in the same prayer: the man who had remembered him in his affection and the woman who had never forgotten him in her hatred,—the constable and the regent.

The prisoner was right. Jacques Aubry's eyes began to become accustomed to the darkness, and he could make out the dying man's features. He was a handsome old man, much emaciated by suffering, with a white beard and a bald head,—such a head as Domenichino dreamed of when painting his Confession of Saint Jerome.

When his prayer was finished, he heaved a deep sigh, and fell back upon the bed; he had swooned.

Jacques thought that he was dead. He ran to the water-jug, however, poured some water in the hollow of his hand, and shook it over his face. The dying man returned to life once more.

"You did well to revive me, young man," said he, "and here is your reward."

"What is that?"

"A dagger."

"A dagger! how did it come into your hands?"

"Wait one moment. One day, when the turnkey brought my bread and water, he put the lamp upon the stool which happened to be standing near the wall. In the wall at that point was a protruding stone, and I saw some letters cut with a knife upon it. I had n't time to read them. But I dug up some earth with my hands, moistened it so as to make a sort of paste, and took an impression of the letters, which formed the word *Ultor*.

"What was the significance of that word, which means *avenger?* I returned to the stone. I tried to shake it. It moved like a tooth in its socket. By dint of patience and persistent efforts I succeeded in removing it from the wall. I immediately plunged my hand into the hole, and found this dagger.

"Thereupon the longing for liberty, which I had almost lost, returned to me in full force; I resolved to dig a passage-way from this to some dungeon near at hand with the dagger, and there concoct some plan of escape with its occupant. Besides, even if it all ended in failure, the digging and cutting was something to occupy my time; and when you have spent twenty years in a dungeon as I have, young man, you will realize what a formidable enemy time is."

Aubry shuddered from head to foot. "Did you ever put your plan in execution?" he inquired.

"Yes, and more easily than I anticipated. After the twelve or fifteen years that I have been here, they have doubtless ceased to think of my escape as a possibility: indeed, it's very likely that they no longer know who I am. They keep me, as they keep the chain hanging from yonder ring. The constable and the regent are dead, and they alone remembered me. Who would now recognize the name of Etienne Raymond, even in this place, if I should pronounce it? No one."

Aubry felt the perspiration starting from every pore as he thought of the oblivion into which this lost existence had fallen.

"Well?" he exclaimed questioningly, — "well?"

"For more than a year," said the old man, "I dug and dug, and I succeeded in making a hole under the wall large enough for a man to pass through."

"But what did you do with the dirt you took from the hole?"

"I strewed it over the floor of my cell, and trod it in by constantly walking upon it."

"Where is the hole?"

"Under my bed. For fifteen years no one has ever thought of moving it. The jailer came down into my cell only once a day. When he had gone, and the doors were closed, and the sound of his footsteps had died away, I would draw out my bed and set to work; when the time for his visit drew near, I would move the bed back to its place, and lie down upon it.

"Day before yesterday I lay down upon it never to rise again. I was at the end of my strength: to-day I am at the end of my life. You are most welcome, young man: you shall assist me to die, and I will make you my heir."

"Your heir!" said Aubry in amazement.

"To be sure. I will leave you this dagger. You smile. What more precious heritage could a prisoner leave you? This dagger is freedom, perhaps."

"You are right," said Aubry, "and I thank you. Whither does this hole that you have dug lead?"

"I had not reached the other end, but I was very near it. Day before yesterday I heard voices in the cell beside this."

"The devil!" said Aubry, "and you think—"

"I think that you will have finished my work in a very few hours."

"Thanks," said Aubry, "thanks."

"And now, a priest. I would much like to see a priest," said the moribund.

"Wait, father, wait," said Aubry; "it is impossible that they would refuse such a request from a dying man."

He ran to the door, this time without stumbling, his eyes being somewhat accustomed to the darkness, and knocked with feet and hands both.

A turnkey came down.

"What's the matter, that you make such an uproar?" he demanded, "what do you want?"

"The old man here with me is dying," said Aubry, "and asks for a priest: can you refuse?"

"Hum!" grumbled the jailer, "I don't know why these fellows must all want priests. It's all right: we'll send him one."

Ten minutes later the priest appeared, carrying the viaticum and preceded by two sacristans, one with the crucifix, the other with the bell.

A solemn and impressive spectacle was the confession of this martyr, who had naught to disclose but the crimes of others, and who prayed for his enemies instead of asking pardon for himself.

Unimaginative as was Jacques Aubry, he fell upon his knees, and remembered the prayers of his childhood, which he thought he had forgotten.

When the prisoner had finished his confession, the priest bowed before him and asked his blessing.

The old man's face lighted up with a smile as radiant as the smile of God's elect; he extended one hand over the priest's head and the other toward Aubry, drew a deep breath, and fell back upon his pillow. That breath was his last.

The priest went out as he had come, attended by his subordinates, and the dungeon, lighted for a moment by the flickering flame of the candles, became dark once more.

Jacques Aubry was alone with the dead. It was a very depressing situation, especially in the light of the reflections to which it gave rise. The man who lay lifeless before him had been consigned to prison an innocent man, had remained there twenty years, and went out at last only because Death, the great liberator, came in search of him.

The light-hearted student could not recognize himself: for the first time he found himself confronted by stern reality; for the first time he looked in the face the bewildering vicissitudes of life, and the calm profundity of death.

Then a selfish thought began to take shape in his heart. He thought of himself, innocent like the dead man, and like him involved in the complications of one of those royal passions which crush and consume and destroy a life. Ascanio and he might disappear, as Etienne Raymond had disappeared: who would think of them?

Gervaise perhaps, Benvenuto Cellini certainly.

But the former could do nothing but weep; and the other confessed his own powerlessness when he cried so loudly for the letter in Ascanio's possession.

His only chance of safety, his only hope, lay in the heritage of the dead man, an old dagger, which had already disappointed the expectations of its two former owners.

Jacques Aubry had hidden the dagger in his breast, and he nervously put his hand upon the hilt to make sure that it was still there.

At that moment the door opened, and men came in to remove the body.

"When shall you bring me my dinner?" Jacques asked. "I am hungry."

"In two hours," the jailer replied.

With that the student was left alone in the cell.

XV.

AN HONEST THEFT.

AUBREY passed the two hours sitting upon his stool, without once moving: his mind was so active that it kept his body at rest.

At the appointed hour the turnkey came down, renewed the water, and changed the bread; this was what, in Châtelet parlance, was called a dinner.

The student remembered what the dying man told him, that the door of his cell would be opened but once in the twenty-four hours; however he still remained for a long while in the same place, absolutely motionless, fearing lest the event that had just occurred should cause some change in the routine of the prison.

He soon observed, through his air-hole, that it was beginning to grow dark. The day just passed had been a well filled day for him. In the morning, the examination by the magistrate; at noon, the duel with Marmagne; at one o'clock, lodged in prison; at three, the prisoner's death; and now his first attempts at securing his freedom.

A man does not pass many such days in his life.

Jacques Aubry rose at last, and walked to the door to listen for footsteps: then, in order that the dirt and the wall might leave no marks upon his doublet, he removed that portion of his costume, pulled the bed away from the corner, and found the opening of which his companion had spoken.

He crawled like a snake into the narrow gallery, which was some eight feet deep, and which, after making a dip under the partition wall, ascended on the other side.

As soon as he plunged his dagger into the earth he knew by the sound that he would very soon accomplish his purpose, which was to open a passage into some place or other. What that place would be only a sorcerer could have told.

He kept actively at work, making as little noise as possible. From time to time he went out of the excavation as a miner does, in order to scatter the loose earth about the floor of his cell; otherwise it would eventually have blocked up the gallery; then he would crawl back, and set to work once more.

While Aubrey was working, Ascanio was thinking sadly of Colombe.

He too, as we have said, had been taken to the Châtelet; he too had been cast into a dungeon. But, it may have been by chance, it may have been at the duchess's suggestion, his quarters were a little less bare, consequently a little more habitable, than the student's.

But what did Ascanio care for a little more or a little less comfort. His dungeon was a dungeon all the same; his captivity a separation. He had not Colombe, who was more to him than light, or liberty, or life. Were Colombe with him in his dungeon, the dungeon would become an abode of bliss, a palace of enchantment.

The poor child had been so happy during the days immediately preceding his arrest! Thinking of his beloved by day, and sitting by her side at night, he had never thought that his happiness might some day come to an end. And if, sometimes, in the midst of his felicity, the iron hand of doubt had clutched his heart, he had, like one threatened by danger from some unknown source, promptly put aside all uneasiness concerning the future that he might lose none of his present bliss.

And now he was in prison, alone, far from Colombe, who was perhaps imprisoned like himself, perhaps a prisoner in some convent, whence she could escape in no other way than by going to the chapel, where the husband whom they sought to force upon her awaited her.

Two redoubtable passions were standing guard at their cell doors; the love of Madame d'Etampes at Ascanio's, the ambition of Comte d'Orbec at Colombe's.

As soon as he was alone in his dungeon, therefore, Ascanio became very sad and down-hearted; his was one of those clinging natures which need the support of some robust organization; he was one of those slender, graceful flowers, which bend before the first breath of the tempest, and straighten up again only in the vivifying rays of the sun.

Had Benvenuto been in his place, his first thought would have been to examine the doors, sound the walls, and stamp upon the floor, to see if one or the other would not afford his quick and combative mind some possible means of escape. But Ascanio sat down upon his bed, let his head fall upon his breast, and whispered Colombe's name. It never occurred to him that one could escape by any possible means from a dungeon behind three iron doors and surrounded by walls six feet thick.

The dungeon was, as we have said, a little less bare and a little more habitable than that assigned to Jacques. It contained a bed, a table, two chairs, and an old rush mat. Furthermore, a lamp was burning upon a stone projection, doubtless arranged for that purpose. Beyond question it was a cell set apart for privileged prisoners.

There was also a great difference in the matter of food: instead of the bread and water which was brought to the student once a day, Ascanio enjoyed two daily repasts, a privilege somewhat neutralized by the consequent necessity of seeing the jailer twice in the twenty-four hours. These repasts, it should be said to the credit of the philanthropic administration of the Châtelet, were not altogether execrable.

Ascanio thought but little of such paltry details: his was one of those delicate feminine organizations which seem to exist on perfume and dew. Without awaking from his reverie he ate a bit of bread, drank a few drops of wine, and continued to think of Colombe and of Benvenuto Cellini; of Colombe as of her to whom all his love was given, of Cellini as of him in whom lay all his hope.

Indeed, up to that moment Ascanio had never been concerned with any of the cares or details of existence. Benvenuto lived for both, and Ascanio was content to breathe, to dream of some lovely work of art, and to love Colombe. He was like the fruit which grows upon a sturdy tree, and draws all its life from the tree.

And even now, perilous as was his situation, if he could have seen Benvenuto Cellini at the moment of his arrest, or at the moment of his incarceration, and Benvenuto had said to him, with a warm grasp of his hand, "Have no fear, Ascanio, for I am watching over you and Colombe," his confidence in the master was so great that, relying upon that promise alone, he would have waited without anxiety for the prison doors to be thrown open, sure that thrown open they would be, in spite of bars and locks.

But he had not seen Benvenuto, and Benvenuto did not know that his cherished pupil, the son of his Stefana, was a prisoner. It would have taken a whole day to carry the intelligence to him at Fontainebleau, assuming that it had occurred to any one to do it, another day to return to Paris, and in two days the enemies of the lovers might gain a long lead upon their defender.

So it was that Ascanio passed the rest of the day and the whole of the night following his arrest without sleep, sometimes pacing back and forth in his cell, sometimes sitting down, and occasionally throwing himself upon the bed, which was provided with white sheets, — a special mark of favor which proved that Ascanio had been particularly commended to the attention of the authorities. During that day and night and the following morning nothing worthy of note occurred, unless it was the regular visit of the jailer to bring his food.

About two o'clock in the afternoon, as nearly as the prisoner could judge by his reckoning of the time, he thought that he heard voices near at hand: it was a dull, indistinct murmur, but evidently caused by the vocal organs of human beings. Ascanio listened and walked toward the point whence the sound seemed to come; it was at one of the corners of his cell. He silently put his ear to the wall and to the ground, and found that the voices apparently came from beneath the floor.

It was evident that he had neighbors who were separated from him only by a thin partition or an equally thin floor. After some two hours the sounds ceased, and all was still once more.

Toward night the noise began again, but this time it was of a different nature. It was not that which would be made by two persons speaking together, but consisted of dull, hurried blows as of some one cutting stone. It came from the same place, did not cease for a second, and seemed to come nearer and nearer.

Absorbed as Ascanio was in his own thoughts, this noise seemed to him deserving of some attention none the less, so he sat with his eyes glued to the spot whence it came. He judged that it must be near midnight, but he did not once think of sleeping, notwithstanding that he had not slept for so many hours.

The noise continued: as it was long past the usual hour for work, it was evidently some prisoner seeking to escape. Ascanio smiled sadly at the thought that the poor devil, who would think for a moment, mayhap, that he was at liberty, would find that he had simply changed his cell.

At last the noise approached so near that Ascanio ran and seized his lamp, and returned with it to the corner; almost at the same moment the earth rose up in that spot, and as it fell away disclosed a human head.

Ascanio uttered an exclamation of wonder, followed by a cry of joy, to which a no less delighted cry made answer. The head belonged to Jacques Aubry.

In an instant, thanks to the assistance rendered by Ascanio to the unexpected visitor who made his appearance in such extraordinary fashion, the two friends were in one another's arms.

As will readily be conceived, the first questions and answers were somewhat incoherent; but at last, after exchanging a few disconnected exclamations, they succeeded in restoring some semblance of order to their thoughts, and in casting some light upon recent events. Ascanio to be sure had almost nothing to say, and everything to learn.

Eventually Aubry told him the whole story: how he had returned to the Hôtel de Nesle simultaneously with Benvenuto; how they had learned almost at the same moment of the arrest of Ascanio and the abduction of

Colombe; how Benvenuto had rushed off to his studio like a madman, shouting, " To the casting! to the casting ! " and he, Aubry, to the Châtelet. Of what had taken place at the Hôtel de Nesle since that time the student could tell him nothing.

But to the general narrative of the Iliad succeeded the private adventures of Ulysses. Aubry described to Ascanio his disappointment at his failure to get committed to prison; his visit to Gervaise, and her denunciation of him to the lieutenant criminal; his terrible examination, which had no other result than the paltry fine of twenty Paris sous, a result most insulting to the honor of Gervaise; and finally his encounter with Marmagne just as he was beginning to despair of procuring his own incarceration. From that point he related everything that had happened to him up to the moment when, utterly in the dark as to what cell he was about to enter, he had thrust his head through the last crust of earth, and discerned by the light of his lamp his friend Ascanio.

Whereupon the friends once more embraced with great heartiness.

" Now, " said Jacques Aubry, " listen to me, Ascanio, for there is no time to lose. "

" But first of all, " said Ascanio, " tell me of Colombe. Where is Colombe ? "

" Colombe ? I can't tell you. With Madame d'Etampes, I think. "

" With Madame d'Etampes ! " cried Ascanio, — " her rival ! "

" So what they say of the duchess's love for you is true, is it ? "

Ascanio blushed and stammered some unintelligible words.

"Oh, you need n't blush for that!" cried Aubry. "Deuce take me! a duchess! and a duchess who 's the king's mistress at that! I should never have any such luck. But let us come back to business."

"Yes," said Ascanio, "let us come back to Colombe."

"Bah! I 'm not talking about Colombe. I 'm talking about a letter."

"What letter?"

"A letter the Duchesse d'Etampes wrote you."

"Who told you that I have a letter from the Duchesse d'Etampes in my possession?"

"Benvenuto Cellini."

"Why did he tell you that?"

"Because he must have that letter, because it is absolutely essential that he should have it, because I agreed to take it to him, because all I have done was done to get possession of that letter."

"But for what purpose does Benvenuto want the letter?"

"Ah! faith, I 've no idea, and it does n't concern me. He said to me, 'I must have that letter.' I said to him, 'Very good, I will get it for you.' I have had myself put in prison in order to get it; so give it me, and I agree to deliver it to Benvenuto. Well, what 's the matter?"

This last question was induced by the cloud which spread over Ascanio's face.

"The matter is, my poor Aubry," said he, "that your trouble is thrown away."

"How so?" cried Aubry. "Have n't you the letter still?"

"It is here," said Ascanio, placing his hand upon the pocket of his doublet.

"Ah! that 's well. Give it to me, and I will take it to Benvenuto."

"That letter will never leave me, Jacques."

"Why so?"

"Because I don't know what use Benvenuto proposes to make of it."

"He means to use it to save you."

"And to crush the Duchesse d'Etampes, it may be. Aubry, I will not help to ruin a woman."

"But this woman seeks to ruin you. This woman detests you: no, I am wrong, she adores you."

"And you would have me, in return for that feeling — "

"Why, it's exactly the same as if she hated you since you don't love her. Besides, it's she who has done all this."

"What! she who has done it?"

"Why, yes, it was she who caused your arrest, and carried off Colombe."

"Who told you that?"

"No one; but who else could it have been?"

"Why the provost, or D'Orbec, or Marmagne, to whom you admit that you told the whole story."

"Ascanio! Ascanio!" cried Jacques in despair, "you are destroying yourself!"

"I prefer to destroy myself, rather than do a dastardly deed, Aubry."

"But this is no dastardly deed, for Benvenuto is the one who undertakes to do it."

"Listen to me, Aubry," said Ascanio, "and don't be angry at what I say. If Benvenuto stood in your place, and should say to me, 'It was Madame d'Etampes, your enemy, who caused your arrest, who carried off Colombe, who now has her in her power and intends to force her to do what she does not wish to do, — I cannot save Colombe unless I have that letter,' — I would make him swear that he would not show it to the king, and then I would give it to him. But Benvenuto is not here, and I am not certain that it is the duchess who is persecuting me. This letter would not be safe in your hands, Aubry: forgive me, but you yourself admit that you are an arrant chatterbox."

"I promise you, Ascanio, that the day I have just passed has aged me ten years."

"You may lose the letter, or, with the best intentions, I know, make an injudicious use of it, Aubry, so the letter will remain where it is."

"But, my dear fellow," cried Jacques, "remember that Benvenuto himself said that nothing but this letter can save you."

"Benvenuto will save me without that, Aubry; Benvenuto has the king's word that he will grant him whatever favor he asks on the day that his Jupiter is safely cast. When you thought that Benvenuto was going mad because he shouted, 'To the casting!' he was beginning to rescue me."

"But suppose the casting should be unsuccessful?" said Aubry.

"There's no danger," rejoined Ascanio with a smile.

"But that sometimes happens to the most skilful founders in France, so I am told."

"The most skilful founders in France are mere schoolboys compared to Benvenuto."

"But how much time is required for the casting?"

"Three days."

"And how much more before the statue can be put before the king?"

"Three days more."

"Six or seven days in all. And suppose Madame d'Etampes forces Colombe to marry D'Orbec within six days?"

"Madame d'Etampes has no power over Colombe. Colombe will resist."

"Very true, but the provost has power over Colombe as his daughter, and King François I. has power over Colombe as his subject; suppose the provost and the king both order her to marry him?"

Ascanio became frightfully pale.

"Suppose that when Benvenuto demands your liberty, Colombe is already the wife of another, what will you do with your liberty then?"

Ascanio passed one hand across his brow to wipe away the cold sweat which the student's words caused to start thereon, while with the other hand he felt in his pocket for the precious letter; but just as Aubry felt certain that he was on the point of yielding, he shook his head as if to banish all irresolution.

"No!" he said, "no! To no one save Benvenuto. Let us talk of something else."

These words he uttered in a tone which indicated that, for the moment at least, it was useless to insist.

"In that case," said Aubry, apparently forming a momentous resolution; "in that case, my friend, if we are to talk on other subjects we may as well do it to-morrow morning, or later in the day, for I am afraid we may remain here for some time. For my own part, I confess that I am worn out by my tribulations of the day and my labor to-night, and shall not be sorry for a little rest. Do you remain here, and I will go back to my own cell. When you want to see me again, do you call me. Meanwhile, spread this mat over the hole I have made, so that our communications may not be cut off. Good night! the night brings counsel, they say, and I hope that I shall find you more reasonable to-morrow morning."

With that, and refusing to listen to the observations of Ascanio, who sought to detain him, Jacques Aubry plunged head first into his gallery, and crawled back to his cell. Ascanio, meanwhile, following up the advice his friend had given him, dragged the mat into the corner of his cell as soon as the student's legs had disappeared. The means of communication between the two cells thereupon disappeared altogether.

He then tossed his doublet upon one of the two chairs which, with the table and the lamp, constituted the furnishings of his apartment, stretched himself out upon the bed, and, overdone with fatigue as he was, soon fell asleep, his bodily weariness carrying the day over his mental torture.

Aubry, instead of following Ascanio's example, although he was quite as much in need of sleep as he, sat down upon his stool, and began to reflect deeply, which, as the reader knows, was so entirely contrary to all his habits, that it was evident that he was meditating some grand stroke.

The student's immobility lasted about fifteen minutes, after which he rose slowly, and, with the step of a man whose irresolution is at an end for good and all, walked to the hole, and crawled into it again, but this time with so much caution and so noislessly, that, when he reached the other end and raised the mat, he was overjoyed to perceive that the operation had not aroused his friend.

That was all that the student wished. With even greater caution than he had theretofore exhibited, he crept stealthily forth from his underground gallery, and approached with bated breath the chair on which Ascanio's doublet lay. With one eye fixed upon the sleeping youth, and his ears on the alert for the slightest sound, he took from the pocket the precious letter so

eagerly coveted by Cellini, and placed in the envelope
a note from Gervaise, which he folded in exactly the
same shape as the duchess's letter, sure that Ascanio
would believe, so long as he did not open it, that lovely
Anne d'Heilly's missive was still in his possession.

As silently as ever he stole back to the mat, raised it,
crawled into the hole once more, and disappeared like the
phantoms who sink through trap-doors at the opera.

It was high time, for he was no sooner back in his
cell, than he heard Ascanio's door grinding on its hinges,
and his friend's voice crying, in the tone of one suddenly
aroused from sleep, —

"Who's there?"

"I," responded a soft voice, "do not be afraid, for it
is a friend."

Ascanio, who was but half dressed, rose at the sound of
the voice, which he seemed to recognize, and saw by
the light of his lamp a veiled woman standing by the
door. She slowly approached him and raised her veil.
He was not mistaken, — it was Madame d'Etampes.

XVI.

WHEREIN IT IS PROVED THAT A GRISETTE'S LETTER, WHEN IT IS BURNED, MAKES AS MUCH FLAME AND ASHES AS A DUCHESS'S.

THERE was upon Anne d'Heilly's mobile features an expression of sadness mingled with compassion, which deceived Ascanio completely, and confirmed him, even before she had opened her mouth, in the impression that she was entirely innocent of any share in the catastrophe of which he and Colombe were victims.

" You here, Ascanio! " she said in a melodious voice; " you, to whom I would have given a palace to live in, I find in a prison! "

" Ah, madame!" cried the youth, " it is true, is it not, that you know nothing of the persecution to which we are subjected ? "

" Did you suspect me for an instant, Ascanio ? " said the duchess; " in that case you have every reason to hate me, and I can only bewail in silence my ill fortune in being so little known to him I know so well."

" No, madame, no, " said Ascanio; " I was told that you were responsible for it all, but I refused to believe it."

" 'T was well done of you ! Ascanio, you do not love me, but with you hatred at least is not synonymous with injustice. You were right, Ascanio; not only am I not responsible for it, but I knew nothing whatever about it. It was the provost, Messire d'Estourville: he learned the whole story, I know not how, told it all to the king, and obtained from him the order to arrest you and recover Colombe."

" And Colombe is with her father ? " demanded Ascanio eagerly.

" No, Colombe is with me."

" With you, madame ! " cried the young man. " Why with you ? "

" She is very lovely, Ascanio," murmured the duchess, " and I can understand why you prefer her to all the women in the world, even though the most loving of them all offers you the richest of duchies."

" I love Colombe, madame," said Ascanio, " and you know that love, which is a treasure sent from Heaven, is to be preferred to all earthly treasures."

" Yes, Ascanio, yes, you love her above everything. For a moment I hoped that your passion for her was only a passing fancy ; I was mistaken. Yes, I realize now," she added with a sigh, " that to keep you apart any longer would be to run counter to God's will."

" Ah, madame! " cried Ascanio, clasping his hands, " God has placed in your hands the power to bring us together. Be noble and generous to the end, madame, and make two children happy who will love you and bless you all their lives."

" Yes," said the duchess. " I am vanquished, Ascanio ; yes, I am ready to protect and defend you ; but alas ! it may be too late even now."

" Too late ! what do you mean ? " cried Ascanio.

" It may be, Ascanio, it may be that at this moment I am lost myself."

" Lost, madame! how so, in God's name ? "

" For having loved you."

" For having loved me ! You, lost because of me ! "

"Yes, imprudent creature that I am, lost because of you; lost because I wrote to you."

"How so? I do not understand you, madame."

"You do not understand that the provost, armed with an order from the king, has directed a general search to be made at the Hôtel de Nesle? You do not understand that this search, the principal purpose of which is to find proofs of your affair with Colombe, will be most rigorously carried out in your bedroom."

"What then?" demanded Ascanio, impatiently.

"Why," continued the duchess, "if they find that letter, which in a moment of frenzy I wrote to you, if it is recognized as mine, if it is laid before the king, whom I was then deceiving, and whom I was willing to betray for you, do you not understand that my power is at an end from that moment? Do you not understand that I can then do nothing either for you or for Colombe? Do you not understand, in short, that I am lost?"

"Oh!" cried Ascanio, "have no fear, madame! There is no danger of that; the letter is here; it has never left me."

The duchess breathed freely once more, and the expression of her face changed from anxiety to joy.

"It has never left you, Ascanio!" she repeated; "it has never left you! To what sentiment, pray tell me, do I owe the fact that that fortunate letter has never left you?"

"To prudence, madame," murmured Ascanio.

"Prudence! mon Dieu! mon Dieu! I am wrong once more! And yet I surely should be convinced ere this. Prudence! Ah well!" she added, seeming to make a powerful effort to restrain her feelings, "in that case, as I have naught but your prudence to thank, Ascanio, do you think it very prudent to keep it upon your person.

when they may come to your cell at any moment and search you by force? do you think it prudent, I say, to keep a letter which, if it is found, will put the only person who can save you and Colombe in a position where it will be impossible for her to help you?"

"Madame," said Ascanio, in his melodious voice, and with that tinge of melancholy which all pure hearts feel when they are forced to doubt, "I know not if the purpose to save Colombe and myself exists at the bottom of your heart as it does upon your lips; I know not whether the desire to see that letter again, and nothing more, is the motive of your visit to me; I know not whether, as soon as you have it in your possession, you may not lay aside this *rôle* of protectress which you have assumed, and become our enemy once more; but this I do know, madame, that the letter is yours, that it belongs to you, and that the moment you claim it I cease to have the right to keep it from you."

Ascanio rose, went straight to the chair upon which his doublet lay, put his hand in the pocket, and took out a letter, the envelope of which the duchess recognized at a glance.

"Here, madame," he said, "is the paper you are so anxious to possess, and which can be of no use to me, while it may injure you seriously. Take it, tear it up, destroy it. I have done my duty; you may do what you choose."

"Ah! yours is indeed a noble heart, Ascanio!" cried the duchess, acting in obedience to one of those generous impulses which are sometimes found in the most corrupt hearts.

"Some one comes, madame! take care!" cried Ascanio.

"True," said the duchess.

At the sound of approaching footsteps she hastily

thrust the paper into the flame of the lamp, which consumed it in an instant. The duchess did not let it drop
until the flame had almost scorched her fingers, when the
letter, three fourths consumed, drifted slowly downward:
when it reached the floor it was entirely reduced to
ashes, but the duchess was not content until she had
placed her foot upon them.

At that moment the provost appeared in the doorway.

"I was told that you were here, madame," he said,
looking uneasily from the duchess to Ascanio, "and I
hastened to descend and place myself at your service.
Is there aught in which I, or they who are under my
orders, can be of any use to you?"

"No, messire," she replied, unable to conceal the feeling of intense joy which overflowed from her heart upon
her face. "No, but I am none the less obliged to you
for your readiness and your good will; I came simply to
question this young man whom you arrested, and to ascertain if he is really as guilty as he was said to be."

"And what is your conclusion?" queried the provost,
in a tone to which he could not refrain from imparting a
slight tinge of irony.

"That Ascanio is less guilty than I thought. I beg
you, therefore, messire, to show him every consideration
in your power. The poor child is in wretched quarters.
Could you not give him a better room?"

"We will look to it to-morrow, madame, for you know
that your wishes are commands to me. Have you any
other commands, and do you wish to continue your examination?"

"No, messire," was the reply, "I know all that I
wished to know."

With that the duchess left the dungeon, darting at
Ascanio a parting glance of mingled gratitude and passion.

The provost followed her and the door closed behind them.

"Pardieu!" muttered Jacques Aubry, who had not lost a word of the conversation between the duchess and Ascanio. "Pardieu! it was time."

It had been Marmagne's first thought on recovering consciousness to send word to the duchess that he had received a wound which might well prove to be mortal, and that before he breathed his last he desired to impart to her a secret of the deepest moment. Upon receipt of that message the duchess hastened to his side. Marmagne then informed her that he had been attacked and wounded by a certain student named Jacques Aubry, who was endeavoring to gain admission to the Châtelet in order to get speech of Ascanio and carry to Cellini a letter that was in Ascanio's possession.

The duchess needed to hear no more, and, bitterly cursing the passion which had led her once more to overstep the limits of her ordinary prudence, she hurried to the Châtelet although it was two o'clock in the morning, demanded to be shown to Ascanio's cell, and there enacted the scene we have described, which had ended in accordance with her wishes so far as she knew, although Ascanio was not altogether deceived.

As Jacques Aubry said, it was high time.

But only half of his task was accomplished, and the most difficult part remained to do. He had the letter which had come so near being destroyed forever; but in order that it should have its full effect it must be in Cellini's hands, not in Jacques Aubry's.

Now Jacques Aubry was a prisoner, very much a prisoner, and he had learned from his predecessor that it was no easy matter to get out of the Châtelet, once one was safely lodged therein. He was therefore, we might say, in much the same plight as the rooster who found the pearl, greatly perplexed as to the use to be made of his treasure.

To attempt to escape by resorting to violence would be utterly vain. He might with his dagger kill the keeper who brought his food, and take his keys and his clothes; but not only was that extreme method repugnant to the student's kindly disposition, — it did not afford sufficiently strong hopes of success. There were ten chances to one that he would be recognized, searched, relieved of his precious letter, and thrust back into his cell.

To attempt to escape by cunning was even less hopeful. The dungeon was eight or ten feet underground, there were huge iron bars across the air-hole through which the one faint ray of light filtered into his cell. It would take months to loosen one of those bars, and, suppose one of them to be removed, where would the fugitive then find himself? — in some courtyard with insurmountable walls, where he would inevitably be found the next morning?

Bribery was his only remaining resource; but, as a consequence of the sentence pronounced by the lieutenant criminal, whereby Gervaise was awarded twenty Paris sous for the loss of her honor, the prisoner's whole fortune was reduced to ten Paris sous, a sum utterly inadequate to tempt the lowest jailer of the vilest prison, and which could not decently be offered to the turnkey of a royal fortress.

Jacques Aubry was therefore, we are forced to confess, in the direst perplexity.

From time to time it seemed as if a hopeful idea passed through his mind; but it was evident that it was likely to entail serious consequences, for each time that it returned, with the persistence characteristic of hopeful ideas, Aubry's face grew perceptibly darker, and he heaved deep sighs, which proved that the poor fellow was undergoing an internal conflict of the most violent description.

This conflict was so violent and so prolonged that Aubry did not once think of sleep the whole night long: he passed the time in striding to and fro, in sitting down and standing up. It was the first time that he had ever kept vigil all night for purposes of reflection; his previous experiences in that line had been on convivial occasions only.

At daybreak the struggle seemed to have ended in the complete triumph of one of the opposing forces, for Jacques heaved a more heart-breaking sigh than any he had yet achieved, and threw himself upon his bed like a man completely crushed.

His head had hardly touched the pillow when he heard steps on the staircase, the key grated in the lock, the door turned upon its hinges, and two officers of the law appeared in the doorway; they were the lieutenant criminal and his clerk.

The annoyance of the visit was tempered by the student's gratification in recognizing two old acquaintances.

"Aha! my fine fellow," said the magistrate, recognizing Aubry, "so it's you, is it, and you succeeded after all in getting into the Châtelet? *Tudieu!* what a rake you are! You seduce young women and run young noblemen through the body! But beware! a nobleman's life is more expensive than a grisette's honor, and you'll not be quit of this affair for twenty Paris sous!"

Alarming as the worthy magistrate's words undoubtedly were, the tone in which he uttered them reassured the prisoner to some extent. This jovial-faced individual, into whose hands he had had the good luck to fall, was such a good fellow to all appearance that it was impossible to think of him in connection with anything deadly. To be sure it was not the same with his clerk, who nodded his head approvingly at each word that fell from his principal's lips. It was the second time that Jacques Aubry had seen the two men side by side, and, deeply engrossed as he was by his own precarious situation, he could not forbear some internal reflections upon the whimsical chance which had coupled together two beings so utterly opposed to each other in character and feature.

The examination began. Jacques Aubry made no attempt at concealment. He declared that, having recognized the Vicomte de Marmagne as a man who had on several occasions betrayed his confidence, he seized his page's sword and challenged him; that Marmagne had accepted the challenge, and that after exchanging a few thrusts the viscount fell. More than that he did not know.

" You know no more than that! you know no more than that! " muttered the judge. " Faith, I should say that that was quite enough, and your affair's as clear as day, especially as the Vicomte de Marmagne is one of Madame d'Etampes's great favorites. So it seems that she has complained of you to the higher powers, my boy."

" The devil! " exclaimed the scholar, beginning to feel decidedly ill at ease. " Tell me, Monsieur le Juge, is the affair so bad as you say? "

" Worse! my dear friend, worse! I am not in the habit of frightening those who come before me; but I give you warning of this, so that if you have any arrangements to make — "

" Arrangements to make! " cried the student. " Tell me, Monsieur le Lieutenant Criminel, for God's sake! do you think my life 's in danger? "

"Certainly it is, certainly. What! you attack a noble-man in the street, you force him to fight, you run a sword through him, and then you ask if your life's in danger! Yes, my dear friend, yes, — in very great danger."

"But such affairs happen every day, and I don't see that the guilty ones are prosecuted."

"True, among gentlemen, my young friend. Oh! when it pleases two gentlemen to cut each other's throats, it's a privilege of their rank, and the king has nothing to say; but if the common people take it into their head some fine day to fight with gentlemen, as they are twenty times as numerous, there would soon be no more gentlemen, which would be a great pity."

"How many days do you think my trial will last?"

"Five or six, in all likelihood."

"What!" cried the student, "five or six days! No more than that?"

"Why should it? The facts are clear enough; a man dies, you confess that you killed him, and justice is satisfied. However," added the judge, assuming a still more benevolent expression, "if two or three days more would be agreeable to you —"

"Very agreeable."

"Oh well! we will spin out the report, and gain time in that way. You are a good fellow at heart, and I shall be delighted to do something for you."

"Thanks," said the student.

"And now," said the judge, rising, "have you any further request to make?"

"I would like to see a priest: is it impossible?"

"No; it is your right."

"In that case, Monsieur le Juge, ask them to send one to me."

" I will do your errand. No ill will, my young friend."

" Good lack ! on the contrary, I am deeply grateful."

" Master Student," said the clerk in an undertone, stepping to Aubrey's side, " would you be willing to do me a favor ? "

" Gladly," said Aubrey ; " what might it be ? "

" It may be that you have friends or relatives to whom you intend to bequeath all your possessions ? "

" Friends ? I have but one, and he 's a prisoner like myself. Relatives ? I have only cousins, and very distant cousins at that. So, say on, Master Clerk, say on."

" Monsieur, I am a poor man, father of a family, with five children."

" What then ? "

" I have never had any opportunities in my position, which I fill, as you can testify, with scrupulous probity. All my confrères are promoted over my head."

" Why is that ? "

" Why ? Ah ! why ? I will tell you."

" Do so."

" Because they are lucky."

" Aha ! "

" And why are they lucky

" That 's what I would ask you, Master Clerk."

" And that 's what I am about to tell you, Master Student."

" I shall be very glad to know."

" They are lucky," — here the clerk lowered his voice a half-tone more, — " they are lucky because they have the rope a man was hanged with in their pocket: do you understand ? "

" No."

" You 're rather dull. You will make a will, eh ? "

"A will! why should I?"

"Dame! so that there may be no contest among your heirs. Very good! write in your will that you authorize Marc-Boniface Grimoineau, clerk to Monsieur le Lieutenant Criminel, to claim from the executioner a bit of the rope you are hanged by."

"Ah!" said Aubry, in a choking voice. "Yes, now I understand."

"And you will grant my request?"

"To be sure!"

"Young man, remember what you have promised me. Many have made the same promise, but some have died intestate, others have written my name, Marc-Boniface Grimoineau so badly that there was a chance for cavilling; and others still, who were guilty, monsieur, on my word of honor very guilty, have been acquitted, and gone off elsewhere to be hanged; so that I was really in despair when you fell in my way."

"Very well, Master Clerk, very well; if I am hanged, you shall have what you want, never fear."

"Oh, you will be, monsieur, you will be, don't you doubt it!"

"Well, Grimoineau," said the judge.

"Here I am, monsieur, here I am. So it's a bargain, Master Student?"

"It's a bargain."

"On your word of honor?"

"On my word!"

"I think that I shall get it at last," muttered the clerk as he withdrew. "I will go home and tell my wife and children the good news."

He left the cell on the heels of the lieutenant criminal, who was grumbling good-humoredly at having to wait so long.

XVII.

WHEREIN IT IS PROVED THAT TRUE FRIENDSHIP IS
CAPABLE OF CARRYING DEVOTION TO THE MARRY-
ING POINT.

AUBRY, once more alone, was soon more deeply absorbed in thought than before; and the reader will agree
that there was ample food for thought in his conversation
with the lieutenant criminal. We hasten to say, however, that one who could have read his thoughts would
have found that the situation of Ascanio and Colombe,
depending as it did upon the letter in his possession,
occupied the first place, and that before thinking of himself, a thing which he proposed to do in good time, he
deliberated as to what was to be done for them.

He had been meditating thus for half an hour more or
less, when the door of his cell opened once more, and
the turnkey appeared on the threshold.

"Are you the man who sent for a priest?" he growled.

"To be sure I am," said Jacques.

"Deuce take me, if I know what they all want with a
damned monk," muttered the turnkey; "but what I do
know is that they can't leave a poor man in peace for
five minutes. Come in, come in, father," he continued,
standing aside to allow the priest to pass, "and be quick
about it."

With that he closed the door, still grumbling, and
left the new comer alone with the prisoner.

"Was it you who sent for me, my son?" the priest asked.

"Yes, father," replied the student.

"Do you wish to confess?"

"No, not just that: I wish to talk with you concerning a simple case of conscience."

"Say on, my son," said the priest, seating himself upon the stool, "and if any feeble light that I can give you will help you — "

"It was to ask your advice that I ventured to send for you."

"I am listening."

"Father," said Aubry, "I am a great sinner."

"Alas!" said the priest; "happy is the man who acknowledges it."

"But that is not all; not only am I a great sinner myself, as I said, but I have led others into sin."

"Is there any way of undoing the harm you have done?"

"I think so, father, I think so. She whom I dragged with me into the pit was an innocent young girl."

"You seduced her, did you?"

"Seduced; yes, father, that is the word."

"And you wish to atone for your sin?"

"That at least is my intention."

"There is but one way to do it."

"I know it well, and that is why I have been undecided so long: if there were two ways I would have chosen the other."

"You wish to marry her?"

"One moment, no! I will not lie: no, father, I do not wish to do it, but I am resigned."

"A warmer, more devoted feeling would be much better."

" What would you have, father? There are people who are born to marry, and others to remain single. Celibacy was my vocation, and nothing less than my present situation, I swear — "

" Very well, my son, the sooner the better, as you may repent of your virtuous intentions."

" What will be the earliest possible moment? " Aubry asked.

" Dame ! " said the priest, " as it is a marriage *in extremis*, there will be no difficulty about the necessary dispensations, and I think that by day after to-morrow — "

" Day after to-morrow let it be," said the student with a sigh.

" But the young woman? "

" What of her ? "

" Will she consent ? "

" To what ? "

" To the marriage."

" Pardieu ! will she consent? That she will, with thanks. Such propositions are n't made to her every day."

" Then there is no obstacle ? "

" None."

" Your parents ? "

" Absent."

" And hers ? "

" Unknown."

" Her name ? "

" Gervaise-Perrette Popinot."

" Do you wish me to tell her of your purpose ? "

" If you will kindly take that trouble, father, I shall be truly grateful."

" She shall be informed this very day."

"Tell me, father, tell me, could you possibly hand her a letter?"

"No, my son: we who are admitted to minister to the prisoners have sworn to deliver no message for them to any person until after their death. When that time comes, I will do whatever you choose."

"Thanks, it would be useless; marriage it must be, then," muttered Aubry.

"You have nothing else to say to me?"

"Nothing, except that, if you doubt the truth of what I say, and if she makes any objection to granting my request, you will find in the office of the lieutenant-criminal a complaint lodged by said Gervaise-Perrette Popinot, which will prove that what I have said is the exact truth."

"Rely upon me to smooth away all obstacles," replied the priest, who realized that Jacques's proposed action was not prompted by enthusiasm for the marriage, but that he was yielding to necessity; "and two days hence — "

"Two days hence — "

"You will have restored her honor to the woman whose honor you took from her."

"Alas!" muttered the student with a deep sigh.

"Ah, my son!" said the priest, "the more a sacrifice costs you, the greater pleasure it affords to God."

"By Mahomet's belly!" cried Jacques; "in that case God should be very grateful to me! go, father, go!"

Indeed, Jacques had had to overcome very bitter opposition in his own mind before arriving at such a resolution. As he had told Gervaise, he had inherited his antipathy to the marriage tie from his father, and nothing less than his friendship for Ascanio, and the thought that it was he who had caused his ruin, together with the incentive afforded by the noblest examples of self-sacrificing devotion to be found in history, — nothing less than all of this was necessary to bring him to the pitch of abnegation at which he had now arrived.

But, the reader may ask, where lies the connection between the marriage of Gervaise and Aubry, and the happiness of Ascanio and Colombe, and how did Aubry expect to save his friend by marrying his mistress? To such a question I can only answer that the reader lacks penetration; to which the reader may retort, to be sure, that it is not his business to have that quality. In that case, I beg him to take the trouble to read the end of this chapter, which he might have passed over had he been endowed with a more subtle intellect.

When the priest had gone, Aubry, recognizing the impossibility of drawing back, seemed to become more tranquil. It is characteristic of resolutions, even the most momentous, to bring tranquillity in their wake: the mind which has wrestled with its perplexity is at rest; the heart which has fought against its sorrow is, as it were, benumbed.

Jacques remained passive in his cell, until, having heard sounds in that occupied by Ascanio, which he supposed to be caused by the entrance of the jailer with his breakfast, he concluded that they would surely be left in peace for a few hours. He waited some little time after the noise had ceased, then crawled into his underground gallery, passed through it, and raised the mat with his head.

Ascanio's cell was plunged in most intense darkness.

Aubry called his friend's name in a low tone, but there was no reply. The cell was untenanted.

Aubry's first feeling was one of joy. Ascanio was free, and if Ascanio was free there was no need for him to — But almost immediately he remembered what was said the night before about providing him with better quarters. It was plain that the suggestion of Madame d'Etampes had been heeded, and the sounds he heard were caused by his friend's being moved.

Aubry's hope was as dazzling, therefore, but as evanescent, as a flash of lightning. He let the mat fall and crawled backward into his cell. Every source of consolation was taken from him, even the presence of the friend for whom he had sacrificed himself.

He had no resource left but reflection. But he had already reflected so long, and his reflections had led to such a disastrous result, that he preferred to sleep.

He threw himself upon his bed, and as he was very much in arrears in the matter of sleep, it was not long before he was entirely unconscious of his surroundings, notwithstanding the perturbed condition of his mind.

He dreamed that he was condemned to death and hanged; but through the deviltry of the hangman, the rope was badly greased, and his neck was not broken. He was buried in due form, none the less, and in his dream was beginning to gnaw his arms, as men buried alive always do, when the clerk, determined to have his bit of rope, came to secure it, opened the coffin in which he was immured, and restored his life and liberty.

Alas! it was only a dream, and when the student awoke his life was still in great danger, and his liberty altogether non-existent.

The evening, the night, and the next day passed away, and brought him no other visitor than his jailer. He tried to ask him a few questions, but could not extract a word from him.

In the middle of the second night, as Jacques was in the midst of his first sleep, he was awakened with a start by the grinding of his door upon its hinges. However soundly a prisoner may be sleeping, the sound of an opening door always awakens him.

The student sat up in bed.

"Up with you, and dress yourself," said the jailer's harsh voice; and Aubry could see by the light of the torch he held, the halberds of two of the provost's guards behind him.

The second branch of his order was unnecessary; as the student's bed was entirely unprovided with bed-clothes, he had lain down completely dressed.

"Where do you propose to take me, pray?" demanded Jacques, still asleep with one eye.

"You are very inquisitive," said the jailer.

"But I would like to know."

"Come, come; no arguing, but follow me."

Resistance was useless, so the prisoner obeyed.

The jailer walked first, then came Aubry, and the two guards brought up the rear of the procession.

Jacques looked around with an inquietude which he did not seek to conceal. He feared a nocturnal execution; but one thing comforted him, he saw no priest or hangman.

After a few moments he found himself in the first room to which he was taken at the time of his coming to the prison; but instead of escorting him to the outer door, which he hoped for an instant that they would do, so prone to illusions does misfortune render one, his guide opened a door at one corner of the room and entered an inner corridor leading to a courtyard.

The prisoner's first thought on entering the court-yard, where he felt the fresh air and saw the starlit sky, was to fill his lungs, and lay in a stock of oxygen, not knowing when he might have another opportunity.

The next moment he noticed the ogive windows of a fourteenth century chapel on the other side of the yard, and began to suspect what was in the wind.

The truth-telling instinct of the historian compels us to state that at the thought his strength wellnigh failed him.

However, the memory of Ascanio and Colombe, and the grandeur of the self-sacrifice about to be consummated, sustained him in his distress. He walked with a firm step toward the chapel, and when he stood in the doorway everything was explained.

The priest stood by the altar; in the choir a woman was waiting; the woman was Gervaise.

Half-way up the choir he met the governor of the Châtelet.

"You desired to make reparation, before your death, to the young woman whose honor you stole from her: your request was no more than just and it is granted."

A cloud passed over the student's eyes; but he put his hand over Madame d'Etampes's letter, and his courage returned.

"Oh, my poor Jacques!" cried Gervaise, throwing herself into the student's arms: "oh, who could have dreamed that this hour which I have so longed for would strike under such circumstances!"

"What wouldst thou have, my dear Gervaise?" cried the student, receiving her upon his breast. "God knows those whom he should punish and those whom he should reward: we must submit to God's will."

"Take this," he added beneath his breath, slipping Madame d'Etampes's letter into her hand; "for Benvenuto and for him alone!"

"What's that?" exclaimed the governor, walking hastily toward them; "what's the matter?"

" Nothing; I was telling Gervaise how I love her. "

" As she will not, in all probability, have time to ascertain the contrary, protestations are thrown away; go to the altar and make haste. "

Aubry and Gervaise went forward in silence to the waiting priest. When they were in front of him they fell upon their knees and the mass began.

Jacques would have been very glad of an opportunity to exchange a few words with Gervaise, who, for her part, was burning up with the desire to express her gratitude to Aubry; but two guards stood beside them listening to every word and watching every movement. It was very fortunate that a momentary feeling of sympathy led the governor to allow them to exchange the embrace under cover of which the letter passed from Jacques's hands to Gervaise's. That opportunity lost, the close surveillance to which they were subjected would have rendered Jacques's devotion of no avail.

The priest had received his instructions, doubtless, for he cut his discourse very short. It may be, too, that he thought it would be trouble thrown away to enjoin due regard to his duties as a husband and father upon a man who was to be hanged within two or three days.

The discourse at an end, the benediction given, the mass said, Aubry and Gervaise thought they would be allowed to speak together privately for a moment, but not so. Despite the tears of Gervaise, who was literally dissolved in them, the guards forced them to part.

They had time, however, to exchange a glance. Aubry's said, " Remember my commission. " Gervaise's replied, " Never fear; it shall be done to-night, or to-morrow at latest. "

Then they were led away in opposite directions. Gervaise was politely escorted to the street door, and Jacques was politely taken back to his cell.

As the door closed upon him, he heaved a deeper sigh than any of those he had perpetrated since he entered the prison: he was married.

Thus it was that Aubry, like another Curtius, plunged headlong, through devotion, into the hymeneal gulf.

XVIII.

THE CASTING.

Now, with our readers' permission, we will leave the Châtelet for a moment, and return to the Hôtel de Nesle.

The workmen responded quickly to Benvenuto's cries, and followed him to the foundry.

They all knew him as he appeared when at work; but never had they seen such an expression upon his face, never such a flame in his eyes. Whoever could have cast him in a mould at that moment, as he was on the point of casting his Jupiter, would have endowed the world with the noblest statue ever created by the genius of an artist.

Everything was ready: the wax model in its envelope of clay, girt round with iron bands, was awaiting in the furnace which surrounded it the hour of its life. The wood was all arranged: Benvenuto set fire to it in four different places, and as it was spruce, which the artist had been long collecting that it might be thoroughly dry, the fire quickly attacked every part of the furnace, and the mould was soon the centre of an immense blaze. The wax thereupon began to run out through the air-holes while the mould was baking: at the same time the workmen were digging a long ditch beside the furnace, into which the metal was to be poured in a state of fusion, for Benvenuto was anxious not to lose a moment, and to proceed to the casting as soon as the mould was thoroughly baked.

For a day and a half the wax trickled from the mould; for a day and a half, while the workmen divided into watches and took turn and turn about like the sailors on a man-of-war, Benvenuto was constantly on hand, hovering about the furnace, feeding the fire, encouraging the workmen. At last he found that the wax had all run out, and that the mould was thoroughly baked; this completed the second part of his work; the last part was the melting of the bronze and the casting of the statue. When that stage was reached the workmen, who were utterly unable to comprehend such superhuman strength and such an intensity of passion, endeavored to induce Benvenuto to take a few hours' rest; but that would mean so many hours added to Ascanio's captivity and the persecution of Colombe. Benvenuto refused. He seemed to be made of the same bronze of which he was about to make a god.

When the ditch was dug, he wound stout ropes about the mould, and with the aid of windlasses prepared for that purpose, he raised it with every possible precaution, swung it out over the ditch, and let it down slowly until it was on a level with the furnace. He fixed it firmly in place there by piling around it the dirt taken from the ditch, treading it down, and putting in place, as the dirt rose about the mould, the pieces of earthen pipe which were to serve as air-holes. All these preparations took the rest of the day. Night came. For forty-eight hours Benvenuto had not slept nor lain down, nor even sat down. The workmen implored, Scozzone scolded, but Benvenuto would hear none of it: he seemed to be sustained by some more than human power, and made no other reply to the entreaties and scolding than to assign to each workman his task, in the short, stern tone of an officer manœuvring his troops.

Benvenuto was determined to begin the casting at once: the energetic artist, who was accustomed to see all obstacles yield before him, exerted his imperious power upon himself; he ordered his body to act, and it obeyed, while his companions were obliged to withdraw, one after another, as in battle wounded soldiers leave the field and seek the hospital.

The casting furnace was ready: it was filled with round ingots of brass and copper, symmetrically piled one upon another, so that the heat could pass between them, and the fusion be effected more quickly and more completely. He set fire to the wood around it as in the case of the other furnace, and as it was mostly spruce, the resin which exuded from it, in conjunction with the combustible nature of the wood, soon made such a fierce flame that it rose higher than was anticipated, and lapped the roof of the foundry, which took fire at once, being of wood. At the sight of this conflagration, and more especially at the heat which it gave forth, all the artist's comrades, save Hermann, drew back; but Hermann and Benvenuto were a host in themselves. Each of them seized an axe and cut away at the wooden pillars which upheld the roof, and in an instant it fell in. Thereupon Hermann and Benvenuto with poles pushed the burning fragments into the furnace, and with the increased heat the metal began to melt.

But Benvenuto had at last reached the limit of his strength. For nearly sixty hours he had not slept, for twenty-four he had not eaten, and during the whole of that time he was the soul of the whole performance, the axis upon which the whole operation turned. A terrible fever took possession of him: a deathly pallor succeeded

to his usual high color. In an atmosphere so intensely
hot that no one could live beside him, he felt his limbs
tremble and his teeth chatter as if he were amid the
snows of Lapland. His companions remarked his condition and drew near to him. He tried to resist, to deny
that he was beaten, for in his eyes it was a disgrace to
yield even before the impossible; but at last he was fain
to confess that his strength was failing him. Fortunately, the fusion was nearly accomplished: the most
difficult part of the operation was past, and what remained to be done was mere mechanical work. He
called Pagolo; Pagolo did not reply. But the workmen
shouted his name in chorus and he at last appeared; he
said that he had been praying for the successful issue of
the casting.

"This is no time to pray!" cried Benvenuto, "and
the Lord said, 'He who works prays.' This is the
time for work, Pagolo. Hark ye: I feel that I am dying; but whether I die or not, my Jupiter must live.
Pagolo, my friend, to thee I intrust the management of
the casting, sure that thou canst do it as well as I, if
thou wilt. Understand, Pagolo, the metal will soon be
ready; thou canst not mistake the proper degree of heat.
When it is red thou wilt give a sledge hammer to Hermann, and one to Simon-le-Gaucher. — My God! what
was I saying? Ah, yes! — Then they must knock out
the two plugs of the furnace; the metal will flow out,
and if I am dead you will tell the king that he promised
me a boon, and that you claim it in my name, and that
it — is — O my God! I no longer remember. What
was I to ask the king? Ah, yes! — Ascanio — Seigneur
de Nesle — Colombe, the provost's daughter — D'Orbec
— Madame d'Etampes — Ah! I am going mad!"

Benvenuto staggered and fell into Hermann's arms,

who carried him off like a child to his room, while Pagolo, intrusted with the superintendence of the work, gave orders for it to go on.

Benvenuto was right: he was going mad, or rather a terrible delirium had taken possession of him. Scozzone, who doubtless had been praying as Pagolo had, hurried to his side; but Benvenuto continued to cry, "I am dying! I am dying! Ascanio! Ascanio! what will become of Ascanio?"

A thousand delirious visions were crowding in upon his brain: Ascanio, Colombe, Stefana, all appeared and disappeared like ghosts. In the throng which passed before his eyes was Pompeo the goldsmith, whom he slew with his dagger; and the keeper of the post-house at Sienna, whom he slew with his arquebus. Past and present were confounded in his brain. Now it was Clement VII. who detained Ascanio in prison; again it was Cosmo I. who sought to force Colombe to marry D'Orbec. Then he would appeal to Queen Eleanora, thinking he was addressing Madame d'Etampes, and would implore and threaten her by turns. Then he would make sport of poor weeping Scozzone, and bid her beware lest Pagolo should break his neck clambering around on the cornices like a cat. Intervals of complete prostration would succeed these paroxysms, and it would seem as if he were at the point of death.

This agonizing state of affairs endured three hours. Benvenuto was in one of his periods of torpor when Pagolo suddenly rushed into the room, pale and agitated, crying: —

"May Jesus and the Virgin help us, master! for all is lost now, and we can look nowhere but to Heaven for help."

Worn out, half conscious, dying as he was, these

words, like a sharp stiletto, reached the very bottom of his heart. The veil which clouded his intellect was torn away, and, like Lazarus rising at the voice of the Lord, he rose upon his bed, crying: —

"Who dares to say that all is lost when Benvenuto still lives?"

"Alas! I, master," said Pagolo.

"Double traitor!" cried Benvenuto, "is it written that thou shalt forever prove false to me? But never fear! Jesus and the Virgin whom you invoked just now are at hand, to bear aid to men of good will, and punish traitors!"

At that moment he heard the workmen lamenting and crying: —

"Benvenuto! Benvenuto!"

"He is here! he is here!" cried the artist, rushing from his room, pale of face, but with renewed strength and clearness of vision. "Here he is! and woe to them who have not done their duty!"

In two bounds Benvenuto was at the foundry; he found all the workmen, whom he had left so full of vigor and enthusiasm, in a state of utter stupefaction and dejection. Even Hermann the colossus seemed to be dying of fatigue; he was tottering on his legs and was compelled to lean against one of the supports of the roof which remained standing.

"Now listen to what I say," cried Benvenuto in an awful voice, falling into their midst like a thunderbolt. "I don't as yet know what has happened, but I swear to you beforehand that it can be remedied, whatever it may be, — upon my soul it can! Now that I am present, obey me on your lives! but obey passively, without a word, without a gesture, for the first man who hesitates I will kill.

"So much for the ill disposed.

"I have but one word to say to those who are disposed to do their duty: the liberty and happiness of Ascanio, your companion of whom you are all so fond, will follow the successful issue of this task. To work!"

With that Cellini approached the furnace to form his own opinion of what had taken place. The supply of wood had given out, and the metal had cooled, so that it had turned to cake, as the professional phrase goes.

Benvenuto at once determined that the disaster could be repaired. Pagolo's watchfulness had relaxed in all likelihood,- and he had allowed the heat of the fire to abate: the thing to be done was to make the fire as hot as ever, and to reduce the metal to a liquid state once more.

"Wood!" cried Benvenuto, "wood! Go look for wood wherever it can possibly be found; go to the bakers, and buy it by the pound if necessary; bring every stick of wood that there is in the house to the smallest chip. Break in the doors of the Petit-Nesle, Hermann, if Dame Perrine does n't choose to open them; everything in that direction is lawful prize, for it's an enemy's country. Wood! wood!"

To set the example Benvenuto seized an axe and attacked the two posts which were still standing: they soon fell with the last remnants of the roof, and Benvenuto at once pushed the whole mass into the fire: at the same time his comrades returned from all directions laden with wood.

"Ah!" cried Benvenuto, "now are you ready to obey me?"

"Yes! yes!" cried every voice, "yes! we will do whatever you bid us do, so long as we have a breath of life in our bodies."

" Select the oak then, and throw on nothing but oak at first: that burns more quickly, and consequently will repair the damage sooner."

Immediately oak began to rain down upon the fire, and Benvenuto was obliged to cry enough.

His energy infected all his comrades; his orders, even his gestures, were understood and executed on the instant. Pagolo alone muttered from time to time between his teeth : —

" You are trying to perform impossibilities, master: it is tempting Providence."

To which Cellini's only reply was a look which seemed to say, " Never fear; we have an account to settle hereafter."

Meanwhile, notwithstanding Pagolo's sinister predictions, the metal began to fuse anew, and to hasten the fusion Benvenuto at intervals threw a quantity of lead into the furnace, stirring up the lead and copper and brass with a long bar of iron, so that, to borrow his expression, the metal corpse began to come to life again. At sight of the progress that was making, Benvenuto was so elate that he was unconscious of fever or weakness; he too came to life once more.

At last the metal began to boil and seethe. Benvenuto at once opened the orifice of the mould and ordered the plugs of the furnace to be knocked out, which was done on the instant; but, as if this immense work was to be a veritable combat of Titans to the end, Benvenuto perceived, as soon as the plugs were removed, not only that the metal did not run freely enough, but that there was some question as to whether there was enough of it. Thereupon, with one of those heaven-sent inspirations which come to none but artists, he cried: —

" Let half of you remain here to feed the fire, and the rest follow me ! "

With that he rushed into the house, followed by five of his men, and an instant later they all reappeared, laden with silver plate, pewter, bullion, and pieces of work half completed. Benvenuto himself set the example, and each one cast his precious burden into the furnace, which instantly devoured everything, bronze, lead, silver, rough pig-metal, and beautiful works of art, with the same indifference with which it would have devoured the artist himself if he had thrown himself in.

Thanks to this reinforcement of fusible matter, the metal became thoroughly liquefied, and, as if it repented of its momentary hesitation, began to flow freely. There ensued a period of breathless suspense, which became something very like terror when Benvenuto perceived that all of the bronze did not reach the orifice of the mould: he sounded with a long rod and found that the mould was entirely filled without exhausting the supply of metal.

Thereupon he fell upon his knees and thanked God: the work was finished which was to save Ascanio and Colombe: now would God permit that the result should fulfil his hopes?

It was impossible to know until the following day.

The night that followed was, as can readily be imagined, a night of agony, and, worn out as Benvenuto was, he slept for a very few moments only, and his sleep even for those few moments was far from being restful. His eyes were hardly closed before real objects gave place to imaginary ones. He saw his Jupiter, the king of the gods in beauty as well as power, as shapeless and deformed as his son Vulcan. In his dream he was unable to understand this catastrophe. Was it the fault of the mould? Was it the fault of the casting? Had he made a miscalculation? or was destiny making sport of him? At the sight his temples throbbed furiously, and he awoke with his heart jumping, and bathed in perspiration. For some time his mind was so confused that he could not separate fact from vision. At last, however, he remembered that his Jupiter was still hidden in the mould, like a child in its mother's womb. He recalled all the precautions he had taken. He implored God not only to make his work successful, but to do a merciful deed. Thereupon he became somewhat calmer, and fell asleep again — under the weight of the never-ending weariness which seemed to have laid hold on him forever — only to fall into a second dream as absurd and as terrifying as the first.

Day broke at last, and with its coming Benvenuto shook himself clear of all symptoms of drowsiness: in an instant he was on his feet and fully dressed, and hastened at once to the foundry.

The bronze was evidently still too hot to be exposed to the air, but Benvenuto was in such haste to ascertain what he had still to fear, or what he might hope, that he could not contain himself, and began to uncover the head. When he put his hand to the mould he was so pale that one would have thought him at the point of death.

"Are you still sick, master?" inquired a voice, which he recognized as Hermann's; "you vould do much petter to stay in your ped."

"You are wrong, Hermann, my boy," said Benvenuto, amazed to find him astir so early, "for I should die in my bed. But how happens it that you are out of bed at this hour?"

"I vas taking a valk," said Hermann, blushing to the whites of his eyes; "I like much to valk. Shall I help you, master?"

E. VAN MUYDEN

"No, no!" cried Benvenuto; "no one but myself is to touch the mould! Wait, wait!"

And he began gently to uncover the head. By a miraculous chance there was just the necessary amount of metal. If it had not occurred to him to throw all his silver plate and other objects into the furnace, the head would have been missing and the casting a failure.

Fortunately the head was not missing, and was wonderfully beautiful.

The sight of it encouraged Benvenuto to expose the other portions of the body one after another. Little by little the mould fell away like bark, and at last Jupiter, freed from head to foot from his trammels, appeared in all the majesty befitting the sovereign of Olympus. In no part of the work had the bronze betrayed the artist, and when the last morsel of clay fell away, all the workmen joined in a shout of admiration; for they had come out one by one and gathered about Cellini, who did not even notice their presence, so absorbed was he by the thoughts to which this complete success gave rise.

But at the shout, which made him too a god, he raised his head, and said with a proud smile : —

"We shall see if the King of France will refuse the first boon asked by the man who has made such a statue!"

The next instant, as if he repented his first impulse of pride, which was entirely characteristic of him, he fell upon his knees, and with clasped hands rendered thanks to the Lord aloud.

As he was finishing his prayer Scozzone ran out to say that *Madame* Jacques Aubry desired to speak to him in private, having a letter from her husband, which she could hand to none but Benvenuto.

Benvenuto made Scozzone repeat the name twice, for

he had no idea that the student was in the hands of a lawful wife.

He obeyed the summons none the less, leaving his companions swollen with pride in their master's renown. Pagolo meanwhile, on scrutinizing the statue more closely, observed that there was an imperfection in the heel, some accident having prevented the metal from filling every part of the mould.

XIX.

JUPITER AND OLYMPUS.

ON the same day that Benvenuto removed his statue from the mould, he sent word to François I. that his Jupiter was cast, and asked him on what day it was his pleasure that the King of Olympus should appear before the King of France.

François replied that his cousin, the Emperor, and he were to hunt in the forest of Fontainebleau on the following Thursday, and that he need do nothing more than have his statue transported to the grand gallery of the château on that day.

The reply was very short; it was evident that Madame d'Etampes had strongly prejudiced the king against his favorite artist. But Benvenuto — was it through pride or confidence in God? — said simply, with a smile, —

"It is well."

It was Monday. Benvenuto caused the Jupiter to be loaded upon a wagon, and rode beside it, not leaving it for an instant, lest some mishap might befall it. On Thursday, at ten o'clock, statue and artist were at Fontainebleau.

To any one who saw Benvenuto, though it were only to see him ride by, it was evident that pride and radiant hope were triumphant in his heart. His conscience as an artist told him that he had executed a *chef-d'œuvre*, and his honest heart that he was about to perform a meritorious action. He was doubly joyous, therefore, and carried his head high, like a man who, having no hatred in his heart, was equally without fear. The king was to see his Jupiter, and could not fail to be pleased with it; Montmorency and Poyet would remind him of his promise; the Emperor and the whole court would be present, and François could not do otherwise than as he had given his word to do.

Madame d'Etampes, with less innocent delight, but with quite as much ardent passion, was maturing her plans. She had triumphed over Benvenuto at the time of his first attempt to confound her by presenting himself at her own hôtel and at the Louvre. The first danger was safely past, but she felt that the king's promise to Benvenuto was a second equally great danger, and it was her purpose, at any cost, to induce his Majesty to disregard it. She therefore repaired to Fontainebleau one day in advance of Cellini, and laid her wires with the profound feminine craft which in her case almost amounted to genius.

Cellini was destined very soon to feel its effects.

He had no sooner crossed the threshold of the gallery where his Jupiter was to be exhibited, than he felt the blow, recognized the hand that had dealt it, and stood for a moment overwhelmed.

This gallery, ordinarily resplendent with paintings by Rosso, which were in themselves enough to distract the attention from almost any masterpiece, had been embellished during the last three days by statues sent from Rome by Primaticcio, — that is to say, the marvels of antique sculpture, the types sanctified by the admiration of twenty centuries, were there before him, challenging comparison, crushing all rivalry. Ariadne, Venus, Hercules, Apollo, even Jupiter himself, the great Olympian Jove, — ideal figures, dreams of genius, eternities in bronze, — formed, as it were, a supernatural assemblage which it was impious to approach, a sublime tribunal whose judgment every artist should dread.

There was something like profanation and blasphemy in the thought of another Jupiter insinuating himself into that Olympus, of Benvenuto throwing down the gauntlet to Phidias, and, notwithstanding his trust in his own merit, the devout artist recoiled.

Furthermore, the immortal statues had taken possession of all the best places, as it was their right to do, and there was no place left for Cellini's poor Jupiter but some dark corner which could only be reached by passing under the stately and imposing glances of the ancient gods.

Benvenuto stood in the doorway with bowed head, and with an expression in which sadness and artistic gratification were mingled.

"Messire Antoine Le Maçon," he said to the king's secretary, who stood beside him, " I ought to and will send my Jupiter back instantly; the disciple will not attempt to contend with the masters; the child will not attempt to contend with his parents; my pride and my modesty alike forbid."

"Benvenuto," replied the secretary, "take the advice of a sincere friend, — if you do that, you are lost. I tell you this between ourselves, that your enemies hope to discourage you, and then to allege your discouragement as a proof of your lack of skill. It will be useless for me to make excuses for you to the king. His Majesty, who is impatient to see your work, would refuse to listen, and, with Madame d'Etampes continually urging him to do it, would withdraw his favor from you forever. She anticipates that result, and I fear it. It's with the living, not with the dead, Benvenuto, that you have to contend."

"You are right, messire," the goldsmith rejoined, "and I understand you perfectly. Thank you for reminding me that I have no right to have any self-esteem here."

"That's all right, Benvenuto. But let me give you one more bit of advice. Madame d'Etampes is too fascinating to-day not to have some perfidious scheme in her head: she took the king and the Emperor off for a ride in the forest with irresistible playfulness and charm; I am afraid for your sake that she will find a way to keep them there until dark."

"Do you think it?" cried Benvenuto, turning pale. "Why, if she succeeds in doing that, I am lost; for my statue would then have to be exhibited by artificial light, which would deprive it of half its merit."

"Let us hope that I am mistaken," said Le Maçon, "and see what comes to pass."

Cellini waited in painful suspense. He placed his Jupiter in as favorable a light as possible, but he did not conceal from himself the fact that its effect would be comparatively slight by twilight, and that after nightfall it would be positively bad. The duchess's hatred had reckoned no less accurately than the artist's skill; she anticipated in 1541 a trick of the critics of the nineteenth century.

Benvenuto watched the sun sink toward the horizon with despair at his heart, and listened eagerly to every sound without the château. Except for the servants the vast structure was deserted.

Three o'clock struck; thenceforth the purpose of Madame d'Etampes could not be mistaken, and her success was beyond question. Benvenuto fell upon a chair, utterly crushed. All was lost: his renown first of all. That feverish struggle, in which he had been so near succumbing, and which he had already forgotten because he had thought that it made his triumph sure, would have no other result than to put him to shame. He gazed sorrowfully at his statue, around which the shadows of night were already beginning to fall, and whose lines began to appear less pure.

Suddenly an inspiration came to him; he sprang to his feet, called little Jehan, whom he had brought with him, and rushed hastily from the gallery. Nothing had yet occurred to suggest the king's return. Benvenuto hurried to a cabinet-maker in the town, and with his assistance and that of his workmen made, in less than an hour, a stand of light-colored oak, with four rollers, which turned in every direction, like casters.

He trembled now lest the king should return too soon: but at five o'clock the work was completed, night had fallen, and the crowned heads had not returned to the château. Madame d'Etampes, wherever she was, was in a fair way to triumph.

In a very short time Benvenuto had the statue in place upon the almost invisible stand. Jupiter held in his left hand the sphere representing the world, and in his right, a little above his head, the thunderbolt, which he seemed to be on the point of launching into space: amid the tongues of the thunderbolt the goldsmith concealed a lamp.

These preparations were hardly completed when a flourish of trumpets announced the return of the king and the Emperor. Benvenuto lighted the lamp, stationed little Jehan behind the statue, by which he was entirely concealed, and awaited the king's coming, not without trepidation, evidenced by the violent beating of his heart.

Ten minutes later the folding-doors were thrown wide open, and François I. appeared, leading Charles V. by the hand.

The Dauphin, Dauphine, the King of Navarre, and the whole court followed the two monarchs; the provost, his daughter, and D'Orbec were among the last. Colombe was pale and dejected, but as soon as she espied Cellini, she raised her head, and a smile of sublime confidence appeared upon her lips and lighted up her face.

Cellini met her glance with one which seemed to say, " Have no fear; whatever happens, do not despair, for I am watching over you."

As the door opened, little Jehan, at a signal from his master, gave the statue a slight push, so that it moved softly forward upon its smoothly rolling stand, and, leaving the antique statues behind, went to meet the king, so to speak, as if it were alive. Every eye was at once turned in its direction. The soft light of the lamp falling from above produced an effect much more agreeable than daylight.

Madame d'Etampes bit her lips.

" Methinks, Sire," said she, " that the flattery is a little overdone, and that it was for the king of earth to go to meet the king of heaven."

The king smiled, but it was easy to see that the flattery did not offend him; as his wont was, he forgot the artist for his art, saved the statue half the journey by walking to meet it, and examined it for a long time in silence. Charles V., who was by nature an astute politician rather than a great artist, although he did one day, in a moment of good humor, pick up Titian's pencil, — Charles V. and the courtiers, who were not entitled to an opinion, waited respectfully to hear that of François before pronouncing their own.

There was a moment of silent suspense, during which Benvenuto and the duchess exchanged a glance of bitter hatred.

Suddenly the king cried, —

"It is beautiful! it is very beautiful! and I confess that my expectations are surpassed."

Thereupon every one overflowed in compliments and extravagant praise, the Emperor first of all.

"If one could conquer artists like cities," said he to the king, "I would declare war on you instantly, to win this one, my cousin."

"But, after all," interrupted Madame d'Etampes, in a rage, "we do not even look at the beautiful antique statues a little farther on, which have somewhat more merit, perhaps, than our modern gewgaws."

The king thereupon walked toward the antique statues, which were lighted from below by the torches, so that the upper portions were in shadow; they were beyond question much less effective than the Jupiter.

"Phidias is sublime," said the king, "but there may be a Phidias in the age of François I. and Charles V., as there was in the age of Pericles."

"Oh, we must see it by daylight," said Anne, bitterly; "to appear to be is not to be: an artificial light is not art. And what is that veil? is it to conceal some defect, Master Cellini, tell us frankly?"

She referred to a very light drapery thrown over the statue to give it more majesty.

Thus far Benvenuto had remained beside his statue, silent, and apparently as cold as it; but at the duchess's words, he smiled disdainfully, shot lightning from his black eyes, and, with the sublime audacity of a heathen artist, snatched the veil away with his powerful hand.

He expected that the duchess would burst forth with renewed fury.

But by an incredible exertion of her will power, she smiled with ominous affability, and graciously held out her hand to Cellini, who was amazed beyond measure by this sudden change of tactics.

"I was wrong," she said aloud, in the tone of a spoiled child; "you are a great sculptor, Cellini; forgive my critical remarks; give me your hand, and let us be friends henceforth. What say you?"

She added in an undertone, with extreme volubility: "Think well of what you are about to ask, Cellini. Let it not be the marriage of Colombe and Ascanio, or I swear that Colombe, Ascanio, and yourself, all three, are undone forever!"

"And suppose I request something else, madame," said Benvenuto, in the same tone; "will you second my request?"

"Yes," said she, eagerly; "and I swear that, whatever it may be, the king will grant it."

"I have no need to request the king's sanction to the marriage of Colombe and Ascanio, for you will request it yourself, madame."

The duchess smiled disdainfully.

"What are you whispering there?" said François.

"Madame la Duchesse d'Etampes," Benvenuto replied, "was obliging enough to remind me that your Majesty had promised to grant me a boon in case you were content with my work."

"And the promise was made in my presence, Sire," said the constable, coming forward; "in my presence and Chancelier Poyet's. Indeed, you bade my colleague and myself remind you —"

"True, constable," interposed the king, good-humoredly; "true, if I failed to remember myself; but I remember famously, on my word! So your intervention, while it is perfectly agreeable to me, is quite useless. I promised Benvenuto to grant whatever boon he might ask when his Jupiter was cast. Was not that it, constable? Have I a good memory, chancellor? It is for you to speak, Master Cellini: I am at your service; but I beg you to think less of your own merit, which is immense, than of our power, which is limited; we make no reservations, saving our crown and our mistress."

"Very good, Sire," said Cellini," since your Majesty is so well disposed toward your unworthy servitor, I will ask for the pardon of a poor student, who fell into a dispute upon the Quai du Châtelet with the Vicomte de Marmagne, and in self-defence passed his sword through the viscount's body."

Every one marvelled at the moderation of his request, and Madame d'Etampes most of all; she gazed at Benvenuto with an air of stupefaction, and as if she thought that she could not have heard aright.

"By Mahomet's belly!" exclaimed François, "you do well to invoke my right of pardon in that matter, for I heard the chancellor himself say yesterday that it was a hanging affair."

"Oh, Sire!" cried the duchess, "I intended to speak to you myself concerning that young man. I have had news of Marmagne, who is improving, and who sent word to me that he sought the quarrel, and the student — What is the student's name, Master Benvenuto?"

"Jacques Aubry, Madame la Duchesse."

"And the student," continued Madame d'Etampes, hurriedly, "was in no wise in the wrong; and so, Sire, instead of rebuking Benvenuto, or cavilling at him, grant his request promptly, lest he repent of having been of modest."

"Very well," said François; "what you desire shall be done, master; and as he gives twice who gives quickly, — so says the proverb, — let the order to set this young man at liberty be despatched to-night. Do you hear, my dear chancellor?"

"Yes, Sire; and your Majesty shall be obeyed."

"As to yourself, Master Benvenuto," said François, "come to me on Monday at the Louvre, and we will adjust certain matters of detail in which you are interested, and which have been somewhat neglected of late by my treasurer."

"But your Majesty knows that admission to the Louvre — "

"Very good! very good! the person who gave the order can rescind it. It was a war measure, and as you now have none but friends at court, everything will be re-established upon a peace footing."

"As your Majesty is in a granting mood," said the duchess, "I pray you to grant a trifling request which I prefer, although I did not make the Jupiter."

"No," said Benvenuto in an undertone, "but you have often acted the part of Danaë."

"What is your request?" said François, who did not hear Benvenuto's epigram. "Say on, Madame la Duchesse, and be sure that the solemnity of the occasion can add nothing to my desire to be agreeable to you."

"Very well, Sire; your Majesty might well confer upon Messire d'Estourville the great honor of signing on Monday next the marriage contract of my young friend, Mademoiselle d'Estourville, with Comte d'Orbec."

"Why, I should be conferring no favor upon you by so doing," rejoined the king, "but I should afford myself a very great pleasure, and should still remain your debtor, I swear."

"So it is agreed, Sire, for Monday?" asked the duchess.

"For Monday," said the king.

"Madame la Duchesse," said Benvenuto, under his breath, "do you not regret that the beautiful lily you ordered Ascanio to execute is not finished, that you might wear it upon such an occasion?"

"Of course I regret it," was the reply; "but it's impossible, for Ascanio is in prison."

"Very true, but I am free; I will finish it and bring it to Madame la Duchesse."

"Oh! upon my honor! if you do that I will say —"

"You will say what, madame?"

"I will say that you are a delightful man."

She gave her hand to Benvenuto, who gallantly imprinted a kiss upon it, after asking the king's permission with a glance.

At that moment a slight shriek was heard.

"What is that?" the king asked.

"Sire, I ask your Majesty's pardon," said the provost, "but my daughter is ill."

"Poor child!" murmured Benvenuto; "she thinks that I have abandoned her."

XX.

A PRUDENT MARRIAGE.

BENVENUTO would have returned to Paris the same evening, but the king was so persistent that he could not avoid remaining at the château until the following morning.

With the rapidity of conception and promptness of decision which were characteristic of him, he determined to arrange for the next day the *dénouement* of a transaction which he began long before. It was a collateral matter which he wished to have off his hands altogether before devoting himself entirely to Ascanio and Colombe.

He remained at the château to supper on that evening and until after breakfast on the Friday, and not until noon did he set out on his return journey, accompanied by little Jehan, after taking leave of the king and Madame d'Etampes.

Both were well mounted, and yet, contrary to his wont, Cellini did not urge his horse. It was evident that he did not wish to enter Paris before a certain hour, and it was seven o'clock in the evening when he alighted at Rue de la Harpe.

Furthermore, instead of betaking himself at once to the Hôtel de Nesle, he called upon one of his friends named Guido, a physician from Florence; and when he had made sure that his friend was at home, and could conveniently entertain him at supper, he ordered little

Jehan to return alone, to say that he had remained at Fontainebleau and would not return until the next day, and to be ready to open the door when he should knock. Little Jehan at once set out for the Hôtel de Nesle, promising to abide by his instructions.

The supper was served, — but before they took their places at the table Cellini asked his host if he did not know some honest and skilful notary whom he could send for to prepare a contract that could not be assailed. He recommended his son in law, who was immediately summoned.

He arrived as they were finishing their supper, some half-hour later. Benvenuto at once left the table, closeted himself with him, and bade him draw up a marriage contract leaving the names in blank. When they had read and re-read the contract, as drawn up, to make sure that there was no flaw in it, Benvenuto paid him handsomely, put the contract in his pocket, borrowed from his friend a second sword of just the length of his own, put it under his cloak, and, as it had become quite dark, started for the Hôtel de Nesle.

When he reached his destination, he knocked once; but though he knocked very gently, the door immediately opened. Little Jehan was at his post.

Cellini questioned him: the workmen were at supper and did not expect him until the morrow. He bade the child maintain the most absolute silence as to his arrival, then crept up to Catherine's room, to which he had retained a key, entered softly, closed the door, concealed himself behind the hangings, and waited.

After a short time, he heard a light footstep on the staircase. The door opened a second time, and Scozzone entered, lamp in hand; she took the key from the outside, locked the door, placed the lamp on the chimney-

piece, and sat down in a large arm-chair, so placed that
Benvenuto could see her face.

To his vast astonishment, that face, formerly so open
and joyous and animated, was sad and thoughtful. The
fact was that poor Scozzone was in the throes of something very like remorse.

We have seen her when she was happy and thought-
less: then Benvenuto loved her. So long as she was
conscious of that love, or rather of that kindly feeling in
her lover's heart, so long as the hope of becoming the
sculptor's wife some day was present like a golden cloud
in all her dreams, so long she maintained herself at the
level of her anticipations, and made atonement for her
past by her love. But as soon as she discovered that
she had been deceived by appearances, and that what she
had mistaken for passion on Cellini's part was at most a
mere whim, she descended the ladder of hope round by
round. Benvenuto's smile, which had made that faded
heart blossom anew, was taken from her, and the heart
lost its freshness once more.

With her childish light-heartedness her childish purity had gradually vanished; her old nature, powerfully
assisted by ennui, gently recovered the upper hand.
A newly painted wall keeps its colors in the sun and
loses them in the rain: Scozzone, abandoned by Cellini
for some unknown mistress, was no longer held to him
save by a remnant of her pride. Pagolo had long paid
court to her: she spoke to Cellini of his love, thinking
that his jealousy would be aroused. Her expectation
was not realized: Cellini, instead of losing his temper,
began to laugh, and, instead of forbidding her to see
Pagolo, actually ordered her to receive him. Thereafter
she felt that she was entirely lost; thereafter she abandoned her life to chance with her former indifference,

and let it blow about in the wind of circumstances like a poor, fallen withered leaf.

Then it was that Pagolo triumphed over her indifference. After all was said, Pagolo was young; Pagolo, aside from his hypocritical expression, was a handsome youth; Pagolo was in love, and was forever repeating to her that he loved her, while Benvenuto had long since ceased to tell her so. The words, " I love you," are the language of the heart, and the heart always feels the need of speaking that language more or less ardently with some one.

Thus, in a moment of idleness, of anger, perhaps of illusion, Scozzone had told Pagolo that she loved him; she had told him so without really loving him; she had told him so with Cellini's image in her heart and his name upon her lips.

Then it immediately occurred to her that the day might come when Cellini, weary of his mysterious, unavailing passion, would return to her, and, if he found her constant, notwithstanding his express orders, would reward her devotion, not by marriage, for the poor girl had lost her last illusion in that regard, but by some remnant of esteem and compassion which she might take for a resurrection of his former love.

It was such thoughts as these which made Scozzone sad and thoughtful, and caused her to feel remorse.

In the midst of her silent reverie, she started and raised her head. She heard a light step on the stairway, and the next moment a key was rapidly turned in the lock, and the door opened.

" How did you come in? Who gave you that key, Pagolo? " she cried, rising from her chair. " There are only two keys to that door, — one is in my possession and the other in Cellini's."

" Ah! my dear Catherine," laughed Pagolo, "you 're a capricious creature: sometimes you open your door to a fellow, and again you keep it closed; and when one attempts to enter by force, even though you have given him a right to do it, you threaten to call for help. So you see I had to resort to stratagem."

" Oh yes! tell me that you stole the key from Cellini, without his knowledge; tell me that he does n't know you have it, for if he gave it to you I should die of shame and chagrin."

" Set your mind at rest, my lovely Catherine," said Pagolo, locking the door, and sitting down near the girl, whom he forced to a seat beside him. " No, Benvenuto does n't love you, it is true: but he 's like those misers who have a treasure of which they make no use themselves, but which they won't allow anybody else to touch. No, I made the key myself. He who can do great things can do small things. Tell me if I love you, Catherine, when my hands, which are accustomed to making pearls and diamonds bloom on golden stalks, consented to shape an ignoble piece of iron. It is true, wicked one, that the ignoble piece of iron was a key, and that the key unlocked the door of paradise."

With that, Pagolo would have taken Catherine's hand, but, to the vast amazement of Cellini, who did not lose a word or a gesture of this scene, Catherine repulsed him.

" Well, well," said Pagolo, " is this whim likely to last long, pray ? "

" Look you, Pagolo," said Catherine, in a melancholy tone, which went to Cellini's heart; " I know that when a woman has once yielded she has no right to draw back afterward; but if the man for whom she has been so weak has a generous heart, — when she says to him that she was acting in good faith at the time, because she had lost her reason, but that she was mistaken, — it is that man's duty, believe me, not to take an unfair advantage of her momentary error. Well, Pagolo, I tell you this: I yielded to you, and yet I did not love you; I loved another, and that other Cellini. Despise me you may, — indeed you ought, — but torment me no more, Pagolo."

"Good!" exclaimed Pagolo, "good! you arrange the matter marvellously well, upon my word! After the time you compelled me to wait for the favor with which you now reproach me, you think that I will release you from a definite engagement which you entered into of your own free will? No, no! And when I think that you are doing all this for Benvenuto, for a man who is twice your age or mine, for a man who does n't love you, for a man who despises you, for a man who treats you as a courtesan!"

"Stop, Pagolo, stop!" cried Scozzone, blushing with shame and jealousy and rage. "Benvenuto does n't love me any more, that is true; but he did love me once, and he esteems me still."

"Very good! Why does n't he marry you, as he promised to do?"

"Promised? Never. No, Benvenuto never promised to make me his wife; for if he had promised, he would have done it. I aspired to mount so high as that: the aspiration led me to hope that it might be so; and when the hope had once taken shape in my heart, I could not confine it there, it overflowed, and I boasted of a mere hope as if it were a reality. No, Pagolo, no," continued Catherine, letting her hand fall into the apprentice's with a sad smile, — "no, Benvenuto never promised me aught."

"Then, see how ungrateful you are, Scozzone!" cried Pagolo, seizing her hand, and mistaking what was simply a mark of dejection for a return to him; "you repulse me, who have promised you and offered you all that Benvenuto, by your own admission, never promised or offered you, while I am convinced that if he were standing there — he who betrayed you — you would freely make to him the confession you so bitterly regret having made to me, who love you so dearly."

"Oh if he were here!" cried Scozzone, "if he were here, Pagolo, you would remember that you betrayed him through hatred, while I betrayed him because I loved him, and you would sink into the ground!"

"Why so?" demanded Pagolo, bold as a lion because he believed Benvenuto to be far away; "why so, if you please? Hasn't every man the right to win a woman's love when that woman doesn't belong to another? If he were here, I would say to him: 'You abandoned Catherine, — poor Catherine, who loved you so well. She was in despair at first, until she fell in with a kind-hearted, worthy fellow, who appreciated her at her true worth, who loved her, and who promised her what you would never promise her, — to make her his wife. He has inherited your rights, and that woman belongs to him.' Tell me, Catherine, what reply your Cellini could make to that?"

"None at all," said a stern, manly voice behind the enthusiastic Pagolo, — "absolutely none at all."

At the same instant a powerful hand fell upon his shoulder, nipped his eloquence in the bud, and threw him to the floor, as pale and terrified as he had been boastful and rash a moment before.

It was a strange picture: Pagolo on his knees, bent double, with colorless cheeks, and deadly terror depicted on his features; Scozzone, half risen from her chair, motionless and dumfounded, like a statue of Astonishment; and lastly, Benvenuto standing with folded arms, a sword in its sheath in one hand, a naked sword in the other, with an expression in which irony and menace struggled for the mastery.

There was a moment of awful silence, Pagolo and Scozzone being equally abashed beneath the master's frown.

"Treachery!" muttered Pagolo, "treachery!"

"Yes, treachery on your part, wretch!" retorted Cellini.

"You asked to see him, Pagolo," said Scozzone; "here he is."

"Yes, here he is," said the apprentice, ashamed to be thus treated before the woman he was so anxious to please; "but he is armed, and I have no weapon."

"I have brought you one," said Cellini, stepping back, and throwing down the sword he held in his left hand at Pagolo's feet.

Pagolo looked at the sword, but made no movement.

"Come," said Cellini, "pick up the sword and stand up yourself. I am waiting."

"A duel?" muttered the apprentice, whose teeth were chattering with terror; "am I able to fight a duel on equal terms with you?"

"Very well," said Cellini, passing his weapon from one hand to the other, "I will fight with my left hand, and that will make us equal."

"I fight with you, my benefactor?—you, to whom I owe everything? Never! never!"

A smile of profound contempt overspread Benvenuto's face, while Scozzone recoiled without seeking to conceal the disgust which showed itself in her expression.

"You should have remembered my benefactions before stealing from me the woman I intrusted to your honor and Ascanio's," said Benvenuto. "Your memory has come back to you too late. On guard, Pagolo! on guard!"

"No! no!" murmured the coward, falling back upon his knees.

"As you refuse to fight like an honest man," said Benvenuto, "I propose to punish you as a scoundrel."

He replaced his sword in its sheath, drew his dagger, and walked slowly toward the apprentice without the slightest indication either of anger or compassion upon his impassive features.

Scozzone rushed between them with a shriek; but Benvenuto, without violence, with a motion of his arm as irresistible as that of a bronze statue endowed with life, put her aside, and the poor girl fell back half dead upon her chair. Benvenuto walked on toward Pagolo, who receded as far as the wall. There the master overtook him, and said, putting his dagger to his throat, —

"Commend your soul to God: you have five minutes to live."

"Mercy!" cried Pagolo in an inarticulate voice; "do not kill me! mercy! mercy!"

"What!" said Cellini, "you know me, and, knowing me, seduced the woman who belonged to me. I know all, I have discovered everything, and you hope that I will spare you! You are laughing at me, Pagolo, you are laughing at me."

Benvenuto himself laughed aloud as he spoke; but it was a strident, terrible laugh, which made the apprentice shudder to his marrow.

"Master! master!" cried Pagolo, as he felt the point

of the dagger pricking his throat; "it was she, not I: yes, she led me into it."

"Treachery, cowardice, and slander! I will make a group of those three monsters some day," said Benvenuto, "and it will be a hideous thing to see. She led you into it, you reptile! Do you forget that I was here and heard all that you said?"

"O Benvenuto," murmured Catherine, "you know that he lies when he says that, do you not?"

"Yes, yes," said Benvenuto, "I know that he lies when he says that, as he lied when he said that he was ready to marry you; but never fear, he shall be punished for the double lie."

"Yes, punish me," cried Pagolo, "but be merciful: punish me, but do not kill me."

"You lied when you said that she led you into it?"

"Yes, I lied; yes, I am the guilty one. I loved her madly; and you know, master, what love will lead a man to do."

"You lied when you said that you were ready to marry her?"

"No, no, master; then I didn't lie."

"So you really love Scozzone?"

"Oh, yes, indeed I love her!" replied Pagolo, realizing that the only way of lessening his guilt in Cellini's eyes was to attribute his crime to the violence of his passion; "yes, I love her."

"And you say again that you were not lying when you proposed to marry her?"

"I was not lying, master."

"You would have made her your wife?"

"If she had not belonged to you, yes."

"Very well, then, take her: I give her to you."

"What do you say? You are joking, are you not?"

"No, I never spoke more seriously: look at me if you doubt it."

Pagolo glanced furtively at Cellini, and saw plainly in his face that the judge might at any moment give place to the executioner; he bowed his head, therefore, with a groan.

"Take that ring from your finger, Pagolo, and put it on Catherine's."

Pagolo passively obeyed the first portion of the order, and Benvenuto motioned to Scozzone to draw near. She obeyed.

"Put out your hand, Scozzone," continued Benvenuto.

Again she obeyed.

"Now do the rest."

Pagolo placed the ring upon Scozzone's finger.

"Now," said Benvenuto, "that the betrothal is duly accomplished, we will pass to the marriage."

"Marriage!" muttered Pagolo; "we can't be married in this way; we must have notaries and a priest."

"We must have a contract," rejoined Benvenuto, producing the one prepared under his orders. "Here is one all ready, in which the names only need to be inserted."

He placed the contract upon a table, took up a pen and handed it to Pagolo.

"Sign, Pagolo," said he, "sign."

"Ah! I have fallen into a trap," muttered the apprentice.

"Eh? what's that?" exclaimed Benvenuto, without raising his voice, but imparting to it an ominous accent. "A trap? Where is the trap in this? Did I urge you to come to Scozzone's room? Did I advise you to tell her that you wished to make her your wife? Very good! make her your wife, Pagolo, and when you are

her husband our *rôles* will be changed; if I come to her
room, it will be your turn to threaten, and mine to be
afraid."

"Oh, that would be too absurd!" cried Catherine,
passing from extreme terror to hysterical gayety, and
laughing aloud at the idea which the master's words
evoked.

Somewhat reassured by the turn Cellini's threats had
taken, and by Catherine's peals of laughter, Pagolo
began to look at matters a little more reasonably. It
became plain to him that Cellini wished to frighten him
into a marriage for which he felt but little inclination:
he considered, therefore, that that would be rather too
tragic a termination of the comedy, and that he might
perhaps, with a little resolution, make a better bargain.

"Yes," he muttered, translating Scozzone's gayety
into words, "yes, it would be very amusing, I agree,
but unfortunately it cannot be."

"What! it cannot be!" cried Benvenuto, as amazed
as a lion might be to find a fox demurring to his
will.

"No, it cannot be," Pagolo repeated; "I prefer to die:
kill me!"

The words were hardly out of his mouth when Cellini
was upon him. Pagolo saw the dagger gleaming in the
air, and threw himself to one side, so swiftly and successfully that the blow which was intended for him
simply grazed his shoulder, and the blade, impelled by
the goldsmith's powerful hand, penetrated the wainscoting to the depth of several inches.

"I consent," cried Pagolo. "Mercy! Cellini, I consent; I am ready to do anything." And while the
master was withdrawing the dagger, which had come in
contact with the wall behind the wainscoting, he ran to

the table where the contract lay, seized the pen, and wrote his name. The whole affair had taken place so rapidly that Scozzone had no time to take part in it.

"Thanks, Pagolo," said she, wiping away the tears which terror had brought to her eyes, and at the same time repressing an inclination to smile; "thanks, dear Pagolo, for the honor you consent to confer upon me; but it's better that we should understand each other thoroughly now, so listen to me. Just now you would have none of me, and now I will have none of you. I don't say this to mortify you, Pagolo, but I do not love you, and I desire to remain as I am."

"In that case," said Benvenuto, with the utmost coolness, "if you won't have him, Scozzone, he must die."

"Why," cried Catherine, "it is I who refuse him."

"He must die," rejoined Benvenuto; "it shall not be said that a man insulted me, and went unpunished. Are you ready, Pagolo?"

"Catherine," cried the apprentice, "Catherine, in Heaven's name take pity on me! Catherine, I love you! Catherine, I will love you always! Sign, Catherine! Catherine be my wife, I beg you on my knees!"

"Come, Scozzone, decide quickly," said Cellini.

"Oh!" said Catherine, pouting, "tell me, master, don't you think you are rather hard on me, who have loved you so dearly, and who have dreamed of something so different? But," cried the fickle child, passing suddenly from melancholy to merriment once more, "Mon Dieu! Cellini, see what a piteous face poor Pagolo is making! Oh, for Heaven's sake, put aside that lugubrious expression, Pagolo, or I will never consent to take you for my husband! Really, you are too absurd!"

"Save me first, Catherine," said Pagolo; "then we will laugh, if you choose."

"Oh well! my poor boy, if you really and truly wish it—"

"Yes, indeed I do!"

"You know what I have been, you know what I am?"

"Yes, I know"

"You are not deceived in me?"

"No."

"You will not regret it?"

"No! no!"

"Then give me your hand. It's very ridiculous, and I hardly expected it; but, no matter, I am your wife."

She took the pen and signed, as a dutiful wife should do, below her husband's signature.

"Thanks, Catherine, thanks!" cried Pagolo; "you will see how happy I will make you."

"If he is false to that promise," said Benvenuto, "write to me, Scozzone, and wherever I may be I will come in person to remind him of it."

As he spoke, Cellini slowly pushed his dagger back into its sheath, keeping his eyes fixed upon the apprentice; then he took the contract, folded it neatly, and put it in his pocket, and said to Pagolo, with the withering sarcasm which was characteristic of him: —

"Now, friend Pagolo, although you and Scozzone are duly married according to the laws of men, you are not in God's sight, and the Church will not sanctify your union until to-morrow. Until then your presence here would be in contravention of all laws, divine and human. Good night, Pagolo."

Pagolo turned pale as death; but as Benvenuto

pointed imperatively to the door, he backed out of the room.

"No one but you, Cellini, would ever have had such an idea as that," said Catherine, laughing as if she would die. "Hark ye, my poor Pagolo," she said, as he opened the door, "I let you go because the law requires it; but never fear, Pagolo, I swear by the Blessed Virgin, that when you are my husband no man, not even Benvenuto himself, will find me anything but a virtuous wife.

"O Cellini!" she added, gayly, when the door was closed, "you give me a husband, but relieve me of his presence for to-day. It is so much time gained: you owed me this reparation."

XXI.

RESUMPTION OF HOSTILITIES.

THREE days after the scene we have described, a scene of quite another sort was in preparation at the Louvre.

Monday, the day appointed for signing the contract, had arrived. It was eleven o'clock in the morning when Benvenuto left the Hôtel de Nesle, went straight to the Louvre, and with anxious heart but firm step ascended the grand staircase.

In the reception-room, into which he was first ushered, he found the provost and D'Orbec, who were conferring with a notary in the corner. Colombe, pale and motionless as a statue, was seated on the other side of the room, staring into vacancy. They had evidently moved away from her so that she could not hear, and the poor child had remained where they placed her.

Cellini passed in front of her, and let these words fall upon her bowed head: —

"Have courage: I am here."

Colombe recognized his voice, and raised her head with a cry of joy; but before she had time to question her protector, he had already entered the adjoining room.

An usher drew aside a tapestry portière, and the goldsmith passed into the king's cabinet.

Nothing less than these words of cheer would have availed to revive Colombe's courage: the poor child be-

lieved that she was abandoned, and consequently lost.
Messire d'Estourville had dragged her thither, half dead,
despite her faith in God and in Benvenuto. As they
were setting out, she was conscious of such a feeling
of despair at her heart, that she implored Madame
d'Etampes to allow her to enter a convent, promising
to renounce Ascanio provided that she might be spared
Comte d'Orbec. But the duchess wanted no half victory; in order that her purpose might be attained, it
was essential that Ascanio should believe in the treachery of his beloved, and so she sternly refused to listen
to poor Colombe's prayers. Thereupon, Colombe summoned all her courage, remembering that Benvenuto
bade her be strong and brave, even at the altar's foot,
and with occasional sinkings of the heart allowed herself
to be taken to the Louvre, where the king was to sign
the contract at noon.

There again her strength failed her for a moment; for
but three chances now remained, to touch the king's
heart with her prayers, to see Benvenuto arrive, or to
die of grief.

Benvenuto had come; Benvenuto had told her to hope,
and Colombe's courage revived once more.

On entering the king's cabinet, Cellini found Madame
d'Etampes alone: it was all that he desired; he would
have solicited the honor of seeing her had she not been
there.

The duchess was thoughtful in her hour of triumph,
and yet, with the fatal letter burned — burned by herself — she was fully convinced that she had nothing to
fear. But although she was reassured as to her power,
she contemplated with dismay the perils that threatened
her love. It was always thus with the duchess: when
the anxiety attendant upon her ambition was at rest,

the ardent passions of her heart devoured her. Her dream, in which pride and passion were mingled, was to make Ascanio great while making him happy. But she knew now that Ascanio, although of noble origin, (for the Gaddis, to which family he belonged, were patricians of long standing at Florence,) aspired to no other glory than that of being a great artist.

If his hopes were ever fixed upon anything, it was some beautifully shaped vase, or ewer, or statue; if he ever longed for diamonds or pearls, it was so that he might make of them, by setting them in chased gold, lovelier flowers than those which heaven waters with its dew. Titles and honors were nothing to him if they did not flow from his own talent, and were not the guerdon of his personal renown; what part could such a useless dreamer play in the active, agitated life of the duchess? In the first storm the delicate plant would be destroyed, with the flowers which it already bore and the fruit of which it gave promise. It might be that he would allow himself to be drawn into the schemes of his royal mistress through discouragement or through indifference; but in that case, a pale and melancholy shadow, he would live only in his memories of the past. Ascanio, in fine, appeared to the Duchesse d'Etampes, as he really was, an exquisite, fascinating personality, so long as he remained in a pure, untroubled atmosphere; he was an adorable child, who would never become a man. He could devote himself to sentiments, but never to ideas; born to enjoy the outpourings of a mutual affection, he would inevitably go down in the first terrific onset of the struggle for supremacy and power. He was the man needed to satisfy Madame d'Etampes's passion, but not to keep pace with her in her ambitious schemes.

Such was the tenor of her reflections when Benvenuto entered: the clouds of her thought hovering about her darkened her brow.

The two adversaries eyed each other narrowly: the same satirical smile appeared upon their lips at the same time; the glances they exchanged were twin brothers, and indicated that they were equally prepared for the struggle, and that the struggle would be a desperate one.

"Well and good! he is a rough fighter," thought Anne, "whom it will be a pleasure to overcome, a foeman worthy of my steel. But to-day there are, in truth, too many chances against him, and there will be no great glory in overthrowing him."

"Beyond question, Madame d'Etampes," said Benvenuto to himself, "you are a masterful woman, and more than one contest with a strong man has given me less trouble than this I have entered upon with you. You may be sure, therefore, that, while fighting courteously, I shall none the less fight with all the weapons at my disposal."

There was a moment's silence while the combatants delivered themselves of these brief monologues aside. The duchess was the first to break the silence.

"You are punctual, Master Cellini," said she. "His Majesty is to sign Comte d'Orbec's contract at noon, and it is now only a quarter past eleven. Permit me to make his Majesty's excuses: he is not behindhand, but you are beforehand."

"I am very happy, madame, that I arrived too early, as my impatience procures me the honor of a *tête-à-tête* with you, — an honor I should have requested most urgently, had not chance, to which I return my thanks, anticipated my wishes."

"Good lack, Benvenuto!" said the duchess; "does defeat incline you to flattery?"

"Not my own defeat, madame, but that of other persons. I have always considered it peculiarly meritorious to pay my court to one in disgrace; and here is the proof of it, madame."

As he spoke, Benvenuto drew from beneath his cloak Ascanio's golden lily, which he had completed that morning. The duchess exclaimed with wonder and delight. Never had her eyes beheld such a marvellous jewel, never did one of the flowers found in the enchanted gardens of the "Thousand and One Nights" so dazzle the eyes of peri or fairy.

"Ah!" cried the duchess, putting forth her hand to take the flower, "you promised me, Benvenuto, but I confess that I did not rely upon your promise."

"Why should you not rely upon it, madame?" laughed Benvenuto. "You insult me."

"Oh! if you had promised to perform a revengeful, instead of a gallant act, I should have been much more certain that you would redeem your promise punctually."

"Who told you that I did not promise both?" retorted Benvenuto, drawing back his hand, so that the lily was still in his control.

"I do not understand you," said the duchess.

"Do you not think," said Benvenuto, pointing to the diamond shimmering in the heart of the flower — the diamond which she owed to the corrupting munificence of Charles V. — "that when mounted in the guise of a dewdrop, the earnest given to bind a certain bargain which is to set off the Duchy of Milan from France has a fine effect?"

"You speak in enigmas, my dear goldsmith; unfortu-

nately the king will soon be here, and I have n't time to
guess them."

"I will tell you the answer, then.   It is an old proverb, *Verba volant, scripta manent*, which, being in-
terpreted, means, 'What is written is written.'"

"Ah! that's where you are in error, my dear goldsmith; what is written is burned: so do not think to
frighten me as you would a child, and give me the lily
which belongs to me."

"One instant, madame; I ought to warn you that
while it is a magic talisman in my hands, it will lose
all its virtue in yours.   My work is even more valuable
than you think.   Where the multitude sees only a
jewel, we artists sometimes conceal an idea.   Do you
wish me to show you this idea, madame?   Nothing is
easier: look, all that is necessary is to press this invisible spring.   The stalk opens, as you see, and in the
heart of the flower we find, not a gnawing worm, as in
some natural flowers and some false hearts, but something similar, worse it may be, — the dishonor of the
Duchesse d'Etampes, written with her own hand and
signed by her."

As he spoke, Benvenuto pressed the spring, opened
the stalk, and took out the letter.   He slowly unfolded
it, and showed it, open, to the duchess, pale with wrath,
and stricken dumb with dismay.

"You hardly expected this, did you, madame?" said
Benvenuto, coolly, folding the letter once more, and
replacing it in the lily.   "If you knew my ways,
madame, you would be less surprised.   A year ago I
concealed a ladder in a statuette; a month ago I concealed a maiden in a statue.   What was there that I could
hide away in a flower to-day?   A bit of paper, that was
all, and that is what I have done."

"But that letter," cried the duchess, "that infernal letter I burned with my own hands: I saw the flame and touched the ashes!"

"Did you read the letter you burned?"

"No! no! madwoman that I was, I did not read it!"

"That is too bad, for you would be convinced now that the letter of a grisette will make as much flame and ashes as the letter of a duchess."

"Why, then, Ascanio, the dastard, deceived me!"

"Oh madame! pray pause! Do not suspect that pure and innocent child, who, even if he had deceived you, would have done no more than turn against you the weapons you used against him. Oh no, no! he did not deceive you; he would not purchase his own life or Colombe's by deceit! No, he was himself deceived."

"By whom? Pray tell me that."

"By a mere boy, a student, the same who wounded your trusty retainer, Vicomte de Marmagne; by one Jacques Aubry, in short, whom it is likely that the Vicomte de Marmagne has mentioned to you."

"Yes," murmured the duchess, "yes, Marmagne did tell me that this student, this Jacques Aubry, was seeking to gain access to Ascanio in order to secure that letter."

"And it was after that that you paid Ascanio a visit. But students are active, you know, and ours had already anticipated you. As you left the Hôtel d'Etampes, he was creeping into his friend's cell, and as you entered it, he went out."

"But I didn't see him; I saw nobody."

"One doesn't think to look everywhere; if you had done so, you would, in due course, have raised a certain mat, and under that mat would have found a hole communicating with the adjoining cell."

" But Ascanio, Ascanio ? "

" When you entered he was asleep, was he not ? "

" Yes."

" Very good! during his sleep, Aubry, to whom he had refused to give the letter, took it from his coat pocket, and put a letter of his own in its place. You were misled by the envelope, and thought that you were burning a note from Madame la Duchesse d'Etampes. Not so, madame; you burned an epistle penned by Mademoiselle Gervaise-Perrette Popinot."

" But this Aubry, who wounded Marmagne, this clown, who almost murdered a nobleman, will pay dear for his insolence; he is in prison and condemned to death."

" He is free, madame, and owes his freedom in great measure to you."

" How so ? "

" Why, who but he was the poor prisoner whose pardon you joined me in urging upon King François ? "

" Oh insane fool that I was! " muttered the duchess, biting her lips till the blood ran. She looked Benvenuto squarely in the eye for a moment, then continued, in a panting voice, —

" On what condition will you give me that letter ? "

" I think I have allowed you to guess, madame."

" I am not skilled in guessing: tell me."

" You must ask the king to bestow Colombe's hand upon Ascanio."

" Go to! " rejoined Anne with a forced laugh; " you little know the Duchesse d'Etampes, Master Goldsmith, if you fancy that my love will yield to threats."

" You did not reflect before answering me, madame."

" I stand by my answer, however."

" Kindly permit me to sit down unceremoniously,

madame, and to talk plainly with you a moment," said Benvenuto, with the dignified familiarity peculiar to superior men. "I am only an humble sculptor, and you are a great duchess; but let me tell you that, notwithstanding the distance which separates us, we were made to understand each other. Do not assume those queenly airs: they will have no effect. It is not my purpose to insult you, but to enlighten you, and your haughty manner is out of place because your pride is not at stake."

"You are a strange man, upon my word," said Anne, laughing in spite of herself. "Say on, I am listening."

"I was saying, Madame la Duchesse," continued Benvenuto, coolly, "that, despite the difference in our fortunes, our positions are almost the same, and that we could understand each other, and perhaps mutually assist each other. You cried out when I suggested that you should renounce Ascanio; it seemed to you impossible and mad, and yet I had set you an example, madame."

"An example?"

"Yes, as you love Ascanio, I loved Colombe."

"You?"

"I. I loved her as I had never loved but once. I would have given my blood, my life, my soul for her, and yet I gave her to Ascanio."

"Truly a most unselfish passion," sneered the duchess.

"Oh! do not make my suffering matter for raillery, madame; do not mock at my agony. I have suffered keenly; but I realized that the child was no more made for me than Ascanio for you. Listen, madame: we are both, if I may be pardoned for the comparison, of those exceptional and uncommon natures which lead an existence of their own, have feelings and emotions peculiar to themselves, and rarely find themselves in accord with others. We both obey, madame, a sovereign idol, the worship of which has expanded our hearts and placed us higher than mankind. To you, madame, ambition is all in all; to me, art. Now our divinities are jealous, and exert their sway always and everywhere. You desired Ascanio as a crown, I desired Colombe as a Galatea. You loved as a duchess, I as an artist. You have persecuted, I have suffered. Oh! do not think that I wrong you in my thoughts; I admire your energy, and sympathize with your audacity. Let the vulgar think what they will: from your point of view it is a great thing to turn the world upside down in order to make a place for the person one loves. I recognize therein a strong and masterful passion, and I admire characters capable of such heroic crimes; but I also admire superhuman characters, for everything which eludes foresight, everything outside the beaten paths, has an attraction for me. Even while I loved Colombe, madame, I considered that my domineering, unruly nature would be ill mated with that pure angelic soul. Colombe loved Ascanio, my harmless, sweet-natured pupil; my rough, vigorous temperament would have frightened her. Thereupon, in a loud, imperative tone, I bade my love hold its peace, and as it remonstrated I called to my assistance my art divine, and by our united efforts we floored the rebellious passion and held it down. Then Sculpture, my true, my only mistress, touched my brow with her burning lips, and I was comforted. Do as I have done, Madame la Duchesse, leave these children to their angel loves and do not disturb them in their heaven. Our domain is earth, with its sorrows, its conflicts, and its intoxicating triumphs. Seek a refuge against suffering in ambition;

unmake empires to distract your thoughts; play with the kings and masters of the world to amuse yourself. That would be well done, and I would applaud your efforts. But do not wreck the peace and happiness of these poor innocents, who love each other with such a pure, sweet love, before the face of God and the Virgin Mary."

" Who are you, Master Benvenuto Cellini? I do not know you," said the duchess in blank amazement. " Who are you?"

" Vrai Dieu! a man among men, as you are a woman among women," rejoined the goldsmith, laughing with his customary frankness; "and if you do not know me, you see that I have a great advantage over you, for I do know you, madame."

" It may be so," said the duchess, "but it is my opinion that a woman among women loves better and more earnestly than a man among men, for she snaps her fingers at your superhuman abnegation, and defends her lover with beak and claws to the last gasp."

" You persist, then, in refusing to give Ascanio to Colombe?"

" I persist in loving him myself."

" So be it. But if you will not yield with good grace, beware! I am somewhat rough when I am roused, and may make you cry out a little in the *mêlée*. You have reflected fully, have you not? You refuse once for all your consent to the union of Ascanio and Colombe."

" Most emphatically, yes."

" Very good! to our posts!" cried Benvenuto, "for the battle is on."

At that moment the door opened and an usher announced the king.

XXII.

A LOVE MATCH.

FRANÇOIS appeared on the threshold, giving his hand to Diane de Poitiers, with whom he had come from the bedside of his sick son.   Diane, inspired by her hatred, had a vague feeling that her rival was threatened with humiliation, and did not choose to miss the gratifying spectacle.

As for the king, he saw nothing, suspected nothing; he believed Madame d'Etampes and Benvenuto to be entirely reconciled, and as he saw them talking together when he entered, he saluted them both at once, with the same smile, and the same inclination of the head.

"Good morrow, my queen of beauty; good morrow, my king of artists," he said; "what are you talking about so confidentially?   You seem both to be deeply interested."

"Mon Dieu! Sire, we are talking politics," said Benvenuto.

"And what particular subject exercises your faculties? Tell me, I beg."

"The question which engrosses everybody at present, Sire," continued the goldsmith.

"Ah! the Duchy of Milan."

"Yes, Sire."

"Well, what were you saying of it?"

"We do not agree, Sire; one of us maintains that the Emperor might well refuse to give you the Duchy of

Milan, and yet redeem his promise by giving it to your
son Charles."

"Which of you makes that suggestion?"

"I think that it was Madame d'Etampes, Sire."

The duchess became pale as death.

"If the Emperor should do that, it would be infamous
treachery," said François; "but he'll not do it."

"In any event, even if he does not do it," said
Diane, joining in the conversation, "it will not be, I
am assured, for lack of advice given him to that effect."

"Given by whom?" cried the king. "By Mahomet's
belly! I would be glad to know by whom?"

"Bon Dieu! do not be so disturbed, Sire," rejoined
Benvenuto; "we said that as we said other things, —
simple conjectures, put forward by us in desultory talk.
Madame la Duchesse and I are but bungling politicians,
Sire. Madame la Duchesse is too much of a woman to
think of aught beside her toilet, although she has no
need to think of that; and I, Sire, am too much of an
artist to think of aught beside art. Is it not so,
Madame la Duchesse?"

"The truth is, my dear Cellini," said François, "that
each of you has too glorious a part to play to envy
others aught that they may have, even though it were
the Duchy of Milan. Madame la Duchesse d'Etampes
is queen by virtue of her beauty, and you are king by
virtue of your talent."

"King, Sire?"

"Yes, king; and although you haven't, as I have,
three lilies in your crest, you have one in your hand,
which seems to me to be lovelier than any that ever
blossomed in the brightest sunlight or upon the fairest
field in all heraldry."

"This lily is not mine, Sire; it belongs to Madame

d'Etampes, who commissioned my pupil Ascanio to make it; but as he could not finish it, and as I realized Madame d'Etampes's desire to have so rich a jewel in her possession, I set to work myself and finished it, wishing with all my heart to make it the symbol of the treaty of peace which we ratified the other day in your Majesty's presence."

"It is marvellously beautiful," said the king, putting out his hand to take it.

"Is it not, sire?" rejoined Benvenuto, withdrawing it as if without design, "and the young artist, whose *chef-d'œuvre* it is, certainly deserves to be magnificently rewarded."

"Such is my purpose," interposed the duchess; "I have in store for him a recompense which a king might envy him."

"But you know, madame, that the recompense to which you refer, splendid as it is, is not that upon which his heart is fixed. What would you have, madame? We artists are whimsical creatures, and often the thing which would, as you say, arouse a king's envy, is viewed by us with disdainful eye."

"Nevertheless," said Madame d'Etampes, as an angry flush overspread her face, "he must be content with what I have set apart for him; for I have already told you, Benvenuto, that I would accord him no other save at the last extremity."

"Very well, you may confide to me what his wishes are," said François to Benvenuto, once more putting out his hand for the lily, "and if it's not too difficult a matter, we will try to arrange it."

"Observe the jewel carefully, Sire," said Benvenuto, placing the stalk of the flower in the king's hand; "examine it in detail, and your Majesty will see that any compensation whatsoever must fall short of the value of such a masterpiece."

As he spoke, Benvenuto darted a keen glance at the duchess; but her self-control was so perfect, that not a muscle of her face moved as she saw the lily pass from the artist's hand to the king's.

"'T is really miraculous," said the king. "But where did you find this superb diamond which glistens in the heart of the flower?"

"I did not find it, Sire," replied Cellini, with charming affability; "Madame d'Etampes furnished it to my pupil."

"I was not aware that you owned this diamond, madame; whence came it to your hands, pray?"

"Why, probably from the place where most diamonds come from, Sire; from the mines of Guzarate or Golconda."

"There is a long story connected with that diamond, Sire, and if your Majesty cares to hear it, I will tell it you. The diamond and I are old acquaintances, for this is the third time it has passed through my hands. In the first place, I set it in the tiara of our Holy Father, the Pope, where its effect was marvellous; then, by order of Clement VII., I mounted it upon a missal which his Holiness presented to the Emperor Charles V.; and as the Emperor desired to carry it constantly about him, as a resource doubtless in an emergency, I set the diamond, which is worth more than a million, in a ring, Sire. Did not your Majesty observe it on the hand of your cousin, the Emperor?"

"Yes, I remember," cried the king; "yes, on the day of our first interview he had it on his finger. How comes the diamond in your possession, duchess?"

"Yes, tell us," cried Diane, whose eyes shone with

joy, " how came it about that a diamond of that value passed from the Emperor's hands to yours ? "

" If the question were put to you, madame," retorted Madame d'Etampes, " the answer would not be far to seek, assuming that you confess certain matters to any other than your confessor."

" You do not answer the king's question, madame," rejoined Diane.

" Yes," said François, " how comes the diamond in your possession ? "

" Ask Benvenuto," said Madame d'Etampes, hurling a last defiance at her enemy; " Benvenuto will tell you."

" Tell me, then," said the king, " and instantly: I am weary of waiting."

" Very good, Sire," said Benvenuto; " I must confess to your Majesty that at sight of this diamond strange suspicions awoke in my mind, as in yours. It was while Madame d'Etampes and myself were at enmity, you must know, and I should not have been sorry to learn some little secret which might injure her in your Majesty's eyes. So I followed the scent, and I learned — "

" You learned ? "

Benvenuto glanced hastily at the duchess, and saw that she was smiling. The power of resistance which she manifested pleased him, and, instead of putting an end to the struggle brutally with one stroke, he resolved to prolong it, like an athlete, sure of victory in the end, who, having fallen in with an antagonist worthy of him, resolves to display all his strength and all his skill.

" You learned — " the king repeated.

" I learned that she purchased it of Manasseh, the Jew. Yes, Sire, know this and govern yourself accordingly: it seems that since he entered France your cousin, the Emperor, has scattered so much money along the road, that he is reduced to putting his diamonds in pawn; and Madame d'Etampes, with royal magnificence, gathers in what the imperial poverty cannot retain."

"Ah! by my honor as a gentleman, 't is most diverting!" cried François, doubly flattered in his vanity as lover, and in his jealousy as king. "But, fair lady," he added, addressing the duchess, "methinks you must have ruined yourself in order to make such an acquisition, and it is for us to repair the disordered state of your finances. Remember that we are your debtor to the value of the diamond, for it is so magnificent that I am determined that it shall come to you from a king's hand at least, if not from an emperor's."

"Thanks, Benvenuto," said the duchess in an undertone; "I begin to believe, as you claim, that we were made to understand each other."

"What are you saying?" cried the king.

"Oh, nothing, Sire! I was apologizing to the duchess for my first suspicion, which she deigns to pardon, — a favor which is the more generous on her part, in that the lily gave birth to another suspicion."

"What was that?" demanded the king, while Diane, whose hate was too keen to allow her to be deceived by this comedy, devoured her triumphant rival with her eyes.

Madame d'Etampes saw that she was not yet quit of her indefatigable foe, and a shadow of dread passed across her face, but it should be said, in justice to her courage, only to disappear immediately.

Furthermore, she availed herself of the king's preoccupation, caused by Benvenuto's words, to try to gain possession of the lily; but Benvenuto carelessly placed himself between the king and her.

"What was the suspicion? Oh!" the goldsmith said with a smile, "it was so infamous that I am not sure that I shouldn't be ashamed of having had it, and that it would not add to my offence to be so shameless as to avow it. I must have an express command from your Majesty before I should dare — " '

"Dare, Cellini! I command you!" said the king.

"So be it. In the first place," said Cellini, "I confess with an artist's candid pride, that I was surprised to see Madame d'Etampes intrust the apprentice with a task which the master would have been happy and proud to execute for her. You remember my apprentice, Ascanio, Sire? He is a charming youth, who might venture to pose for Endymion, upon my word."

"Well! what then?" said the king, his brows contracting at the suspicion which began to gnaw his heart.

This time it was evident that, for all her self-control, Madame d'Etampes was on the rack. In the first place she read malicious curiosity in the eyes of Diane de Poitiers, and in the second place she was well aware that, while François might have forgiven treason to the king, he certainly would not forgive infidelity to the lover. However, as if he did not notice her agony, Benvenuto continued: —

"I reflected upon the beauty of my Ascanio, and it occurred to me — forgive me, mesdames, if there was anything in the thought which seems to cast a reflection upon the French, but I am accustomed to the ways of our Italian princesses, who, in love, it must be confessed, are very weak creatures — it occurred to me that a sentiment which had little connection with art — "

" Master," said François, frowning darkly, " reflect before you speak."

" I apologized beforehand for my temerity, and asked to be permitted to hold my peace."

" I bear witness to that," said Diane; " you yourself bade him speak, Sire, and now that he has begun — "

" It is always time to stop," said Madame d'Etampes, " when one knows that what one is about to say is a falsehood."

" I will stop if you choose, madame," said Benvenuto; " you know that you have but to say the word."

" Yes, but I choose that he shall continue. You are right, Diane; there are matters here which must be probed to the bottom. Say on, monsieur, say on," said the king, keeping his eyes fixed upon the sculptor and the duchess.

" My conjectures were taking a wide range when an incredible discovery opened a new field to them."

" What was it ? " cried the king and Diane de Poitiers in the same breath.

" I am getting in very deep," whispered Cellini to the duchess.

" Sire," said she, " you do not need to hold the lily in your hand to listen to this long discourse. Your Majesty is so accustomed to hold a sceptre in a firm grasp, that I fear the fragile flower may be broken in your fingers."

As she spoke, the duchess, with one of those smiles which belonged to her alone, put out her hand to take the jewel.

" Forgive me, Madame la Duchesse," said Cellini; " but as the lily plays an important part throughout my story, permit me to enforce my words with ocular demonstration."

"The lily plays an important part in the story you have to tell, master?" cried Diane, snatching the flower from the king's hand with a movement swift as thought. "In that case, Madame d'Etampes is right, for if the story is at all what I suspect, it is much better that the lily should be in my hands than in yours, Sire; for, purposely or not, your Majesty might, by some uncontrollable impulse, break it."

Madame d'Etampes became terribly pale, for she deemed herself lost; she hastily seized Benvenuto's hand, and her lips opened to speak, but almost immediately she thought better of it. Her hand let the artist's fall, and her lips closed again.

"Say what you have to say," she muttered through her clenched teeth, — "if you dare!" she added in so low a tone that Benvenuto alone could hear.

"Yes, and measure your words, my master," said the king.

"And do you, madame, measure your silence," said Benvenuto.

"We are waiting!" cried Diane, unable to restrain her impatience.

"Fancy, Sire, and you, madame, fancy that Ascanio and Madame la Duchesse d'Etampes corresponded."

The duchess looked about to see if there were not at hand some weapon with which she could silence the goldsmith's tongue forever.

"Corresponded?" echoed the king.

"Yes, corresponded; and the most extraordinary thing is that the subject of this correspondence between Madame la Duchesse d'Etampes and the humble carver's apprentice was love."

"The proofs, master! you have proofs, I trust!" cried the king, in a rage.

"O mon Dieu! yes, Sire," replied Benvenuto. "Your Majesty must understand that I should not have allowed myself to form such suspicions without proofs."

"Produce them instantly, then," said the king.

"When I say that I have them, I am in error: your Majesty had them a moment since."

"I!" cried the king.

"And Madame de Poitiers has them now."

"I!" cried Diane.

"Yes," rejoined Benvenuto, who, amid the king's wrath, and the hatred and terror of the two most powerful women in the world, was perfectly cool and complacent. "Yes, for the proofs are in the lily."

"In the lily?" cried the king, snatching the flower from the hands of Diane de Poitiers, and examining it with a careful scrutiny, in which love of art had no share. "In this lily?"

"Yes, Sire, in the lily," Benvenuto repeated. "You know that it is so, madame," he continued in a meaning tone, toward the gasping duchess.

"Let us come to terms," she whispered; "Colombe shall not marry D'Orbec."

"That is not enough," returned Cellini; "Ascanio must marry Colombe."

"Never!" exclaimed Madame d'Etampes.

Meanwhile the king was turning the fatal lily over and over in his fingers, his suspense and wrath being the more poignant in that he dared not express them openly.

"The proofs are in the lily! in the lily!" he repeated; "but I can see nothing in the lily."

"Because your Majesty does not know the secret of opening it."

"There is a secret. Show it me, messire, on the instant, or rather — "

François made a movement as if to crush the flower, but both women cried out, and he checked himself.

" Oh Sire! it would be a pity," cried Diane; " such a charming toy! Give it to me, Sire, and I promise you that if there is a secret I will find it."

Her slender, active fingers, to which hatred lent additional subtlety, passed over all the rough places on the jewel, felt in all the hollows, while the Duchesse d'Etampes, half fainting, followed with haggard eyes her investigations, which for a moment were without result. But at last, whether by good luck, or a rival's instinct of divination, Diane touched the precise spot on the stalk.

The flower opened.

The two women cried out again at the same moment; one with joy, the other with dismay. The duchess darted forward to tear the lily from Diane's hand, but Benvenuto held her back with one hand, while with the other he showed her the letter which he had taken from its hiding place. A swift glance at the flower showed her that the hiding place was empty.

" I agree to everything," said the duchess, completely crushed, and too weak to maintain such a contest.

" On the Gospel?" said Benvenuto.

" On the Gospel."

" Well, master," said the king, impatiently, " where are the proofs? I see a recess very cleverly hollowed out in the stalk, but there is nothing within it."

" No, sire, there is nothing," said Benvenuto.

" True, but there might have been something," suggested Diane.

" Madame is right," said Benvenuto.

" Master!" cried the king through his clenched teeth. " do you know that it may be dangerous for you to

prolong this pleasantry, and that stronger men than you
have repented playing with my anger ? "

" For that reason I should be in despair were I to
incur it, Sire," rejoined Cellini, without losing his com-
posure; " but there is nothing in the present circumstances
to arouse it, for I trust your Majesty did not take my
words seriously. Should I have dared to bring so grave
an accusation so lightly ? Madame d'Etampes can show
you the letters this lily contained, if you are curious to
see them. They are in fact concerned with love, but
it is the love of my poor Ascanio for a noble demoiselle,
— a passion which at first seems insane and impossible,
doubtless; but my Ascanio, like the true artist he is,
fancying that a beautiful jewel falls not far short of
equalling in value a beautiful maiden, applied to
Madame d'Etampes as to a special providence, and
made this lily his messenger. Now, you know, Sire, that
Providence can do anything, and you will not be jealous
of this particular one, I fancy, since, while doing a
kindly action, she attributes part of the credit to you.
That is the solution of the enigma, Sire, and if all the
beating about the bush I have indulged in has offended
your Majesty, I pray you to forgive me in consideration
of the familiarity to which you have been graciously
pleased to admit me."

This quasi academic harangue changed the face of
affairs. As Benvenuto went on, Diane's brow grew
dark, while the wrinkles vanished from that of Madame
d'Etampes, and the king resumed his smiling good
humor. When Benvenuto had finished, —

" Forgive me, fair duchess," said François, " for having dared to suspect you for an instant. Tell me what
I can do to redeem my offence and earn my forgiveness."

" Grant the request which Madame la Duchesse

d'Etampes is about to make, as your Majesty heretofore granted the one that I made."

" Speak for me, Master Cellini, since you know what it is that I wish," said the duchess with better grace than Cellini would have thought possible.

" Very well: since Madame la Duchesse apppoints me to be her mouthpiece, Sire, you must know that she desires your all-powerful intervention in favor of poor Ascanio's passion."

" Yes, yes! " laughed the king; " I agree with all my heart to assist in making the comely apprentice a happy man.   What is the name of his sweetheart? "

" Colombe d'Estourville, sire."

" Colombe d'Estourville! " cried François.

" I pray your Majesty to remember that it is Madame d'Etampes who proffers this request.   Come, madame, add your prayers to mine," he added, causing a corner of the letter to protrude from his pocket, " for if you are silent much longer, his Majesty will think that you make the request solely from a desire to oblige me."

" Is it true that you desire this marriage, madame? " inquired François.

" Yes, Sire," murmured Madame d'Etampes; " I do desire it — earnestly."

The adverb was extracted by a fresh exhibition of the letter.

" But how do I know," said the king, " that the provost will accept for his son in law a nameless, penniless youth? "

" In the first place, Sire," Benvenuto replied, " the provost, being a loyal subject, will surely have no other will than his king's.   In the second place, Ascanio is not nameless; he is a Gaddo Gaddi, and one of his ancestors was Podesta of Florence.   He is a goldsmith, it is true, but in Italy it is no disgrace to belong to that guild. Furthermore, even if he could boast of no ancient nobility, as I am at liberty to insert his name in the letters patent which have been forwarded to me by your Majesty's directions, he will be a nobleman of recent creation. Oh, think not that it requires any sacrifice on my part to resign in his favor. To reward my Ascanio is to reward myself twice over. So it is settled, Sire, that he is Seigneur de Nesle, and I will not let him want for money. He may, if he will, lay aside his profession, and buy a company of lances, or an appointment at court. I will provide the funds."

"And we shall look to it, you may be sure, that your generosity does not lighten your purse too much."

"Then I may consider, Sire — "

"Ascanio Gaddo Gaddi, Seigneur de Nesle, let it be!" cried the king, laughing heartily: the certainty that Madame d'Etampes was faithful to him had put him in a joyous humor.

"Madame," said Cellini, in an undertone, " you cannot in conscience leave the Seigneur de Nesle at the Châtelet; it was well enough for Ascanio."

Madame d'Etampes called an officer of the guards, and whispered a few words, the concluding ones being these : —

"In the king's name!"

"What are you doing, madame?" demanded François.

"Madame d'Etampes is simply sending a messenger for the bridegroom that is to be, Sire," interposed Cellini.

"Where?"

"Where Madame d'Etampes, who knew the king's kindness of heart, bade him await your Majesty's pleasure."

Fifteen minutes later, the door of the apartment opened, in which were assembled Colombe, the provost, D'Orbec, the Spanish ambassador, and almost the whole court, except Marmagne, who was still confined to his bed. An usher cried, —

"The king!"

François I. entered, leading Diane de Poitiers, and followed by Benvenuto, upon one of whose arms was leaning the Duchesse d'Etampes, and on the other Ascanio, each of them being as pale as the other.

At the announcement made by the usher, all the courtiers turned, and all were paralyzed for a moment when they saw this strange group.

Their astonishment redoubled when the king, stepping aside to allow the sculptor to pass in front of him, said in a loud voice : —

"Master Benvenuto, take our place for the moment, and our authority; speak as if you were the king, and be obeyed as a king should be."

"Beware, Sire," replied the goldsmith: "in order to fill your place fittingly, I propose to be magnificent."

"Go on, Benvenuto," said François laughingly; "every magnificent stroke will be a bit of flattery for me."

"Very good, Sire; that puts me at my ease, and I will praise you as much as I can. Do not forget," he continued, "all you who hear me, that the king is speaking by my mouth. Messieurs les Notaires, you have prepared the contract which his Majesty deigns to sign? Insert the names of the contracting parties."

The two notaries seized their pens and made ready to write the names in the two copies of the contract, one of which was to remain in the archives and the other in their office.

"Of the one part," continued Cellini, "the noble and puissant demoiselle, Colombe d'Estourville."

"Colombe d'Estourville," repeated the notaries, mechanically, while the auditors listened in open-mouthed astonishment.

"Of the other part," continued Cellini, "the most noble and puissant Ascanio Gaddi, Seigneur de Nesle."

"Ascanio Gaddi!" cried the provost and D'Orbec in the same breath.

"A mere artisan!" added the provost bitterly, turning toward the king.

"Ascanio Gaddi, Seigneur de Nesle," repeated Benvenuto, unmoved, "upon whom his Majesty bestows letters of naturalization and the office of Superintendent of the Royal Châteaux."

"If his Majesty so commands, I will obey," said the provost; "but — "

"Ascanio Gaddi," continued Benvenuto, "out of regard for whom his Majesty grants to Messire Robert d'Estourville, Provost of Paris, the title of Chamberlain."

"Sire, I am ready to sign," said D'Estourville, vanquished at last.

"Mon Dieu! mon Dieu!" murmured Colombe, falling back into her chair, "is not all this a dream?"

"And what of me?" cried D'Orbec.

"As for you," rejoined Cellini, continuing his royal functions; "as for you, Comte d'Orbec, I spare you the inquiry which I should be justified in ordering into your conduct. Clemency is a kingly virtue, no less than generosity, is it not, Sire? But here are the contracts, all prepared; let us sign, messieurs, let us sign!"

"He plays the king to perfection," cried François, as happy as a monarch on a vacation.

He passed the pen to Ascanio, who signed with a trembling hand; Ascanio then passed the pen to Colombe, to whose assistance Madame Diane had gone in pure kindness of heart. The hands of the lovers met, and they almost swooned.

Next came Madame Diane, who passed the pen to the Duchesse d'Etampes, who passed it to the provost, the provost to D'Orbec, and D'Orbec to the Spanish ambassador.

Below all these great names Cellini wrote his own in a firm, distinct hand. And yet he was not the one who had made the least painful sacrifice.

After writing his name, the Spanish ambassador drew nigh the duchess.

" Our plans still hold, madame ? " he asked.

" Mon Dieu ! " she replied, " do what you choose: what matters France or the world to me ? "

The duke bowed. As he resumed his place, his nephew, a young and inexperienced diplomat, re-marked : —

" So it is the Emperor's purpose that not the King of France, but his son, shall be Duke of Milan ? "

" Neither the one nor the other will be," replied the ambassador.

Meanwhile other signatures were being affixed.

When every one had written his name as a subscriber to the happiness of Colombe and Ascanio, Benvenuto walked up to the king, and knelt upon one knee before him.

" Sire," said he, " having issued commands as king I now prefer a request as your Majesty's humble and grateful servant. Will your Majesty deign to grant me one last favor ? "

" Say on, Benvenuto, say on ! " returned François,

who was in a granting mood, and who discovered anew that it was the prerogative of royalty wherein, take it for all in all, a king finds the most pleasure; "what do you desire?"

"To return to Italy, sire," said Benvenuto.

"What does this mean?" cried the king; "you wish to leave me when you have so many masterpieces still in hand for me? I'll not have it."

"Sire," replied Benvenuto, "I will return, I give you my word. But let me go, let me see my country once more, for I feel the need of it just now. I do not talk of my suffering," he continued, lowering his voice and shaking his head sadly, "but I have many causes of sorrow which I could not describe, and nothing but the air of my native land can heal my wounded heart. You are a great and generous king, to whom I am deeply attached. I will return, Sire, but let me go now and be cured in the bright sunlight of the South. I leave with you Ascanio, my brain, and Pagolo, my hand; they will suffice to carry out your artistic dreams until my return; and when I have received the soft kisses of the breezes of Florence, my mother, I will return to you, my king, and death alone shall part us."

"Go if you will," said François, sadly; "it is fitting that art should be free as the swallows: go!"

He gave Benvenuto his hand, which the artist kissed with all the fervor of heartfelt gratitude.

As they withdrew, Benvenuto found himself by the duchess's side.

"Are you very angry with me, madame?" said he, slipping into her hand the fatal letter which, like a magic talisman, had accomplished impossibilities.

"No," said the duchess, overjoyed to have it in her possession at last; "and yet you defeated me by means—"

" Go to! " said Benvenuto; " I threatened you with them, but do you think I would have used them ? "

" God in heaven! " cried the duchess, as if the light had suddenly come to her; " that is what it is to have thought that you were like myself! "

The next day, Ascanio and Colombe were married in the chapel at the Louvre, and, notwithstanding the rules of etiquette, the young people obtained permission for Jacques Aubry and his wife to be present.

It was a signal favor, but we must agree that the poor student had well merited it.

XXIII.

MARIAGE DE CONVENANCE.

A WEEK later, Hermann solemnly espoused Dame Perrine, who brought him as her marriage portion twenty thousand Tours livres, and the assurance that he would soon be a father.

We hasten to say that this assurance had much more to do with the honest German's determination than the twenty thousand Tours livres.

On the evening following the marriage of Colombe and Ascanio, Benvenuto set out for Florence, despite the entreaties of the young husband and wife.

During his stay in Italy, he cast the statue of Perseus, which still adorns the square of the Old Palace, and which was his most beautiful work, — for no other reason, perhaps, than that he executed it at the period of his greatest sorrow.

THE END.